D0742978

THE VALANCOURT BOOK OF HORROR STORIES

VOLUME TWO

THE VALANCOURT BOOK OF
HORROR STORIES

VOLUME TWO

edited by
JAMES D. JENKINS & RYAN CAGLE

VALANCOURT BOOKS
Richmond, Virginia
2017

Published by Valancourt Books, Richmond, Virginia
http://www.valancourtbooks.com

ISBN 978-1-943910-76-2 (hardcover)
ISBN 978-1-943910-77-9 (trade paperback)
Also available as an electronic book.

All Valancourt Books publications are printed on acid free paper
that meets all ANSI standards for archival quality paper.

Cover by M. S. Corley
Set in Dante MT

CONTENTS

ACKNOWLEDGMENTS

The Editors acknowledge with thanks permission to include the following stories:

'Samhain' © 1991 by Bernard Taylor. Originally published in *Final Shadows*, edited by Charles F. Grant. Reprinted by permission of the author and A.M. Heath, Ltd.

'The Bell' © 1946 by Beverley Nichols. Originally published in *Strand Magazine*. Reprinted by permission of Eric Glass, Ltd.

'The Elemental' © 1974 by R. Chetwynd-Hayes. Originally published in *The Elemental and Other Stories*. Reprinted by permission of the author's estate.

'The Creatures in the House' © 1980 by Robert Westall. Originally published in *You Can't Keep Out the Darkness*, edited by Peggy Woodford. Reprinted by permission of the Laura Cecil Agency.

'Halley's Passing' © 1987 by Michael McDowell. Originally published in *Twilight Zone*. Reprinted by permission of The Otte Company.

'The Nice Boys' © 1965 by Isabel Colegate. Originally published in *Horror Anthology*, edited by Syd Bentlif. Reprinted by permission of the author and Janklow & Nesbit.

'Tudor Windows' © 2017 by the Trustees of the Estate of the late Nevil Shute Norway. Published by permission of A.P. Watt, Ltd.

'Camera Obscura' © 1965 by Basil Copper. Originally published in *The Sixth Pan Book of Horror Stories*. Reprinted by permission of the author's estate.

'The Boys Who Wouldn't Wake Up' © 2017 by Stephen Gregory. Published by permission of the author.

EDITORS' FOREWORD

OUR FIRST COLLECTION OF HORROR STORIES received such a positive response that we decided to assemble a second volume of tales by Valancourt authors, and, if possible, to make this one even better than the last.

The fourteen tales in Volume Two span almost two hundred years – Thomas De Quincey's Gothic story of a demonic pact, 'The Dice', dates from 1823, while Stephen Gregory's quiet ghost story 'The Boys Who Wouldn't Wake Up' is a brand new tale appearing for the first time in this volume – a period during which horror has developed and evolved into numerous permutations: Gothic horror, penny dreadfuls, Sensation fiction, ghost stories, monster tales, Lovecraftian or cosmic horror, *contes cruels*, tales of unease, quiet horror, folk horror, weird fiction, and countless others. In this book we have taken a broad view of the term 'horror stories', so readers will find many different modes of horror represented and that no two stories here are alike.

As in the first volume we have tried to assemble a mix of both well-known horror authors and literary writers not ordinarily thought of as contributors to the genre. Fans of the rich period of horror fiction that arose in the 1970s and '80s will find rare stories by authors whose names are readily recognizable, such as Michael McDowell, Bernard Taylor, Basil Copper, and R. Chetwynd-Hayes. But readers will also discover excellent and creepy tales by Isabel Colegate, an award-winning literary novelist, Beverley Nichols, best known for his light-hearted gardening books, and a never-before-published story by Nevil Shute, the bestselling author of novels of aviation and adventure. Reflecting Valancourt Books' commitment to unearthing and republishing works from the more distant literary past, we have also selected Romantic and Victorian-era gems by De Quincey, Mary Elizabeth Braddon, and John

Buchan, as well as forgotten tales from the early twentieth century by John Metcalfe and Russell Thorndike, neglected masters of the genre.

Of the fourteen stories in the book, two have never before been published anywhere and four others have never previously been reprinted; most of the rest have not been available in print for at least the past quarter-century. Each story is prefaced with a brief introduction about the author and his or her other works, including titles available from Valancourt. If you're at all like us, you're constantly looking to expand your reading horizons and discover new authors whose works you've previously missed, and we hope that this book – in addition to supplying some welcome Halloween shivers – also helps you find a new favourite author or two.

Meanwhile, while you prepare to sit back and enjoy these fine horror stories, we had better get back to work on Volume Three . . .

James D. Jenkins & Ryan Cagle
Publishers, Valancourt Books
July 2017

Bernard Taylor

SAMHAIN

One of the finest authors to emerge from the horror publishing boom of the late 1970s and early '80s, BERNARD TAYLOR *is the author of ten novels and several nonfiction true crime books. His first novel,* The Godsend *(1976), the story of the horrible things that happen to an ordinary family who adopt a sweet-looking little girl, was a bestseller and adapted for a film.* Sweetheart, Sweetheart *(1977) was chosen for inclusion in* Horror: 100 Best Books *(1990) and was named by Charles L. Grant as the best ghost story he had ever read. Both of these novels, along with* The Moorstone Sickness *(1982), are available from Valancourt Books. 'Samhain' first appeared in Grant's anthology* Final Shadows *(1991), and is reprinted for the first time here. As with Taylor's 'Out of Sorts', which appeared in Volume One, it is a wicked little tale laced with dark humour and with a surprising – and surprisingly nasty – ending.*

WEARING HER TRACK SUIT, Doris stood gasping for breath as the lift took her up to the fifth floor, the top of the apartment building. A minute later at the door of the flat she discovered that she'd come out without her keys and she rang the bell and waited impatiently for Arthur to answer. Then at last, after the fourth ring, the door was opened. She helped it aside with an angry shove and stepped into the hall.

'Arthur,' she gasped (she still hadn't got her breath back), 'didn't you hear me ringing?'

He shook his head. 'No, I'm sorry, dear; I was in the bedroom going through my underwear. You know – I think I need to get some more.'

'You need to get a hearing aid, that's what you need.' With her words she turned away and strode into the kitchen where she poured herself a glass of water. She would have liked a

Coke but there was no sense in half killing yourself to take off a few pounds and then put it all straight back on again. As she stood there slowly sipping the water Arthur came to the open doorway and stood looking at her with the inane smile that always infuriated her so.

'How was the running?' he asked.

Her answer was clipped, cold. 'If you mean the jogging, it was fine.'

'Yes. Yes, of course – jogging.' He nodded. 'I have to hand it to you – you've got more energy than I have. If *I* tried a run round the park I'd be dead before I got halfway.'

It's a pity you don't try it then, a voice inside her head snapped, *and save me all the trouble you're putting me to.* She kept silent, though, and turned and rinsed the empty glass under the tap.

As she dried the glass and put it away Arthur said solicitously, 'I'll bet you're hungry, are you? Would you like me to make you some breakfast?'

'You?' She looked at him with contempt. 'You know very well you're useless in the kitchen. You're as incompetent there as you are everywhere else.' She paused. 'Besides, I'm trying to lose weight, you know that. I've got some pride – even if you haven't.'

He looked hurt. 'What does that mean?'

'It means it wouldn't hurt *you* to lose a few pounds, either. You do know what this weekend is, don't you?'

He nodded. 'Of course. The thirty-first. Halloween.'

'*Halloween?*' There was disgust in her tone. 'Yes, that's what *they* call it, those idiots out there.' She gestured with an impatient hand, taking in the rest of the world. '*I* prefer to call it by its proper name.'

'Samhain?'

'Of *course* Samhain.'

'All right – Samhain – but so what?'

She made a short, mocking sound of derision. '*So what?* he asks. *So what?* Maybe it doesn't bother you, the thought of stripping off and dancing around in the nude in front of all our friends. Maybe you don't give it a second thought. Maybe you're happy with your body the way it is. If so, then you've got a lot to be happy about – because there's a lot of it. Personally, if it were me, I'd want to do something about it.'

He frowned. 'Oh, come on, Doris, what can I do about it? I'm fifty-six years old. I'm not a young man anymore. Besides, there'll be plenty there older than I am. Plenty.'

He looked hurt and she gave a sigh. 'Oh – forget it, Arthur. I won't say anything else. It doesn't make any difference anyway. You never listen.'

She pushed past him and went into the lounge where she flopped down into her easy chair, took off her shoes, put her feet up on the footstool and closed her eyes. After a few moments she heard him come into the room, and then she heard his voice again, irritatingly considerate as always:

'Are you asleep?'

Without opening her eyes she said, 'Of course I'm not asleep.'

'I just wondered.' A pause. 'Would you like a cup of coffee?'

She opened her eyes, about to say no, then gave a grudging shrug. 'Yes, why not. If you think you can manage it.'

'Doris, of course I can manage it.' He started off across the room. 'You want it black?'

'Of course black. I always have it black.'

'Yes, of course.'

She turned her head and watched his thick, heavy body move through the doorway, then she sighed, got to her feet and stretched. There was a mirror near the window and she stepped in front of it and looked at herself. She didn't look at all bad for her forty-three years, she thought. And holding herself like this – erect and with her stomach drawn in – she looked *years* younger. Trouble was, it was impossible to sustain the effort. You forgot, and with the forgetting everything sagged again. She must get into the habit of holding herself well; work on her posture as well as everything else. After all, soon she'd be free again . . .

As she looked at her reflection she thought again of the

thirty-first. Tomorrow. Everything depended on tomorrow. Tomorrow would see the end to her problems and the beginning of a new life. And the day would bring other bonuses too: at the meeting she'd see that young male witch, the new initiate from Lyddiard, Steve Walker. She hadn't seen him since the initiation ceremony back at the end of April, the Feast of Beltane, but she remembered him well enough: tall, tanned, good-looking and with an obvious taste for older women. Not that she regarded herself as old, Satan forbid, but when he was only in his late twenties one had to acknowledge the age difference. Thinking of him now she remembered how he had smiled at her – and in such a very special way. He'd had his clothes on then, of course, but even so they hadn't been able to disguise the firmness, the clean, muscular lines of his body. Not like Arthur with his pale flab.

She pictured Arthur as he'd be at the dance – as usual making a complete idiot of himself. Some people had no dignity at all. Well, at least *she* knew how to go on. And when *she* danced nobody was going to snigger or look the other way. With the thought she did a couple of steps in front of the mirror. It looked good – and *she* looked pretty good too – a damned sight better than that stupid Shirley Goldberg. Sure Shirley Goldberg's figure was a lot firmer and more up-together these days – but so it should be – she'd spent enough on cosmetic surgery. And it showed, of course. There was no way of disguising those scars. Those scars – good Satan, in the cold weather Shirley Goldberg looked as if she'd been pressed against a wire fence.

Arthur came back into the room then and she sat down and took the cup of coffee he handed her. Looking down at it, she said impatiently, 'I said *black,* Arthur. Can't you ever get anything right?'

As he moved back to the kitchen with the offending cup of coffee she reflected on her loathing of him. And it would never change now, she knew that – which was one reason she had decided to get rid of him and look out for a newer model. Well, she had to. They couldn't go on as they were. With him around she had no future at all. Oh, yes, she could leave him, of course – but what good would that do? She'd just be giving up her home in this flat to go and find someplace on her own – and someplace not nearly as comfortable – and almost certainly she'd have to get a job of some kind too. No, she couldn't afford to leave Arthur – and as she couldn't bear the thought of continuing to live with him either, then there was only one thing to be done.

Which she was in the process of taking care of right now. And so much trouble it was, too. She had never dreamed. All those sessions in the coven's library for a start, doing all that research. It was mind-blowingly tedious – but it was the only way to do things, she had no doubt of that.

Thinking of the library, she thought of the books she'd been studying. It hadn't been easy getting access to them. It had surprised her just how closely they were guarded. She had told the coven librarian that she was taking a degree course on the ancient arts. And he had believed her, the fool. She remembered his grave expression as he had brought the old, leather-bound volumes and placed them before her. 'Be careful with them, won't you?' he had said. 'And do remember that they mustn't be taken out of this room. We wouldn't want them falling into the wrong hands, would we? If that happened, there's no telling where the mischief would stop.'

Mischief. *Mischief* – it seemed such a pathetic little word when applied to the act of murder. Not that anyone was going to construe it as murder. It would be put down to heart failure. Simple. She smiled to herself. And now her researches were finished, and she had all the answers she wanted. And now, too, she had the stone and the nail. And this evening she'd have the clay portrait as well.

After a few moments Arthur approached with a fresh cup of coffee – black this time – in his hand. As she took it from him she said, 'I'll be out this evening, you haven't forgotten that, have you?'

'Oh, yes, of course.' He nodded. 'Your art class. I wasn't sure that you'd still be going – what with the feast and everything tomorrow.'

Still going? 'Of course I'm still going,' she said witheringly. Wild horses wouldn't keep her away.

'How are you getting on?' he asked.

'Fine. I'm getting on fine.'

'You must really enjoy it, your clay modelling – these past few weeks you've been so keen.'

She shrugged. 'Yes – I do enjoy it.'

'Maybe I could come with you one evening. It might be interesting.'

She tried to picture him in the art studio, making a hash of everything. What an embarrassment he would be. 'Oh, I don't think it would appeal to you at all,' she said.

'Oh . . . What are you making?'

'This and that.'

'What, exactly?'

'I've been modelling a figure.'

'All this time? Just one? It must be huge.'

'No – it's quite small.'

'But it's been weeks.'

'I've been trying to get it right.'

'I see. And are you nearly there, you think?'

'Nearly there. This evening it'll be finished.'

'Well, that's nice.'

Well, that's nice, the voice in her head mimicked. *You wouldn't think it was so nice if you knew whose figure I was modelling, you old fool.* She wondered for a moment how he would react if she told him that the model was of *him* . . . She frowned momentarily at the thought of her work in the class. Getting his likeness had proved so difficult. It would have been easy if she had some real artistic ability – but she hadn't and that was it. Anyway, after several poor starts she'd been getting on better over the past few sessions and now, this evening, at last, it would be done.

The idea for the clay model was one of the things she'd got from her researches in the library. Not that such means were that secret. On the contrary, she supposed it must be one of the most commonly known methods of disposing of someone. Even so, however, she didn't intend relying on some half-baked old wives' tales handed down; she meant to get it right – which was why she'd gone to the experts.

And that, too, was why she had chosen the thirty-first – that was the day when the spells would be at their most potent. Strange, really, she thought, most people today had no idea what the day really meant – and what it had meant since early times. *Samhain* – that was the real meaning of the thirty-first of October. Samhain, one of the two great witches' festivals of the year – a celebration of fire and the dead and the powers of darkness. In the modern world the thirty-first was generally recognized only as All Hallows' Eve, and celebrated only by children with turnip lanterns, silly masks, games and dressing up. Still, it could be worse, she supposed; in America they made even more nonsense out of the whole thing with their ridiculous trick-or-treating. Huh – if any children came to *her* door carrying bags of flour or whatever and begging for sweets, they'd get something they weren't prepared for, the little monsters. Mind you, that's what came from too much civilization. Thank Satan England hadn't gone *that* far – *yet*. Though it probably would in time. They did say that what America had one day England got the next.

When she was out of the shower and dry again she moved to a chest and opened the bottom drawer. From a small cardboard box she withdrew a long, rusty nail and a large, smooth stone. With these and the clay image she had no doubt of success. They'd be enough to kill Arthur ten times over.

That evening at art class she finished the clay model and carefully placed it in the small box she had brought with her for the purpose. As she did so the instructor, a tall woman with a face like a dispossessed spaniel, came to her, looked over her shoulder and said, 'All done, then, Mrs Armstrong?'

'Yes, all done.'

'I'm curious,' the instructor said, 'as to what you want it for...'

Doris turned to her and gave a bleak smile. 'Are you?' She put the lid on the box and sealed it with tape. Let the stupid woman be curious; she wasn't going to satisfy her curiosity. What was more, she wouldn't be coming back to the class after this evening; there'd be no need to.

That night as she lay awake in bed thinking of tomorrow and the festival she could hear Arthur's snoring through the wall. That was something else she wouldn't have to put up with for much longer. Just a little while and he'd never snore again.

The thirty-first. It had rained during the night but the morning was clear, bright and promising.

Over the breakfast table Arthur, as usual, was clearly unhappy about his eggs, and she watched, secretly pleased, as he pushed them to one side. 'Aren't you going to eat your eggs?' she said.

He frowned. 'You know I don't like them like this, Doris,' he said. 'I tell you every morning and next day they're just the same. Sometimes I think you just don't make the effort.'

She looked at him over her coffee cup, hating him. She was glad that his scrambled eggs were like rubber. Glad. If he'd been pleased with them she'd have been disappointed. And he was wrong to say that she didn't make the effort. She *did*. She had to have ways of showing her loathing for him and the eggs were one of those ways. 'I worked hard to prepare those eggs for you,' she said reproachfully.

After a few moments under her glare he pulled the plate back before him. 'I'll try to eat a little,' he murmured.

She watched then as he braced himself and dug a fork into the solid yellow mass. Added to his incompetence he had no guts, either. What a wimp. Any other man would have thrown the mess at the wall – which was what it deserved. Not Arthur, though; he put up with it. All the inedible food she had served up to him every morning for the past twenty years, and he accepted it all, ate it all. Her contempt for him grew.

When the evening came she went into her bedroom and took from the box the small clay figure. Then she put on her coat, took her door key and went quietly out of the room. A short ride down in the lift and a few minutes later she was leaving the foyer and stepping out into the late October evening. Moving to the garden behind the apartment block, she stepped over the grass to the ornamental pool where water cascaded into its centre from a little waterfall. She had always despised it so, this pathetic little attempt at re-creating nature; now she wouldn't have changed it for anything.

At the side of the pool she looked around, eyes glancing up at the windows of the overlooking flats. She could see no one looking out at her. Then, carefully unwrapping the little clay figure, she stepped closer to the edge of the pool, leaned over and placed the figure on the lip of the waterfall. The water surging over the stone was icy cold. She pressed the figure firmly onto the stone, wedging it in. Then, satisfied that it was secure, she stepped back and looked at it. As she did so she thought of the words she had read in the book in the coven library: *Make ye a picture of clay, like unto the shape of thine enemy, and then, on the night of Samhain or Beltane place it in a running stream till it be worn away.* Well, it was in a running stream now – and it wasn't going to last long by the looks of things; already, even as she watched, the limbs were beginning to crumble . . .

Back upstairs she went straight to her room and began to get ready.

Well before nine o'clock she was dressed and eager to get away. Emerging from her room she came to a stop before the hall mirror and put down her bag – heavier this evening – and made a last survey of her appearance. She had taken great trouble with her makeup, and she had been to the hairdresser just that afternoon. She'd hardly eaten all day, either, and felt about as slim as she had felt in a long while. Under her floor-length deep-blue velvet cloak, her warm ceremonial robe fell to her ankles. Beneath it she wore nothing. She was ready. Now if only Arthur would hurry up, they could get going.

'Arthur?' she shouted in the direction of his bedroom. 'Come on, will you? We're going to be late.'

When he appeared a few minutes later she shook her head in exasperation. 'I thought you were getting ready,' she said.

'I *am* ready.'

'But – you've got your Burberry on.'

'I know.'

'You don't mean to say you're going in that, do you?'

'Why not? I shall take it off when we get there.'

'You'll take it off *now*. You can't go there looking like that. Where's your cloak? All the others will arrive in cloaks.'

'Oh, Doris, for Luci's sake – I can't stand that cloak. Every year I wear it, and I feel like an idiot.'

'Well, you'll look like an idiot in *that*. And how d'you think *I'm* going to feel? Of course that doesn't matter to you, does it? – showing me up. And stop blaspheming – I keep telling you!' She continued to glare at him. 'Well, I'm not going with you looking like that, so you can just go and put on your cloak.'

After a moment's hesitation he went away. When he came back a couple of minutes later Doris still wasn't happy. 'What's up with your cloak?' she asked, frowning. 'It's not hanging right. You look like a badly tied bag of laundry.'

He shrugged. 'Well – it's probably my underwear.'

'You're wearing *underwear?*'

'Two sets.'

'Tell me you're joking.'

'What's wrong? I shall be cold. It's not *that* warm, in case you hadn't noticed. I don't want to catch pneumonia.'

'You talk as if this were the Dark Ages. Haven't you ever heard of central heating? The Goldbergs' house will be very warm and comfortable. And we shan't be outside for more than a minute or so. For Hell's sake, go and take it off at once.'

'Oh, Doris, must I?'

'Of course you must. Oh, my Lord, what a picture! Everybody else dancing around in the total nude and you in your Fruit of the Loom Y-fronts. It makes me shudder to think of it.' She shook her head. 'You don't take any of this seriously, do you?'

'Satan Almighty, Doris,' he sighed, 'we go through this every year. If you want the truth, I'd much rather stay home tonight and watch TV.'

'Yes, that's all you're fit for. Look at you – a descendant of one of the greatest witches who ever lived and now, tonight of all nights, instead of wanting to go and celebrate our main festival you'd rather stay in and watch TV. And *stop blaspheming.*' She glared at him for a second, then turned, opened the door and strode toward the lift.

The Goldbergs, who were hosting the festival this year, were longtime members of the coven and lived in wide grounds in the heart of the countryside some miles west of Trowbridge. Arthur had wanted to drive but after experiencing a little difficulty getting the car out of the garage Doris had ordered him out of the driver's seat. 'My Lord, how can you be so *incompetent!*' she'd snapped as she got behind the wheel. They set off then and got there just after ten, and as Doris steered the Ford Capri along the drive she saw ahead of her a large number of other cars. A rough count gave a number somewhere above forty. She was pleased and her excitement took another surge.

She kept very close to the edge of the driveway as she pulled the car to a stop. A moment later Arthur opened the door, looked down and groaned. 'Can't you move it out a little, Doris? It's so muddy here; I'll mess up my shoes.'

Doris had known exactly what she was doing and she just shook her head and sighed a long-suffering sigh. 'Oh, Arthur, stop being such a damned wimp, will you.' She switched off the ignition, got out of the car and started off toward the front of the house. Arthur caught up with her just as she reached the front door where the porch was brightly illuminated by colourful lanterns.

The door was opened by Ralph Goldberg, dressed in a long robe with a gold-coloured sash tied loosely at the place where his waist used to be. He greeted them with smiles and words of welcome, at the same time raising his right hand above his head, thumb and pinky extended, in a salute to the devil. Doris repeated the gesture – as did Arthur in a halfhearted way – then they were taking off their outer garments and putting them into Ralph's arms. After that they moved through the hall into

the main lounge where the rest of the party revelers were con-
gregated.

'Shall we be sacrificing any chickens?' Steve Walker asked. 'I
hope so. I've been looking forward to that.' He, Shirley Goldberg and Doris were standing together in the centre of the
crowd of chattering people with glasses of mulled wine in their
hands. At his question Shirley shook her head.

'No, I'm afraid not. Ralph got the order in too late and there
weren't any available. All they had left were dead ones – fresh or
frozen. We could have got some live turkeys but I couldn't face
the thought of being faced with eating turkey for days on end
afterward. It's bad enough at Christmas when you have to keep
up appearances.'

The party was well on and Doris was looking forward to the
dance and then to being alone with Steve. She hadn't really had
a chance to talk to him so far – not with Shirley Goldberg and
other people milling around all the time. It wouldn't be long
now, though, she thought. For the moment, however, Shirley
was holding the reins and, in her customary name-dropping
way, was holding the floor too – and was obviously out to
impress.

'I got in touch with Joan last night,' she was saying.

'Joan?' Doris asked. 'Joan who?'

'Joan who? Joan of Arc, of course.'

'Oh, that Joan. How was she?'

'Still very bitter.'

'Well, it's understandable, isn't it?'

Shirley nodded. 'Very bitter. I told her – you ought to get
some kind of counselling – or therapy. I mean, it's eating away
at her. Though I suppose it's to be expected after what they did
to her. Some people – they've got a lot to answer for.'

'Right.'

'Mind you, in many ways she only had herself to blame –
and I as good as told her so. I mean, once you start admitting
that you're hearing voices, then people are going to get your
number pretty damn quick. Sure to. Still, she had a hard time,

there's no denying, and it was rotten luck on her – being set up like that – being made to carry the can for the inefficiency of our armies. Still, she should have kept her mouth shut. If she'd done that, she could be alive today.'

'I suppose you're right.'

'Of course I'm right. There are procedures that have to be adhered to. You can't go yelling your mouth off and going about things in a half-assed way. You've got to do things *right* . . .'

Shirley's voice droned on while Doris repeated her words: *You've got to do things right. Right* – and that's how *she* was doing things.

Turning slightly, she saw Arthur sitting near the window in conversation with Thelma Winnecky, a young, blond widow from Purton. Then, glancing above Arthur's head, she saw through the window Ralph Goldberg on the lawn setting light to the bonfire. She looked at her watch. Eleven forty-five. The dancing would start very soon. She hadn't much time.

'Will you excuse me for a moment, please . . . ?' She smiled at Shirley – who was still in full flood – and briefly pressed Steve's hand. Then, turning, she moved from the room.

In the cloakroom near the front door she took from her bag the large, smooth, pale stone she had brought and, with her nail file, carefully scratched Arthur's name upon it. Then she put it back into the bag along with the nail, put on her cloak and went out into the hall, where she opened the front door and slipped out into the night.

Moving swiftly, she walked out onto the drive where the cars were parked. When she got to the Ford she stepped carefully over to the near-side door and, taking a small torch from her purse, shone its beam down at the spot where Arthur had stepped (so complainingly, the wimp!) onto the soft, muddy earth of the verge. And – yes! – very clearly the light picked out the shape of his footprints. Three of them, two right and one left – and as cleanly indented as if he'd worked at it. She smiled, reached back into her bag and took out the nail and the stone.

Holding the nail up against the dull light of the sky, she looked at it. It appeared to be just an ordinary, if rather old-fashioned, nail. It was *not* ordinary, though, and it had cost a bomb – not to mention the difficulty she'd had in getting hold of it. Well, it wasn't something you could get in the local super-market or even in some fancy ironmonger's shop. What did you do – walk in and say, 'I'd like one coffin nail, please?' No, she'd had to go to some old hag of a witch in Frome and pay a fortune – in cash. Cash on the nail, so to speak.

Anyway, she'd got the nail – and it would be worth it, every penny. After a quick glance around she carefully placed the nail's point into the indented heel of Arthur's left footprint, then with the stone she hammered it into the ground. *On the night of Samhain take ye a naile from a coffin that has been buried in the earth,* the book had said, *and put it in the footprint of thy foe. Very soon thereafter thy foe shall sicken and perish.* The nail went in easily; the soil was quite soft. She straightened and looked down. No sign of it. She smiled, turned and moved away.

She didn't reenter the house straightaway but went round to the back where Ralph Goldberg was tending the fire and feeding it with wood. As he did so it crackled and blazed and shot out sparks and made swift moving shadows against the backcloth of the house. He looked around at her and smiled as she approached. 'Came out to get a breath of air, did you, Doris?' he asked.

She nodded, returning his smile. 'Yes – and to see how it's all going.'

'Oh, we'll be ready in a minute.' He threw on more wood. 'I want to get a good blaze going first. We don't want anyone to catch cold.'

'Right.' It was funny how things had changed over the years, she thought. Everyone was so comfort-conscious today. In the old days they'd have danced naked round the fire, either till the fire went out or till they dropped. Not now; now the actual dance around the fire was only a token thing – a quick dash naked out into the chill air, link hands and dance around the fire a couple of times and then back indoors to finish the celebra-tions in the warm.

Ralph glanced at his watch, adjusted a burning log on the

fire and gave a nod of satisfaction. 'I think we might as well start now.' He moved off toward the patio door, then paused briefly and looked back. 'Aren't you coming in to disrobe . . . ?'

'Yes, in a minute – I'll be right there.' As she spoke she put out her hands toward the heat of the flames and then turned to watch as he went on into the house.

As soon as he had gone she dipped her right hand into her bag and took out the stone. In the flickering light of the fire she looked at it. Arthur's name stood out clearly. (*Choose thy time with care, then take ye a stone, writ with the name of thine adversary* . . .) A quick glance toward the patio window and she took a step forward. (*. . . and place it in fire . . .*) She muttered a little prayer, took a breath and cast the stone into the heart of the flames.

And it was done. Everything was done. All she had to do now was wait. And she wouldn't have to wait very long. Within twelve hours of the hour of midnight Arthur would be dead.

She sat at the breakfast bar in the Goldbergs' kitchen drinking coffee. She had been there for a long time. There had been no sign of Arthur for a long while and she sat tense and expectant, waiting at any moment for someone to come in and say that he was dead, had been found lying dead in one of the Goldbergs' many spare bedrooms or on some sofa in some other part of the house. It looked as if he'd had a heart attack, they would say, and she would cry and try to look brave in the face of her great tragedy.

The thought should have cheered her more than it did. Oh, yes, she was glad, very glad, when she thought of Arthur getting out of her hair, out of her life at last, but when she thought of Steve Walker it was another matter. She'd seen hardly anything of him after their chat over cocktails and the dance around the fire. He had been close to her then as they'd all circled the crackling flames, and the grasp of his hand in hers had been firm and full of promise. But soon afterward he had just vanished. Then, later, wandering about the huge house alone, she had come upon two people in a room, lying together on a rug, limbs threshing, their movements accompanied by groans

and sighs and muttered words. She'd backed out, but not before
she had realized who the two were. One was Steve, she was
sure. And the other? No mistaking that voice. Shirley Goldberg.

Later, while nursing a coffee, her disappointment and her
anger, she'd put her robe back on; there didn't seem much point
in doing otherwise. There was no one else around now – the
others had all gone off long since to different rooms, either in
pairs or groups of three, four, five or six. Now, sitting in the
kitchen she turned at the sound of approaching footsteps and
braced herself for the news. The door opened.

'Arthur . . .' She gaped at him.

He looked a little sheepish. "Ah – there you are. I was wondering.'

Then her bitterness at the evening's disappointment flared
up. 'Where the hell have you been?' she rapped out.

'Been? I haven't been anywhere.'

She shook her head in contempt and exasperation. 'Well – I
want to go home. I've had enough.'

'But they'll be serving breakfast soon.'

'I don't want any breakfast. I just want to go home.' She
waited, then when he didn't move she said, 'Didn't you hear
me? I said I want to go home.'

He looked at her, sighed and nodded. 'Yes, dear. Whatever
you say.'

They slipped away without saying their good-byes to anyone,
and when they got outside she left Arthur for a moment, went
round to the back of the house and looked at the remains of
the bonfire. Now it was just a pile of cold ashes. Poking into
it with a stick, she uncovered the stone she had put there last
night. Bending, she picked it up, blew off the dust and looked at
it closely. And suddenly she felt a little touch of pleasure in the
midst of her frustration and dissatisfaction. On the stone there
was not a sign of Arthur's name. (*If the fire shall destroy the name
then so shall the owner of that name be destroyed . . .*) The name had
been burned clean away. With a little smile she dropped the
stone back into the ashes and went to join Arthur where he sat
waiting in the car.

When they got back to Stratton she put the car away while Arthur went on upstairs. She didn't follow him immediately, but first went toward the communal garden in the centre of which lay the ornamental pool and the little waterfall. When she reached the pool she looked at the lip of the stone over which the water ran and saw that there was no trace left of the clay figure. It was gone, without trace. The water had completely worn it away.

And all at once the depression that had hung over her since Steve's betrayal was lifted. What did it matter, anyway? He meant nothing to her. And there were plenty of other men in the world. And soon, very soon, with Arthur gone, she would be free to play the field. She looked at her watch. Just after six. There was very little time to go now. It could happen at any moment. She turned and looked up toward the windows of the flat. 'Arthur,' she whispered, 'your hours are numbered.'

Upstairs in the flat she pushed open his bedroom door and found him getting ready for bed. He turned to her and gave a little shrug. 'I thought I'd just have a nap for a while . . .'

Hiding the elation that was growing within her, she took in the look of exhaustion on his face and said, 'Don't you want any breakfast?' After all, she said to herself, every condemned man was entitled to a good breakfast.

He shook his head. 'No, thanks. I'm feeling very tired. I'm too old for all those goings-on. Staying up all night, cavorting around. I think I'll give it a miss next year.'

You certainly will, Doris thought, then aloud she said, 'Didn't you get any sleep at the Goldbergs'? There were enough beds.'

'Oh, I dozed a bit,' he said. 'But nothing much.' He climbed into bed and pulled the covers up over him. 'But I think I'll sleep now all right.'

She stayed there in the room until he was settled and then crept out into the hall. After a while she began to move around the flat doing odd little chores – for no other reason than simply to keep herself occupied. Then after a while she crept to his bedroom, silently pushed open the door and looked in. The curtains were drawn against the light, but in the gloom she could hear the sound of his breathing. The suspense was unbearable. When was it going to happen?

Later, just before eleven, she quietly went back into his room and in the half-light stood listening to the sound of his breathing. It sounded strange: slow and faint, with touches of harshness as if the breaths came with difficulty. She moved closer to the bed and looked down at him. His flesh had a gray-ish look about it – a dead look. She called his name but he made no response. Carefully she reached in beneath the bed cover, located his wrist and felt his pulse. Sweet Lord, it was only just discernible – only the faintest little flutter there.

Letting him go, she stepped back from the bed. Now all she had to do was wait. Smiling, she turned and left the room.

Taking the morning paper into the sitting room, she settled in her favorite chair. It was impossible to concentrate, though, and in the end she just gave in to the warm, sparkling thoughts that crowded her mind and, closing her eyes, she laid back her head and let the thoughts take over.

A sudden sound brought her head toward the door, and she realized that she had been sleeping.

Arthur was standing there in his dressing gown. He smiled at her. 'You should have gone to bed and had a real nap, like I did,' he said. 'You look as if you could do with it.'

She gaped at him, speechless. When she had found her voice she said, 'How do you feel?'

He nodded, smiling. 'Oh, much better now after my rest.'

'That's good,' she murmured. 'You look better.'

She gazed at him, realizing that her words were true – he *did* look better. So much better. For one thing his colour was better than it had been for years – and also he seemed to be holding himself so much straighter – and she saw too an unaccustomed suppleness in his movement as he turned, stepped toward the window, opened it and breathed in the fresh air.

'Now,' he said, turning to smile back at her, 'I could really eat some breakfast.'

She nodded and, almost in a daze, got up and started off

toward the kitchen, Arthur walking behind her. 'I've already mixed the eggs,' he said. 'I just have to finish them off.'

'No, *I'll* do it,' she retorted quickly.

'I really don't mind, Doris. Honestly.'

She had reached the kitchen table now and she turned back to face him. She had never hated him so much. Scathingly she said, *'You'll* do it, Arthur? *You?'* She laughed. 'Dear Hell, the most inefficient, incompetent man this side of the English Channel. I should let *you* loose in my kitchen? That'll be the day.'

Ten minutes later she moved to the breakfast table, where she placed before him a plate of scrambled eggs. Then, setting down in her own place the two lightly boiled eggs she had prepared so perfectly, she sat and began to eat.

As she ate – without looking at him – she waited for him to complain. There was silence, though, and at last she lifted her head and gazed at him. He sat there, very still, just looking down at his plate. And, dear Satan, he looked better than he had for ages. Nothing had worked – not the clay image, nor the coffin nail nor the stone. But how could it be? She had done everything exactly according to the book. Or at least she had tried to. Then what had gone wrong? Was it that the name on the stone hadn't quite disappeared in the fire? Was it that the nail she had bought hadn't come from a coffin? Was it that the clay model hadn't been quite faithful enough in its likeness? Or was it perhaps because there had been no live chickens at the festival and therefore no blood had been spilled . . . ? The questions went on churning through her mind. Whatever had happened, though, it hadn't worked. He was still here.

Thrusting the thoughts, the questions from her mind, she waited for him to speak, to say something about the eggs. Yet still he said nothing. That wasn't like him; and this time she had truly excelled herself; there was no way that anyone could eat the food she had put before him. Every bit of her seething hatred and frustration had gone into its preparation. He had to react soon.

And then, as she watched him he gave a little sigh, pushed

the empty plate away from him, got up from the table and moved toward the kitchen. 'What's the matter?' she called after him. 'You feel sick?'

When he came back a few seconds later she turned to him as he approached. He had a weird, calm look about him that she had never seen before. And suddenly she was afraid. 'Arthur,' she said, 'don't look at me like that.'

'I've told you, Doris,' he said, shaking his head, 'I've told you over and over again – I don't like my eggs like that.'

Calmly, he raised the hatchet in his right hand and brought it down. Very efficiently, more than competently, and without an ounce of wasted effort, he split her skull from crown to jaw with one clean downward blow. Then, aiming the ax from the side, he struck a second time and severed her head from her neck.

Later, when he had cleaned up the mess, he beat up more eggs and scrambled them the way he liked.

Beverley Nichols

THE BELL

Despite his vast output, which comprises some sixty volumes of fiction, nonfiction, drama, and autobiography, BEVERLEY NICHOLS *(1898-1983) seems to have written only one contribution to the horror genre, the excellent short tale 'The Bell', originally published in* Strand Magazine *in 1946 and last reprinted nearly thirty years ago. Nichols is best remembered today for his books on gardening, which have been continuously in print since their original appearance in the 1930s and remain highly enjoyable, written in a lively and extremely humorous style. During his lifetime he was also well known as a mystery writer (Somerset Maugham cited him as one of the top five British authors in the genre) and an author of children's books. Though it is to be regretted Nichols did not write more horror, it is clear that he himself believed in the paranormal: in his autobiography* Twenty-Five *(1926) he describes a chilling visit he made to a reputedly haunted house, and in* Powers that Be *(1966) he recounts authenticated cases of the supernatural and paranormal. Nichols's early novel* Crazy Pavements *(1927), an updating of Oscar Wilde's* The Picture of Dorian Gray *set amongst the world of the Bright Young Things in 1920s London has been reissued by Valancourt Books as part of our series of rediscovered gay-interest fiction.*

'WELL, HUGH,' said Mrs Lupton, giving a final pat to the pillow, 'you're sure there's nothing more you want?'

Hugh shook his head, and sighed deeply. 'No, my dear. Nothing.'

'In that case I shall be going. The night's growing wilder, and it's past ten o'clock. Mrs Jenkins will come round from the vicarage in the morning, in plenty of time to give you breakfast. Of course, she won't be able to come permanently, but I can easily spare her till you're settled.' She bent down and gave her brother an affectionate peck. 'Good-night, my dear.'

'Good-night.'

She went to the door and turned off the switch. The room was now illuminated only by the green glow from the reading-lamp. In this light Hugh looked very wan and frail. She hated to leave him all alone like this, but then it wasn't as if he were *ill,* though, of course, his heart had never been strong. It was simply a matter of nerves, and though she loved her brother she did think he was being unreasonable.

She obeyed an impulse to speak her mind.

'Hugh, dear, before I go, *do* try not to take it so badly.'

'I can't help it. Frank was with me for forty years. And I feel as if I'd killed him.'

'That's morbid, Hugh, and you know it.'

'He was going to the village on an errand for me when that car ran over him.'

'What has that got to do with it? The car skidded. It was no more your fault than it was mine. It was an act of God.'

'God moves in a mysterious way.' He frowned. And then . . . 'Of course, if I had wished him to die, nothing could have been more convenient, could it?'

'Wished Frank to die? Frank, of all people? But he was the perfect servant!'

'He was too perfect. He never let me do anything for myself.'

'But, my dear, you never showed the least desire to.'

'Didn't I?' He shifted impatiently on the pillow. 'Didn't I?' he repeated. And then, as though he were speaking to himself. 'Maybe not, in the last fifteen or twenty years. You see, by then, he'd got me.'

' "Got" you?'

'Where he wanted. And that was *there.*' He pressed his thumb on the counterpane; she noticed that his hand was trembling. 'He knew I couldn't move an inch without him. It was like a sort of slavery.'

'Hugh . . . You sound as if you hated him.'

'Do I?' he laughed, but there was little mirth in his voice.

'Perhaps he made me hate myself. If life hadn't been so easy, if I'd had to fend for myself, to do my own thinking, even to do my own packing . . .'

'Well?'

'Things might have been different. I might have had adventures. I might have met people.'

'Do you mean women?'

'Perhaps. Frank was jealous of everyone, you know. He was even jealous of you.' He shrugged his shoulders. 'Anyway, it's all too late now.'

He seemed to have drifted far away. Mrs Lupton's kind face was troubled. She had never seen her brother like this before. But then – now she came to think of it – she had never seen him without Frank. All these years, all their lives, Frank – tall, dark, inscrutable Frank – had been hovering somewhere in the background, handing a drink, drawing the curtains, silently, discreetly, serving and watching. It was as though he were with them at this moment. And then, just as she was reproving herself for such thoughts, her heart seemed to freeze.

For she saw that her brother was reaching for the bell.

It lay just above his head – a little bronze button set into the wall. He had lifted his hand over his shoulder, and his finger was groping over the wall's surface.

'Hugh!' Her voice rang out sharply. 'What are you doing?'

He blinked and stared at her. His hand fell down again. He smiled sheepishly.

'Old habits die hard,' he muttered.

There was silence, except for the faint ticking of the bedside clock. Then he spoke again.

'I wonder' – it was as though he were speaking to himself – 'I wonder how many thousand times I have rung that bell? And always it's been answered. I'd lie back, and count nine. One, two, three, four, five, six, seven, eight – nine. And at exactly nine, I'd hear the swing of the green baize door into the hall. Then, if it were stormy weather, there'd be a little tinkle from the Japanese wind bells, as the draught blew down the passage. After that, there'd be three steps on the marble pavement. Then silence, till he reached the top of the staircase. It always creaked, that top step. Then three more steps, and the door opened . . .'

'Hugh!' Try as she would, Mrs Lupton could not prevent her voice from trembling, for Hugh was staring at the door. 'I simply will not listen to this sort of talk.'

He smiled, and seemed to pull himself together.

'I'm sorry, my dear. I was only reminiscing.'

'Well – they're very unhealthy reminiscences.' She stepped forward and gave him a final peck. 'Tomorrow I shall look for some nice old housekeeper who'll make you forget all about – everything.' She felt a sudden aversion to mentioning Frank's name. 'And now, once again, good-night.'

'Good-night, my dear.'

She went out, shutting the door softly behind her. As she began the descent of the staircase, she gave a sudden start as she trod on the top step; she had never noticed that it creaked before.

The hall was bitterly cold and very dimly lit; the electricity must be running down now that Frank was no longer there to tend the little independent plant. It was incredible, she thought, as she groped for the handle of the front door, how much that man had done for Hugh.

She flung open the doors, and the wind rushed in with such force that she staggered back as though she had been pushed aside by some violent intruder. As she pushed it to again, she heard the tinkle of the Japanese wind bells. They seemed to be laughing at her.

Hugh could not sleep.

He switched off the light – noticing as he did so that the power was growing very faint – and lay back staring into the darkness, making plans.

Now that his sister was gone, he felt a curious exhilaration. Life, which had previously been so safe, so ordered, and – frankly – so *dull*, had suddenly become, through Frank's death, dangerous, chaotic, and exciting. If he went abroad, as he well might, he would not have to stay at the best hotels, as he had always done, for forty years, lest he should risk Frank's disapproval. He would not even have to take a dinner-jacket. He could go where he pleased, stay as long as he liked, be shabby, meet artists, gamblers, adventurers. It was not too late – he was only sixty – he might have ten years of life, even now.

Of course, there would be drawbacks. This house – for example. If he stayed in this house, he would need at least three servants to take Frank's place. A man and his wife, and a gardener as well. But then, why need he stay in this house? Would he ever have stayed in it, if it had not been for Frank? It was far too large, too lonely, too gloomy. But he would never have dared to suggest to Frank that they should move. Frank would have been hurt; he would have taken it as a personal reflection on his service – his perfect, all-absorbing, devoted service.

All that was changed now.

Hugh sat up in bed, and switched on the light once more. Even this little act gave him a sense of freedom, for in the old days he would have hesitated, in case Frank, with that weird sixth sense of his, had seen the light and come to ask if there was anything he wanted.

Hugh lay back, letting his mind drift, enjoying the sensuous pleasure of the warm bed in contrast to the tempestuous night outside. But gradually, perhaps because the room was growing colder and the night more wild, his mood changed. He felt restless, fidgety.

He shifted from one side to another, and now and then he paused, tense and rigid, because he had a curious idea that he had heard a sound, far below. He told himself not to be a fool; the old house was full of sounds on a night like this.

What really worried him was his hand, his right hand; he could not keep it still. It plucked nervously at the blanket, straying hither and thither; it seemed to have an independent life of its own. One would have said that it was searching for something, that it was trying to obey some order that it could not, as yet, understand.

And then, suddenly, Hugh realized that without his knowledge or desire his hand was moving – moving slowly, very slowly, in the direction of the bell.

His eyes were wide with terror, but his hand continued to move, nearer, ever nearer. It was being dragged by an irresistible force; and he noticed that the fingers of this hand were numb and cold, though the rest of his body was warm.

He longed to call for help; his lips moved convulsively; but no words came. By a supreme effort of will he held his arm rigid, digging his fingers into the plaster till he could have cried with pain. But the wall seemed cold and slippery, like ice; inch by inch his fingers slid nearer. And now they were touching the little brass ring round the bell itself, and now they were sliding over it – and now ... 'O God, give me strength!' ... his heart cried within him. But no strength came.

Far below came the familiar ring. It seemed to echo all through the empty house, like a voice, calling down the deserted corridors, through the lonely hall, calling for someone who was not there.

Who was not there?

His arm dropped to his side, like a dead thing. His head sank forward; he lay crouched, waiting, like an animal in hiding.

And he began to count nine.

One, two, three – four, five, six – seven ... eight ... nine.

He waited. The seconds ticked by. If ... if ... anyone were coming ... surely he would have heard some sound by now?

But there was no sound save the moan of the wind and the fitful lash of the rain on the windows.

A sob of relief escaped him; and though he was trembling violently, he felt the blood surging back into his arm, warming the icy fingers. Slowly he lifted his head, and raised his hand to his eyes, staring at it.

It was just an ordinary hand – wrinkled, white, with the gold signet ring on the second finger; yes – it was his own hand – and look! It obeyed his own commands. He had no desire to ring the bell any longer. His eyes filled with tears of gratitude; he even began to laugh.

And then the laugh died in his throat. For in the distance, he heard the swing of the green baize door. And the faint tinkle of the Japanese wind bells.

Silence again. His teeth were clenched in expectation, but not yet had he completely surrendered to the wild beast of terror. A part of his conscious brain was working, trying desperately to comfort him, to tell him that his fears were only creatures of the storm, that a window was open, that the door was swinging in the wind.

'Why this long pause' – his conscious brain demanded – 'if anything is below? Why are the seconds again ticking by, with nothing happening?' It was this same conscious brain that supplied the answer.

'Because the thing that is down below is hurt, is wounded – the thing is only dragging itself towards me under a sense of terrible compulsion.'

No sooner had this answer flashed across his mind than the next sound came – the step on the marble pavement – then another, and another – very slowly, as though the thing were dragging its feet in agony.

He was conscious of a sharp pain in his heart. But he knew that at all costs he must get out of bed, and cross the room and himself open the door before the thing that was mounting the stairs could open it. If only he could open the door in time he knew that at last, at the end of his life, he would prove himself the master and not the servant. But if he could not reach it, he knew that the door would be opened by the thing, and that this slavery was on him for ever, beyond the grave.

Gasping, entreating, muttering little prayers, he staggered out of bed. As he did so, the light from the bedside lamp flickered – flickered again – and once again. The electric plant, which Frank had always managed so perfectly, was failing. The room was almost dark.

But there was still time ... still time. He staggered to the door, and reached for the handle. As he did so, he heard a creak. It was the top step.

He sank to his knees. At that very moment, the light went out. Moaning pitifully, he groped for the handle in the darkness.

As he touched it, it turned very slowly, from the other side.

R. Chetwynd-Hayes

THE ELEMENTAL

R. CHETWYND-HAYES (1919-2001) *was a prolific author of horror fiction, publishing over a dozen novels and more than twenty volumes of short stories; he also edited numerous paper-back horror anthologies in the 1970s, including volumes of the* Armada Monster Book *and* Fontana Book of Great Ghost Stories *series. Although Chetwynd-Hayes never wrote a bestseller, he was consistently among England's top earners of public lend-ing rights, meaning that his books were among the most frequently borrowed from British libraries. Chetwynd-Hayes's stories usually feature a mixture of horror and humour, and he often wrote about monsters, both traditional ones like vampires and werewolves and others of his own creation, such as the Shadmock and the Jumpity-Jim. His brilliant collection of interlinked monster stories,* The Monster Club *(1976), was adapted for a cult classic film version in 1981 starring Vincent Price and John Carradine and has been republished by Valancourt, as has a volume of Chetwynd-Hayes's complete vampire tales,* Looking for Something to Suck *(1997). 'The Elemental', which showcases the author's trademark blend of the horrific and humorous, first appeared in 1974 and has not been reprinted in more than twenty-five years.*

'THERE'S AN ELEMENTAL SITTING NEXT TO YOU,' said the fat woman in the horrible flower-patterned dress and amber beads.

Reginald Warren lowered his newspaper, glanced at the empty seats on either side, shot an alarmed look round the car-riage in general, then took refuge behind his *Evening Standard* again.

'He's a killer,' the fat woman insisted.

Reginald frowned and tried to think rationally. How did you tackle a nutty fat woman?

'Thank you,' he said over the newspaper, 'I'm obliged.'

Then he tried to immerse himself in the exploits of a company secretary who had swindled his firm out of thirty thousand pounds. He had not progressed further than the first paragraph when the newspaper shook violently, and a little pyramid formed just above an advertisement for Tomkins Hair Restoring Tonic. He jerked the paper downwards and it was at once skewered on the sharp point of an extremely lethal ladies' umbrella.

'Look, madam,' he spluttered, 'this really is too much.'

'And I really do think you should listen to me, ducks,' the fat lady insisted, completely unmoved by his outburst. 'This is a particularly nasty specimen – a real stinker, and he's growing stronger by the minute.'

Reginald stared longingly at the communication cord, but he had been conditioned from birth to regard this interesting facility as something never to be pulled. Apart from which the old dear looked harmless. She was just batty.

'Have you been feeling weak, run down, rather tired lately?' the fat lady enquired solicitously. 'Don't bother to answer that – I can see you have. He's been feeding on you. They do, you know, nasty, vicious things. I must say I haven't seen a homicidal one before. Sex-starved ones, yes, alcoholic ones, quite often, but killers, they are rare. In a way you are privileged.'

'What . . .' Reginald felt he should display some interest, if only to humour her, 'What exactly is an el . . . ?'

'An elemental?' The fat woman settled back and assumed the air of an expert revealing professional mysteries to a layman. 'Generally speaking it is a spirit of air, fire and water, but the 'orrible thing that's attached itself to you, is something that's trapped between the planes. It sort of lusts after the pleasures of the flesh. It sucks – yes, that's the word – sucks the juices of the soul. You follow me?'

Reginald was incapable of coherent speech; he nodded.

'Good.' She beamed, then fumbled in her handbag and produced a pair of spectacles. 'Let's have a butcher's.' She adjusted the spectacles firmly on her nose and stared intently at a spot immediately to Reginald's left. 'Ah, yes, my word yes. Tut-tut. He's firmly embedded, I fear. His right arm is deep in your left shoulder – ah – he's not happy about my interest . . .' She shook a clenched fist. 'Don't you glare at me, you dirty little basket, I've got your measure, me lad. Yes, I have.'

A shocked expression made her lips pucker and she hurriedly removed the spectacles and replaced them in her bag.

'He spat at me,' she stated.

'Oh dear, I am sorry,' Reginald was completely powerless to subdue the urge to rub his left shoulder, and the fat lady smiled grimly.

'I'm afraid you won't rub 'im off, dear. Not in a lifetime will you rub 'im off.'

The train roared into Hillside Station, and Reginald greeted its appearance much as a Red-Indian-besieged cowboy welcomed the arrival of the U.S. cavalry.

'My station.' He pulled a suitcase from the luggage rack. 'Thank you very much.'

'Wait.'

The fat lady was fumbling in her handbag. 'I've got one somewhere.'

She upturned the bag and its contents tumbled out on to the seat.

'Really, don't bother.' Reginald had the door open. 'Must go . . .'

'Ah!' She produced a scrap of pasteboard. 'My professional card. "Madame Orloff, Clairvoyant Extraordinary. Séances, private sitting, palmistry, full psychic service guaranteed." I can take care of your little problem in no time at all . . .'

Reginald snatched the card from her outstretched hand, slammed the door, and sprinted for the ticket-barrier. Madame Orloff jerked down the carriage window and shouted after his retreating figure:

'Special reduced rates for five sittings, and a bumper free gift of a genuine crystal-ball if you sign up for ten!'

Susan was waiting for him at the station entrance; she was white and gold and wore a backless sun-suit. He instantly forgot the fat lady, banished the last lingering thought of elementals to that dark world which had always lurked at the back of his mind, and drank in her cool beauty. The blood sang through his veins when he kissed her, and he wanted to say beautiful words, but instead: 'It was hot in town.'

'Poor darling.' She slid her hand over his arm and they walked slowly towards the car. 'You look tired. But never mind, seven lazy days in the country is what you need.'

'Seven days of mowing grass, clipping hedges, hoeing, and chopping wood.' He laughed, and the sound was young, care-free. 'What have you been doing today?'

She opened the car door.

'Get in, I'll drive. Doing? Cleaning windows, Hoovering carpets, airing the bed, everything that's needed in a cottage that hasn't been lived in for three months. Did you remember to turn off the gas and lock the flat door before you left?'

He climbed in beside her and settled back with a sigh of content.

'Yes, and I cancelled the milk and papers, turned on the burglar-alarm, and flushed the loo.'

'Good.'

She swung the car out of the station forecourt and they glided smoothly under an archway of trees that linked arms over the narrow road. He closed his eyes and the occasional beam of sunlight flashed across his round, pleasant face.

'I shall sleep tonight. God, I feel tired, drained dry, almost as if . . .'

He stopped, opened his eyes, then frowned.

'As if what?' Susan cast an anxious glance sideways. 'Look, don't you think you ought to see a doctor? I mean it's not like you to be so whacked.'

He forced a laugh.

'Nonsense. It's this hot weather and the stuffy atmosphere in town. No, give me three or four days of this country air, plus three square meals prepared by your fair hand, and I'll be raring to go.'

'I don't cook *square* meals. They're very much *with-it* meals.

But honestly, you do look peaky. I'm going to make you put your feet up.'

He grinned. 'I don't need any encouragement.'

The car shot out from under the trees and the sunlight hit them like a blast from a furnace. Reginald opened the glove-compartment and took out two pairs of sunglasses. He handed one to Susan and donned the other himself.

'We must have anti-glare windscreens installed. Bloody dangerous when the light hits you like that.'

Susan changed gear.

'Don't swear, darling. It's not like you.'

'I'm not swearing. Bloody is a perfectly respectable word these days.'

'But it doesn't sound right coming from you. You're not a bloody type.'

'Oh!' He grimaced, then sank back in his seat. Presently Susan's voice came to him again.

'Darling, I don't want to nag, but don't hump your left shoulder. It makes me think of the Hunchback of Notre-Dame.'

He jerked his head sideways and a little cold shiver rang down his spine.

'What?'

She laughed happily; she was gold and ivory in the afternoon sunlight.

'That made you sit up. "Oh, man, your name is vanity." '

They swept round a bend in the road, and there was the cottage nestling like a broody hen behind the neatly-trimmed privet hedge. Susan unlocked the front door and Mr Hawkins barked happily and reared up on his hind legs, begging to have his ears tickled. 'Down, you monster.' She patted his silky head, then went quickly through the little hall and disappeared into the kitchen. Reginald said: 'Hullo, boy, how are you?' and Mr Hawkins began to wag his tail, but after one or two cautious sniffs turned about and ran into the living-room.

'I think Mr Hawkins has gone off me,' Reginald said on entering the kitchen where Susan was examining a roast that was half out of the oven.

'About fifteen minutes more,' she announced. 'What did you say?'

'I said, I think Mr Hawkins has gone off me. Seems I don't smell right or something.'

'Probably thinks you need a bath. Why not have one before dinner? I've laid out a pair of slacks, and a white shirt; you'll feel much fresher afterwards.'

'Hey . . .' He crept up behind her. 'Are you suggesting I stink?'

She looked back at him, her eyes laughing.

'If your best friend won't tell you, why should I?'

He was but two feet from her, his hand raised above her gleaming white shoulder, and he bellowed with mock rage.

'Is that the way you speak to your lord and master? I've a good mind to . . .'

She pulled a saucepan on to the gas ring, then reached up to a wall cupboard and took down two dinner-plates which she placed in the slotted plate-rack.

'Be a good boy and go have your bath.'

'Right.' He shrugged as he turned towards the door. 'I'll wallow in soap suds and sprinkle *Eau-de-Cologne* under my armpits.'

'Oh, don't! That hurt!'

He stared back at her in astonishment; she was rubbing her right shoulder, her face screwed up in a grimace of pain.

'What are you talking about?'

'Don't play the innocent. You know darn well – you hit me.'

He laughed, imagining this to be some sort of joke, the point of which would become clear in due course.

'Don't be silly, I haven't touched you.'

She was performing an almost comical convulsion in an effort to rub the afflicted shoulder. 'Look, there's only two of us here, and I certainly didn't hit myself.'

'I tell you, I was nowhere near you.'

She turned back to the stove, adjusted the gas, then switched on an extractor-fan. 'It's not important, so there's no need to lie.'

Reginald took a deep breath, and made an effort to speak calmly.

'For the last time, I did not hit you, I was nowhere near you, and I don't like being called a liar.'

She made a great business of opening and closing doors, her face set in angry lines. 'Go and have your bath. Dinner will soon be ready.'

Reginald stamped out of the kitchen. In the hall he almost trod on Mr Hawkins, who yelped and streaked towards the living-room.

Dinner began in an atmosphere that would have gladdened the heart of an Eskimo; a thaw set in when the sweet was served, and warmth returned with the coffee.

'Darling,' he murmured, 'please believe me, I didn't . . .'

She interrupted with a radiant smile.

'Forget it. If a man can't beat his wife, who can he beat?'

'But . . .'

'Not another word. What are we going to do after dinner? Watch television, read, or go to bed?'

'Let's take Mr Hawkins for a walk, then pop in the *Plough* for a quick one.'

'OK.' She began to collect the empty coffee cups. 'I'll wash up, then we'll be off.'

'Give you a hand?' Reginald half-rose from his chair.

'No, you don't, this lot won't take me more than ten minutes. In any case, you always break something. Sit in the armchair and read the local rag – there's an uplifting article on pig-raising.'

'If you insist.'

He got up from the table, then slumped down in an arm-chair, where, after a fruitless attempt at interest in local events, he tossed the newspaper to one side and closed his eyes. The muted sounds made by Susan in the kitchen were pleasant; they told him all was well in his safe little world. They reminded him he had an adoring, beautiful young wife, a good job that he tackled with ease, a flat in town, a cottage in the country, money in the bank. He smiled, and this wonderful sense of security drew him gently into the quiet realms of sleep.

He came awake with a start. The rattle of plates still came from the kitchen; far away on the main by-pass a heavy van sent its muted roar across fields that dozed in the hot evening sun; Mr Hawkins sat under the table and glared at his owner. Reginald blinked, then yawned as he spoke.

'What's the matter with you?'

The dog's usually placid, brown velvet eyes were fierce; his body was rigid, and, even as Reginald spoke, he bared his teeth and growled.

'What the hell!'

Reginald sat upright, and instantly Mr Hawkins retreated and took refuge under a chair, where he crouched, growling and watching his master with a terrible intensity.

'Susan!' Reginald called out, 'what the hell's wrong with this dog?'

Susan came out of the kitchen wiping her hands on a towel, her face creased into an expression of amused enquiry.

'So far as I know, nothing. Why?'

'Well, look at him.' Reginald pointed at the snarling dog, who backed farther away under the chair until all that could be seen was a pair of gleaming eyes and bared teeth. 'Anyone would think I was Dracula's mother looking for her feeding bottle. I say, you don't suppose he's got rabies, do you?'

'Good heavens, no.' Susan crouched down and called softly: 'Mr Hawkins, come on boy.'

Mr Hawkins ran to her, his tail wagging feebly, and he whimpered when she patted his head and stroked his soft coat.

'Poor old chap, has the heat got you down? Eh? Do you want nice walkies? Eh? Nice walkies?'

Mr Hawkins displayed all the signs of intense pleasure at this prospect, and performed a little dance of pure joy.

'He's all right,' Susan said, straightening up. 'It must have been your face that put him off.'

'Well, he put the fear of God into me,' Reginald rose. 'He hasn't been normal since I arrived. Perhaps we ought to take him to a vet.'

'Nonsense, he's fine.' Susan went out into the hall and the dog scampered after her. 'It must have been the heat that got him down. Do you think I need a coat?'

'No, go as you are and shock the natives.' Reginald grinned, then frowned when he saw a six-inch-long mark that marred her right shoulder. 'No, come to think of it, perhaps you'd better put on a jacket or something. It may be chilly before we get back.'

She took a thin satin shawl down from the hall stand.

'I'll wear this. There isn't a breath of wind, and I wouldn't be surprised if there's a storm before morning.'

Mr Hawkins was flattened against the front door, and when Reginald opened it, he growled low in his throat before scampering madly along the garden path and out through a hole in the hedge. Reginald smiled grimly as he closed the door and followed Susan towards the gate.

'There's something bothering that damned dog.'

Out in the narrow road Susan took his arm and they walked slowly under a steel-blue sky.

'Don't be so silly. He's frisky. Just heat and sex.'

'Ah!' Reginald nodded. 'I know then how he feels. What a combination.' They left the roadway, climbed a stile and walked ankle-deep through lush summer grass, as the dying sun painted the far-away hillsides golden-brown. Mr Hawkins raced happily back and forth, sniffing at rabbit holes, saluting trees, reliving the days when his forebears acknowledged neither man nor beast as master, and Susan sighed.

'Heaven must be eternity spent in walking through an English field at sunset.'

'And hell,' Reginald retorted, 'must be eternity spent in a tube train during the rush hour.'

They walked for a few minutes in silence; Susan adjusted her shawl, and Reginald watched her, a tiny frown lining his forehead.

'Susan, did something really . . . ?'

'Did something really what?'

He shook his head. 'Nothing. Forget it.'

'No, tell me. What were you going to say?'

'It wasn't important.' He patted the hand that lay on his arm. 'Just a passing thought.'

The sun had set when they once again walked up the garden path, and a full moon lit up the cottage and surrounding countryside, painting the red-bricked walls, the neat little garden, with a cold silver hue. Susan was laughing softly, and Reginald was frowning; he looked tired and drawn.

'Honestly, you must admit it was funny.' She inserted the latch-key, then opened the door and led the way into the hall. 'That little girl . . .'

'Yes, yes, you've been through it three times before,' Reginald snapped, but his irritability only provoked further laughter.

'But . . .' She opened the living-room door and switched on the light. 'But in front of a crowd of beer-boozy layabouts this little mite pointed at you and said . . .' For a moment Susan could not continue, then she wiped her eyes . . . and said, "Ugly man making faces at me." '

'All right,' Reginald glared at Mr Hawkins, who was watching him from under the table. 'All right, so it was funny. Let's forget it, shall we?'

'But you should have seen your face. I thought for a moment you were going to be sick.'

Reginald slumped into a chair and absentmindedly rubbed his left shoulder.

'Say, ugly face, you don't want anything else to drink after all that beer, do you?'

'No, and cut it out.'

'Come on, now.' She sat on the arm of his chair. 'Where's your sense of humour? She was only a little thing, and probably tired out. I mean to say, you weren't really making faces at her, were you?'

'Of course not.'

'Well then, why so grumpy?'

'I don't know.' He spoke softly, 'I honestly don't know.'

'Let's go to bed,' she whispered, 'and dream away the dark-footed hours.'

'Yup.' He rose, then smiled down at her; she slid an arm about his neck and laid a soft cheek against his own.

'You are the most beautiful man in the whole world,' she said.

He nodded.

'I guess you're right at that.'

Their laughter mingled when he carried her up the stairs, and Mr Hawkins stood in the hallway and watched their ascending figures with worried eyes.

The curtains were drawn back, the soft moonlight kept shadows at bay, and they lay side by side and waited for the silence to summon sleep.

'Think of all the bunny-rabbits peacefully asleep in their burrows,' she whispered.

'Or think of them eating Farmer Thing-a-bob's cabbages,' he murmured.

She giggled.

'Are you sleepy?'

'Somewhat.'

'Why do you insist on sleeping on the right hand side of the bed?'

'That's a darn fool question.' He stirred uneasily and widened the space between them. 'Because it's man's prerogative, I guess.'

There was a full minute of blessed silence.

'Darling, if you must hold my hand, don't press so hard.'

His voice came from the half world where sleep and consciousness hold an even balance.

'I'm not holding your hand.'

'But, darling, you are, and you must cut your nails.'

'Stop blathering and go to sleep.'

Suddenly her body began to thresh wildly, and her cry of protest rose to a terrified scream.

'Reginald, what are you doing? No . . . oh, my God!'

For a second he imagined she must be playing some silly joke, that this was a not very subtle way of informing him she was not prepared to sleep, then the violent threshing of her legs, the choking gasps, made him sit up and fumble frantically for the light switch. As lamplight blasted darkness, hurled it back against the walls, she leapt from the bed and stood facing him, gasping, massaging her throat, staring with fear-crazed eyes. He was dimly aware of a faint smell, sweet, cloying, like dead flowers.

'What's wrong?' He climbed out of bed and she backed to the wall, shaking her head.

'Keep away from me.'

'What the hell . . . ?'

He moved round the foot of the bed then stopped when he saw her expression of terror deepen. At that moment, truth reared up in his brain, but he ignored it, crushed it under the weight of his disbelief, and he whispered:

'You know I would do nothing to hurt you.'

Her whisper matched his and it was as though they were in some forbidden place, afraid lest a dreaded guardian heard their voices.

'You tried to choke me. Awful hands with nails like talons, and a foul breath that I can still smell.'

He could scarcely utter the next words.

'Could that have been me?'

The awful fear on her face was dreadful to watch, and truth was uncoiling again, would not be denied.

'Then – who was it?'

'Get back into bed,' he urged. 'Please, I will sit on a chair. I won't come near you, I promise.'

The beautiful eyes still watched him as she moved to obey, but the moment her hand touched the pillow, she recoiled.

'The smell – the stench, it's still here.'

They went downstairs and seated themselves in the living-room, far apart, like strangers who may never meet again, and his voice bridged the great gulf that separated them.

'There was a woman on the train. She said she was a medium.' She waited for his next words as though they were venomous snakes being offered on a silver tray.

'She said I had an elemental attached to my left shoulder. Apparently it is feeding off me, growing stronger by the minute.'

Susan did not move or betray the slightest sign she had understood or even heard what he said.

'A few hours ago, I guess, we would have laughed at the very idea.' Reginald was staring at the empty fireplace, even giving the impression he was addressing it rather than the silent girl who sat clutching her dressing-gown with white fingers. 'It would have been a great giggle, a funny story to tell our friends over a drink. Now . . .'

They sat opposite each other for the remainder of the dark hours. Once, Mr Hawkins howled from his chosen place in the empty hall. They ignored him.

Reginald found the card in his jacket pocket and read the inscription aloud.

MADAME ORLOFF
Clairvoyant Extraordinary

15 Disraeli Road,
Clapham, London, S.W.4.

He dialled the telephone number at the foot of the card and waited; presently a voice answered.

'Madame Orloff, Clairvoyant Extraordinary, messages from beyond a speciality, speaking.'

Reginald cleared his throat.

'My name is Reginald Warren. I don't suppose you remember me – we met on a train yesterday . . .'

'Yes, indeed I do.' The voice took on a joyful tone. 'You're the man with the nasty little E. I expect you want me to get cracking on the 'orrible little basket.'

'Well,' Reginald lowered his voice, 'last night it tried to strangle my wife.'

'What's that? Speak up, my dear man. It did what?'

'Tried to strangle my wife,' Reginald repeated.

'Yes, I expect it did. I told you it was a homicidal. Now look, stay put, I'll have to belt down there. It's a bit of a bind because I had two table-tapping sessions and one poltergeist on the books for this afternoon. Still, it can't be helped. Let me have your address.'

Reginald parted with his address with the same reluctance that he would have experienced had he given up his soul.

'The Oak Cottage, Hawthorne Lane, Hillside, Surrey.'

'Right.' The cheerful voice had repeated the address, word by word. 'Be with you about three. I wouldn't eat too hearty if I were you. He seems to be putting on weight if he's been up to his little tricks so soon. You may have a materialization, although I doubt it at this stage. His main objective is to get inside you. Take over. Follow me?'

'Yes,' Reginald swallowed, 'I think so.'

'Good man. See you at three. Can I get a cab at the station?'

'No, but I'll pick you up.'

'Not on your nelly.' The voice assumed a shocked tone. 'He'll most likely try to run you off the road if he knows I'm coming. I'll hire a car – and add the cost to my bill, of course.'

'Of course,' Reginald agreed, 'anything at all.'

Madame Orloff arrived at five minutes past three; she crossed her fingers and waved at Mr Hawkins, who promptly made a bolt for the stairs.

'Poor little dear,' she sighed. 'Animals always spot them first, you know. Animals and some small children. Now let's have a butcher's.'

She put on her spectacles and studied Reginald with keen interest.

'My, my, we have grown. Yes indeed, he's sucking up the old spiritual fluids like a baby at its mother's breast.' She bent forward and sniffed, looking rather like a well-fed bulldog who is eagerly anticipating its dinner. 'Pongs too, don't he?'

'How did it become attached to me?' Reginald asked, aware that Susan was watching their visitor with an expression that was divided between horror and amazement. 'I mean, I was all right up to yesterday.'

'Been in a tube train lately?' Madame Orloff asked. He nodded.

'Thought so. That damned Underground is packed with them during the rush hour. I once saw a bank clerk with six of 'em clinging to him like limpets, and he picked up two more between Charing Cross and Leicester Square. Wouldn't listen to me, of course.'

She turned her attention to Susan, who cringed as the heavy figure came towards her.

'You're a pretty dear, and sensitive too, I fear. You must watch yourself, poppet, keep off animal foods – and I should wear a sprig of garlic if I were you. They can't stand garlic or clean thoughts. Think clean and religious thoughts, dear. Try to picture the Archbishop of Canterbury taking a bath. Now . . .' She rolled up her sleeves. 'Let's see if we can get 'im dislodged. Sit yourself down, lad. No, not in an easy-chair, this plain straight-backed one is the ticket, and angel-love, will you draw the curtains? Light is apt to put me off me stroke.'

Reginald was seated on a dining-room chair, the sunlight was diffused through blue nylon curtains, and the room looked cool, peaceful, a place where one might doze away the years. Susan whimpered.

'I'm frightened. Don't let her do it.'

'Hush, dear.' Madame Orloff twisted her head round. 'We must dislodge the basket, or he'll be at your throat again, as sure as a preggers cat has kittens.'

She put a large beringed hand on either side of Reginald's head, and closed her eyes.

'I don't follow the usual formula, so don't be surprised at anything I might say. It's just ways and means of concentrating me powers.'

She began to jerk Reginald's head backwards and forwards while intoning a little rhyming ditty in a high-pitched voice.

> 'Black, foul thing from down below,
> Get you hence, or I'll bestow
> A two-footed kick right up your bum
> That'll make your buttocks come through your tum.'

She writhed, jerked, made the amber beads rattle like bones in a box, all the while jerking Reginald's head and pressing down on his temples, then gave vent to a roar of rage.

'No you don't, you black-hearted little basket! Try to bite, would you? Get out, out – out – out . . .

> 'Get right out or I'll bash your snout,
> Go right under, or get your number,
> No more kicks, or you'll pass bricks,
> No more crying, it's no use trying,
> Out-a-daisy, you're driving me crazy.'

Madame Orloff snatched her hands from Reginald's head and flopped down in a chair, where she sat mopping her sweat-drenched face with a large red handkerchief.

'Must have a breather, dear. Strewth, he's made me sweat like a pig. I've tackled some 'ard ones in me time, but he takes the biscuit.' She clenched her fist and shook it in Reginald's direction. 'You can grin at me like a cat that's nicked the bacon, but I'll get your measure yet.' She turned to Susan. 'Get us a glass of water, there's a dear.'

Susan ran from the room, and Madame Orloff shook her head.

'You'll have to watch that one. She's hot stuff, attracts 'em like flies to cow dung, if you get my meaning. She's soft and pliable, and they'll slide into her as easy as a knife going into butter. You back already, dear? Mustn't run like that, you'll strain something.'

She drank greedily from the glass that Susan handed her then rubbed her hands.

'Thirsty work this. Well, as the bishop said to the actress "let's have another go." '

She got up and once again took Reginald's head between her hands. Her face wore an expression of grim determination.

'Now, dear, I want you to help me. Strain. That's the word, dear. Strain. Possession is rather like having constipation. You have to strain. Keep repeating "Old Bill Bailey" to yourself. It'll help no end. Ready?'

Reginald tried to nod but was unable to do so due to Madame's firm hold, so he muttered, 'Yes' instead.

'Right – strain.

> 'Nasty horsie that's had no oats,
> This little bunny ain't afraid of stoats,

(Strain man – Old Bill Bailey)

> Coal black pussy, he's no tom,
> He's had his op, so get you gone.'

Madame raised her voice to a shout, and a large blue vase on the mantelpiece suddenly crashed onto the tiled hearth.

'Strain – Old Bill Bailey – come on, we've got 'im! Out – out – get yer skates on ...

> 'Out of the window, out through the door,
> There's no marbles here, he'll keep you poor,
> Don't grind your teeth ...'

A chair went tumbling across the floor, books came hurling from their shelves, a rug left the floor and wrapped itself round the ceiling lamp, and a cold wind tugged at the window curtains. Madame Orloff lowered her voice, but it was still clear, unexpectedly sad.

> 'Lonely wanderer of the starless night,
> You must not stay, it is not right,
> Blood is for flesh, and flesh is for blood,
> We live for an hour, then are lost in the flood
> That sweeps us away into fathomless gloom,
> We spend eternity in a darkened room.'

'Please stop!' Susan's voice was lost amid the howling wind, but Madame Orloff's cry of triumph rang out.

'Strain – strain ... he's coming out. Aye, he's coming out as smooth as an eye leaving its socket. He's fighting every inch of the way, but old Ma Perkins was one too many for him. Out you go, my beauty, out you go, down to the land where black mountains glow with never-quenched fire, and white worms crawl from the corrupt earth, even as maggots seethe from a carcass on a hot afternoon. Go . . . *go* . . .'

The cold wind died, hot air seeped back into the room; all around lay wrecked pictures, scattered books, broken furniture. An ugly crack disfigured the polished surface of a table. Susan was crying softly, Reginald was white-faced, looking like a man who has survived a long illness. Madame Orloff rose, pulled open the window curtains, then looked about with an air of satisfaction.

'A bit of a ruddy mess, but then, as someone once said, you can't make an omelette without breaking eggs. 'Fraid me services come a bit high, dear. I'll want fifty nicker for this little do.'

'Worth every penny,' Reginald rose somewhat unsteadily to his feet. 'I can't thank you enough, Madame, I feel like . . .'

'A feather, eh?' Madame Orloff beamed. 'A great weight lifted off yer shoulders? I know what you mean. I remember an old geezer down in Epsom; he had a nasty attached to him that was as big as a house. Ruddy great thing, had a lust for rice puddings, made the poor old sod eat three at one sitting. When I got shot of it, he leapt about like a two-year-old. Said he felt like floating. Well . . .' She took up her handbag. 'Mustn't keep that car waiting any longer – the fare will cost you a fortune.' She put a hand under Susan's chin and tilted her head; the blue eyes were bright with tears.

'Cheer up, ducks. It's all over now. Nothing to worry your pretty little head about any more.'

'You must stay for dinner,' Susan said softly. 'We can't let you go like this . . .'

'Thanks all the same, but I've got a sitting laid on for six o'clock, so I'll leave you to clear up the mess. Don't trouble to see me out. I'm quite capable of opening and closing a door.'

From the hallway she looked back.

'I should keep away from the Underground during the rush hour, Mr Warren. The place is a cesspit – everything from a damn nuisance poltergeist to a vampire-elemental. See you.'

The front-door slammed and Reginald gathered Susan up

into his arms; he patted her shaking shoulders and murmured. 'There, there, it's all over now. It's all over.' They sat in the twilight, younger than youth, older than time, and rejoiced in each other.

'You are wonderful,' she said.

'True,' he nodded.

'And awfully conceited.'

'Self-confidence,' he corrected. 'The weak are vain, the strong self-confident.'

'And what am I?'

'White, gold and tinged with pink.'

'I like that.' She snuggled up to him and Mr. Hawkins dozed peacefully on the hearthrug.

Presently –

'What's that?'

She sat up. Fear was in waiting, ready to leap into her eyes.

'Nothing.' He pulled her back. 'Just nerves. It's all over now.'

'I thought I heard someone knocking.'

'There's no one to come knocking at our door. No one at all.'

Mr Hawkins whimpered in his sleep, and somewhere above, a floorboard creaked.

'The wood contracting,' he comforted her. 'The temperature is falling, so the wood contracts. We must not let imagination run away with us.'

'Reginald . . .' She was staring up at the ceiling. 'Madame Orloff – she got it loose from you, and I am grateful, but suppose – '

Another floorboard creaked and a bedroom door slammed.

'Suppose – it's – still here?'

He was going to say 'Nonsense', laugh at her fears, but Mr Hawkins was up on his four legs, his coat erect, growling fiercely as he glared at the closed door. Heavy footsteps were on the landing, pacing back and forth, making the ceiling lamp shake, breaking now and again into a kind of skipping dance.

Susan screamed before she collapsed into merciful oblivion, and at once the sounds ceased, to be replaced by a menacing silence.

Reginald laid Susan down upon the sofa and crept on tip-toe towards the door. When he opened it a wave of foul-smelling cold air made him gasp, then, with courage born of desperation, he went out to the hall and peered up into the gloom-haunted staircase.

It was coming down. A black blob that was roughly human-shaped, but the face was real – luminous-green; the eyes, red; a bird's-nest thatch of black hair. It was grinning, and the unseen feet were making the stairs tremble. Reginald, aware only that he must fight, picked up a small hall table and flung it straight at the approaching figure. Instantly, something – some invisible force – hurled him against the front door, and he lay on the door-mat powerless to move. The Thing moved slowly down the stairs, and for a hell-bound second the red eyes glared down at the prostrate man before it clumped into the living-room. The door slammed, and Mr Hawkins howled but once.

Minutes passed and Reginald tried to move, but the power had gone from his legs. Also, there was a dull pain in the region of his lower spine, and he wondered if his back were broken. At last, the living-room door slid open, went back on its hinges with a protesting creak as though wishing to disclaim all responsibility for that which was coming out. Susan walked stiff-legged into the hall, white-faced, clothes torn, but her face was lit by a triumphant smile, and Reginald gasped out aloud with pure relief.

'Darling, thank heavens you're safe. Don't be alarmed – it flung me against the door, but I think I've only sprained something. Give me a hand up and we'll get the hell out of here.'

She moved closer, still walking with that grotesque stiff-legged gait. Her head went over to one side, and for the first time he saw her eyes. They were mad – mad – mad . . . Her mouth opened, and the words came out in a strangled, harsh tone.

'Life . . . life . . . life . . . flesh . . . flesh . . . flesh . . . blood . . .'

'Susan!' Reginald screamed and tried to get up, but collapsed as a blast of pain seared his back; he could only watch with dumb horror as she swung her stiff left leg round and began to hobble towards the broken table that lay on the bottom stair. She had difficulty in bending over to pick up the carved walnut leg, and even more difficulty in straightening up, but she gripped the leg firmly in her right hand, and the grimace on her face could have denoted pleasure.

'You ... denied ... me ... life,' the harsh voice said. 'You ... denied ... me ... life ...'

She, if the thing standing over Reginald could still be so called, looked down with red-tinted eyes, horror in ivory and gold, and he wanted even then to hold her, kiss away the grotesque lines from around the full-lipped mouth, murmur his great love, close those dreadful eyes with gentle fingers. Then the carved walnut leg came down and smashed deep into his skull, and the world exploded, sent him tumbling over and over into eternity.

Presently the Thing which had been Susan went out into the evening that was golden with the setting sun. It drank deep of the cool air, for storm clouds were pouring in from the west and soon there would be rain.

It went stiff-legged down the garden path, and out into the roadway. There was still much killing to be done.

Mary Elizabeth Braddon

HERSELF

MARY ELIZABETH BRADDON (1835-1915) *was a prolific author of Victorian popular fiction, producing more than eighty novels, along with numerous short stories and articles; she also founded and edited the magazine* Belgravia. *Braddon is remembered as the queen of 'Sensation' fiction, a genre that became extremely popular in England in the 1860s and '70s, with plots involving crime and murder and often incorporating then-controversial elements such as adultery and bigamy. But Braddon also deserves to be known for her Gothic and horror stories, some of which, like 'Herself', rank among the best of their era. Two of Braddon's novels have appeared in scholarly editions from Valancourt:* Thou Art the Man (1894), *a murder mystery that incorporates Victorian theories of disease and criminality, and* Dead Love Has Chains (1907), *a psychological novel about the relationship between a woman disgraced by having had a child out of wedlock and a man who has previously been committed as insane and is in danger of relapsing. 'Herself', in our opinion one of the very best of Braddon's Gothic tales, was originally published in the Sheffield* Weekly Telegraph's *Christmas number in 1894 and has very seldom been anthologized.*

CHAPTER I

'AND YOU INTEND TO KEEP THE ORANGE GROVE for your own occupation, Madam,' interrogates the lawyer gravely, with his downward-looking eyes completely hidden under bushy brows.

'Decidedly,' answered my friend. 'Why, the Orange Grove is the very best part of my fortune. It seems almost a special Providence, don't you know, Helen,' pursued Lota, turning to me, 'that my dear old grandfather should have made himself a winter home in the south. There are the doctors always teasing me about my weak chest, and there is a lonely house and gardens and orange groves waiting for me in a climate invented on purpose for weak chests. I shall live there every winter of my life, Mr Dean.'

The eminently respectable solicitor allowed a lapse of silence before he replied.

'It is not a lucky house, Miss Hammond.'

'How not lucky?'

'Your grandfather only lived to spend one winter in it. He was in very good health when he went there in December – a strong, sturdy old man – and when he sent for me in February to prepare the will which made you his sole heiress, I was shocked at the change in him – broken – wasted – nerves shattered – a mere wreck.

'It was not merely that he was aged – he was mentally changed – nervous, restless, to all appearance unhappy.'

'Well, didn't you ask him why?' demanded Lota, whose impetuous temper was beginning to revolt against the lawyer's solemnity.

'My position hardly warranted my questioning Mr Hammond on a matter so purely personal. I saw the change, and regretted it. Six weeks later he was gone.'

'Poor old gran'pa. We were such friends when I was a little thing. And then they sent me to Germany with a governess – poor little motherless mite – and then they packed me off to Pekin where father was Consul and there he died, and then they sent me home again – and I was taken up by the smartest of all my aunts, and had my little plunge in society, and always exceeded my allowance; was up to my eyes in debt – for a girl. I suppose a man would hardly count such bills as I used to owe. And then Gran'pa took it into his head to be pleased with me; and here I am – residuary legatee. I think that's what you call me?' with an interrogative glance at the lawyer, who nodded a grave assent, 'and I am going to spend the winter months in my villa near Taggia. Only think of that, Helen, Taggia – Tag-gi-a!'

She syllabled the word slowly, ending with a little smack of her pretty lips as if it were something nice to eat, and she looked at me for sympathy.

'I haven't the faintest idea what you mean by Tag-gi-a,' said I. 'It sounds like an African word.'

'Surely you have read Dr Antonio.'

'Surely I have not.'

'Then I have done with you. There is a gulf between us. All that I know of the Liguria comes out of that delightful book. It taught me to pine for the shores of the Mediterranean when I was quite a little thing. And they show you Dr Ruffini's house at Taggia. His actual house, where he actually lived.'

'You ought to consider, Miss Hammond, that the Riviera has changed a good deal since Ruffini's time,' said the lawyer. 'Not that I have anything to say against the Riviera *per se*. All I would advise is that you should winter in a more convenient locality than a romantic gorge between San Remo and Alassio. I would suggest Nice, for instance.'

'Nice. Why, someone was saying only the other day that Nice is the chosen rendezvous of all the worst characters in Europe and America.'

'Perhaps that's what makes it such an agreeable place,' said the lawyer. 'There are circles and circles in Nice. You need never breathe the same atmosphere as the bad characters.'

'A huge towny place,' exclaimed Lota. 'Gran'pa said it was not better than Brighton.'

'Could anything be better than Brighton?' asked I.

'Helen, you were always a Philistine. It was because of the horridness of Nice and Cannes that gran'pa bought a villa – four times too big for him – in this romantic spot.'

She kissed the white house in the photograph. She gloated over the wildness of the landscape, in which the villa stood out, solitary, majestic. Palms, olives, cypress – a deep gorge cutting through the heart of the picture – mountains romantically remote – one white crest in the furthest distance – a foreground of tumbled crags and threads of running water.

'Is it really real?' she asked suddenly, 'not a photographer's painted background? They have such odious tricks, those photographers. One sits for one's picture in a tidy South Kensington studio, and they send one home smirking out of a primeval forest, or in front of a stormy ocean. Is it real?'

'Absolutely real.'

'Very well, Mr Dean. Then I am going to establish myself there in the first week of December, and if you want to be very careful of me for gran'pa's sake all you have to do is to find me a thoroughly respectable major-domo, who won't drink my wine or run away with my plate. My aunt will engage the rest of my people.'

'My dear young lady, you may command any poor services of mine; but really now, is it not sheer perversity to choose a rambling house in a wild part of the country when your ample means would allow you to hire the prettiest bijou-villa on the Riviera?'

'I hate bijou houses, always too small for anybody except some sour old maid who wants to over-hear all her servants say about her. The spacious rambling house – the wild solitary landscape – those are what I want, Mr Dean. Get me a butler who won't cut my throat, and I ask no more.'

'Then madam, I have done. A wilful woman must have her way, even when it is a foolish way.'

'Everything in life is foolish,' Lota answered, lightly. 'The people who live haphazard come out just as well at the end as your ineffable wiseacres. And now that you know I am fixed as Fate, that nothing you can say will unbend my iron will, do, like a darling old family lawyer whom I have known ever since I began to know one face from another, do tell me why you object to the Orange Grove. Is it the drainage?'

'There is no drainage.'

'Then that's all right,' checking it off on her forefinger. 'Is it the neighbours?'

'Need I say there are no neighbours?' pointing to the photograph.

'Number two satisfactory.'

'Is it the atmosphere? Low the villa is not; damp it can hardly be, perched on the side of a hill.'

'I believe the back rooms are damp. The hill side comes too near the windows. The back rooms are decidedly gloomy, and I believe damp.'

'And how many rooms are there in all?'

'Nearer thirty than twenty. I repeat it is a great rambling house, ever so much too large for you or any sensible young lady.'

'For the sensible young lady, no doubt,' said Lota, nodding impertinently at me. 'She likes a first floor in Regency Square, Brighton, with a little room under the tiles for her maid. I am not sensible, and I like lots of rooms; rooms to roam about in, to furnish and unfurnish, and arrange and rearrange; rooms to see ghosts in. And now, dearest Mr Dean, I am going to pluck out the heart of your mystery. What kind of ghost is it that haunts the Orange Grove? I know there is a ghost.'

'Who told you so?'

'You. You have been telling me so for the last half-hour. It is because of the ghost you don't want me to go to the Orange Grove. You might just as well be candid and tell me the whole story. I am not afraid of ghosts. In fact, I rather like the idea of having a ghost on my property. Wouldn't you, Helen, if you had property?'

'No,' I answered, decisively. 'I hate ghosts. They are always associated with damp houses and bad drainage. I don't believe you would find a ghost in Brighton, not even if you advertised for one.'

'Tell me all about the ghost,' urged Lota.

'There is nothing to tell. Neither the people in the neighbourhood nor the servants of the house went so far as to say the Orange Grove was haunted. The utmost assertion was that time out of mind the master or the mistress of that house had been miserable.'

'Time out of mind. Why, I thought gran'pa built the house twenty years ago.'

'He only added the front which you see in the photograph. The back part of the house, the larger part, is three hundred years old. The place was a monkish hospital, the infirmary belonging to a Benedictine monastery in the neighbourhood, and to which the sick from other Benedictine houses were sent.'

'Oh, that was ages and ages ago. You don't suppose that the ghosts of all the sick monks, who were so inconsiderate as to die in my house, haunt the rooms at the back?'

'I say again, Miss Hammond, nobody has ever to my knowledge asserted that the house was haunted.'

'Then it can't be haunted. If it were the servants would have seen something. They are champion ghost-seers.'

'I am not a believer in ghosts, Miss Hammond,' said the friendly old lawyer, 'but I own to a grain of superstition on one point. I can't help thinking there is such a thing as "luck." I have seen such marked distinctions between the lucky and unlucky people I have met in my professional career. Now, the Orange Grove has been an unlucky house for the last hundred years. Its bad luck is as old as its history. And why, in the name of all that's reasonable, should a beautiful young lady with all the world to choose from insist upon living at the Orange Grove?'

'First, because it is my own house; next, because I conceived a passion for it the moment I saw this photograph; and thirdly, perhaps because your opposition has given a zest to the whole thing. I shall establish myself there next December, and you must come out to me after Christmas, Helen. Your beloved Brighton is odious in February and March.'

'Brighton is always delightful,' answered I, 'but of course I shall be charmed to go to you.'

CHAPTER II

AN EARTHLY PARADISE

I was Lota's dearest friend, and she was mine. I had never seen anyone quite so pretty, or quite so fascinating then: I have never seen anyone as pretty or as fascinating since. She was no Helen, no Cleopatra, no superbly modelled specimen of typical loveliness. She was only herself. Like no one else, and to my mind better than everybody else – a delicately wrought ethereal creature, all spirit and fire and impulse and affection, flinging herself with ardour into every pursuit, living intensely in the present, curiously reckless of the future, curiously forgetful of the past.

When I parted with her at Charing Cross Station on the first of December it was understood that I was to join her about the middle of January. One of my uncles was going to Italy at that time, and was to escort me to Taggia, where I was to be met by my hostess. I was surprised, therefore, when a telegram arrived before Christmas, entreating me to go to her at once.

I telegraphed back: 'Are you ill?'

Answer: 'Not ill; but I want you.'

My reply: 'Impossible. Will go as arranged.'

I would have given much, as I told Lota in the letter that followed my last message, to have done what she wished; but family claims were too strong. A brother was to marry at the beginning of the year, and I should have been thought heartless had I shirked the ceremony. And there was the old idea of Christmas as a time for family gatherings. Had she been ill, or unhappy, I would have cancelled every other claim, and gone to her without one hour's delay, I told her; but I knew her a creature of caprices, and this was doubtless only one caprice among many.

I knew that she was well cared for. She had a maiden aunt with her, the mildest and sweetest of spinsters, who absolutely adored her. She had her old nurse and slave, a West Indian half-caste, who had accompanied her from Pekin, and she had –

'Another, and a dearer one still.'

Captain Holbrook, of the Stonyshere Regiment, was at San Remo. I had seen his name in a travelling note in the *World*, and I smiled as I read the announcement, and thought how few of his acquaintance would know as well as I knew the magnet which attracted him to quit San Remo rather than go to Monte Carlo or Nice. I knew that he loved Violetta Hammond devotedly, and that she had played fast and loose with him, amused at his worship, accepting all his attentions in her light happy manner, and giving no heed to the future.

Yes, my pretty, insouciante Lota was well cared for, ringed round with exceeding love, guarded as faithfully as a god in an Indian temple. I had no uneasiness about her, and I alighted in a very happy frame of mind at the quiet little station at Taggia, beside the tideless sea, in the dusk of a January evening.

Lota was on the platform to welcome me, with Miss Elderson, her maternal aunt, in attendance upon her, the younger lady muffled in sealskin from head to foot.

'Why Lota,' said I, when we had kissed, and laughed a little with eyes full of tears, 'you are wrapped up as if this were Russia, and to me the air feels balmier than an English April.'

'Oh, when one has a hundred guinea coat one may as well wear it,' she answered carelessly. 'I bought this sealskin among my mourning.'

'Lota is chillier than she used to be,' said Miss Elderson, in her plaintive voice.

There was a landau with a pair of fine strong horses waiting to carry us up to the villa. The road wound gently upward, past orange and lemon groves, and silvery streamlets, and hanging woods, where velvet dark cypresses rose tower-like amidst the silvery grey of the olives, and so to about midway between the valley, where Taggia's antique palaces and church towers gleamed pale in the dusk, and the crest of the hill along which straggled the white houses of a village. The after-glow was rosy in the sky when a turn of the road brought our faces towards the summer-like sea, and in that lovely light every line in Lota's face was but too distinctly visible. Too distinctly, for I saw the cruel change which three months had made in her fresh young beauty. She had left me in all the bloom of girlhood, gay, careless, brimming over with the joy of life and the new delight of that freedom of choice which wealth gives to a fatherless and motherless girl. To go where she liked, do as she liked, roam the world over, choosing always the companions she loved – that had been Lota's dream of happiness, and if there had been some touch of self-love in her idea of bliss there had been also a generous and affectionate heart, and unfailing kindness to those whom Fate had not used so kindly.

I saw her now a haggard, anxious-looking woman, the signs of worry written too plainly on the wan pinched face, the lovely eyes larger but paler than of old, and the markings of nervous depression visible in the droop of the lips that had once been like Cupid's bow.

I remembered Mr Dean's endeavour to dissuade her from occupying her grandfather's villa on this lovely hill, and I began to detest the Orange Grove before I had seen it. I was prepared to find an abode of gloom – a house where the foul miasma from some neighbouring swamp crept in at every open window, and hung grey and chill in every passage; a house whose too obvious unwholesomeness had conjured up images of terror, the spectral forms engendered of slackened nerves, and sleepless nights. I made up my mind that if it were possible for a bold and energetic woman to influence Lota Hammond I would be that woman, and whisk her off to Nice or Monte Carlo before she had time to consider what I was doing.

There would be a capital pretext in the Carnival. I would declare that I had set my heart upon seeing a Carnival at Nice; and once there I would take care she never returned to the place that was killing her. I looked, with a thrill of anger, at the mild sheep-faced aunt. How could she have been so blind as not to perceive the change in her niece? And Captain Holbrook! What a poor creature, to call himself a lover, and let the girl he loved perish before his eyes.

I had time to think while the horses walked slowly up the hill-road, for neither the aunt nor the niece had much to say. Each in her turn pointed out some feature in the view. Lota told me that she adored Taggia, and doted on her villa and garden; and that was the utmost extent of our conversation in the journey of more than an hour.

At last we drove round a sharpish curve, and on the hill-side above us, looking down at us from a marble terrace, I saw the prettiest house I had ever seen in my life; a fairy palace, with lighted windows, shining against a background of wooded hills. I could not see the colours of the flowers in the thickening gloom of night, but I could smell the scent of the roses and the fragrant-leaved geraniums that filled the vases on the terrace.

Within and without all was alike sparkling and lightsome; and so far as I could see on the night of my arrival there was not a corner which could have accommodated a ghost. Lota told me that one of her first improvements had been to install the electric light.

'I love to think that this house is shining like a star when the people of Taggia look across the valley,' she said.

I told her that I had seen Captain Holbrook's name among the visitors at San Remo.

'He is staying at Taggia now,' she said. 'He grew rather tired of San Remo.'

'The desire to be nearer you had nothing to do with the change?'

'You can ask him if you like,' she answered, with something of her old insouciance. 'He is coming to dinner tonight.'

'Does he spend his days and nights going up and down the hill?' I asked.

'You will be able to see for yourself as to that. There is not much for anyone to do in Taggia.'

* * * * *

Captain Holbrook found me alone in the salon when he came; for, in spite of the disadvantages of arrival after a long journey, I was dressed before Lota. He was very friendly, and seemed really glad to see me; indeed, he lost no time in saying as much with a plainness of speech which was more friendly than flattering.

'I am heartily glad you have come,' he said, 'for now I hope we shall be able to get Miss Hammond away from this depressing hole.'

Remembering that the house was perched upon the shoulders of a romantic hill, with an outlook of surpassing loveliness, and looking round at the brilliant colouring of an Italian drawing-room steeped in soft clear light, and redolent of roses and carnations, it seemed rather hard measure to hear of Lota's inheritance talked of as 'a depressing hole'; but the cruel change in Lota herself was enough to justify the most unqualified dislike of the house in which the change had come to pass.

Miss Elderson and her niece appeared before I could reply, and we went to dinner. The dining-room was as bright and gracious of aspect as all the other rooms which I had seen, everything having been altered and improved to suit Lota's somewhat expensive tastes.

'The villa ought to be pretty,' Miss Elderson murmured plaintively, 'for Lota's improvements have cost a fortune.'

'Life is so short. We ought to make the best of it,' said Lota gaily.

We were full of gaiety, and there was the sound of talk and light laughter all through the dinner; but I felt that there was a forced note in our mirth, and my own heart was like lead. We all went back to the drawing-room together. The windows were open to the moonlight, and the faint sighing of the night wind among the olive woods. Lota and her lover established themselves in front of the blazing pine logs, and Miss Elderson asked me if I would like a stroll on the terrace. There were fleecy white shawls lying about ready for casual excursions of this kind, and the good old lady wrapped one about my shoulders with motherly care. I followed her promptly, foreseeing that she was as anxious to talk confidentially with me as I was to talk with her.

My eagerness anticipated her measured speech. 'You are unhappy about Lota,' I asked.

'Very, very unhappy.'

'But why haven't you taken her away from here? You must see that the place is killing her. Or perhaps the dreadful change in her may not strike you, who have been seeing her every day – ?'

'It does strike me; the change is too palpable. I see it every morning, see her looking a little worse, a little worse every day, as if some dreadful disease were eating away her life. And yet our good English doctor from San Remo says there is nothing the matter except a slight lung trouble, and that this air is the very finest, the position of this house faultless, for such a case as hers, high enough to be bracing, yet sheltered from all cold winds. He told me that we could take her no better place between Genoa and Marseilles.'

'But is she to stop here, and fade, and die? There is some evil influence in this house. Mr Dean said as much; something horrible, uncanny, mysterious.'

'My dear, my dear!' ejaculated the amiable invertebrate creature, shaking her head in solemn reproachfulness, 'can you, a good Churchwoman, believe in any nonsense of that sort?'

'I don't know what to believe; but I can see that my dearest friend is perishing bodily and mentally. The three months in which we have been parted have done the work of years of declining health. And she was warned against the house; she was warned.'

'There is nothing the matter with the house,' that weak-brained spinster answered pettishly. 'The sanitary engineer from Cannes has examined everything. The drainage is simply perfect –'

'And your niece is dying!' I said, savagely, and turned my back upon Miss Elderson.

I gazed across the pale grey woods to the sapphire sea, with eyes that scarcely saw the loveliness they looked upon. My heart was swelling with indignation against this feeble affection which would see the thing it loved vanishing off the earth, and yet could not be moved to energetic action.

CHAPTER III

'SOMETIMES THEY FADE AND DIE'

I tested the strength of my own influence the next day, and I was inclined to be less severe in my judgment of the meek spinster, after a long morning in the woods with Lota and Captain Holbrook, in which all my arguments and entreaties, backed most fervently by an adoring lover, had proved useless.

'I am assured that no place could suit my health better,' Lota said, decisively, 'and I mean to stay here till my doctor orders me to Varese or home to England. Do you suppose I spent a year's income on the villa with the idea of running away from it? I am tired to death of being teased about the place. First it is auntie, and then it is Captain Holbrook, and now it is young Helen. Villa, gardens, and woods are utterly lovely, and I mean to stay.'

'But if you are not happy here?'

'Who says I am not happy?'

'Your face says it, Lota.'

'I am just as happy here as I should be anywhere else,' she answered, doggedly, 'and I mean to stay.'

She set her teeth as she finished the sentence, and her face had a look of angry resolve that I had never seen in it before. It seemed as if she were fighting against something, defying something. She rose abruptly from the bank upon which she had been sitting, in a sheltered hollow, near the rocky cleft where a ruined oil mill hung mouldering on the brink of a waterfall; and she began to walk up and down very fast, muttering to herself with frowning brows:

'I shall stay! I shall stay!' I heard her repeating, as she passed me.

*   *   *   *   *

After that miserable morning – miserable in a climate and a scene of loveliness where bare existence should have been bliss – I had many serious conversations with Captain Holbrook, who was at the villa every day, the most wonderful and devoted of lovers. From him I learnt all that was known of the house in which I was living. He had taken infinite pains to discover any reason, in the house or the neighbourhood, for the lamentable change in Lota, but with the slightest results. No legend of the supernatural was associated with the Orange Grove; but on being questioned searchingly an old Italian physician who had spent his life at Taggia, and who had known Ruffini, confessed that there was a something, a mysterious something, about the villa which seemed to have affected everybody who lived in it, as owner or master, within the memory of the oldest inhabitant.

'People are not happy there. No, they are not happy, and sometimes they fade and die.'

'Invalids who come to the South to die?'

'Not always. The Signorina's grandfather was an elderly man; but he appeared in robust health when he came. However, at that age, a sudden break up is by no means wonderful. There were previous instances of decay and death far more appalling, and in some ways mysterious. I am sorry the pretty young lady has spent so much money on the villa.'

'What does money matter if she would only go elsewhere?'

She would not. That was the difficulty. No argument of her lover's could move her. She would go in April, she told him, at the season for departure; but not even his persuasion, his urgent prayers, would induce her to leave one week or one day sooner than the doctor ordered.

'I should hate myself if I were weak enough to run away from this place,' she said; and it seemed to me that those words were the clue to her conduct, and that she was making a martyr of herself rather than succumb to something of horror which was haunting and killing her.

Her marriage had been fixed for the following June, and George Holbrook was strong in the rights of a future husband; but submissive as she was in all other respects, upon this point she was stubborn, and her lover's fervent pleading moved her no more than the piteous entreaties of her spinster aunt.

I began to understand that the case was hopeless, so far as Lota's well-being depended upon her speedy removal from the Orange Grove. We could only wait as hopefully as we could for April, and the time she had fixed for departure. I took the earliest opportunity of confiding my fears to the English physician; but clever and amiable as he was, he laughed all ideas of occult influence to scorn.

'From the moment the sanitary engineer – a really scientific man – certified this house as a healthy house, the last word was said as to its suitableness for Miss Hammond. The situation is perfect, the climate all that one could desire. It would be folly to move her till the spring is advanced enough for Varese or England.'

What could I say against this verdict of local experience? Lota was not one of those interesting and profitable cases which a doctor likes to keep under his own eye. As a patient, her doctor only saw her once in a way; but he dropped in at the villa often as a friend, and he had been useful in bringing nice people about her.

I pressed the question so far as to ask him about the rooms at the back of the house, the old monkish rooms which had served as an infirmary in the seventeenth and eighteenth centuries. 'Surely those rooms must be cold and damp?'

'Damp, no. Cold, yes. All north rooms are cold on the Riviera – and the change from south to north is perilous – but as no one uses the old monkish rooms their aspect can make little difference.'

'Does not Miss Hammond use those rooms sometimes?'

'Never, I believe. Indeed, I understood Miss Elderson to say that the corridor leading to the old part of the house is kept locked, and that she has the key. I take it the good lady thinks that if the rooms are haunted it is her business to keep the ghosts in safe custody – as she does the groceries.'

'Has nobody ever used these rooms since the new villa was built?' I asked.

'Mr Hammond used them, and was rather attached to that part of the house. His library is still there, I believe, in what was once a refectory.'

'I should love to see it.'

'You have only to ask Miss Elderson.'

I did ask Miss Elderson without an hour's delay, the first time I found myself alone with her. She blushed, hesitated, assured me that the rooms contained nothing worth looking at, and fully confessed that the key was not come-atable.

'I have not lost it,' she said. 'It is only mislaid. It is sure to turn up when I am looking for something else. I put it in a safe place.'

Miss Elderson's places of safety had been one of our stock jokes ever since I had known Lota and her aunt; so I was inclined to despair of ever seeing those mysterious rooms in which the monks had lived. Yet after meditating upon the subject in a long ramble on the hill above the villa I was inclined to think that Lota might know more about that key than the good simple soul who had mislaid it. There were hours in every day during which my friend disappeared from the family circle, hours in which she was supposed to be resting inside the mosquito curtains in her own room. I had knocked at her door once or twice during this period of supposed rest; and there had been no answer. I had tried the door softly, and had found it locked, and had gone away believing my friend fast asleep; but now I began to wonder whether Lota might not possess the key of those uninhabited rooms, and for some strange capricious motive spend some of her lonely hours within those walls. I made an investigation at the back of the villa the following day, before the early coffee and the rolls, which we three spinsters generally took in the verandah on warm sunny mornings, and most of our mornings were warm. I found the massive Venetian shutters firmly secured inside, and affording not a glimpse of the rooms within. The windows looked straight upon the precipitous hill, and these northward-facing rooms must needs be dark and chilly at the best of times. My curiosity was completely baffled. Even if I had been disposed to do a little housebreaking there was no possibility of opening those too solid-looking shutters. I tugged at the fastenings savagely, but made no more impression than if I had been a fly.

CHAPTER IV

SUNSHINE OUTSIDE, BUT ICE AT THE CORE

For the next four days I watched Lota's movements.

After our morning saunter – she was far too weak now to go further than the terraced paths near the villa, and our sauntering was of the slowest – my poor friend would retire to her room for what she called her afternoon rest, while the carriage, rarely used by herself, conveyed her aunt and me for a drive, which our low spirits made ineffably dreary. Vainly was that panorama of loveliness spread before my eyes – I could enjoy nothing; for between me and that romantic scene there was the image of my perishing friend, dying by inches, and obstinately determined to die.

I questioned Lota's maid about those long afternoons which her mistress spent in her darkened room, and the young woman's answers confirmed my suspicions.

Miss Hammond did not like to be disturbed. She was a very heavy sleeper.

'She likes me to go to her at four o'clock every afternoon to do her hair, and put on her teagown. She is generally fast asleep when I go to her.'

'And her door locked?'

'No, the door is very seldom locked at four. I went an hour earlier once with a telegram, and then the door was locked, and Miss Hammond was so fast asleep that she couldn't hear me knocking. I had to wait till the usual time.'

On the fourth day after my inspection of the shutters, I started for the daily drive at the accustomed hour; but when we had gone a little way down the hill, I pretended to remember an important letter that had to be written, and asked Miss Elderson to stop the carriage, and let me go back to the villa, excusing my desertion for this afternoon. The poor lady, who was as low-spirited as myself, declared she would miss me sadly, and the carriage crept on, while I climbed the hill by those straight steep paths which shortened the journey to a five minutes' walk.

The silence of the villa as I went softly in at the open hall door suggested a general siesta. There was an awning in front of the door, and the hall was wrapped in shadow, the corridor beyond darker still, and at the end of this corridor I saw a flitting figure in pale grey – the pale Indian cashmere of Lota's neat morning frock. I heard a key turn, then the creaking of a heavy door, and the darkness had swallowed that pale grey figure.

I waited a few moments, and then stole softly along the passage. The door was half open, and I peered into the room beyond. It was empty, but an open door facing the fireplace showed me another room – a room lined with bookshelves, and in this room I could hear footsteps pacing slowly to and fro, very slowly, with the feeble tread I knew too well.

Presently she turned, put her hand to her brow as if remembering something, and hurried to the door where I was standing.

'It is I, Lota!' I called out, as she approached me, lest she should be startled by my unexpected presence.

I had been mean enough to steal a march upon her, but I was not mean enough to conceal myself.

'You here!' she exclaimed.

I told her how I had suspected her visits to these deserted rooms, and how I had dreaded the melancholy effect which their dreariness must needs exercise upon her mind and health.

'Do you call them dreary?' she asked, with a curious little laugh. 'I call them charming. They are the only rooms in the house that interest me. And it was just the same with my grandfather. He spent his declining days in these queer old rooms, surrounded by these queer old things.'

She looked round her, with furtive, wandering glances, at the heavy old bookshelves, the black and white cabinets, the dismal old Italian tapestry, and at a Venetian glass which occupied a narrow recess at the end of the inner room, a glass that reached from floor to ceiling, and in a florid carved frame, from which the gilding had mostly worn away.

Her glance lingered on this Venetian glass, which to my uneducated eye looked the oldest piece of furniture in the room. The surface was so clouded and tarnished that although Lota and I were standing opposite it at a little distance, I could see no reflection of ourselves or of the room.

'You cannot find that curious old glass very flattering to your vanity,' I said, trying to be sprightly and careless in my remarks, while my eyes were watching that wasted countenance with its hectic bloom, and those too brilliant eyes.

'No, it doesn't flatter, but I like it,' she said, going a little nearer the glass, and then suddenly drawing a dark velvet curtain across the narrow space between the two projecting bookcases.

I had not noticed the curtain till she touched it, for this end of the long room was in shadow. The heavy shutters which I had seen outside were closed over two of the windows, but the shutters had been pushed back from the third window, and the casements were open to the still, soft air.

There was a sofa opposite the curtained recess. Lota sank down upon it, folded her arms, and looked at me with a defiant smile.

'Well, what do you think of my den?' she asked.

'I think you could not have chosen a worse.'

'And yet my grandfather liked these rooms better than all the rest of the house. He almost lived in them. His old servant told me so.'

'An elderly fancy, which no doubt injured his health.'

'People choose to say so, because he died sooner than they expected. His death would have come at the appointed time. The day and hour were written in the Book of Fate before he came here. The house had nothing to do with it – only in this quiet old room he had time to think of what was coming.'

'He was old, and had lived his life; you are young, and life is all before you.'

'All!' she echoed, with a laugh that chilled my heart.

I tried to be cheerful, matter of fact, practical. I urged her to abandon this dismal library, with its dry old books, airless gloom, and northern aspect. I told her she had been guilty of an unworthy deceit in spending long hours in rooms that had been especially forbidden her. She made an end of my pleading with cruel abruptness.

'You are talking nonsense, Helen. You know that I am doomed to die before the summer is over, and I know that you know it.'

'You were well when you came here; you have been growing worse day by day.'

'My good health was only seeming. The seeds of disease were here,' touching her contracted chest. 'They have only developed. Don't talk to me, Helen; I shall spend my quiet hours in these rooms till the end, like my poor old grandfather. There need be no more concealment or double dealing. This house is mine, and I shall occupy the rooms I like.'

She drew herself up haughtily as she rose from the sofa, but the poor little attempt at dignity was spoilt by a paroxysm of coughing that made her glad to rest in my arms, while I laid her gently down upon the sofa.

The darkness came upon us while she lay there, prostrate, exhausted, and that afternoon in the shadow of the steep hill was the first of many such afternoons.

From that day she allowed me to share her solitude, so long as I did not disturb her reveries, her long silences, or brief snatches of slumber. I sat by the open window and worked or read, while she lay on the sofa, or moved softly about the room, looking at the books on the shelves, or often stopping before that dark Venetian glass to contemplate her own shadowy image.

I wondered exceedingly in those days what pleasure or interest she could find in surveying that blurred shadow of her faded beauty. Was it in bitterness she looked at the altered form, the shrunken features – or only in philosophical wonder such as Marlborough felt, when he pointed to the withered old form in the glass – the poor remains of peerless manhood and exclaimed: 'That was once a man.'

I had no power to withdraw her from that gloomy solitude. I was thankful for the privilege of being with her, able to comfort her in moments of physical misery.

Captain Holbrook left within a few days of my discovery, his leave having so nearly expired that he had only just time enough to get back to Portsmouth, where his regiment was stationed. He went regretfully, full of fear, and his last anxious words were spoken to me at the little station on the sea shore.

'Do all you can to bring her home as soon as the doctor will let her come,' he said. 'I leave her with a heavy heart, but I can do no good by remaining. I shall count every hour between now and April. She has promised to stay at Southsea till we are married, so that we may be near each other. I am to find a pretty villa for her and her aunt. It will be something for me to do.'

My heart ached for him in his forlornness, glad of any little duty that made a link between him and his sweetheart. I knew that he dearly loved his profession, and I knew also that he had offered to leave the army if Lota liked – to alter the whole plan of his life rather than be parted from her, even for a few weeks. She had forbidden such a sacrifice; and she had stubbornly refused to advance the date of her marriage, and marry him at San Remo, as he had entreated her to do, so that he might take her back to England, and establish her at Ventnor, where he believed she would be better than in her Italian paradise.

He was gone, and I felt miserably helpless and lonely without him – lonely even in Lota's company, for between her and me there were shadows and mysteries that filled my heart with dread. Sitting in the same room with her – admitted now to constant companionship – I felt not the less that there were secrets in her life which I knew not. Her eloquent face told some sad story which I could not read; and sometimes it seemed to me that between her and me there was a third presence, and that the name of the third was Death.

She let me share her quiet afternoons in the old rooms, but though her occupation of these rooms was no longer concealed from the household, she kept the privilege of solitude with jealous care. Her aunt still believed in the siesta between lunch and dinner, and went for her solitary drives with a placid submission to Lota's desire that the carriage and horses should be used by somebody. The poor thing was quite as unhappy as I, and quite as fond as Lota; but her feeble spirit had no power to struggle against her niece's strong will. Of these two the younger had always ruled the elder. After Captain Holbrook's departure the doctor took his patient seriously in hand, and I soon perceived a marked change in his manner of questioning her, while the stethoscope came now into frequent use. The casual weekly visits became daily visits; and in answer to my anxious questions I was told that the case had suddenly assumed a serious character.

'We have something to fight against now,' said the doctor; 'until now we have had nothing but nerves and fancies.'

'And now?'

'The lungs are affected.'

This was the beginning of a new sadness. Instead of vague fears, we had now the certainty of evil; and I think in the dreary days and weeks that followed, the poor old aunt and I had not one thought or desire, or fear, which was not centred in the fair young creature whose fading life we watched. Two English nurses, summoned from Cannes, aided in the actual nursing, for which trained skill was needed; but in all the little services which love can perform Miss Elderson and I were Lota's faithful slaves.

I told the doctor of her afternoons spent in her grandfather's library; and I told him also that I doubted my power, or his, to induce her to abandon that room.

'She has a fancy for it, and you know how difficult fancies are to fight with when anyone is out of health.'

'It is a curious fact,' said the doctor, 'that in every bad case I have attended in this house my patient has had an obstinate preference for that dull, cold, room.'

'When you say every bad case, I think you must mean every fatal case,' I said.

'Yes. Unhappily the three or four cases I am thinking of ended fatally; but that fact need not make you unhappy. Feeble, elderly people come to this southern shore to spin out the frail thread of life that is at breaking point when they leave England. In your young friend's case sunshine and balmy air may do much. She ought to live on the sunny side of the house; but her fancy for her grandfather's library may be indulged all the same. She can spend her evenings in that room, which can be made thoroughly warm and comfortable before she enters it. The room is well built and dry. When the shutters are shut and the curtains drawn, and the temperature carefully regulated, it will be as good a room as any other for the lamp-light hours; but for the day let her have all the sunshine she can.'

I repeated this little lecture to Lota, who promised to obey.

'I like the queer, old room,' she said, 'and, Helen, don't think me a bear if I say that I should like to be alone there sometimes, as I used to be before you hunted me down. Society is very nice for people who are well enough to enjoy it, but I'm not up to society, not even your's and auntie's. Yes, I know what you are going to say. You sit like a mouse, and don't speak till you are spoken to; but the very knowledge that you are there, watching me and thinking about me, worries me. And as for the auntie, with her little anxious fidgettings, wanting to settle my footstool, and shake up my pillows, and turn the leaves of my books, and always making me uncomfortable in the kindest way, dear soul – well, I don't mind confessing that she gets on my nerves, and makes me feel as if I should like to scream. Let me have one hour or two of perfect solitude sometimes, Helen. The nurse doesn't count. She can sit in the room, and you will know that I am not going to die suddenly without anybody to look on at my poor little tragedy.'

She had talked longer and more earnestly than usual, and the talking ended in a fit of coughing which shook the wasted frame. I promised that all should be as she wished. If solitude were more restful than even our quiet companionship, she should be sometimes alone. I would answer for her aunt, as for myself.

The nurses were two bright, capable young women, and were used to the caprices of the sick. I told them exactly what was wanted: a silent unobtrusive presence, a watchful care of the patient's physical comfort by day and night. And henceforth Lota's evenings were spent for the most part in solitude. She had her books, and her drawing-board, on which with light, weak hand she would sketch faint remembrances of the spots that had charmed us most in our drives or rambles. She had her basket overflowing with scraps of fancy work, beginnings of things that were to have no end.

'She doesn't read very long, or work for more than ten minutes at a time,' the nurse told me. 'She just dozes away most of the evening, or walks about the room now and then, and stands to look at herself in that gloomy old glass. It's strange that she should be so fond of looking in the glass, poor dear, when she can scarcely fail to see the change in herself.'

'No, no, she must see, and it is breaking her heart. I wish we could do away with every looking-glass in the house,' said I, remembering how pretty she had been in the fresh bloom of her happy girlhood only six months before that dreary time.

'She is very fond of going over her grandfather's papers,' the nurse told me. 'There is a book I see her reading very often – a manuscript book.'

'His diary, perhaps,' said I.

'It might be that; but it's strange that she should care to pore over an old gentleman's diary.'

Strange, yes; but all her fancies and likings were strange ever since I had entered that unlucky house. In her thought of her lover she was not as other girls. She was angry when I suggested that we should tell him of her illness, in order that he might get leave to come to her, if it were only for a few days.

'No, no, let him never look upon my face again,' she said. 'It is bad enough for him to remember me as I was when we parted at the station. It is ever so much worse now – and it will be – oh, Helen, to think of what must come – at last!'

She hid her face in her hands, and the frail frame was convulsed with the vehemence of her sobbing. It was long before I could soothe her; and this violent grief seemed the more terrible because of the forced cheerfulness of her usual manner.

CHAPTER V

'SEEK NOT TO KNOW'

We kept early hours at the villa. We dined at seven, and at eight Lota withdrew to the room which she was pleased to call her den. At ten there was a procession of invalid, nurse, aunt, and friend to Lota's bedroom, where the night nurse, in her neat print gown and pretty white cap, was waiting to receive her. There were many kisses and tender good-nights, and a great show of cheerfulness on all sides, and then Miss Elderson and I crept slowly to our rooms – exchanging a few sad words, a few sympathetic sighs, to cry ourselves to sleep, and to awake in the morning with the thought of the doom hanging over us.

I used to drop in upon Lota's solitude a little before bedtime, sometimes with her aunt, sometimes alone. She would look up from her book with a surprised air, or start out of her sleep.

'Bedtime already?'

Sometimes when I found her sleeping, I would seat myself beside her sofa, and wait in silence for her waking. How picturesque, how luxurious, the old room looked in the glaring light of the wood, which brightened even the grim tapestry, and glorified the bowls of red and purple anemones and other scentless flowers, and the long wall of books, and the velvet curtained windows, and shining brown floor. It was a room that I too could have loved were it not for the shadow of fear that hung over all things at the Orange Grove.

I went to the library earlier than usual one evening. The clock had not long struck nine when I left the drawing room. I had seen a change for the worse in Lota at dinner, though she had kept up her pretence of gaiety, and had refused to be treated as an invalid, insisting upon dining as we dined, scarcely touching some things, eating ravenously of other dishes, the least wholesome, laughing to scorn all her doctor's advice about dietary. I endured the interval between eight and nine, stifling my anxieties, and indulging the mild old lady with a game of bezique, which my wretched play allowed her to win easily. Like most old people her sorrow was of a mild and modified quality, and she had, I believe, resigned herself to the inevitable. The careful doctor, the admirable nurses, had set her mind at ease about dear Lota, she told me. She felt that all was being done that love and care could do, and for the rest, well, she had her church

services, her prayers, her morning and evening readings in the
well-worn New Testament. I believe she was almost happy.

'We must all die, my dear Helen,' she said, plaintively.

Die, yes. Die when one had reached that humdrum stage on
the road of life where this poor old thing was plodding, past
barren fields and flowerless hedges – the stage of grey hairs, and
toothless gums, and failing sight, and dull hearing – and an old-
fashioned, one-idead intellect. But to die like Lota, in the pride
of youth, with beauty and wealth and love all one's own! To lay
all this down in the grave! That seemed hard, too hard for my
understanding or my patience.

*   *   *   *   *

I found her asleep on the sofa by the hearth, the nurse sitting
quietly on guard in her armchair, knitting the stocking which
was never out of her hands unless they were occupied in the
patient's service. Tonight's sleep was sounder than usual, for
the sleeper did not stir at my approach, and I seated myself in
the low chair by the foot of the sofa without waking her.

A book had slipped from her hand, and lay on the silken
coverlet open. The pages caught my eye, for they were in manuscript, and I remembered what the nurse had said about Lota's
fancy for this volume. I stole my hand across the coverlet, and
possessed myself of the book, so softly that the sleeper's sensitive frame had no consciousness of my touch.

A manuscript volume of about two hundred pages in a neat
firm hand, very small, yet easy to read, so perfectly were the
letters formed and so evenly were the lines spaced.

I turned the leaves eagerly. A diary, a business man's diary,
recording in commonplace phraseology the transactions of
each day, Stock Exchange, Stock Exchange – railways – mines
– loans – banks – money, money, money, made or lost. That was
all the neat penmanship told me, as I turned leaf after leaf, and
ran my eye over page after page.

The social life of the writer was indicated in a few brief sentences. 'Dined with the Parkers: dinner execrable; company

stupid; talked to Lendon, who has made half a million in Mexican copper; a dull man.'

'Came to Brighton for Easter; clear turtle at the Ship good; they have given me my old rooms; asked Smith (Suez Smith, not Turkish Smith) to dinner.'

What interest could Lota possibly find in such a journal – a prosy commonplace record of losses and gains, bristling with figures?

This was what I asked myself as I turned leaf after leaf, and saw only the everlasting repetition of financial notes, strange names of loans and mines and railways, with contractions that reduced them to a cypher. Slowly, my hand softly turning the pages of the thick volume, I had gone through about three-fourths of the book when I came to the heading, 'Orange Grove', and the brief entries of the financier gave place to the detailed ideas and experiences of the man of leisure, an exile from familiar scenes and old faces, driven back upon self-commune for the amusement of his lonely hours.

This doubtless was where Lota's interest in the book began, and here I too began to read every word of the diary with closest attention. I did not stop to think whether I was justified in reading the pages which the dead man had penned in his retirement, whether a licence which his grand-daughter allowed herself might be taken by me. My one thought was to discover the reason of Lota's interest in the book, and whether its influence upon her mind and spirits was as harmful as I feared.

I slipped from the chair to the rug beside the sofa, and, sitting there on the ground, with the full light of the shaded reading-lamp upon the book, I forgot everything but the pages before me.

The first few pages after the old man's installation in his villa were full of cheerfulness. He wrote of this land of the South, new to his narrow experience, as an earthly paradise. He was almost as sentimental in his enthusiasms as a girl, as if it had not been for the old-fashioned style in which his raptures expressed themselves these pages might have been written by a youthful pen.

He was particularly interested in the old monkish rooms at the back of the villa, but he fully recognised the danger of occupying them.

'I have put my books in the long room which was used as a refectory,' he wrote, 'but as I now rarely look at them there is no fear of my being tempted to spend more than an occasional hour in the room.'

Then after an interval of nearly a month:

'I have arranged my books, as I find the library the most interesting room in the house. My doctor objects to the gloomy aspect, but I find a pleasing melancholy in the shadow of the steep olive-clad hill. I begin to think that this life of retirement, with no companions but my books, suits me better than the pursuit of money making, which has occupied so large a portion of my later years.'

Then followed pages of criticism upon the books he read – history, travels, poetry – books which he had been collecting for many years, but which he was now only beginning to enjoy.

'I see before me a studious old age,' he wrote, 'and I hope I may live as long as the head of my old college, Martin Routh. I have made more than enough money to satisfy myself, and to provide ample wealth for the dear girl who will inherit the greater part of my fortune. I can afford to fold my hands, and enjoy the long quiet years of old age in the companionship of the master spirits who have gone before. How near, how living they seem as I steep myself in their thoughts, dream their dreams, see life as they saw it! Virgil, Dante, Chaucer, Shakespeare, Milton, and all those later lights that have shone upon the dullest lives and made them beautiful – how they live with us, and fill our thoughts, and make up the brightest part of our daily existence.'

I read many pages of comment and reverie in the neat, clear penmanship of a man who wrote for his own pleasure, in the restful solitude of his own fire-side.

Suddenly there came a change – the shadow of the cloud that hung over that house:

'I am living too much alone. I did not think I was of the stuff which is subject to delusions and morbid fancies – but I was wrong. I suppose no man's mind can retain its strength of fibre without the friction of intercourse with other minds of its own calibre. I have been living alone with the minds of the dead, and waited upon by foreign servants, with whom I hardly exchange half a dozen sentences in a day. And the result is what no doubt any brain-doctor would have foretold.

'I have begun to see ghosts.

'The thing I have seen is so evidently an emanation of my own mind – so palpably a materialisation of my own self-consciousness, brooding upon myself and my chances of long life – that it is a weakness even to record the appearance that has haunted me during the last few evenings. No shadow of dying monk has stolen between me and the lamplight; no presence from the vanished years, revisiting places. The thing which I have seen is myself – not myself as I am – but myself as I am to be in the coming years, many or few.

'The vision – purely self-induced as I know it to be – has not the less given a shock to the placid contentment of my mind, and the long hopes which, in spite of the Venusian's warning, I had of late been cherishing.

'Looking up from my book in yesterday's twilight my casual glance rested on the old Venetian mirror in front of my desk; and gradually, out of the blurred darkness, I saw a face looking at me.

'My own face as it might be after the wasting of disease, or the slow decay of advancing years – a face at least ten years older than the face I had seen in my glass a few hours before – hollow cheeks, haggard eyes, the loose under-lip drooping weakly – a bent figure in an invalid chair, an aspect of utter helplessness. And it was myself. Of that fact I had no shadow of doubt.

'Hypochondria, of course – a common form of the malady, – perhaps this shaping of the imagination into visions. Yet, the thing was strange – for I had been troubled by no apprehensions of illness or premature old age. I had never even thought of myself as an old man. In the pride bred of long immunity from illness I had considered myself exempt from the ailments that are wont to attend declining years. I had pictured myself living to the extremity of human life, and dropping peacefully into the centenarian's grave.

'I was angry with myself for being affected by the vision, and I locked the door of the library when I went to dress for dinner, determined not to re-enter the room till I had done something – by outdoor exercise and change of scene – to restore the balance of my brain. Yet when I had dined there came upon me so feverish a desire to know whether the glass would again show me the same figure and face that I gave the key to my major-domo, and told him to light the lamps and make up the fire in the library.

'Yes, the thing lived in the blotched and blurred old glass. The dusky surface, which was too dull to reflect the realities of life, gave back that vision of age and decay with unalterable fidelity. The face and figure came and went, and the glass was often black – but whenever the thing appeared it was the same – the same in every dismal particular, in all the signs of senility and fading life.

' "This is what I am to be twenty years hence," I told myself, "A man of eighty might look like that."

'Yet I had hoped to escape that bitter lot of gradual decay which I had seen and pitied in other men. I had promised myself that the reward of a temperate life – a life free from all consuming fires of dissipation, all tempestuous passions – would be a vigorous and prolonged old age. So surely as I had toiled to amass fortune so surely also had I striven to lay up for myself long years of health and activity, a life prolonged to the utmost span.'

*   *   *   *   *

There was a break of ten days in the journal, and when the record was resumed the change in the writing shocked me. The neat firm penmanship gave place to weak and straggling characters, which, but for marked peculiarities in the formation of certain letters, I should have taken for the writing of a stranger.

'The thing is always there in the black depths of that damnable glass – and I spend the greater part of my life watching for it. I have struggled in vain against the bitter curiosity to know the worst which the vision of the future can show me. Three days ago I flung the key of this detestable room into the deepest well on the premises; but an hour afterwards I sent to Taggia for a blacksmith, and had the lock picked, and ordered a new key, and a duplicate, lest in some future fit of spleen I should throw away a second key, and suffer agonies before the door could be opened.

' "Tu ne quaesieris, scire nefas – "

'Vainly the poet's warning buzzes and booms in my vexed ear – repeating itself perpetually, like the beating of a pulse in my brain, or like the ticking of a clock that will not let a man sleep.

' "Scire nefas – scire nefas."

'The desire to know more is no stranger than reason.

'Well, I am at least prepared for what is to come. I live no longer in a fool's paradise. The thing which I see daily and hourly is no hallucination, no materialisation of my self-consciousness, as I thought in the beginning. It is a warning and a prophesy. So shalt thou be. Soon, soon, shalt thou resemble this form which it shocks thee now to look upon.

'Since first the shadow of myself looked at me from the darker shadows of the glass I have felt every indication of approaching doom. The doctor tries to laugh away my fears, but he owns that I am below par – meaningless phrase – talks of nervine decay, and suggests my going to St Moritz. He doubts if this place suits me, and confesses that I have changed for the worse since I came here.'

Again an interval, and then in writing that was only just legible.

'It is a month since I wrote in this book – a month which has realised all that the Venetian glass showed me when first I began to read its secret.

'I am a helpless old man, carried about in an invalid chair. Gone my pleasant prospect of long tranquil years; gone my selfish scheme of enjoyment, the fruition of a life of money-getting. The old Eastern fable has been realised once again. My gold has turned to withered leaves, so far as any pleasure that it can buy for me. I hope that my grand-daughter may get some good out of the wealth I have toiled to win.'

Again a break, longer this time, and again the handwriting showed signs of increasing weakness. I had to pore over it closely in order to decipher the broken, crooked lines pencilled casually over the pages.

'The weather is insufferably hot; but too ill to be moved. In library – coolest room – doctor no objection. I have seen the last picture in the glass – Death – corruption – the cavern of Lazarus, and no Redeemer's hand to raise the dead. Horrible! Horrible! Myself as I must be – soon, soon! How soon?'

And then, scrawled in a corner of the page, I found the date – June 24, 1889.

I knew that Mr Hammond died early in the July of that year.

*　*　*　*　*

Seated on the floor, with my head bent over the pages, and reading more by the light of the blazing logs than by the lamp on the table above me, I was unaware that Lota had awoke, and had raised herself from her reclining position on the sofa. I was still absorbed in my study of those last horrible lines when a pale hand came suddenly down upon the open book, and a laugh which was almost a shriek ran through the silent spaces around us. The nurse started up and ran to her patient, who was struggling to her feet and staring wildly into the long narrow glass in the recess opposite her sofa.

'Look, look!' she shrieked. 'It has come – the vision of Death! The dreadful face – the shroud – the coffin. Look, Helen, look!'

My gaze followed the direction of those wild eyes, and I know not whether my excited brain conjured up the image that appalled me. This alone I know, that in the depths of that dark glass, indistinct as a form seen through turbid water, a ghastly face, a shrouded figure, looked out at me——

'As one dead in the bottom of a tomb.'

A sudden cry from the nurse called me from the horror of that vision to stern reality, to see the life-blood ebbing from the lips I had kissed so often with all a sister's love. My poor friend never spoke again. A severe attack of haemorrhage hastened the inevitable end; and before her heart-broken lover could come to clasp the hand and gaze into her fading eyes, Violetta Hammond passed away.

Robert Westall

THE CREATURES IN THE HOUSE

ROBERT WESTALL (1929-1993) *was the multi-award-winning author of over forty books for young readers. He is the only author to have won the Carnegie Medal twice, for* The Machine Gunners (1975) *and* The Scarecrows (1981), *while* Blitzcat (1989) *won the Smarties Prize and was named by the American Library Association as one of the best books for young adults in the past 25 years. Westall also wrote extensively in the field of the supernatural and has been called the best writer of traditional British ghost stories since M. R. James. Valancourt has previously published his collection* Antique Dust (1989), *his only book written specifically for adults, featuring tales centred on an antique dealer's encounters with the supernatural, as well as his novella* The Stones of Muncaster Cathedral (1991), *and an original collection,* Spectral Shadows, *which comprises three short novels of the supernatural. 'The Creatures in the House', originally published in 1980, was Westall's first published horror story and features two of the author's favourite subjects – the supernatural, and cats.*

D AWN BROKE OVER SOUTHWOLD SEAFRONT.
The wind was blowing against the waves; white horses showed all the way to the horizon, smaller and smaller as if painted by some obsessional Dutch marine artist. On the horizon itself sat a steamship, square as a pan on a shelf, scarcely seeming to move.

Seafront deserted; beach-huts huddled empty in the rain. The only movement was a flaking flap of emulsion-paint on the pier pavilion, tearing itself off in the wind.

Miss Forbes opened her eyes on her last day. Eyes grey and empty as the sea. She eased her body in the velvet reclining rocker in the bay window; luxurious once, now greased black in patches from the day and night shifting of her body. It was some years since she had been to bed. Beds meant sheets and sheets meant washing ... She seldom left the bay window. She took her food off the front doorstep and straight on to the occasional table by her side. Once a week she took the remains to the dustbin. Otherwise there was just the trips to the toilet, and the weekly journey to the dripping tap in the kitchen for a pink-rosed ewerful of water.

She opened her eyes and looked at the sea and wondered what month it was. Her mind was clearer this morning than for a long time. The creature in the house had not fed on her mind for a week. There wasn't much of Miss Forbes' mind left to feed on. A few shreds of memory from the forties; a vague guilt at things not done. The creature itself was weakening. The creature knew a time would come soon when it had nothing to feed on at all. Then it would have to hibernate, like a dormouse or hedgehog. But first the creature must provide for its future, while there was still time. There was something Miss Forbes had to do ...

She rose shakily, after trying to straighten thick stockings of two different tones of grey. She went out into the hall, picked up the 1968 telephone directory, and, her eyes squinting two inches off the page, looked up the solicitor's number.

She had difficulty making the solicitor's girl understand who she was; an old-standing client and a wealthy one. She mentioned the name of partner after partner ... old Mr Sandbach had been dead twenty years ... young Mr Sandbach retired last spring. Yes, she supposed Mr Mason would have to do ... two o'clock?

Then she slowly climbed the stairs, slippered feet carving footprints in dust thicker than the worn staircarpet. In what had once been her bedroom she opened the mirrored wardrobe door, not even glancing at her reflection as it swung out at her.

She began to wash and comb and dress. With spells of sitting down to rest it took three hours. The creature had to lend her its own waning strength. Even then, Miss Forbes scarcely managed. The creature itself nearly despaired.

But between them, they coped. At half past one Miss Forbes

rang for a taxi, the ancient black stick-phone trembling in her hand.

The taxi-driver watched her awestruck in his rear-view mirror. Two things clutched tightly in her gloved hand: a door-key and a big lump of wallpaper with something scrawled on the back in a big childish hand. Like all his kind, he was good at reading things backwards in his mirror.

'I leave all my worldly possessions to my niece, Martha Vickers, providing she is unmarried and living alone at the time of my death. On condition that she agrees, and continues, to reside alone at 17 Marine Parade. Or, if she is unable or unwilling to comply with my wishes, I leave all my possessions to my great-niece, Sarah Anne Walmsley . . .'

The taxi-man shuddered. *He'd* settle for a heart-attack at seventy . . .

'Suppose I spend all the money, sell the house and run?' asked Sally Walmsley. 'I mean what's to stop me?'

'Me, I'm afraid,' said Mr Mason, wiping the thick fur of dust off the hallstand of 17 Marine Parade, and settling his plump pinstriped bottom. 'We are the executors of your aunt's estate . . . we shall have to keep *some* kind of eye on you . . . it could prove unpleasant . . . I hope it won't come to that. Suppose you and I have dinner about once every six months and you tell me what you've been up to . . .' He smiled tentatively, sympathetically. He liked this tall thin girl with green eyes and long black hair. 'Of course, you could contest the will. It wouldn't stand up in court a moment. I couldn't *swear* your aunt was in her right mind the morning she made it. Not of sound testamentary capacity, as we say. But if you break the will, it would have to be shared with all your female aunts and cousins – married and unmarried. You'd get about three thousand each – not a lot.'

'Stuff *them*,' said Sally Walmsley. 'I'll keep what I've got.' She suddenly felt immensely weary. The last six months had happened so fast. Deciding to walk out of art school. Walking out of art school. Trailing London looking for work. Getting a break as assistant art editor of *New Woman*. And then lovely Tony Harrison of Production going back to his fat, frigid suburban cow of a wife. And then this . . .

'I must be off,' said Mr Mason, getting off the hallstand and surveying his bottom for dust in the spotted stained mirror. But he lingered in the door, interminably, as if guilty about leaving her. 'It was a strange business . . . I've dealt with a lot of old ladies, but your aunt . . . she looked . . . faded. Not potty, just *faded*. I kept on having to shout at her, to bring her back to herself.

'The milkman found her, you know. When the third bottle of milk piled up on her doorstep. He always had the rule to let three bottles pile up. Old ladies can be funny. She might have gone away. But there she was, sitting in the bay window, grey as dust.

'He seems to have been her only human contact – money and scribbled notes pushed into the milk bottles. She lived on what he brought – bread, butter, eggs, yoghurt, cheese, orange juice. She seems to have never tried to cook – drank the eggs raw after cracking them into a cup.

'But she didn't die of malnutrition . . . the coroner said it was a viable diet, though not a desirable one. Didn't die of hypothermia, either. It was a cold week in March, but the gas fire was full on, and the room was like an oven . . .' He paused, as if an unpleasant memory had struck him. 'In fact, the coroner couldn't find any cause of death at all. He said she just seemed to have faded away . . . put down good old natural causes. Well, I must be off. If there's any way I can help . . .'

Sally nearly said, 'Please don't go.' But that would have been silly. So she smiled politely while he smiled too, bobbed his head and left.

Sally didn't like that at all. She listened to the silence in the house, and her skin crawled.

A primitive man, a bushman or Aborigine, would have recognized that crawling of the skin. Would have left the spot immediately. Or if the place had been important to him, a cave or spring of water, he would have returned with other primi-

tive men and performed certain rituals. And then the creature
would have left.

But Sally simply told herself not to be a silly fool, and forced
herself to explore.

The library was books from floor to ceiling. *Avant-garde* –
fifty years ago. Marie Stopes, Havelock Ellis, the early Agatha
Christie, Shaw and Wells. Aunt Maude had been a great reader,
a Girton girl, a bluestocking. So what had she read the last ten
years? For the fur of dust lay over the books as it lay over everything else. And there wasn't a magazine or paper in the house.
So what had she *done* with herself, never going out, doing all
her business by post, never putting stamps on her letters till
the bank manager began sending her books of stamps of his
own volition. Even the occasional plumber or meter-reader had
never seen her; only a phone message and the front door open,
with scrawled instructions pinned to it . . .

Aunt Maude might as well have been an enclosed nun . . .

But the house with its wood-planked walls, its red-tiled roof,
its white gothic pinnacles, balconies and many bay windows
was not in bad shape; nowhere near falling down. Nothing
fresh paint wouldn't cure. And there was plenty of money. And
the furniture was fabulously Victorian. Viennese wallclocks, fit
only for the junkshop twenty years ago, would fetch hundreds
now, once their glass cases were cleared of cobwebs, and their
brass pendulums of verdigris. And the dining-room furniture
was Sheraton; genuine, eighteenth-century Sheraton. Oh, she
could make it such a place . . . where people would bother to
come, even from London. Everybody liked a weekend by the
sea. Even Tony Harrison . . . she thrust the thought down savagely. But what a challenge, bringing the place back to life.

So why did she feel like crying? Was it just the dusk of a
November afternoon; the rain-runnelled dirt on the windows?

She reached the top of the house: a boxroom under the roof
with sloping ceiling. A yellow stained-glass window at one end
that made it look as if the sun was always shining outside; the
massed brick of the chimney stacks at the other. A long narrow
tall room; a wrong room that made her want to slam the door

and run away. Instead, she made herself stand and *analyse* her feelings. Simple, really; the stained glass was alienating; the shape of the room was uncomfortable, making you strain upwards and giving you a humiliating crick in the neck. Simple, really, when you had art school training, an awareness of the psychology of shape and colour.

She was still glad to shut the door, go downstairs to the kitchen with its dripping tap, and make herself a cup of tea. She left all the rings of the gas stove burning. *And* the oven. Soon the place was as warm as a greenhouse . . .

In the darkest corner of the narrow boxroom, furthest from the stained-glass window where the sun always seemed to shine, up near the grey-grimed ceiling, the creature stirred in its sleep. It was not the fiercest or strongest of its kind; not quite purely spirit, or rather decayed from pure spirit. It could pass through the wood and glass of doors and windows easily, but it had difficulty with brick and stonework. That was why it had installed Miss Forbes in the bay window: so it could feed on her quickly, when it returned hungry from its long journeys. It fed on humankind, but not all humankind. It found workmen in the house quite unbearable; like a herd of trampling, whistling, swearing elephants. Happy families were worse, especially when the children were noisy. It only liked women, yet would have found a brisk WI meeting an unbearable hell. It fed on women alone; women in despair. It crept subtly into their minds, when they slept or tossed and worried in the middle of the night, peeling back the protective shell of their minds that they didn't even know they had; rather as a squirrel cracks a nut, or a thrush a snail shell; patient, not hurrying, delicate, persistent . . .

Like all wise parasites it did not kill its hosts. Miss Forbes had lasted it forty years; Miss Forbes' great-aunt had lasted nearer sixty.

Now it was awake, and hungry.

Sally hugged her third mug of tea between her hands and stared out of the kitchen window, at the long dead grass and scattered dustbins of the November garden. The garden wall was fifty yards away, sooty brick. There was nothing else to see. She had the conviction that her new life had stopped, that her clockwork was running down. I could stand here forever, she thought in a panic. I must go upstairs and make up a bed; there was plenty of embroidered lavendered Edwardian linen in the drawers. But she hadn't the energy.

I could go out and spend the night in an hotel. But which hotels would be open, in Southwold in November? She knew there was a phone, but the Post Office had cut it off.

Just then, something appeared suddenly on top of the sooty wall, making her jump. One moment it wasn't there; next moment it was.

A grey cat. A tom-cat, from the huge size of its head and thickness of shoulder.

It glanced this way and that; then lowered its forefeet delicately down the vertical brick of the wall, leapt, and vanished into the long grass.

She waited; it reappeared, moving through the long grass with a stalking lope so like a lion's and so unlike a cat indoors. It went from dustbin to dustbin, sniffing inside each in turn, without hope and without success. She somehow knew it did the same thing every day, at the same time. It had worn tracks through the grass.

'Hard luck,' she thought, as the cat found nothing. Then, spitefully, 'Sucker!' She hated the cat, because its search for food was so like her own search for happiness.

The cat sniffed inside the last bin unavailingly, and was about to depart, empty-handed.

'Welcome to the club,' thought Sally bitterly.

It was then that the hailstorm came; out of nowhere, huge hailstones, slashing, hurting. The tom-cat turned, startled, head and paw upraised, snarling as if the hailstorm was an enemy of its own kind; as if to defend itself against this final harshness of life.

Sally felt a tiny surge of sympathy.

It was almost as if the cat sensed it. It certainly turned towards the kitchen window and saw her for the first time. And immediately ran towards her, and leapt on to the lid of a bin directly under the window, hailstones belting small craters in its fur, and its mouth open; red tongue and white teeth exposed in a silent miaow that was half defiance and half appeal.

You can't let this happen to me.

It made her feel like God; the God she had often screamed and wept and appealed to, and never had an answer.

I am *kinder* than God, she thought in a sad triumph, and ran to open the kitchen door.

The cat streaked in, and, finding a dry shelter, suddenly remembered its dignity. It shook itself violently, then shook the wetness off each paw in turn, as a kind of symbol of disgust with the weather outside, then began vigorously to belabour its shoulder with a long pink tongue.

But not for long. Its nose began to twitch; began to twitch quite monstrously. It turned its head, following the twitch, and leapt gently on to the kitchen table, where a packet lay, wrapped in paper.

A pound of mince, bought up in the town earlier, and forgotten. Sally sat down, amused, and watched. All right, she thought, if you can get it, you can have it.

The cat tapped and turned the parcel, as if it was a living mouse. Seemed to sit and think for a moment, then got its nose under the packet and, with vigorous shoves, propelled it to the edge of the table, and sent it thumping on to the stone floor.

It was enough to burst the paper the butcher had put round it. The mince splattered across the stone flags with all the gory drama of a successful hunt. The cat leapt down and ate steadily, pausing only to give Sally the occasional dark suspicious stare, and growling under its breath.

OK, thought Sally. You win. I'd never have got round to cooking it tonight, and there isn't a fridge . . .

The cat extracted and hunted down the last red crumb, and then began exploring the kitchen, pacing along the work-tops, prying open the darkness of the cupboards with an urgent paw.

There was an arrogance about him, a sense of taking possession, that could only make her think of one thing to call him.

When he finally sat down, to wash and survey her with blank
dark eyes she called softly, 'Boss? Boss?'

He gave a short and savage purr and leapt straight on to her
lap, trampling her about with agonizing sharp claws, before
finally settling down, facing outwards, front claws clenched
into her trousered knees. He was big, but painfully thin. His
haunches felt like bone knives under his matted fur. The fat days
must be in the summer, she thought sleepily, with full dustbins
behind every hotel. What do they do in November?

He should have been an agony; but strangely he was a comfort. The gas stove had made the room deliciously warm. His
purring filled her ears.

They slept, twisted together like symbiotic plants, in a
cocoon of contentment.

The creature sensed her sleep. It drifted out of the boxroom
and down the intricately carved staircase, like a darkening of
the shadows; a dimming of the faint beams that crept through
the filthy net curtains from a distant street-lamp.

Boss did not sense it until it entered the kitchen. A she-cat
would have sensed it earlier. But Boss saw it, as Sally would
never see it. His claws tightened in Sally's knee; he rose up and
arched his back and spat, ears laid back against his skull. Sally
whimpered in her sleep, trying to soothe him with a drowsy
hand. But she didn't waken . . .

Cat and creature faced each other. Boss felt no fear, as a
human might. Only hate at an intruder, alien, enemy.

And the creature felt Boss's hate. Rather as a human might
feel a small stone that has worked its way inside a shoe. Not
quite painful; not enough to stop for, but a distraction.

The creature could not harm Boss; their beings had nothing
in common. But it could press on his being; press abominably.

It pressed.

Boss leapt off Sally's knee. If a door had been open, or a
window, Boss would have fled. But no door or window was

open. He ran frantically here and there, trying to escape the black pressure, and finally ended up crouched in the corner under the sink, protected on three sides by brickwork, but silenced at last.

Now the creature turned its attention to Sally, probing at the first layer of her mind.

Boss, released, spat and swore terribly.

It was as if, for the creature, the stone in the shoe had turned over, exposing a new sharp edge.

The creature, exploding in rage, pressed too hard on the outer layer of Sally's mind.

Sally's dream turned to nightmare: a nightmare of a horrible female thing with wrinkled dugs and lice in her long grey hair. Sally woke, sweating.

The creature was no longer there.

Sally gazed woozy-eyed at Boss, who emerged from under the sink, shook himself, and immediately asked to be let out the kitchen door. Very insistently. Clawing at the woodwork.

Sally's hand was on the handle, when a thought struck her. If she let the cat out, she would be *alone*.

The thought was unbearable.

She looked at Boss.

'Hard luck mate,' she said. 'You asked to be let in. You've had your supper. Now bloody earn it!'

As if he sensed what she meant, Boss gave up his attempts on the door. Sally made some tea, and, conscience-stricken, gave Boss the cream off the milk. She looked at her watch. Midnight.

They settled down again.

Three more times that night the creature tried. Three times with the same result. It grew ever more frantic, clumsy. Three times Sally had nightmares and woke sweating, and made tea.

Boss, on the other hand, was starting to get used to things. The last time, he did not even stir from Sally's knee. Just lay tensely and spat. The black weight of the creature seemed less when he was near the human.

After three a.m. cat and girl slept undisturbed. While the creature roamed the stairs and corridors, demented. It began to realize that one day, like Miss Forbes and Miss Forbes' great-aunt, it too might simply cease to exist; like the corpse of a hedgehog, by a country road, it might slowly blow away into particles of dust.

A weak morning sunlight cheered the dead grass of the garden. Sally opened a tin of corned beef and gave Boss his breakfast. He wolfed the lot, and then asked again to be let out, with renewed insistence.

Freedom was freedom, thought Sally sadly. Besides, if he didn't go soon there was liable to be a nasty accident. She watched him go through the grass, and gain the top of the wall with a magnificent leap.

Then he vanished, leaving the world totally empty.

She spent four cups of coffee and five fags gathering her wits; then opened her suitcase, washed at the kitchen sink, and set out to face the world.

It wasn't bad. The sky was pale blue, every wave was twinkling like diamonds as it broke on the beach, and her brave new orange Mini stood parked twenty yards down the road.

But it was Boss she watched for: in the tangled front garden, on the immaculate lawn of the house next door.

Then she looked back at number 17, nervously. It looked all right, from here . . .

'Good morning!' The voice made her jump.

The owner of number 16 was straightening up from behind his well mended fence, a handful of dead brown foliage in one hand.

He was everything she disliked in a man. About thirty. Friendly smile, naive blue eyes, check shirt, folk-weave tie. He offered a loamy paw, having wiped it on the seat of his gardening trousers.

'Just moved in then? My name's Mike Taverner. Dwell here with my mama . . .'

Half an hour later she broke away, her head spinning with a muddling survey of all the best shops in town and what they were best for. The fact that Mr Taverner was an accountant and therefore worked gentleman's hours. That he was quite handy round the house and that anything he could do . . . But it was his subtly pitying look that was worst.

Stuff him! If *he* thought that *she* was going to ask *him* round for coffee . . .

She spent the day using Miss Forbes' money. A huge hand-torch for some reason; a new transistor radio, satisfyingly loud; a check tablecloth; three new dresses, the most with-it that Southwold could offer. She ordered a new gas stove, and gained the promise that the Post Office would re-connect tomorrow . . .

She still had to go home in the end.

She put her new possessions on the kitchen table, all in a mass, and they just seemed to shrink to the size of Dinky Toys. The silence of the house pressed on her skin like a cold moist blanket.

But she was firm. Went upstairs and made the bed in the front bedroom with the bay window. Then sat over her plate of bacon and eggs till it congealed solid, smoking fag after fag. The sounds that came out of the transistor radio seemed like alien code messages from Mars.

She went to bed at midnight, clutching the tranny under one arm, and fags, matches, torch, magazines with the other.

But before she went, she left the kitchen window open six inches. And a fresh plate of mince on the sill. It was like a hundred-to-one bet on the Grand National . . .

Boss left the house determined never to return, and picked up the devious trail through alley and garden, backyard and beach-shelter that marked the edge of his territory, smelling his old trademarks and renewing them vigorously. He stalked and killed a hungry sparrow in one alley; found some cinder-embedded bacon rind in another, but that was all. He was soon hungry again.

By the time dusk was falling, and he rendezvoused at the derelict fishermen's hut with his females, he was very hungry indeed. The memory of the black terror had faded; the memory of the raw mince grew stronger.

He sniffed noses and backsides with one of his females in particular, a big scrawny tortoiseshell with hollow flanks and bulging belly. But he could not settle. The memory of the mince grew to a mountain in his mind; a lovely blood-oozing salty mountain.

Around midnight, he got up and stretched, and headed out again along his well beaten track.

Ten yards behind, weak and limping, the tortoiseshell followed. She followed him further than she had ever ventured before; she was far more hungry than him; her plight far more desperate. And she had smelt the rich raw meat on his breath . . .

The creature felt them enter the house; now there were two sharp stones in its shoe.

It had been doing well before they came. Sally had taken a Mogadon, and lay sleeping on her back, mouth open and snoring, a perfect prey. The creature was feeding gently on the first layer of her mind; lush memories of warmth and childhood, laughter and toys. First food in six months.

Uneasy, it fed suddenly harder; too hard. Sally moaned and swam up slowly from her drugged sleep; sat up and knew with terror that something precious had been stolen from her; was missing, gone for ever.

The creature did not let go of her, hung on with all its strength; it was so near to having her completely.

Sally felt as cold as death under the heaped blankets; the sheets were like clammy winding-sheets, strangling, smothering. She fought her way out of them and reeled about the room, seeking blindly for the door in the dark. Warm, she must get warm or . . .

The kitchen . . . gas stove . . . warm. Desperately she searched the walls for the door, in the utter dark. Curtains, windows, pictures swinging and falling under her grasping hands. She was crying, screaming . . . Was there no door to this black room?

Then the blessed roundness of the door handle, that would not turn under her cold-sweating palm until she folded a piece of her nightdress over it. And then she was going downstairs, half-running, half-falling, bumping down the last few steps on her bottom, in the dim light of the street-lamp through the grimy curtains . . .

The whole place rocked still in nightmare, because the creature still clung to her mind . . .

Twice she passed the kitchen door, and then she found it and broke through, and banged the light on.

Check tablecloth; suitcase; tweed coat. Sally's eyes clutched them, like a drowning man clutches straws. The creature felt her starting to get away, struggling back to the real world outside.

But much worse, the creature felt two pairs of eyes glaring; glaring hate. The tom-cat was crouched on the old wooden draining board, back arched. But the tom was not the worst. The she-cat lay curled on a pathetic heap of old rags and torn-up newspaper under the sink. And her hatred was utterly immovable. And there were five more small sharp stones now in the creature's shoe. A mild squeaking came from within the she-cat's protective legs. Little scraps of blind fur, writhing . . .

Sally's mind gave a tremendous heave and the creature's hold broke. The creature could not stand the she-cat's eyes, utterly rejecting.

It fled back, back up the stairs, right to the boxroom, and coiled itself in the dark corner, between a high shelf and the blackened ceiling.

It knew, as it lapsed into chaos, that there was one room in its house where it dared never go again.

Back in the kitchen, Sally closed the door and then the window, and lit all the rings of the gas stove. The tom-cat shook itself and rubbed against her legs, wanting milk.

'Kittens,' said Sally, 'kittens. Oh you *poor* thing.'

But at that moment there was nothing in the world she wanted more than kittens. She put on a saucepan, and filled it to the brim with milk.

She felt Boss stir on her knee towards dawn. She opened her eyes, and saw him on the windowsill, asking to go out.

'All right,' she said reluctantly. She opened the window. She knew now that he would come back. Besides, the purring heap of cat and kittens, now installed on a heap of old curtains in an armchair, showed no sign of wanting to move. She would not be alone . . .

She left the window open. It was not a very cold night, and the room was now too hot if anything from the gas stove.

She was wakened at eight, by Boss's pounding savage claws on her lap. He made loud demands for breakfast.

And he was not alone. There was a black-and-white female sitting washing itself on the corner of the table; and a white-and-ginger female was curled up with the mother and kittens, busy washing all and sundry. The aunties had arrived.

'Brought the whole family, have you?' she asked Boss sourly. 'Sure there aren't a few grandmas you forgot?'

He gave a particularly savage purr, and dug his claws deeper into her legs.

'OK,' she said. 'How would Tyne-Brand meat loaf do? With pilchards for starters?'

By the time they had finished, the larder was bare. They washed, and Sally ate toast and watched them washing. She thought, I'm bonkers. Only old maids have cats like this. People will think I'm mad. The four cats regarded her with blandly friendly eyes. Somehow it gave her courage to remember the nightmare upstairs . . .

Then the cats rose, one by one. Nudged and nosed each other, stretched, began to mill around.

It reminded her of something she'd once seen; on telly somewhere.

Lionesses, setting off to hunt. That was it. Lionesses setting off to hunt.

But, for God's sake, they'd *had* their breakfast . . .

Boss went to the door and miaowed. Not the kitchen door; the door that led to the nightmare staircase. Mother joined him. And Ginger. And the black-and-white cat she'd christened Chequers.

When she did not open that door, they all turned and stared at her. Friendly; but expectant. Compelling.

My God, she thought. They're going hunting whatever is upstairs. And inviting me to join in . . .

They were the only friends she had. She went; but she picked up Boss before she opened the door. He didn't seem to mind; he settled himself comfortably in her arms, pricking his ears and looking ahead. His body was vibrating. Purr or growl deep in his throat. She could not tell.

The she-cats padded ahead, looked at the doors of the downstairs rooms, then leapt up the stairs. They nosed into everything, talking to each other in their prooky spooky language. They moved as if they were tied to each other and to her with invisible strands of elastic; passing each other, weaving from side to side like a cat's cradle, but never getting too far ahead, or too far apart.

They went from upstairs room to upstairs room, politely standing aside as she opened each door. Leaping on to dust-sheeted beds, sniffing in long-empty chamber-pots.

Each of the rooms was empty; dreary, dusty, but totally empty. Sally wasn't afraid. If anything, little tingling excitements ran through her.

The cats turned to the staircase that led to the boxroom in the roof. They were closer together now, their chirrups louder, more urgent.

They went straight to the door of the narrow room, with the yellow stained-glass window that was always sunshine.

Waited. Braced. Ears back close to the skull.

Sally took a deep breath and flung open the door.

Immediately the cold came, the clammy winding-sheet cold of the night before. The corridor, the stairs twisted and fell together like collapsing stage scenery.

She would have run; but Boss's claws, deep and sharp in her arm, were realler than the cold and the twisting, like an anchor in a storm. She stood. So did the cats, though they crouched close to the floor, huddled together.

Slowly, the cold and twisting faded.

The cats rose and shook themselves, as after a shower of rain, and stalked one by one into the boxroom.

Trembling, Sally followed.

Again the sick cold and twisting came. But it was weaker. Even Sally could tell that. And it didn't last so long.

The cats were all staring at the ceiling at the far end; at a dark grey space between the heavy brickwork of two chimneys; between the ceiling and a high wooden shelf.

Sally stared too. But all she could see was a mass of cobwebs; black rope-like strands blowing in some draught that came through the slates of the roof.

But she knew that her enemy, the enemy who had stolen from her, was there. And for the first time, because the enemy was now so small, no longer filling the house, she could feel anger, red healthy anger.

She looked round for a weapon. There was an old short-bristled broom leaning against the wall. She put down Boss and picked it up, and slashed savagely at the swaying cobwebs, until she had pulled every one of them down.

They clung to the broomhead.

But they were only cobwebs.

Boss gave a long chirrup. Cheerful, pleased, but summoning. Slowly, in obedience, the three she-cats began to back out of the door, never taking their green eyes from the space up near the ceiling.

Sally came last, and closed the door.

They retired back to the kittens, in good order.

Back in the boxroom, the creature was absolutely still. It had learned the bitter limitations of its strength. It had reached the very frontier of its existence.

It grew wise.

Back in the kitchen, there came a knock on the door.

It was Mr Taverner. Was she all right? He thought he had heard screams in the night . . .

'It was only Jack the Ripper,' said Sally with a flare of new-found spirit. 'You're too late – he murdered me.'

He had the grace to look woebegone. He had quite a nice lopsided smile, when he was woebegone. So she offered him a cup of coffee.

He sat down, and the she-cats climbed all over him, sniffing in his ears with spiteful humour. Standing on his shoulders with their front paws on top of his head . . . He suffered politely, with his lopsided grin. 'Have they moved in on you? Once you feed them, they'll never go away . . . they're a menace round Southwold, especially in the winter. I could call the RSPCA for you . . . ?'

'They are *my* cats. I *like* cats.'

He gave her a funny look. 'They'll cost you a bomb to feed . . .'

'I know how much cats cost to feed. And don't think I can't afford to keep a hundred cats if I want to.'

Again he had the grace to shut up.

Things went better for Sally after that. Mike Taverner called in quite often, and even asked her to have dinner with his mother. Mrs Taverner proved not to be an aged burden, but a smart fifty-year-old who ran a dress-shop, didn't discuss hysterectomies, and watched her son's social antics with a wry long-suffering smile.

The kittens grew; the house filled with whistling workmen; the Gas Board came finally to install the new cooker.

And Sally took to sleeping on the couch of a little breakfast room just off the kitchen; where she could get a glimpse of sea in the mornings, and the cats came and went through the serving-hatch.

She slept well, usually with cats coming and going off her feet all night. Sometimes they called sharply to each other, and there was a scurrying of paws, and she would waken sweating. That noise meant the creature from the boxroom was on the prowl.

But it never tried anything, not with the cats around.

And every day, Sally and the cats did their daily patrol into enemy territory. What Sally came to think of, with a nervous giggle, as the bearding of the boxroom.

But the creature never reacted. The patrols became almost a bore, and pairs of cats could be heard chasing each other up and down the first flight of stairs, on their own.

What a crazy life, Sally thought. If Mike Taverner *dreamt*

what was going on, what would he say? Once, she even took him on a tour of the house, to admire the new decorations. Took him right into the boxroom. All the cats came too.

The creature suffered a good deal from Mike's elephantine soul and great booming male voice . . .

But the boundary between victory and defeat is narrow; and usually composed of complacency.

The last night started so happily. Mike was coming to dinner; well, he was better than *nothing*. Sally, in her newest dress and butcher's apron, was putting the finishing touches to a sherry trifle. A large Scotch sirloin steak lay wrapped in a bloody package on the fridge, handy for the gas cooker.

Sally had just nipped into the breakfast room to lay the table when she heard a rustling noise in the kitchen . . .

She rushed back in time to see Boss nosing at the bloody packet.

She should have picked him up firmly; but chose to shoo him away with a wild wave of her arms. Boss, panicking, made an enormous leap for the window. The sherry trifle, propelled by all the strength of his back legs, catapulted across the room and self-destructed on the tiled floor in a mess of cream and glass-shards a yard wide.

Sally went berserk. Threw Boss out of the back door; threw Chequers after him, and slammed the window in Mother's face, just as Mother was coming in.

That only left the kittens, eyes scarcely open, crawling and squeaking in their basket. She would have some peace for once, to get ready.

Maybe Mike was right. Too many cats. Only potty old maids had so many cats. RSPCA . . . good homes.

She never noticed that the kittens had ceased to crawl and squeak and maul each other. That they grew silent and huddled together in one corner of their basket, each trying desperately to get into the middle of the heap of warm furry bodies . . .

She scraped and wiped up the trifle. Made Mike an Instant Whip instead. In a flavour she knew he didn't like. Well, he could lump it. Sitting round her kitchen all day, waiting to have his face fed. Fancy living with *that* face for forty years . . . growing bald, scratching under the armpits of his checked shirt like an ape. He'd only become interested in her seriously when he heard about her money . . . Stuff him. Better to live alone . . .

Mike was unfortunate to ring up at that point. He was bringing wine. Would Chateauneuf du Pape do? How smug he sounded; how sure he had her in his grasp.

He made one of his clumsy teasing jokes. She chose to take it the wrong way. Her voice grew sharp. He whinged self-righteously in protest. Sally told him what she *really* thought of him. He rang off in high dudgeon, implying he would never bother her again.

Good. Good riddance to bad rubbish. Much better living on her own in her beautiful house, without a great clumsy corny man in it . . .

But his rudeness had given her a headache. Might as well take an aspirin and lie down. She suddenly felt cold and really tired . . . sleep it off.

Boss was crazy for the sirloin; Mother was very worked-up about her kittens; and the window-catch was old and rusted. Five minutes' work had the window open. Mother made straight for her kittens and Boss made straight for the meat. Three heaves and he had the packet open, and the kitchen filled with the rich smell of blood. Ginger and Chequers appeared out of nowhere and Mother, satisfied her brood was safe, rapidly joined them in a baleful circle round the fridge.

They were not aware of the creature, in their excitement. It was in the breakfast room with Sally, behind a closed door and feeding quietly.

But Boss was infuriatedly aware of the other cats, as they stretched up the face of the fridge, trying to claw his prize out of his mouth. He sensed he would have no peace to enjoy a morsel. So, arching his neck magnificently to hold the steak clear of the floor, he leapt down, then up to the windowsill and out into the night.

Unfortunately, it was one of those damp nights that accent every odour; and the faintest of breezes was blowing from the north towards the town-centre of Southwold. Several hungry noses lifted to the fascinating new scent.

Within a minute, Boss knew he was no longer alone. Frantically he turned and twisted through his well-known alleyways. But others knew them just as well, and the scent was as great a beacon as the circling beams of Southwold's lighthouse. Even the well-fed domestic tabbies, merely out for an airing, caught it. As for the hungry desperate ones . . .

Boss was no fool. He doubled for home. Came through the window like a rocket, leaving a rich red trail on the yellowed white paintwork and regained the fridge. Another minute, and there were ten strange cats in the room. Two minutes and there were twenty.

Boss leapt for the high shelving in desperate evasion. A whole shelf of pots and pans came down together. The noise beggared description, and there were more cats coming in all the time.

Next door the creature, startled, slipped clumsily in its feeding. Sally came screaming up out of nightmare and ran for the warmth of her kitchen, the creature still entangled in her mind.

To the creature, the kitchenful of cats was like rolling in broken glass. Silently, it fled to the high shelf in the box-room.

It was unfortunate for the creature that Boss had very much the same thought. The hall door was ajar. He was through it in a flash and up the stairs, the whole frantic starving mob in pursuit.

Back in the near-empty kitchen, there came a thunderous knocking on the door. It burst open to reveal Mr Taverner in a not-very-becoming plum-coloured smoking-jacket. He flung his arms round Sally, demanding wildly to know what the matter was.

Sally could only point mutely upstairs.

By the time they got there, Boss, with slashing claws, and hideous growls that filtered past the sirloin steak, was making his last stand in the open boxroom door.

And, confused and bewildered by so many enemies, weak from hunger and shattered by frustration, the creature was cowering up on its shelf, trying to get out into the open air through the thick brickwork of the chimneys. But it was old, old . . .

Boss, turning in desperation from the many claws dabbing at his steak, saw the same high shelf and leapt.

Thirty pairs of ravening cat-eyes followed him.

The creature knew, for the first time in its ancient existence, how it felt to be prey . . .

It lost all desire to exist.

Nobody heard the slight popping noise, because of the din. But suddenly there was a vile smell, a rubbish-tip, graveyard, green-water smell.

And the house was empty of anything but dust and cobwebs, woodlice and woodworm. Empty for ever.

Russell Thorndike

NOVEMBER THE THIRTEENTH

RUSSELL THORNDIKE (1885-1972) *was equally well known in his lifetime as a stage and film actor and as the author of the series of swashbuckling novels recounting the adventures of the smuggler Dr Syn. 'November the Thirteenth', one of Thorndike's rare forays into horror, originally appeared in* Powers of Darkness (1934), *one of the volumes in the famous* Creeps *series published by Philip Allan, and has never before been reprinted. Thorndike seems to have enjoyed penning this macabre story, for over a decade later he revised it and included it in a modified form as a chapter in his* The Master of the Macabre (1947), *a remarkable novel composed of a series of linked tales, most of them rather gruesome and horrific. Both that novel and the author's earlier* The Slype (1927), *a mystery with supernatural overtones that earned comparisons to the works of Dickens, are available from Valancourt.*

EVERYONE IN THE VILLAGE KNEW that there was bad blood between Farmer Quested and the Sexton. How the quarrel had originated nobody knew, but it had grown ever since the Farmer had been elected Vicar's Warden, and as such read the lessons every Sunday. It became violent when Kitty Quested returned from service abroad and set all the lads' hearts hammering at her beauty.

The Sexton's daughter was a poor sickly imbecile, and when she died the village pronounced it a good thing, and laughed when they saw the old man transfer his affection upon the churchyard horse, which was named Scraggybones. That, his beer and his hatred for Quested, were the only things the Sexton loved.

One night when the village was drinking at the Chequers, some wag asked the Sexton whose beetroots he had been stealing.

'Beetroots?' repeated the Sexton. 'Don't like 'em.'

'Then why steal 'em?' asked the wag.

'Haven't,' snapped the Sexton.

The wag pointed to the Sexton's spade. There was a smear upon its blade.

'If you've been amongst my beetroots, old 'un,' put in Farmer Quested, from his corner by the fireplace, 'I'll have the law o' you.' The Sexton chuckled, 'If ever Cephas Quested takes the law o' me, it'll be over something more serious than beetroots, I promise you.'

Just then the Vicar came in, and called for a glass of old ale. He was popular because he was not above drinking in his own parish inn. His arrival checked the angry retort which his Warden was about to make to his Sexton. But it did not check the Sexton's chuckles, which developed into a sinister giggling as the old man cleaned the blade of his spade with his thumb, flicking the bits of dirt across the farmers' knees into the fire. The Vicar, having nodded to all the cronies, addressed himself to his Warden:

'You'll be glad to hear, Quested, that we have started carrying out the improvements you suggested re the churchyard at our last Council Meeting. Our worthy Sexton has been digging up the bones from behind the old wall above the Bier-Walk. Such a pile.' He turned to the doctor. 'As a man of science, I should like you to look them over. Your judgment must sort the Christian from the heathen. I think they're all heathen, buried there long before the Church came, and if so they need not harbour up consecrated ground when we're so short of space.'

'Very foolish to have built a churchyard on the side of a hill,' laughed the doctor. 'Naturally the bones work their way through the cracks in the old wall. Many's the mischievous limb I've prevented from tumbling out upon the Bier-Walk.'

'Yes, it's quite uncanny the way they work themselves out,' agreed the Vicar. 'I suppose it's something to do with the wet soaking through to the lower level. It carries them along.'

'It's not the wet,' contradicted the Sexton, still flicking bits of dirt into the fire. 'If you wants to know what it is, I'll tell you. It's the worms.'

They all laughed at this, which annoyed the old man. 'I tells you THEY finishes what the Sexton begins. When I buries you there,' and he struck the floor with his spade, 'I don't flatter myself you'll stop there. THEY'LL come and scatter you, and never leave you till they've got you where they wants you. They're always on the march manoeuvring the dead.'

'Horrible thought,' laughed the Vicar.

'If there's any truth in Parson's yarns about the dead rising again with their bodies, I'll guarantee some confusion in this churchyard, where Smith's finger-bones have been creeping into Jones' eye-sockets. The Quested marble slab won't keep Cephas still, for all its weight. His mother ain't under it now. They'd shifted her sideways last time I give her a look-up. MAKING ROOM FOR THE NEXT. HA, HA!'

'Stop your blasphemy!' shouted the farmer.

'Now then. Now then,' warned the Vicar.

'More ale,' laughed the Sexton.

'No, you've had enough. Go home,' ordered the Vicar.

'All right, sir,' answered the Sexton. 'But if Farmer Quested wants to see for himself, he'll find me up in the churchyard. I'm going to put away my spade.' The Sexton slapped the blade of it with the flat of his hand, then looked at his enemy, and said, 'Beetroots, eh? I like that.' He turned the spade upside down and began to walk it about the bar-parlour. He looked like a child playing with a doll. 'I never had a pretty daughter, I didn't. Mine was as ugly as sin, as I overheard Farmer Quested say the day of her funeral. But my spade ain't ugly. You're a beauty, ain't you?' He kissed the blade, and catching it up in his arms, hugged it.

'Go home at once,' commanded the Vicar. 'You're drunk.'

'That's good too,' sniggered the Sexton. 'But the best thing I've heard to-night was BEETROOTS,' and clutching his spade in high glee he trotted towards the door, where he collided with Johnny Jolt, the hangman.

'Wait till I gets you, you clumsy digger,' cried Mister Jolt.

'Wait till I gets *you*, you clever stringer,' chuckled the Sexton.

'Birds of a feather,' laughed the doctor.

'You needn't talk, you old poisoner,' chaffed the Vicar.

Everybody laughed, and the wag capped the joke with, 'Where's the body? For the vultures are gathered together.'

Johnny Jolt, fresh from a job at the County Gaol, enlivened the company with gruesome details. Cephas Quested was not listening. No. Cephas Quested was sniffing. Sniffing audibly.

Mister Jolt broke his talk to scowl at his interrupter. Quested sniffed again. 'I recommend hot Hollands for a cold,' snapped the hangman.

Quested took no notice, but sniffed again, then said, 'Can any of you smell anything? What did that Sexton flick in the fire?'

A faint crackle came from the hearth. Cephas Quested leaned forward and stared.

Just then young Piper came in, looking sorry for himself. The wag had a new victim, for the village knew that he had been captivated by the Quested girl.

'Cheer up,' cried the wag. 'There's more than one rosy apple in any orchard. Besides, I ain't sure but that Miss Kitty don't favour you above us all.'

'Then why did she appoint a meeting which she never meant to keep?' answered the dejected lover.

'Where were you to meet my daughter?' demanded the farmer. Young Piper was too miserable to care whether the father was annoyed. 'By the churchyard wall above the Bier-Walk. I was late. I warned her that I might be. She promised to wait.'

'God grant she didn't,' muttered the farmer, still staring into the fireplace.

'But she did, and she is,' laughed the wag, looking through the casement. 'You gave up too soon, my lad. She's up there now. Look.' Young Piper ran to the window. On the other side of the street, high above the chimneys of the shops, stood the church, with its burial ground braced with an ancient wall, from the top of which was suspended a lantern which gave light to the Bier-Walk beneath. The silhouette of a girl stood out against the skyline. She was sitting on the wall with one arm leaning upon the lamp-bracket.

'I could only just have missed her,' cried young Piper, bounding towards the door.

'Stop,' thundered Cephas Quested.

Everyone thought that the farmer was about to play the heavy father against young Piper.

'Do you love my girl?' he asked.

It was not a reasonable question to put in a public bar, but the young man answered bold as brass, 'I do, sir.'

'Then what is the colour of her hair?' asked the farmer. Everyone thought this an odd question.

'The harvest moon tries to copy it, sir,' replied the lover poetically.

'The harvest moon, eh? And what is the colour of this?' The farmer plunged his hand across the fire and drew out a piece of dirt from the hearth-back. He did not seem to notice that he burnt his hand. With his finger and thumb he dangled the piece of dirt from a hair which stuck to it.

'Don't do that,' laughed Johnny Jolt. 'Is a man always to be reminded of his work?'

'If this is what I think it be,' whispered the farmer, 'your work ain't finished to-night, Johnny Jolt.' The farmer's manner was very odd.

'Have they all been drinking?' asked the Vicar of the landlord. The door swung back. Everyone turned at the bang. Young Piper had run out. The wag looked through the window, but started back with his hands over his eyes. The window glass had been shattered in his face. A large bone fell on to the floor. The doctor picked it up. 'A human thigh-bone. Very ancient,' he said.

'The Sexton's throwing bones into the High Street,' cried someone, from the door. Then there arose a murmuring like the rumble of an accumulating storm. It rose and rose. Then the screams of women pierced the growling of the men. Doors banged. Lanterns waved. Lights in every window, and casements thrown wide.

The wag called for someone to pull the glass from his eyes, but everyone was looking through the smashed window up at the churchyard.

The limp form of a girl was being swung to and fro. She was suspended by her skirt, which the little Sexton was gripping with both hands as he stood upon the wall. From the Bier-Walk beneath young Piper was leaping, trying to get the girl from the Sexton's grasp. He looked like a dog jumping for a bone. The news spread like wild-fire. The quarrel of the Sexton and the farmer had come to a head. To what had been the very pretty head of Kitty Quested, but was now horrible, nearly severed as it had been by the Sexton's spade.

There was a great pot-hook hanging in the chimney. The farmer dropped the piece of hair and dirt upon the floor. Somebody repeated young Piper's words, 'Copies the harvest moon.'

Quested seized the pot-hook and wrenched it from the chain, bringing down a quantity of soot and a bat which flew about the room.

Up under the churchyard wall the young man snarled and leapt. He leapt high and touched the body several times, and then the skirt ripped, and what should have been the light form of a girl leaning shyly against her lover, dropped heavily upon a maniac and knocked him to the gravel. The Sexton had no time to gloat upon this horror, for the whole village swarmed like a pack of wolves into the Bier-Walk. They were met with a fusillade of heathen bones.

In the deserted bar-parlour of the Chequers, Johnny Jolt took his tankard of ale to the fireplace, kicked up the logs into a blaze, seated himself in Quested's corner and stretched his long legs towards the warmth. It was not his business to arrest a murderer. He was the hangman, and had to wait for the law to take its course. Besides, it was pleasant to get the chimney-corner to himself after a trying day, and everyone had rushed out of the inn in such excitement, neglecting to finish their tankards. The bar-man brought them one by one for the hang-man to drink. At the risk of offending the whole parish, it was his maxim to keep on good terms with the hangman. That gentleman of ghastly trade closed his eyes. 'What are they doing now?' he yawned. Beer was good. The fireplace was warm. He decided not to return to his lonely cottage till the inn closed for the night. 'What's all that infernal banging noise?' he asked.

'Fireworks,' answered the bar-man, from the window. 'The boys have cleared out the stock left over from Guy Fawkes Day.'

'I wonders there's any left,' drawled the hangman. 'To-day's the thirteenth, ain't it?'

'That's right, Mister Jolt.'

'And what are they letting off fireworks for?'

'Shooting them up at the old Sexton. The kids hate him because he never lets them play around the churchyard. I say, you should look. Everything's a-blaze round him and he don't seem to care. He's flinging bones. They're flinging fireworks, Roman candles, squibs, crackers, flares and whatnot. He don't half look horrible.'

'Why don't they go up and get him?' yawned the hangman. 'I wouldn't let no Sexton throw bones at me.'

'There's no stopping him while that pile lasts,' answered the bar-man. 'And when that's done, he's got his spade. Perhaps he'll start the coffins going soon.'

'Don't be silly,' laughed the hangman. 'He couldn't get 'em out in time.'

'Unless he's got 'em ready,' suggested the barman. 'Sort of humour that would appeal to him.'

'They should attack him from the other side.'

'Climbing up from the gravel pits ain't so easy,' argued the bar-man. 'Besides, it lands you right against the mortuary, which ain't cheerful. Hallo. That's what some of them's done. There's shapes on the dodge in and out behind the grave-stones at his back. They've got up by the mortuary. Ah. Now they've got him.'

A terrible shriek made the hangman open his eyes. 'What now?' he asked.

'He's just seen 'em in time. Hurled a pick at one. Got him too. Now he's over the railings of the Boggesses' Vault. Swinging his spade. Slicing their fingers with it. They're pulling the railings down with a rope.'

'Oh, they've got a rope, have they?'

'Yes, and they've got him, too.'

A great shout arose. The bar-man turned quickly to the hangman. 'They're going to hang him from the lamp-bracket.'

This aroused the hangman's professional curiosity. He got up, and swayed unsteadily in the firelight. 'I must see them do that. Hanging ain't so easy. Let's have a quick noggin of rum, just to keep out the cold and go along.'

The bar-man served the hangman quickly with two or three noggins. Then they went unsteadily along the High Street and up the churchyard steps. The steps proved to Johnny Jolt that he was drunk. When they reached the Bier-Walk the bar-man thought they would never get through the crowd. He reckoned without his companion. Mister Jolt was well known, but his trade made folk avoid him, especially on a day like this, when it was known that he had launched a human soul into eternity. Thus a way was made for him, some shrinking from fear or loathing, others from a desire to see a real hangman carry out the job in hand. 'Here's Johnny Jolt!' they cried, to the amateur executioners, who had already fixed a knot to the lantern-bracket and a noose round the Sexton's neck.

'We'll do it ourselves,' answered Quested. 'This is lynch-law, and no interference.'

'Aye, our turn now, Mister Hangman,' called out young Piper, who was staggering aimlessly about with the body of the unfortunate girl clutched in his arms. He refused madly to put her down, and fearing for his reason, they left him alone.

'Go ahead, then,' laughed the hangman. 'Only you won't make no sort of job of it, I can see, and you'll have the constables after you before you can say "Knife".'

'No we shan't,' answered Quested. 'The Police Sergeant rode off with the Parson for help. They found it convenient to be out of our way. There'll be no rescue here, I promise you. We'll have finished with this devil by the time they gets back.'

'Not at the rate you be going,' scoffed the hangman. His

professional eye was criticizing not only the noose and the length of rope, but the rope itself. They threw the Sexton into the air over the wall. The people on the Bier-Walk pushed back to get clear, but the Sexton fell on top of them, causing a panic, in which women were trampled. The Sexton scrambled to his feet, and without removing the noose from his neck, climbed up the rope and caught hold of the iron bracket in the wall. But they soon dislodged him with a pole, and then they tried pulling him up. He got his fingers inside the noose, and by swinging out from the wall, managed to kick several people in the face with his iron-tipped boots. At last Johnny Jolt's patience was exhausted.

'It's a sin not to work a man off on the first jerk,' he cried.

'You do it. What's wrong?' they answered.

'It's all wrong,' shouted the hangman. 'To begin with – the rope. Where did you get it? Out of the Ark?'

'It's his,' they cried, pointing to the hanging Sexton. 'Used it for lowering coffins.'

'Well, it's too thick for a neck like his. Get a bell-rope from the Tower. He keeps the key in his pocket.' The Sexton was lowered. 'Bind his hands behind him with his neckcloth, which you should have took off in the first place.' The expert was obeyed.

'Now two ringers up the Tower with me to choose a rope.'

Going round and round up the turret steps to the belfry convinced Johnny Jolt how very drunk he was. He chose a rope by lantern light, and sent the ringers up the ladder to the bell-chamber to cut it down. It slipped through the ceiling hole, and lashed the hangman in his face as it fell, which put him in a rage.

Out in the churchyard again the fresh noose was adjusted. They offered no prayer, but Churchwarden Quested pronounced a curse that was shuddering to hear. Young Piper held the corpse of his beloved high up in his arms. It looked as if he were being civil to the last and giving the dead girl every chance of seeing justice done for her. Nobody troubled about the after results. The whole village was in it. Johnny Jolt cared for nothing. He was drunk. Everything was ready. The nerve of the village was strung to breaking point when a great white horse came trotting across the churchyard, in and out of the tombstones, and right into the crowd, which scattered screaming, till someone shouted, 'It's only old Scraggybones, the churchyard horse. The only thing he cares about. String it up beside him.'

Over the branch of a great elm, which stretched across the Bier-Walk, the Sexton's discarded coffin rope was thrown, and before his eyes the Sexton's whimpering pet was pulled up. The poor beast, like his master, managed to lay out more than one of the villagers as it was swung off its feet. 'Courage, Scraggybones,' cried the Sexton. 'I shall be with you in a moment, and then we will ride the Bier-Walk together.'

Johnny Jolt waited for the Sexton to see this piece of savagery completed, and then he made ready the knot, but his victim's words sobered him. He did not like them.

Mockingly asked if he had anything to say, the Sexton turned to Quested, and said, 'It is November the Thirteenth. I shall not forget that date in the place where I am going. I shall ride the horse of Death, and trample you upon the Bier-Walk. Remember.' The hangman tightened the noose, and adjusted the knot to his final satisfaction. As he did so the Sexton spoke to him in a voice that sounded dead, 'It would have been better for you, Mister Jolt, had you stayed within doors. It is an unlucky night for you to be abroad, and before the Calendar has run round many times, you will know that my last words were true. I shall be riding, and you will be thinking, "November the Thirteenth. The Thirteenth of November. I wish I had kept within doors." ' The body was jerked over. The Sexton was dead.

When the Vicar returned with the rescue party the whole village was a-bed, but they found the Sexton beside his horse over the Bier-Walk. The whole village being implicated, nobody was punished, and all kept mum throughout the Inquiry, and after a half-hearted attempt on the part of the authorities to make someone speak, the matter was dropped.

A few years went by. People died and people were born, and the dread night was effaced by more recent happenings. Young Piper never mentioned it, as he had married someone else, and did not care to mention Kitty Quested. And then one night

Cephas Quested did not return home. It was in November, and there was snow upon the Bier-Walk. They found him there on the morning of the Fourteenth. He had been trampled by a horse, for the mark of a great shoe showed livid on his temple. Yes. He had been trampled to death on the Bier-Walk, which was significant. From that day Johnny Jolt became a wreck. He drank more heavily, and his eyes were haunted with a fear. He sought company, but there was none where he was welcome. He was always asking people what day of the week the Thirteenth of November fell on, and whenever that unlucky day came, he moved from his lonely cottage and bought board and lodging at the Chequers Inn for one night.

The inn changed hands, and the new landlord did not approve of Johnny Jolt. He thought that the presence of a drunken hangman kept good custom away, and he did not intend to give the creature house-room upon the Thirteenth of November. The day came, and with it the hangman. He was drunk by noon, but had the sense to sit quiet and soak in the corner. It drew on towards midnight and the cronies left. The ex-hangman – for he had lost his job – steered himself to the bar.

'I always sleep here upon this night,' he enunciated slowly. 'I have done so for many years. It is the night when I cannot sleep in the cottage by myself. I daresay you know the reason.'

'Ah yes, sir,' answered mine host. 'That is quite right. You honour the house every Thirteenth of November, I remember. Now please, sir, I wish to close the doors. Drink up, if you please.'

'I will have one more before going to my room.'

The landlord gave him another. 'I will prepare your room for to-morrow, sir.'

'No, for to-night,' corrected the ex-hangman.

'I thought it was for the thirteenth you ordered it.'

'Well?'

'It is the twelfth now, sir.'

'No, the thirteenth.'

Looking at a calendar the landlord shook his head. But the

drunkard wanted to see for himself. The landlord brought the calendar and leant across the bar. 'Here you are. November. That's right. Here's the Thirteenth. Tuesday as large as life. To-day's Monday, and as you see the Twelfth.'

'So it is,' admitted the drunkard. 'Even the Constable told me wrong.'

'To-morrow then, sir?' queried the landlord, putting away the calendar. 'I'll get the pot-boy to light a lantern for you and pilot you up the church steps. It's your quickest way.'

When they had gone, the landlord chuckled to his wife, 'I'll tell him to-morrow that we were looking at the calendar for next year. I got it to-day on purpose.'

Johnny Jolt chuckled to the pot-boy as they climbed the steps. 'Nearly let myself in for two nights at the inn. Couldn't have run to that, with prices as they are now.'

The pot-boy asked him why he wished to spend a night at the inn when his own cottage was so near.

'For company, lad. Did you never hear the tale of the mad and murderous Sexton?'

'Never, sir,' lied the pot-boy, who wanted to hear it first-hand.

'Then sit down here in the porch, and I'll tell you while my legs get sober.'

The pot-boy thought it stupid of Mister Jolt to drink any more brandy if he really wanted to get sober, but he kept his mouth shut while the ex-hangman talked and drank from the bottle in his hand.

The story was finished about the same time as the brandy. Then Mister Jolt turned to the pot-boy and said, 'Now you see why I spend the Thirteenth at the inn. If there are such things as ghosts that there Sexton will be one, and I ain't taking chances with him. See?'

'But you are. It's the Thirteenth now.'

'What do you mean?' screamed the hangman. 'What's to-night?'

'Well, yesterday was Sunday, and we had Psalms for the Twelfth Evening. The Parson don't make mistakes, I hope.'

'If that's true, I'll break that landlord's neck. But are you sure?'

Before the pot-boy could answer, there came the sound of a galloping horse, and at the same time the church clock began to chime for midnight. Mister Jolt's teeth chattered.

'Listen. What's that?'

'A 'orse galloping,' whimpered the pot-boy.

'Coming close, ain't it?'

'Yus.'

'Stopping, ain't it?'

'Yus.'

'What's that noise?'

'Clock striking twelve.'

'No. The other noise.'

'What? That sort of shuffling scuffle?' snivelled the pot-boy.

'Yes. It's skeleton feet.'

'No. It ain't.'

'What is it then?'

'Dunno.'

'I do. It's the Sexton. The Sexton on his horse. He's ridden up the Bier-Walk. He's dismounting under the bracket. He's come to take me. But I won't be took. I won't. I say I won't.' The hangman swung the lantern round his head, and raising the bottle with his other hand, pointed into the darkness screaming, 'Look.' The pot-boy sprang out of the porch, and the hangman brought the lantern down with a crash on to his head, and then came at him with the bottle. The boy had a dim recollection of thrusting his hand against the madman's throat, and of gripping hard. Then the bottle came down, and he remembered no more.

Half an hour later the landlord and two ostlers came from the Chequers to look for the pot-boy. He was lying insensible upon the pavement. They gave him brandy and brought him round, when he screamed out, 'Mister Jolt. Where's Mister Jolt?' They found Mister Jolt on the Bier-Walk, beneath the lantern-bracket, his arms across his face and his legs crumpled under him.

'He has fallen from the wall,' said one of the ostlers. 'Broke his legs, by the look of it.'

'Drunk. It will give my house a bad name,' muttered the landlord, as he uncovered the dead man's face. When he saw it, he sprang to his feet. 'Run for the doctor. I think he's dead.'

When the doctor came and looked at the distorted face, he said, 'Yes, he is dead. A seizure. I warned him to keep off spirits.'

'He had none to-night at the Chequers,' said the landlord.

'I daresay,' nodded the doctor. 'He carried it with him. See.' He unclasped the dead man's fingers, which were clutching the broken neck of a bottle. 'Hallo. Finger-marks on his throat. How's that?'

The pot-boy looked at the doctor, and stammered, 'It's what he feared, sir. The Sexton's ghost come for him. It's the Thirteenth of November.'

'Nonsense,' snapped the doctor. 'You must have seized him by the throat when he came at you.'

'I was knocked senseless with his lantern,' answered the pot-boy stubbornly.

'Hallo. What's this?' The doctor had turned the dead man's head, and they all saw the mark of a great hoof on his face.

'I couldn't have done that now, could I, sir? It's the Sexton's horse, like when Mister Quested was found here.'

'More likely this, I think,' answered the man of science, lifting a great carthorse-shoe from the gravel. 'He was raving drunk, and he fell on this.'

'Put it down, sir,' whispered the landlord.

'Horseshoes won't harm us. They are lucky,' said the doctor.

'That's been dropped by the Devil's horse,' shuddered an ostler.

The landlord suddenly pulled the doctor's hand from the corpse. 'Look. That proves it,' he cried, and pointed to the wall. From a crevice in the old stones there appeared a gigantic and glossy worm, which slithered and dropped upon the hangman's neck, and slipped in under his shirt before the doctor could free his hand to take it.

And so it became a ghost story. The Sexton's horse had trampled him as it had Cephas Quested, and the Sexton's bony fingers had finished by throttling. Then came the King Worm to claim him, and from that day not a soul who had been at the hanging would venture up the Bier-Walk upon November the Thirteenth.

Michael McDowell

HALLEY'S PASSING

Of the many authors rediscovered by Valancourt, none has proven more popular with readers than MICHAEL MCDOWELL *(1950-1999). McDowell's writing career was relatively short – his first novel,* The Amulet, *appeared in 1979, and his last in 1987 – but quite prolific: under his own name and various pseudonyms he published some thirty volumes of fiction during this span before turning his hand to Hollywood screenwriting* (Beetlejuice, The Nightmare Before Christmas). *His Southern Gothic novels* Cold Moon over Babylon *(1980),* The Elementals *(1981) and* Blackwater *(1983) are among the finest horror novels of their era and are now rightly considered classics of the genre.* 'Halley's Passing', *one of only a handful of short stories McDowell wrote, first appeared in the magazine* Twilight Zone *in 1987 and is reprinted here for the first time in almost thirty years. When she included it in her anthology* The Year's Best Fantasy *(1988), editor Ellen Datlow noted that it was 'unquestionably the most distressingly violent story' in the volume, an observation that holds true for the present book as well. Nine of McDowell's novels are available from Valancourt, and his short story 'Miss Mack' appeared in* The Valancourt Book of Horror Stories, Volume One.

'WOULD YOU LIKE TO KEEP THAT ON YOUR CREDIT CARD?' asked the woman on the desk. Her name was Donna and she was dressed like Snow White because it was Halloween.

'No,' said Mr Farley, 'I think I'll pay cash.' Mr Farley counted out twelve ten-dollar bills and laid them on the counter. Donna made sure there were twelve, then gave Mr Farley change of three dollars and twenty-six cents. He watched to make certain she tore up the charge slips he had filled out two days before. She ripped them into thirds. Original copy, Customer's Receipt, Bank Copy, two intervening carbons – all bearing the impress of Mr Farley's Visa card and his signature – they went into a trash basket that was invisible beneath the counter.

'Good-bye,' said Mr Farley. He took up his one small suitcase and walked out the front door of the hotel. His suitcase was light blue Samsonite with an X of tape underneath the handle to make it recognizable at an airport baggage claim.

It was seven o'clock. Mr Farley took a taxi from the hotel to the airport. In the back of the taxi, he opened his case and took out a black loose-leaf notebook and wrote in it:

> 103185   *Double Tree Inn*
> *Dallas, Texas*
> *Checkout 1900 / $116.74 /*
> *Donna*

The taxi took Mr Farley to the airport and cost him $12.50 with a tip that was generous but not too generous.

Mr Farley went to the PSA counter and picked up an airline schedule and put it into the pocket of his jacket. Then he went to the Eastern counter and picked up another schedule. In a bar called the Range Room he sat at a small round table. He ordered a vodka martini from a waitress named Alyce. When she had brought it to him, and he had paid her and she had gone away, he opened his suitcase, pulled out his black loose-leaf notebook and added the notations:

> *Taxi $10.20 + 2.30 / #1718*
> *Drink at Airport Bar*
> *$2.75 + .75 / Alyce*

He leafed backwards through the notebook and discovered that he had flown PSA three times in the past two months. Therefore he looked into the Eastern Schedule first. He looked on page 23 first because $2.30 had been the amount of the tip to the taxi driver. On page 23 of the Eastern airline schedule were flights from Dallas to Milwaukee, Wisconsin, and Mobile, Alabama. All of the flights to Milwaukee changed in Cincinnati or

St Louis. A direct flight to Mobile left at 9:10 p.m. arriving 10:50 p.m. Mr Farley returned the black loose-leaf notebook to his case and got up from the table, spilling his drink in the process.

'I'm very sorry,' he said to Alyce, and left another dollar bill for her inconvenience.

'That's all right,' said Alyce.

Mr Farley went to the Eastern ticket counter and bought a coach ticket to Mobile, Alabama. He asked for an aisle seat in the non-smoking section. He paid in cash and after taking out his black loose-leaf notebook, he checked his blue Samsonite bag. He went through security, momentarily surrendering a ringful of keys. The flight to Mobile departed Gate 15 but Mr Farley sat in the seats allotted to Gate 13, directly across the way. He read through a copy of *USA Today* and he gave a Snickers bar to a child in a pumpkin costume who trick-or-treated him. He smiled at the child, not because he liked costumes or Halloween or children, but because he was pleased with himself for having been foresightful enough to buy three Snickers bars just in case he ran into trick-or-treating children on Halloween night. He opened his black loose-leaf notebook and amended the notation of his most recent bar tab:

Drink at Airport Bar
$2.75 + 1.75/Alyce

The flight for Mobile began boarding at 8:55. As the announcement was made for the early accommodation of those with young children or other difficulties, Mr Farley went into the men's room.

A Latino man in his twenties with a blue shirt and a lock of hair dangling down his neck stood at a urinal, looking at the ceiling and softly farting. His urine splashed against the porcelain wall of the urinal. Mr Farley went past the urinals and stood in front of the two stalls and peered under them. He saw no legs or feet or shoes but he took the precaution of opening the doors. The stalls were empty, as he suspected, but Mr Farley did not like to leave such matters to chance. The Latino man, looking downwards, flushed the urinal, zipping his trousers and backing away at the same time. Mr Farley leaned down and took the Latino man by the waist. He swung the Latino man around so that he was facing the mirrors and the two sinks in the restroom and could see Mr Farley's face.

'Man –' protested the Latino man.

Mr Farley rolled his left arm around the Latino man's belt and put his right hand on the Latino man's head. Mr Farley pushed forward very swiftly with his right hand. The Latino man's head went straight down towards the sink in such a way that the cold-water faucet, shaped like a Maltese Cross, shattered the bone above the Latino man's right eye. Mr Farley had gauged the strength of his attack so that the single blow served to press the Latino's head all the way down to the porcelain. The chilled aluminum faucet was buried deeply in the Latino man's brain. Mr Farley took the Latino man's wallet from his back pocket, removed the cash and his Social Security card. He gently dropped the wallet into the sink beneath the Latino man's head and turned on the hot water. Mr Farley peered into the sink, and saw blood, blackish and brackish swirling into the rusting drain. Retrieving his black looseleaf notebook from the edge of the left hand sink where he'd left it, Mr Farley walked out of the restroom. The Eastern flight to Mobile was boarding all seats and Mr Farley walked on directly behind a young woman with brown hair and a green scarf and directly in front of a young woman with slightly darker brown hair in a yellow sweater-dress. Mr Farley sat in Seat 4-C and next to him, in Seat 4-A, was a bearded man in a blue corduroy jacket who fell asleep before take-off. Mr Farley reached into his pocket and pulled out the bills he'd taken from the Latino man's wallet. There were five five-dollar bills and nine one-dollar bills. Mr Farley pulled out his own wallet and interleaved the Latino man's bills with his own, mixing them up. Mr Farley reached into his shirt pocket and pulled out the Latino man's Social Security card, cupping it from sight and slipping it into the Eastern Airlines In-Flight Magazine. He turned on the reading light and opened the magazine. The Social Security card read:

IGNACIOS LAZO
424-70-4063

Mr Farley slipped the Social Security card back into his shirt pocket. He exchanged the in-flight magazine for the black loose-leaf notebook in the seat back pocket. He held the notebook in his lap for several minutes while he watched the man in the blue corduroy jacket next to him, timing his breaths by the sweep second hand on his watch. The man seemed genuinely to be asleep. Mr Farley declined a beverage from the stewardess, who did not wear a name tag, and put his finger to his lips with a smile to indicate that the man in the blue corduroy jacket was sleeping and probably wouldn't want to be disturbed. When the beverage cart was one row behind and conveniently blocking the aisle so that no one could look over his shoulder as he wrote, Mr Farley opened the black loose-leaf notebook on his lap, and completed the entry for Halloween:

> *2155/Ignacios Lazo/c*
> *27/Dallas Texas/ Airport/*
> *RR/38/Head onto Faucet*

RR meant Rest Room, and Mr Farley stared at the abbreviation for a few moments, wondering whether he shouldn't write out the words. There was a time when he had been a good deal given to abbreviations, but once, in looking over his book for a distant year, he had come across the notation CRB, and had had no idea what that stood for. Mr Farley since that time had been careful about his notations. It didn't do to forget things. If you forgot things, you might repeat them. And if you inadvertently fell into a repetitious pattern – well then, you just might get into trouble.

Mr Farley got up and went into the rest room at the forward end of the passenger cabin. He burned Ignacios Lazo's Social Security card, igniting it with a match torn from a book he had picked up at the casino at the MGM Grand Hotel in Las Vegas. He waited in the rest room till he could no longer smell the nitrate in the air from the burned match, then flushed the toilet, washed his hands, and returned to his seat.

The flight arrived in Mobile at three minutes past eleven. While waiting for his blue Samsonite bag, Mr Farley went to a Yellow Pages telephone directory for Mobile. His flight from Dallas had been Eastern Flight No. 71, but Mr Farley was not certain there would be that many hotels and motels in Mobile, Alabama, so he decided on number 36, which was half of 72 (the closest even number to 71). Mr Farley turned to the pages advertising hotels and counted down thirty-six to the Oasis Hotel. He telephoned and found a room was available for fifty-six dollars. He asked what the cab fare from the airport would be and discovered it would be about twelve dollars, with tip. The reservations clerk asked for Mr Farley's name, and Mr Farley, looking down at the credit card in his hand, said, 'Mr T. L. Rachman.' He spelled it for the clerk.

Mr Rachman claimed his bag, and went outside for a taxi. He was first in line, and by 11:30 he had arrived at the Oasis Hotel, downtown in Mobile. In the hotel's Shore Room Lounge, a band was playing in Halloween costume. The clerk on the hotel desk was made up to look like a mummy.

'You go to a lot of trouble here for holidays, I guess,' said Mr Rachman pleasantly.

'Anything for a little change,' said the clerk as he pressed Mr Rachman's MasterCard against three copies of a voucher. Mr Rachman signed his name on the topmost voucher and took back the card. Clerks never checked signatures at this point, and they never checked them later either, but Mr Rachman had a practiced hand, at least when it came to imitating a signature.

Mr Rachman's room was on the fifth and topmost floor, and enjoyed a view down to the street. Mr Rachman unpacked his small bag, carefully hanging his extra pair of trousers and his extra jacket. He set his extra pair of shoes, with trees inside, into the closet beneath the trousers and jacket. He placed his two laundered shirts inside the topmost bureau drawer, set his little carved box containing an extra watch and two pairs of cufflinks and a tie clip and extra pairs of brown and black shoelaces on top of the bureau, and set his toiletries case next to the sink in the bathroom. He opened his black loose-leaf note-book and though it was not yet midnight, he began the entry for 110185, beneath which he noted:

> 110185   *Eastern 71 Dallas-Mobile*
>   *Taxi $9.80 + 1.70*
>   *Oasis Hotel/4th St*
>   *T.L. Rachman*

In the bathroom, Mr Rachman took scissors and cut up the Visa card bearing the name Thomas Farley, and flushed away the pieces. He went down to the lobby and went into the Shore Room Lounge and sat at the bar. He ordered a vodka martini and listened to the band. When the bartender went away to the rest room, Mr Rachman poured his vodka martini into a basin of ice behind the bar. When the bartender returned, Mr Rach-man ordered another vodka martini.

The cocktail lounge – and every other bar in Mobile – closed at 1 a.m. Mr Rachman returned to his room, and without ever turning on the light, he sat at his window and looked out into the street. After the laundry truck had arrived, unloaded, and driven off from the service entrance of the Hotel Oasis, Mr Rachman retreated from the window. It was 4:37 on the morn-ing of the first of November, 1985. Mr Rachman pulled the shade and drew the curtains. Towards noon, when the maid came to make up the room, Mr Rachman called out from the bathroom, 'I'm taking a bath.'

'I'll come back later,' the maid called back.

'That's all right,' Mr Rachman said loudly. 'Just leave a couple of fresh towels on the bed.' He sat on the tile floor and ran his unsleeved arm up and down through the filled tub, making splashing noises.

Mr Rachman counted his money at sundown. He had four hundred fifty-eight dollars in cash. With all of it in his pocket, Mr Rachman walked around the block to get his bearings. He had been in Mobile before, but he didn't remember exactly when. Mr Rachman had his shoes shined in the lobby of a hotel that wasn't the one he was staying in. When he was done, he paid the shoe-shine boy seventy-five cents and a quarter tip, and got into the elevator behind a businessman who was carrying a briefcase. The businessman with the briefcase got off on the fourth floor, and just as the doors of the elevator were closing Mr Rachman startled and said, 'Oh this is my floor, too,' and jumped off behind the businessman with the briefcase. Mr Rachman put his hand into his pocket, and jingled his loose change as if he were looking for his room key. The business-man with the briefcase put down his briefcase beside Room 419 and fumbled in his pocket for his own room key. Mr Rachman stopped and patted all the pockets of his jacket and trousers. 'Did I leave it at the desk?' he murmured to himself. The busi-nessman with the briefcase put the key into the lock of Room 419, and smiled a smile that said to Mr Rachman, *It happens to me all the time, too.* Mr Rachman smiled a small embarrassed smile, and said, 'I sure hope I left it at the desk,' and turned and started back down the hall past the businessman with the briefcase.

The businessman and his briefcase were already inside of Room 419 and the door was beginning to shut when Mr Rach-man suddenly changed direction in the hallway and pushed the door open.

'Hey,' said the businessman. He held his briefcase up protec-tively before him. Mr Rachman shut the door quietly behind him. Room 419 was a much nicer room than his own, though he didn't care for the painting above the bed. Mr Rachman smiled, though, for the businessman was alone and that was always easier. Mr Rachman pushed the businessman down on the bed and grabbed the briefcase away from him. The business-man reached for the telephone. The red light was blinking on the telephone telling the businessman he had a message at the desk. Mr Rachman held the briefcase high above his head and then brought it down hard, giving a little twist to his wrist just at the last so that a corner of the rugged leather case smashed against the bridge of the businessman's nose, breaking it. The businessman gaped, and fell sideways on the bed. Mr Rachman raised the case again and brought the side of it down against the businessman's cheek with such force that the handle of the case broke off in his hand and the businessman's cheekbones were splintered and shoved up into his right eye. Mr Rachman took the case in both hands and swung it hard along the length of the businessman's body and caught him square beneath his chin in the midst of a choking scream so that the businessman's lower jaw was shattered, detached, and then embedded in the roof of his mouth. In the businessman's remaining eye was one second more of consciousness and then he was dead. Mr Rachman turned over the businessman's corpse and took out his wallet, discovering that his name was Edward P. Maguire, and that he was from Sudbury, Massachusetts. He had one hundred and thirty-three dollars in cash, which Mr Rachman put into his pocket. Mr Rachman glanced through the credit cards, but took only the New England Bell telephone credit card. Mr Maguire's briefcase, though battered and bloody, had remained locked, secured by an unknown combination. Mr Rachman would have taken the time to break it open and examine its contents but the telephone on the bedside table rang. The hotel desk might not have noticed Mr Maguire's entrance into the hotel, but Mr Rachman did not want to take a chance that Mr Maguire's failure to answer the telephone would lead to an investigation. Mr Rachman went quickly through the dead man's pockets, spilling his change onto the bedspread. He found the key of a Hertz rental car with the tag number indicated on a plastic ring. Mr Rachman pocketed it. He turned the dead man over once more and pried open his shattered mouth. A thick broth of clotting blood and broken teeth spilled out over the knot of Mr Maguire's tie. With the tips of two fingers, Mr Rachman picked out a pointed fragment of incisor, and put it into his mouth, licking the blood from his fingers as he did so. As he peered out into the hallway, Mr Rachman rolled the broken tooth around the roof of his mouth, and then pressed it there with his tongue till its jagged edge drew blood and he could taste it. No one was in the hall, and Mr Rachman walked out of Room 419, drawing it

closed behind him. He took the elevator down to the basement
garage, and walked slowly about till he found Mr Maguire's
rented car. He drove out of the hotel garage and slowly circled
several streets till he found a stationery store that was still open.
Inside he bought a detailed street map of Mobile. He studied
it by the interior roof light of the rented car. For two hours he
drove through the outlying suburbs of the city, stopping now
and then before a likely house, and noting its number on the
map with a black felt-tip marker. At half-past eleven he returned
to the Oasis Hotel and parked the rental car so that it would be
visible from his window. He went up to his room, and noted in
his diary, under 110185:

> 1910/Edward P Maguire/c
> 43/Mobile Alabama/Hotel
> Palafox 419/1133/Jaw and
> Briefcase

On a separate page in the back of the looseleaf notebook, he
added:

> Edward P Maguire
> (110185)/9 Farmer's
> Road/Sudbury MA 01776/
> 617 392 3690

That was just in case. Sometimes Mr Rachman liked to visit
widows. It added to the complexity of the pattern, and so far as
Mr Rachman was concerned, the one important thing was to
maintain a pattern that couldn't be analyzed, that was arbitrary
in every point. That was why he sometimes made use of the
page of notations in the back of the book – because too much
randomness was a pattern in itself. If he sometimes visited a
widow after he had met her husband, he broke up the pattern of
entirely unconnected deaths. Mr Rachman, who was methodi-
cal to the very core of his being, spent a great percentage of his
waking time in devising methods to make each night's work

seem entirely apart from the last's. Mr Rachman, when he was young, had lived in a great city and had simply thought that its very size would hide him. But even in a great city, his very pattern of randomness had become apparent, and he had very nearly been uncovered. Mr Rachman judged that he would have to do better, and he began to travel. In the time since then, he had merely refined his technique. He varied the length of his stays, he varied his acquaintance. That's what he called them, and it wasn't a euphemism – he simply had no other word for them, and really, they were the people he got to know best, if only for a short time. He varied his methods, he varied the time of the evening, and he even varied his variety. Sometimes he would arrange to meet three old women in a row, three old women who lived in similar circumstances in a small geographical area, and then he would move on, and his next acquaintance would be a young man who exchanged his favors for cash. Mr Rachman imagined a perfect pursuer, and expended a great deal of energy in evading and tricking this imaginary hound. Increasingly, over the years Mr Rachman's greatest satisfaction lay in evading this nonexistent, dogged detective. His only fear was that there was a pattern in the carpet he wove which was invisible to him, but perfectly apparent to anyone who looked at it from a certain angle.

No one took notice of Mr Maguire's rented car that night. Next morning Mr Rachman told the chambermaid he wasn't feeling well and would spend the day in bed, so she needn't make it up. But he let her clean the bathroom as she hadn't been able to do the day before. He lay with his arm over his eyes. 'I hope you feel better,' said the chambermaid. 'Do you have any aspirin?'

'I've already taken some,' said Mr Rachman, 'but thank you. I think I'll just try to sleep.'

That night, Mr Rachman got up and watched the rented car. It had two parking tickets on the windshield. At 11:30 p.m. he went downstairs, got into the car, and drove around three blocks slowly, just in case he was being followed. He was not, so far as he could tell. He opened his map of Mobile, and picked the house he'd marked that was nearest a crease. It was 117 Shadyglade Lane in a suburb called Spring Hill. Mr Rachman drove on, to the nearest of the other places he'd marked. He stopped in front of a house on Live Oak Street, about a mile away. No lights burned. He turned into the driveway and waited for fifteen minutes. He saw no movement in the house. He got out of his car, closing the door loudly, and walked around to the back door, not making any effort to be quiet.

There was no door bell so he pulled open the screen door and knocked loudly. He stood back and looked up at the back of the house. No lights came on that he could see. He knocked more loudly, then without waiting for a response he kicked at the base of the door, splintering it in its frame. He went into the kitchen, but did not turn on the light.

'Anybody home?' Mr Rachman called out as he went from the kitchen into the dining room. He picked up a round glass bowl from the sideboard and hurled it at a picture. The bowl shattered noisily. No one came. Mr Rachman looked in the other two rooms on the ground floor, then went upstairs, calling again, 'It's Mr Rachman!'

He went into the first bedroom, and saw that it belonged to a teenaged boy. He closed the door. He went into another bedroom and saw that it belonged to the parents of the teenaged boy. He went through the bureau drawers, but found no cash. The father's shirts, however, were in Mr Rachman's size – 16 ½ x 33 – and he took two that still bore the paper bands from the laundry. Mr Rachman checked the other rooms of the second floor just in case, but the house was empty. Mr Rachman went out the back door again, crossed the back yard of the house, and pressed through the dense ligustrum thicket there. He found himself in the back yard of a ranch house with a patio and a brick barbeque. Mr Rachman walked to the patio and picked up a pot of geraniums and hurled it through the sliding glass doors of the den. Then he walked quickly inside the house, searching for a light switch. A man in pajamas suddenly lurched through a doorway, and he too was reaching for the light switch. Mr Rachman put one hand on the man's shoulder, and with his other he grabbed the man's wrist. Then Mr Rachman gave a twist, and smashed the back of the man's elbow against the edge of a television set with such force that all the bones there shattered at once. Mr Rachman then took the man by the waist, lifted him up and carried him over to the broken glass door. He turned him sideways and then pushed him against the long line of broken glass, only making sure that the shattered glass was embedded deep into his face and neck. When Mr Rachman let the man go, he remained standing, so deep had the edge of broken door penetrated his head and chest. Just in case, Mr Rachman pressed harder. Blood poured out over Mr Rachman's hands. With a nod of satisfaction, Mr Rachman released the man in pajamas and walked quickly back across the patio and disappeared into the shrubbery again. On the other side, he looked back, and could see the lights going on in the house. He heard a woman scream. He took out a handkerchief to cover his bloody hands and picked up the shirts which he'd left on the back porch of the first house. Then he got into his car and drove around till he came to a shopping mall. He parked near half a dozen other cars – probably belonging to night watchmen – and took off his blood-stained jacket. He tossed it out the window. He took off his shirt, and wiped off the blood that covered his hands. He threw that out of the window, too. He put on a fresh shirt and drove back to the Oasis Hotel. He parked the car around the block, threw the keys into an alleyway, and went back up to his room. In his black loose-leaf notebook he wrote, under 110285:

> *1205/unk./mc 35/Spring*
> *Hill (Mobile) Alabama/*
> *$0/Broken glass*

Mr Rachman spent the rest of the night simply reading through his black loose-leaf notebook, not trying to remember what he could not easily bring to mind, but merely playing the part of the tireless investigator trying to discern a pattern. Mr Rachman did not think he was fooling himself when he decided that he could not.

When the chambermaid came the next day, Mr Rachman sat on a chair with the telephone cradled between his ear and his shoulder, now and then saying, 'Yes' or 'No, not at all' or 'Once more and let me check those numbers,' as he made notations on a pad of paper headed up with a silhouette cartouche of palm trees.

Mr Rachman checked out of the Oasis Hotel a few minutes after sundown, and smiled a polite smile when the young woman on the desk apologized for having to charge him for an extra day. The bill came to $131.70 and Mr Rachman paid in cash. As he watched the young woman on the desk tear up the credit card receipt, he remarked, 'I don't like to get near my limit,' and the young woman on the desk replied, 'I won't even apply for one.'

'But they sometimes come in handy, Marsha,' said Mr Rachman, employing her name aloud as a reminder to note it later in his diary. Nametags were a great help to Mr Rachman in his travels, and he had been pleased to watch the rapid spread of their use. Before 1960 or thereabouts, hardly anyone had worn a nametag.

Mr Rachman drove around downtown Mobile for an hour or so, just in case something turned up. Once, driving slowly down an alleyway that was scarcely wider than his car, a prostitute on yellow heels lurched at him out of a recessed doorway, plunging a painted hand through his rolled-down window. Mr Rachman said, 'Wrong sex,' and drove on.

'Faggot!' the prostitute called after him.

Mr Rachman didn't employ prostitutes except in emergencies, that is to say, when it was nearly dawn and he had not managed to make anyone's acquaintance for the night. Then he resorted to prostitutes, but not otherwise. Too easy to make that sort of thing a habit.

And habits were what Mr Rachman had to avoid.

He drove to the airport, and took a ticket from a mechanized gate. He drove slowly around the parking lot, which was out of doors, and to one side of the airport buildings. He might have taken any of several spaces near the terminal, but Mr Rachman drove slowly about the farther lanes. He could not drive very long, for fear of drawing the attention of a guard.

A blue Buick Skylark pulled into a space directly beneath a burning sodium lamp. Mr Rachman made a sudden decision. He parked his car six vehicles down, and quickly climbed out with his blue Samsonite suitcase. He strode towards the terminal with purpose, coming abreast of the blue Buick Skylark. A woman, about thirty-five years old, was pulling a dark leather bag out of the backseat of the car. Mr Rachman stopped suddenly, put down his case and patted the pockets of his trousers in alarm.

'My keys . . .' he said aloud.

Then he checked the pockets of his suit jacket. He often used the forgotten keys ploy. It didn't really constitute a habit, for it was an action that would never appear later as evidence.

The woman with the suitcase came between her car and the recreational vehicle that was parked next to it. She had a handbag over her shoulder. Mr Rachman suddenly wanted very badly to make this one work for him. For one thing, this was a woman, and he hadn't made the acquaintance of a female since he'd been in Mobile. That would disrupt the pattern a bit. She had a purse, which might contain money. He liked the shape and size of her luggage, too.

'Excuse me,' she said politely, trying to squeeze by him.

'I think I locked my keys in my car,' said Mr Rachman, moving aside for her.

She smiled a smile which suggested that she was sorry but that there was nothing she could do about it.

She had taken a single step towards the terminal when Mr Rachman lifted his right leg and took a long stride forward. He caught the sole of his shoe against her right calf, and pushed her down to the pavement. The woman crashed to her knees on the pavement with such force that the bones of her knees shattered. She started to fall forward, but Mr Rachman spryly caught one arm around her waist and placed his other hand on the back of her head. In his clutching fingers, he could feel the scream building in her mouth. He swiftly turned her head and smashed her face into the high-beam headlight of the blue Buick Skylark. He jerked her head out again, and even before the broken glass had spilled down the front of her suit jacket, Mr Rachman plunged her head into the low-beam headlight. He jerked her head out, and awkwardly straddling her body, he pushed her between her Buick and the next car in the lane, a silver VW GTI. He pushed her head hard down against the pavement four times, though he was sure she was dead already. He let go her head, and peered at his fingers in the light of the sodium lamp. He smelled the splotches of blood on his third finger and his palm and his thumb. He tasted the blood, and then wiped it off on the back of the woman's bare leg. Another car turned down the lane, and Mr Rachman threw himself onto the pavement, reaching for the woman's suitcase before the automobile lights played over it. He pulled it into the darkness between the cars. The automobile drove past. Mr Rachman pulled the woman's handbag off her shoulder, and then rolled her beneath her car. Fishing inside the purse for her car keys, he opened the driver's door and unlocked the back door. He climbed into the car and pulled in her bag with him. He emptied its contents onto the floor, then crawled across the back seat and opened the opposite door. He retrieved his blue Samsonite suitcase from beneath the recreational vehicle where he'd kicked it as he struck up his acquaintance with the woman. The occupants of the car that had passed a few moments before walked in front of the Buick. Mr Rachman ducked behind the back seat for a moment till he could no longer hear the voices – a man and a woman. He opened his Samsonite case and repacked all his belongings into the woman's black leather case. He reached into the woman's bag and pulled out her wallet. He took her Alabama driver's license and a Carte Blanche credit card that read A. B. Frost rather than Aileen Frost. He put the ticket in his pocket. Mr Rachman was mostly indifferent to the matter of fingerprints, but he had a superstition against carbon paper of any sort.

Mr Rachman surreptitiously checked the terminal display and found that a plane was leaving for Birmingham, Alabama in twenty minutes. It would probably begin to board in five minutes. Mr Rachman rushed to the Delta ticket counter, and said breathlessly, 'Am I too late to get on the plane to Birmingham? I haven't bought my ticket yet.'

Mark, the airline employee said, 'You're in plenty of time – the plane's been delayed.'

This was not pleasant news. Mr Rachman was anxious to leave Mobile. Aileen Frost was hidden beneath her car, it was true, and might not be found for a day or so – but there was always a chance that someone would find her quickly. Mr Rachman didn't want to be around for any part of the investigation. Also, he couldn't now say, 'Well, I think I'll go to Atlanta instead.' That would draw dangerous attention to himself. Perhaps he should just return to Mr Maguire's car and drive away. The evening was still early. He could find a house in the country, make the acquaintance of anyone who lived there, sit out quietly the daylight hours, and leave early the following evening.

'How long a delay?' Mr Rachman asked Mark.

'Fifteen minutes,' said Mark pleasantly, already making out the ticket. 'What name?'

Not Frost, of course. And Rachman was already several days old.

'Como,' he said, not knowing why.

'Perry?' asked Mark with a laugh.

'Peter,' said Mr Como.

Mr Como sighed. He was already half enamoured of his alternative plan. But he couldn't leave now. Mark might remember a man who had rushed in, then rushed out again because he couldn't brook a fifteen-minute delay. The ticket from Mobile to Birmingham was $89, five dollars more than Mr Como had predicted in his mind. Putting his ticket into the inside pocket of his jacket that did not contain Aileen Frost's ticket to Wilmington, Mr Como went into the men's room and locked himself into a stall. Under the noise of the flushing toilet, he quickly tore up Aileen Frost's ticket, and stuffed the fragments into his jacket pocket. When he left the stall he washed his hands at the sink until the only other man in the rest room left. Then he wrapped the fragments in a paper towel and stuffed that deep into the waste paper basket. Aileen Frost's license and credit card he slipped into a knitting bag of a woman waiting for a plane to Houston.

Mr Como had been given a window seat near the front of the plane. The seat beside him was empty. After figuring his expenses for the day, Mr Como wrote in his black loose-leaf notebook:

> *0745/Aileen Frost/fc*
> *35/Mobile Airport Parking*
> *Lot/$212/Car headlights*

Mr Como was angry with himself. Two airport killings within a week. That was laziness. Mr Como had fallen into the lazy, despicable habit of working as early in the evening as possible. This, even though Mr Como had *never* failed, not a single night, not even when only minutes had remained till dawn. But he tended to fret, and he didn't rest easy till he had got the evening's business out of the way. That was the problem of course. He had no other business. So if he worked early, he was left with a long stretch of hours till he could sleep with the dawn. If he put off till late, he only spent the long hours fretting, wondering if he'd be put to trouble. *Trouble* to Mr Como meant witnesses (whose acquaintance he had to make as well), or falling back on easy marks – prostitutes, nightwatchmen, hotel workers. Or, worst of all, pursuit and flight, and then some sudden, uncomfortable place to wait out the daylight hours.

On every plane trip, Mr Como made promises to himself: he'd use even more ingenuity, he'd rely on his expertise and work at late hours as well as early hours, he'd try to develop other interests. Yet he was at the extremity of his ingenuity, late hours fretted him beyond any pleasure he took in making a new acquaintance, and he had long since lost his interest in any pleasure but that moment he saw the blood of each night's new friend. And even that was only a febrile memory of what had once been a hot true necessity of desire.

Before the plane landed, Mr Como invariably decided that he did too much thinking. For, finally, instinct had never failed him, though everything else – Mr Como, the world Mr Como inhabited, and Mr Como's tastes – everything else changed.

'Ladies and gentlemen,' said the captain's voice, 'we have a special treat for you tonight. If you'll look out the left side of the plane, and up – towards the Pleiades – you'll see Halley's Comet. You'll see it better from up here than from down below. And I'd advise you to look now, because it won't be back in our lifetimes.'

Mr Como looked out of the window. Most of the other passengers didn't know which stars were the Pleiades, but Mr Como did. Halley's Comet was a small blur to the right of the small constellation. Mr Como gladly gave his seat to a young couple who wanted to see the comet. Mr Como remembered the 1910 visitation quite clearly, and that time the comet had been spectacular. He'd been living in Canada, he thought, somewhere near Halifax. It was high in the sky then, brighter than Venus, with a real tail, and no one had to point it out to you. He tried to remember the time before – 1834, he determined with a calculation of his fingernail on the glossy cover of the Delta In-flight magazine. But 1834 was beyond his power of recollection. The Comet was surely even brighter then, but where had he been at that time? Before airports, and hotels, and credit cards, and the convenience of nametags. He'd lived in one place then for long periods of time, and hadn't even kept proper records. There'd been a lust then, too, for the blood, and every night he'd done more than merely place an incrimsoned finger to his lips.

But everything had changed, evolved slowly and immeasurably, and he was not what once he'd been. Mr Como knew he'd change again. The brightness of comets deteriorated with every pass. Perhaps on its next journey around the sun, Mr Como wouldn't be able to see it at all.

Isabel Colegate

THE NICE BOYS

ISABEL COLEGATE *is the author of many acclaimed novels, including* The Shooting Party *(1980), a modern classic set in Edwardian England that won the W. H. Smith Literary Award and was adapted for an award-winning film. 'The Nice Boys', her sole contribution to the horror genre, is an atmospheric tale with a lingering sense of menace set in Venice. It was first published in a now-scarce volume simply entitled* Horror Anthology *(1965) – where it appeared alongside tales by Ray Bradbury, M. R. James, Robert Aickman and others – and it has never previously been reprinted. Colegate's first novel, the darkly comical* The Blackmailer *(1958), recently cited in a BBC.com article as one of 'ten lost books you should read right now', is available from Valancourt.*

October 2

O F COURSE VENICE IS NOT THE SAME. How could it be? Last year was the first time, and with Jacob.

There were two nice boys on the train from Milan. I talked to them. I have been through bad periods before. I know how easy it is to become isolated if you are unhappy.

I asked them for a light.

The one in the corner brought out a box of matches, lit one, and held it out to me with a steady hand.

'What's that on your arm?' he asked. 'A bite?'

I had taken off my coat, and the sleeves of my dress were short. There was a circular bruise on my forearm.

I explained feebly that I had bitten myself in a temper. The travel agency had muddled all my arrangements just when I was fussing about my packing. 'I know it sounds stupid,' I said. 'But it did calm me down as a matter of fact.'

The boy who had lit my cigarette pushed back the sleeve of

his jacket, undid the button of his beautifully white cuff, and showed me his wrist. One side of it was purple and swollen. It was a much more serious bruise than mine.

'That was a bite,' he said.

I wondered what to say.

The other boy said, 'His kid sister did it,' and they both laughed, excessively I thought, but I suppose they were remembering a funny incident.

'She's a terror,' said the first boy.

'How old is she?' I asked. They told me she was eight and called Jean, and then a noisy Italian family moved into the carriage with a lot of luggage and our conversation came to an end for the time being.

We exchanged another non-committal word or two on the journey, about the weather and this or that, and I was rather struck by them. It was not just that they were nice-looking and well-dressed, with good haircuts and Italian shoes, but that they had a certain air of confidence and reserve as if they already had some achievement to their credit. I don't know what the achievement could be. They might have been pop singers; but there would have been fans, and a manager or something. Academic success? They might have been grammar school boys who had won scholarships somewhere; but no, they had more assurance than that. Anyway, whatever its origin, their air of authority was rather charming.

Of course, all young people are confident these days. Confident, independent, and cool. He didn't sink his teeth into his own flesh at three o'clock in the morning after hours of sobbing and screaming with jealous misery. I wish I had his self-control.

October 5

I am glad I came. Venice is wonderfully soothing, wonderfully sad.

I remember my very first impression, which was one of gaiety; but that was misleading. I remember going down the Grand Canal in a launch – boats dashing about through the choppy water, the sun on buildings of pure fantasy – it was so active, startling, beautiful, such a glorious joke. I remember standing up and laughing, and Jacob watching me with surprise and pleasure. Later I discovered the Venice I loved best, the Venice of regret.

We stayed for two nights at the Gritti Palace, but then it became obvious that my money was not going to last, and so we moved to this same seedy pensione where I am now, not far from the Accademia bridge. The pale German woman is still the proprietress. She does not remember me, thank goodness. I was right to come. It is easy to be sad here, and when I am sad I am not enraged. Besides, Venice's glory is all over too.

I was rather nervous when I came in. I was afraid she would ask about Jacob. I could not decide whether to deny having been here before, or to say 'He is busy,' or to say 'He has married someone younger, prettier, and richer than I am.' I need not have bothered. She hardly looked at me; but when she saw my English passport she said, 'I see you have more terrible murders in London.' She was not interested in me, only in some idea she had about a gas-lit London where sadistic murderers pad through the fog about their dreadful business: some foreigners do have this picture of London in their minds. I asked her if she had ever been there and she said no. 'It is terrible,' she said. 'These poor girls.' Someone has evidently been chopping up prostitutes again. She seemed to have a morbid interest in the whole business.

When we were here before the sun was shining. This time it is misty and damp. Appropriate, perhaps. Loneliness, damp, melancholy, the seediness of a place from which the glory has fled. I went to Torcello in the water-bus, simply to be on the lagoon again, and visit those dead islands, grass on stone, quiet water over fallen palaces; and felt a sort of happiness. How soon will all Venice slide into the sea?

The boys from the train are staying in the pensione. They were signing themselves in when I came in this evening. I greeted them, and saw that they had written 'N. Bray, S. Brook'. Seeing where I was looking the one who had been writing said with a smile, 'He's Sig. I'm Poney.' Sig is slightly smaller and quieter, Poney darker, more handsome and less intense. They seem unlikely names.

October 9

The fog has come. Damp cold fog has flopped over Venice, making the whole place mysteriously different. The people seem to accept it with a certain gloomy relish. They say it is better than the floods they often have at this time of the year.

There is nothing to do. I walk endlessly. Everyone seems to have disappeared: only occasionally another human being pads past in the fog, muffled to the eyes, a stranger. The little restaurant round the corner where I often go for lunch is usually empty, the student waiters have disappeared and only the close-faced husband and wife who own it are there. And the cats. There are always cats in Venice.

I begin to think it may be lucky that I could not keep my room after November the first. Apparently the German woman closes down then and goes for a holiday, to her mother in Munich, she told me. She's an odd woman. She seems to have no family here, or friends. She has struck up some sort of relationship with the two boys. They order her about in a rather disagreeable manner: they are really awfully arrogant, but she seems to like it. There is something slavish in her attitude as she fetches and carries for them.

They have the room next to mine. Last night I was awake until about five. I had taken my last sleeping pill, and when it didn't work I began to panic. I walked up and down, tried to read, did exercises. It was no good. All the agony came back. I am so bloody jealous. It is hardly sane. I hate it, but what can I do? Here she is at that party, leaning against the door – how pleased with her own looks – and Jacob walking towards her, unsteadily because he is a bit drunk, and I recognize with a shock that the curve of her cheek and chin is rather like mine – and I am lost in the endless torture of imagining them together, of remembering his love-making and imagining him making love to her. He said, 'She's awfully sweet really, you'd like her.' Unimaginable cruelty.

At some stage in the night I opened my window and leaned out into the fog. The water of the little canal below slopped gently against its walls. Someone laughed, quite close to me. I shut the window quickly and leant against the wall for a moment. The laugh had come from the next room and had sounded so spiteful that I thought for a moment that the two boys must have been watching me and were laughing at my agony. It was half-past three. I had seen them go upstairs at about eleven. I listened, and could just hear a murmur of voices, then a series of bumps. After a moment I opened the window again very slightly, but I could still only hear the voices without being able to make out what they were saying. Evidently it was not me they were interested in. And then I heard someone cry out 'The King!' in a harsh high voice. 'The King! The King!' Then the laugh again. Then silence. I shut the window.

I don't know what the explanation was. They didn't look in the least tired this morning, which is more than could be said for me. They were talking to Frau Engels when I came down, about the famous London murders again. It was not prostitutes apparently, but a respectable family in a respectable suburb who were found dead in their beds one morning, having all been murdered and mutilated during the night. It does seem extraordinary and horrible. They had no enemies. I imagine Jacob's wife – but no, of course I don't want her to be murdered – sometimes I could be half in love with her in a sort of way. Today I feel sick and tired. Lack of sleep gives me indigestion, my obsession makes me feel guilty: I must try to distract myself, but my will seems hopelessly weak.

I asked Frau Engels about the boys when they had gone.

'They are charming,' I said to start the conversation. 'Are they on holiday?'

'Yes.' She did not seem particularly keen to talk, but I persisted.

'What part of England do they come from?' I asked.

'They are from – what do you call it? – a home,' she said.

'What sort of home?' I asked, startled.

'They are from very distinguished parentage,' she said portentously.

'Oh, yes?' I did not understand.

'They have been supported in this home for orphans by their fathers who were both from high up in the English aristocracy, but who were not married with their mothers.'

'I see. That sort of home. But how have they money? I mean, to buy those clothes and come for holidays in Venice?'

'From their fathers, who gave them much money when they attained eighteen years.'

'But do they know their fathers then?'

'They know, but they cannot tell.'

And then an elderly Italian couple who were staying in the pensione came up to ask whether it was not possible to stay after November 1st: their daughter was joining them and they hoped the weather might have improved by then.

'It is impossible, I am so very sorry, but on the first I must everything close.' She gave her remote correct smile, and I walked out into the fog.

In order to reach the vaporetto stop I had to cross the small canal which ran beside the pensione, and as I turned across the little humped bridge, the boys materialized out of the fog and crossed with me, one on each side. They did not speak at first, and nor did I. Finally Sig said, in a mild conversational tone, 'What were you talking to the old bag about?'

'Frau Engels?' I said. 'We were talking about you as a matter of fact.'

'What did she say?' asked Sig.

'She said she believed you were both orphans.'

They laughed. Sig's is the high, hard laugh, the other is a kind of low giggle, rather sexy: it struck me that neither sounded genuinely amused.

'She's just a stupid old bag,' said Sig. 'She fancies Poney, that's all.'

'She'd like to eat me,' said Poney, in a bored sort of way.

'Hardly the verb I'd have chosen,' said Sig. They talk in a semi-facetious, slangy, private joke sort of way which is often awkward. I suppose that may be how schoolboys talk, I don't know.

'Aren't you orphans then?' I asked.

'We come from respectable middle-class backgrounds,' said Sig. 'We live in Epping, my dear, that respectable middle-class suburb where you may be chopped into little pieces as you lie a-sleeping.'

'We were so frightened we ran away from home,' said Poney in a baby voice. 'We were afraid of the nasty man with the chopper. We suck our thumbs you see.'

'Where are you going?' asked Sig as I slowed down.

'I am going to look at the pictures here,' I said, turning towards the Accademia. 'There's nothing much else to do in the fog is there?'

'Do you know one of these palaces is for sale?' said Sig.

'I had heard it was.'

'We're thinking of buying it,' said Sig casually.

'But you must be millionaires!'

'Oh, we're all right for money,' said Sig. 'Cheery-bye.' They glided away into the fog.

I can't make up my mind whether they are ridiculous or offensive. They would be ridiculous but for something peculiar about their partnership. I don't know whether it is a homosexual relationship or not: it might be that that makes them seem so close, so set apart from the common run of men.

October 15

I cannot sleep. And the fog is still here.

Last night two girls appeared for dinner at the pensione. The boys were out, but everyone else was there, that is to say, the elderly Italian couple, the two moderately attractive French sisters and the daughter of one of them, the solitary Italian who looks like some sort of minor businessman, and myself. That, with the boys, is the sum of the guests at the moment. An Italian brother and sister who live next door do the waiting, and Frau Engels herself cooks.

The girls were nice-looking and well dressed. They spoke with American accents. One was dark and curly-haired, the other wore glasses but had quite good features. They both wore little hats. They immediately drew attention to themselves by being appallingly rude. They complained loudly of the dreary decor before they went in to dinner. At dinner they ordered the waiter about most disagreeably and soon sent for Frau Engels herself in order to complain of the food. It annoyed me intensely to see how she took it from them, padding backwards and forwards with a cringing anxiety to please, quite different from her usual frosty attitude towards her guests.

I finished my meal as quickly as I could and went upstairs. I had not been there long before I heard someone going into the next room, and the sound of voices and laughter. I decided to go and read downstairs. As I passed the boys' room the door opened. Frau Engels came out laughing and carrying some clothes. Behind her I caught a glimpse of Sig, still half-dressed, in women's clothes.

As soon as I saw it I wondered why I had not realized before that the American girls were in fact Sig and Poney. All the same the transformation had been alarmingly convincing. I didn't really like it. I didn't like the way they had abused her and she had cringed. I didn't like their pleasure in having deceived us all. There was no question of throwing off the disguise and allowing us to share the joke: there they were in the bedroom laughing at us. I don't like them. I don't know why I ever thought they were nice boys. I think there is something unpleasant about them.

October 18

Sinus trouble back at its very worst. A constant headache that nothing seems to cure. I don't know why I don't leave. My will seems to have been weakened by the lowering insinuations of the soggy fog: why doesn't it go? I wander and wander, waiting for the fog to clear and the sun to come out. I have nothing in my head, no thought, no will, nothing. Except pain. I wander, and lean over bridges, and watch the slack water. Pain pain go away, Come again another day. Immeasurable pain, Last night my dreaming soul was king again.

I hate those boys. They shouted again last night, something

about the king. I think they have orgies up there night after night. There's something suspicious about the way they are always so clean. Only guilty people wash as much as they do.

Also they are morbid. They came in this morning as I was drinking coffee in the dreary little sitting-room, and sat down beside me. They were carrying newspapers.

'Haven't caught him yet, I see,' said Sig.

'Caught who?' I asked.

'This murderer.'

'Oh.'

'Aren't you interested then?' asked Poney.

'Not particularly,' I said.

'Don't you think there's something about it though?' said Poney encouragingly. 'I mean these people lying there safe in their snug little beds in their snug little house, and suddenly bash, bash, they're all in pieces?' He gave his rather charming boyish smile. 'Not interesting?'

I smiled feebly, too tired to talk to them.

Sig laughed his nasty laugh and Poney's smile widened.

'That'll teach them, won't it?' he said.

'Teach them what?' I said.

'Teach them who's master,' said Poney quietly.

'He who wields the axe,' said Sig.

'Ah,' said Poney. 'He must have been a great man all right, that killer, don't you think so?'

'No,' I said flatly.

'Don't you like us?' said Sig suddenly.

'Good Heavens I – I hardly know you,' I said, embarrassed.

'At first you seemed to like us,' Sig went on, watching me intently. 'Now you don't seem so friendly. Do we offend you?'

'No, no, of course not.'

'But there is something about us you find yourself resenting? Have you ever tried hypnosis? For your headaches I mean?'

'How did you know I have headaches.'

'I can see. Have you ever been hypnotized?' He was staring at me much too hard.

'No,' I said.

'I should think you'd be a bad subject,' he said, leaning back in his chair.

'Sig could do it,' said Poney confidently.

'I could. But no one else. She'd withstand anyone else. What is it about us that annoys you?'

'I think you're talking nonsense. I'm not annoyed by you.'

He was leaning forward again. 'Is it that you feel the power coming from us?'

'Power?'

'That you feel we're in some way set apart.'

'You seem to feel that yourselves. I had noticed that.'

'Do you know what sets us apart?' said Sig very quietly. His gaze had become unbearably intense by now. 'Do you know what it is? Our *virtue*.'

A moment's peculiar silence. And then they both noticeably relaxed, and laughed briefly, and looked like two prankish schoolboys.

I can't make them out.

October 21

A horrible day.

It started well. The fog had cleared and the sun was shining. Everything seemed to have changed. My headache was no better, but I felt calmer, convalescent almost. I took the vaporetto to San Marco and sat in the Piazza to have some coffee. The place was quite crowded; everyone seemed to have gathered there to see Venice reborn.

I saw the boys moving in my direction, and sat back behind my paper hoping they would pass: but they had seen me, and paused, though they did not sit down.

'Got them yet?' Poney asked, gesturing slightly towards my paper.

'Got what?' I said.

'The murderers.'

I wondered vaguely why he used the plural.

'It doesn't say so,' I said. 'Lovely morning, isn't it?'

'More like it, isn't it?' agreed Poney. 'We're off to that

crooked old house agent again,' and they walked off through the tables, neat, spruce, untouchable.

Then in the evening there was a question of moving some furniture. Frau Engels was making preparations for shutting up her house and wanted, for some reason, to move several pieces of furniture from downstairs up into one of the empty bedrooms. There were several chairs, three Viennese-looking cabinets, and a big mahogany cupboard. She asked the boys to help her. Seriously they removed their well-cut jackets, rolled up the sleeves of their impeccably clean white shirts, and set to work. They lifted the heavy furniture with no difficulty at all; and I saw the muscles in their arms. The two Frenchwomen and the daughter of one of them were coming in at the time, and were much impressed.

'But how is it you do this?' one of the Frenchwomen asked them. 'You are weight-lifters?'

'It's nothing really,' said Poney.

'It's a matter of training,' said Sig, remotely.

'But you do this training for what?' she asked. 'You are athletes?'

'We just keep in training,' said Sig.

'You never know when it may come in useful,' said Poney.

They went on with their work. The Frenchwomen passed them admiringly and went upstairs. The boys began showing off, to each other more than to anyone else.

Poney flexed his muscles and lifted a small chair, pretending it was a great weight.

'The strong man,' said Sig. 'Nothing he can't do.'

'You're not bad yourself,' said Poney. 'Come on, let's see those muscles now.'

Sig lifted one of the little cabinets which really did look heavy. Poney put down his chair and lifted the pair of cabinets. They stood side by side swaying slightly, then gently lowered the weights without faltering in their control.

'Not bad, not bad,' said Poney again.

'You're the best,' said Sig, who was breathing rather heavily. 'You're the king of the weight-lifters.'

'You could lift a heavy man.'

'You could hold one down.'

'You know your judo.'

'You could lift a heavy axe.'

'You could have gone into that house in Woodbridge Road. You could have dealt with that fat family.'

'You could have wielded that axe.'

'You could have taken it in turns with me.'

'You could have smothered the parents.'

'You could have despatched the two girls, wham, wham, all gone.'

'You could have swung that axe.'

'You could have swopped their heads ...' Here Poney became lost in his low giggle. Sig joined in. They bent over the furniture, laughing. Then each taking one side of one of the cabinets, they began to carry it towards the stairs.

'Ah, we could have swung it,' said Sig, calm after his laughter.

'We could have swung it,' echoed Poney in his deeper voice.

And suddenly I knew that they had.

They were murderers.

With absolute certainty and terror, I knew that they were murderers.

'You are not well?' Frau Engels was looking at me strangely.

'Oh, yes, I – I have a bit of a headache.' I did not dare to say more because I felt certain that she would think me mad. Besides, she was so strangely fascinated by the boys. Unless she knew already, and this was the secret of their relationship? Or perhaps she merely sensed in them a depth of evil which appealed to some perverted leaning of her own? She offered me aspirin. I refused, but asked if she had any back numbers of English papers. She led me to a cupboard and left me to look for what I wanted.

I soon found it. I read everything I could see about the Epping murders. A family of four, father, mother, and two daughters had been found dead and mutilated. The crime was described as being of appalling brutality. No one had seen or heard a thing. They had lived in a detached house in its own garden in a high-class suburban street. They had had no enemies. The father had worked in a City office, the two girls had been to a local school, were popular at the tennis club, and looked quite pretty from the photographs. There were interviews with the various young friends – no, Jean and Pam had no special boy-friends, everybody had liked them, Jean was on the committee of the tennis club, Pam was keener on riding, they were the most popular girls in the neighbourhood. The parents went to Church, the mother was a member of the local Women's Institute. Here was something. And yet I was hardly surprised to read it. 'Mrs Bray, Chairman of the local branch, said at her home in nearby Forest Avenue, that Mrs Anderson had been a regular attender at W.I. Meetings. "It hardly bears thinking of," she said.' Poney's name was Bray. I had seen him writing it in the Register when they first arrived.

Before dinner I found them sitting in the tiny bar next to the dining-room drinking fruit juice (they never touch alcohol). It was an effort to go and sit beside them, but I made it.

'Whereabouts in Epping do you live?' I began, ordering whisky. 'I used to know it slightly.'

'Forest Avenue,' said Poney. 'We both do.'

'Isn't that quite near where the murder was?'

'I thought you weren't interested in the murder,' said Sig.

'I'm not particularly,' I said. 'But it becomes more interesting if you knew the people.'

'We didn't,' said Sig firmly.

I did not dare to pursue it. Their faces had become closed and uninformative. Poney patted his already immaculately tidy hair and said, 'I wonder what's for jolly old dins.'

'How are you getting on with your house-hunting?' I asked.

'We've gone off it,' said Poney. 'It seems you can't rely on the weather here. We're going to Sardinia in a few days to look around there.'

'Was anything stolen from the house where the murder was?' I asked before I could stop myself.

'Hey, what's the . . .' began Poney, but Sig interrupted him. He said very clearly, 'Some valuable jewellery I believe.'

'What's the big interest suddenly?' said Poney.

'Oh, I don't know,' I said. 'Tell me about Sardinia. I believe it's lovely there.'

'So old Aga Khan says,' said Poney, stroking his hair again. 'He's looking out a decent plot for us.'

Then the bell went for dinner.

I don't know what to do.

It is late now and I have locked myself into my bedroom. My headache has come back and I cannot sleep. I can just hear their voices next door. They talk so much alone in their room. What do they do in there?

They have some horrible thing between them. I felt it from the beginning. They are linked by some fantasy they have built up about power and violence, I am sure of it. Perhaps the girls snubbed them at a local dance. One of the girls was called Jean. Didn't they tell me that was the name of Poney's little sister, when he was showing me his bruise from a bite? Jean. I'm sure they said Jean. Perhaps they simply chose the Anderson family because they were so obviously harmless. This made it more of a joke, a clever trick. They enjoy fooling people; as they enjoyed letting us all think they were two American girls the other night, to score off the rest of the world, to build up their sense of isolation and superiority. I suppose they are mad, if to live in a world of fantasy is mad; or perhaps Sig is mad and Poney merely bad, and utterly corrupted. Heaven knows what appalling rituals may be going on in the next room even now – that shout of 'The King!' – what shall I do if I hear it again tonight? But what can I do? Who would believe me? I have no friends in Venice. Frau Engels is useless. What about the other people in the pensione? Those unimaginative-looking French-women with the daughter, the bored businessman, the doddering old couple – what use would they be? I can't go to the British Consul unless I can offer something more positive than just my own conviction. In a way the people I know best, though only in the most, casual way, are the couple who run the little restaurant round the corner, Mario and his wife. I don't even particularly like them, but we have talked a certain amount. I think I will try and say something to them tomorrow. In the meantime I can do nothing but sit behind my locked door and listen to the murmurs and occasional bumps from the next room.

October 28

I think I did hear the shout, but it may have been a dream. I took three sleeping pills. It was too many and I have felt terrible all day.

I lunched at the restaurant. I said to Mario, 'Do you ever see those two young English boys who are staying at my pensione?'

'Yes, they have been in once or twice,' he answered in his good English. 'Architectural students, they told me. They seemed nice boys. I lent them a guide book.'

'They are not architectural students,' I said.

He looked surprised.

'They lie to everyone, they live in a complete fantasy,' I said. 'Look, if I tell you something, will you take it seriously, will you give me your advice?'

He said he would, and sat down at my table, looking worried. It was difficult to go on.

'I have reason to believe,' I said. 'In fact I know, that they have committed a terrible crime.'

He looked down at the table cloth in silence. I felt I was doing badly.

'I know it sounds absurd,' I said. 'But I am quite sure about this. I wouldn't say so otherwise. You must believe me.'

But he didn't. He listened politely as I told him of my suspicions, and then he told me that he thought I was mistaken.

'When the fog comes I sometimes have strange ideas myself. You told me you had been having sinus trouble and bad headaches. You don't think you could be mistaken about these boys?'

'I know I am not mistaken.'

But I could see it was no good. All I could do was to make him say that if at any stage I needed help I could come to him.

'But of course,' he said, standing up with obvious relief. 'We are your friends.'

During the day I managed to see the Frenchwomen and the elderly couple. I asked them whether they thought there was anything odd about the boys. They all said no, they thought them charming. I did not go on.

I do not know what to do. They might do it again, kill someone I mean.

October 31

I notice them more now. I notice the black hairs on the back of Poney's hands, and the tight line between the eyebrows on Sig's white face. I notice how they both have the same strutting walk, how close they walk and how they never touch. I notice the metallic tone in Sig's voice, the sleepy softness in Poney's. I notice how light they are on their feet, how controlled; and yet I've seen, in Sig's eyes only and only when he is looking at Poney, an occasional doubt. I think this must be when the veil of fantasy momentarily twitches. I don't think Poney doubts. He has been handed his myth and he is living it out.

I watch them. I think they are watching me. I want to go, but I must stay. They are bound to make some move, and then I can send for help and run away myself. But I can't leave them, knowing what I do. I am not yet so disgusted with the human race. They must be caught, and stopped.

What will they do? I lurk about the pensione, pretending to read, watching them. The other guests look at me oddly, wondering what I am doing, but I can't talk, not yet. I feel ill and desperately anxious.

November 1

And now it is all over.

The next morning I followed them to the Piazza and sat down a few tables away to drink some coffee. A girl whom I knew slightly in London came up to speak to me. She said that some friends of hers, with whom she was staying, were giving a party that night after dinner. Would I like to come?

I had not seen anyone from London for some time. Indeed for the last few days I had had no conversation except with other people at the pensione. I said I would go to the party.

Later when I was in my bedroom changing I heard the voices of the boys and Frau Engels in the next room. I opened the window and leaned out. I heard Frau Engels sobbing, 'No,' and the two voices together, one high and one low, repeating, 'Yes, yes, yes, yes.'

I finished changing quickly and went downstairs. What else could I do? What could I tell to whom? Who would be concerned to know what went on in a bedroom between a middle-aged proprietress of the pensione and her two young lodgers: who would do more than shrug knowingly?

I stayed late at the party. Not so much because it was a good party as because I did not want to go back to the pensione. It was a boring party really. My friend's friends were stuffy Italians who lived in a comfortable little flat at the top of a fine flaking palazzo. One or two of the other people there looked quite interesting, but my Italian was not good enough to find out whether the impression was misleading, and I spent most of the evening talking to an American professor and his wife. I almost forgot about the boys, but not quite. I stayed until I was too tired to stay any longer. Then I walked out into the damp darkness. The vaporetto was still running. I got off at the Accademia bridge and walked towards the pensione, along the narrow way between the houses, over the little canal and up to the door. It was open. No one was at the desk. There was a light on the stairs, none in the hall.

I moved quietly towards the stairs. There was a sound above me. I stopped. There was silence. I went on. Another soft dragging sound, very slight. I went on. The weak bulb revealed the landing much as usual, shadowy, the faded Turkish carpet, the row of doors, mine, theirs, the Frenchwomen's, the couple's, the businessman's: Frau Engels slept on the top floor.

The faint sound seemed to come from the businessman's room. There were shoes outside some of the doors, ready for the maid to clean when she came in in the morning – the two

Frenchwomen's and the daughter's, and the elderly couple's –
there were none outside the businessman's door, or the boys',
or mine. There were long shadows beside the shoes. They were
not shadows. They were marks. Something had been spilt. But
beside all the shoes? I moved closer. All the shoes had a long
dark stain coming from them. They were neatly placed outside
the doors but surrounded by this dark wet stain. But the shoes
were not empty. They had feet in them. There was a lot of
blood.

A handle turned quietly. The businessman's door opened
very slightly. A hand came out holding a pair of shoes. It placed
them neatly outside the door.

I ran, stumbling on the stairs.

I battered on the door of the restaurant.

At last they came.

'It's happened. They've done it again. They've killed everyone in the pensione.'

'All right. Steady now. Come in.'

Mario and his wife were both there, in their nightclothes,
looking startled, and then annoyed. I saw the beginnings of disbelief on their faces and for the first time in my life I collapsed
into hysterics.

They slapped my face, made me swallow several pills, and
put me to bed. I kept begging them to hurry, to get the police,
to go round there before it was too late. They promised they
would, and left me. I must have been quite heavily drugged
because I fell asleep almost immediately.

And in the morning, unbelievably, they had done nothing.

I woke, heavy-headed, at nine o'clock, dressed as quickly as I
could and went downstairs. They were in the kitchen drinking
coffee.

'What happened?' I said.

The wife did not look at me. Mario said quite kindly, 'You
had a nightmare.'

'But the police . . . ?'

'We didn't want to wake them in the middle of the night.
Now come and have some coffee.'

I made a great effort and remained calm.

'Please will you come round there with me now.'

Mario came.

The pensione seemed very quiet as we approached. The front door was still open. We walked into the dim hall. A figure moved slowly towards us from the kitchen door. It was Frau Engels. Her face was very white except for where several raw red scratches ran down one side of it.

'Good morning, Frau Engels,' said Mario, in English for my sake. 'Have you had an accident?'

'It was in the fog. I walked into a tree,' she said brusquely. 'Have you come to collect your luggage, madame?'

But I had already passed her without answering and was running up the stairs. The stains were still there. I burst into the boys' room. It was empty. Their clothes and luggage had gone. I went into the next room, and the next. They were all empty. There was no sign of anyone.

Frau Engels and Mario had followed me up the stairs. I confronted them.

'Where are they?' I said. 'Where are the boys?'

'They left this morning,' she said, looking at me with the coldest hatred. 'Everybody left this morning.'

'Why?'

'It is November the 1st. I told you. I am closing down.'

'These stains . . .'

She explained them away. She said they were varnish, which had run when the wooden boards had been stained brown. I tried to insist that they should send for the police and have the stains tested to prove that they were blood. I asked where the two servants were, but Frau Engels said they had already left for a holiday with their family in Naples. I heard Mario murmur to her in Italian that he would telephone for a doctor.

'I go to get the police,' he said to me soothingly as he turned to go downstairs.

'No,' I said. 'I'll take my luggage now and come back later with the British Consul.'

I packed and left. I went to the hotel where my acquaintance from London was staying. I found her and told her my story. I took her with me back to the pensione. It was locked and shuttered. Frau Engels had left.

It is of course an impossible story. I can hardly blame people for not wanting to believe it. Only I know it is true. I am not a hysterical or deluded person.

Frau Engels also knows that I know that it is true. I do not know to what extent she was involved or whether her appalling association with the boys is still going on, but it seems likely that she may somehow or other have told them about my return to the pensione.

This is the horror with which I have to live.

They will find me. One day I shall take a train. I shall settle myself in my corner seat, open the paperback I have bought to read on the journey. And I shall look up. And there will be two nice boys sitting opposite me.

John Buchan

THE WATCHER BY THE THRESHOLD

JOHN BUCHAN (1875-1940) *was a barrister, diplomat, historian, editor, publisher, war correspondent, Director of Intelligence during the Lloyd George administration, Member of Parliament, and Governor General of Canada – and somehow still found time to publish some one hundred books, nearly forty of them fiction. His works include historical Scottish novels like* Sir Quixote of the Moors *(1895), republished by Valancourt, as well as a number of extremely successful adventure novels such as* Prester John *(1910),* The 39 Steps *(1915; adapted for a 1935 Alfred Hitchcock film) and* Greenmantle *(1916). Like several other authors in this volume, Buchan is not commonly thought of as a writer of horror, which is perhaps unfortunate, since he wrote around twenty supernatural tales which at their best are very good indeed and have counted H. P. Lovecraft among their admirers. Several of these stories, including 'The Watcher by the Threshold' (first published in* Blackwood's *Magazine in December 1900) were collected in Buchan's* The Watcher by the Threshold and Other Tales *(1902).*

A CHILL EVENING IN THE EARLY OCTOBER of the year 189– found me driving in a dogcart through the belts of antique woodland which form the lowland limits of the hilly parish of More. The Highland express, which brought me from the north, took me no farther than Perth. Thence it had been a slow journey in a disjointed local train, till I emerged on the platform at Morefoot, with a bleak prospect of pot stalks, coal heaps, certain sour corn lands, and far to the west a line of moor where the sun was setting. A neat groom and a respectable trap took the edge off my discomfort, and soon I had forgotten my sacrifice and found eyes for the darkening landscape. We were driving through a land of thick woods, cut at rare intervals by old long-frequented highways. The More, which at Morefoot is an open sewer, became a sullen woodland stream, where the brown leaves of the season drifted. At times we would pass an ancient lodge, and through a gap in the trees would come a glimpse of chipped crowstep gable. The names of such houses, as told me by my companion, were all famous. This one had been the home of a drunken Jacobite laird, and a king of north country Medmenham. Unholy revels had waked the old halls, and the devil had been toasted at many a hell-fire dinner. The next was the property of a great Scots law family, and there the old Lord of Session, who built the place, in his frouzy wig and carpet slippers, had laid down the canons of Taste for his day and society. The whole country had the air of faded and bygone gentility. The mossy roadside walls had stood for two hundred years; the few wayside houses were toll bars or defunct hostelries. The names, too, were great: Scots baronial with a smack of France, – Chatelray and Riverslaw, Black Holm and Fountainblue. The place had a cunning charm, mystery dwelt in every cranny, and yet it did not please me. The earth smelt heavy and raw; the roads were red underfoot; all was old, sorrowful, and uncanny. Compared with the fresh Highland glen I had left, where wind and sun and flying showers were never absent, all was chilly and dull and dead. Even when the sun sent a shiver of crimson over the crests of certain firs, I felt no delight in the prospect. I admitted shamefacedly to myself that I was in a very bad temper.

I had been staying at Glenaicill with the Clanroydens, and for a week had found the proper pleasure in life. You know the house with its old rooms and gardens, and the miles of heather which defend it from the world. The shooting had been extraordinary for a wild place late in the season; for there are few partridges, and the woodcock are notoriously late. I had done respectably in my stalking, more than respectably on the river, and creditably on the moors. Moreover, there were pleasant people in the house – and there were the Clanroydens. I had had a hard year's work, sustained to the last moment of term, and a fortnight in Norway had been disastrous. It was therefore with real comfort that I had settled myself down for another ten days in Glenaicill, when all my plans were shattered by Sibyl's letter. Sibyl is my cousin and my very good friend, and in old days when I was briefless I had fallen in love with her many times. But she very sensibly chose otherwise, and married a man Ladlaw – Robert John Ladlaw, who had been at school with me. He was a cheery, good-humoured fellow, a great sportsman, a justice of the peace, and deputy lieutenant for his county, and something of an antiquary in a mild way. He had a box in Leicestershire to which he went in the hunting season, but from February till October he lived in his moorland home. The place was called the House of More, and I had shot at it once or twice in recent years. I remembered its loneliness and its comfort, the charming diffident Sibyl, and Ladlaw's genial welcome. And my recollections set me puzzling again over the letter which that morning had broken into my comfort. 'You promised us a visit this autumn,' Sibyl had written, 'and I wish you would come as soon as you can.' So far common politeness. But she had gone on to reveal the fact that Ladlaw was ill; she did not know how, exactly, but something, she thought, about his heart. Then she had signed herself my affectionate cousin, and then had come a short, violent postscript, in which, as it were, the fences of convention had been laid low. 'For Heaven's sake, come and see us,' she scrawled below. 'Bob is terribly ill, and I am crazy. Come at once.' To cap it she finished with an afterthought: 'Don't bother about bringing doctors. It is not their business.'

She had assumed that I would come, and dutifully I set out. I could not regret my decision, but I took leave to upbraid my luck. The thought of Glenaicill, with the woodcock beginning to arrive and the Clanroydens imploring me to stay, saddened my journey in the morning, and the murky, coaly, midland country of the afternoon completed my depression. The drive through the woodlands of More failed to raise my spirits. I was anxious about Sibyl and Ladlaw, and this accursed country had always given me a certain eeriness on my first approaching it. You may call it silly, but I have no nerves and am little susceptible to vague sentiment. It was sheer physical dislike of the rich deep soil, the woody and antique smells, the melancholy roads and trees, and the flavor of old mystery. I am aggressively healthy and wholly Philistine. I love clear outlines and strong colours, and More with its half tints and hazy distances depressed me miserably. Even when the road crept uphill and the trees ended, I found nothing to hearten me in the moorland which succeeded. It was genuine moorland, close on eight hundred feet above the sea, and through it ran this old grass-grown coach road. Low hills rose to the left, and to the right, after some miles of peat, flared the chimneys of pits and oil works. Straight in front the moor ran out into the horizon, and there in the centre was the last dying spark of the sun. The place was as still as the grave save for the crunch of our wheels on the grassy road, but the flaring lights to the north seemed to endow it with life. I have rarely had so keenly the feeling of movement in the inanimate world. It was an unquiet place, and I shivered nervously. Little gleams of loch came from the hollows, the burns were brown with peat, and every now and then there rose in the moor jags of sickening red stone. I remembered that Ladlaw had talked about the place as the old Manann, the holy land of the ancient races. I had paid little attention at the time, but now it struck me that the old peoples had been wise in their choice. There was something uncanny in this soil and air. Framed in dank mysterious woods and a country of coal and ironstone, at no great distance from the capital city, it was a sullen relic of a lost barbarism. Over the low hills lay a green pastoral country with bright streams and valleys, but here, in this peaty desert, there were few sheep and little cultivation. The House of More was the only dwelling, and, save for the ragged village, the wilderness was given over to the wild things of the hills. The shooting was good, but the best shooting on earth would not persuade me to make my abode in such a place. Ladlaw was ill; well, I did not wonder. You can have uplands without air, moors that are not health-giving, and a country life which is more arduous than a townsman's. I shivered again, for I seemed to have passed in a few hours from the open noon to a kind of dank twilight.

We passed the village and entered the lodge gates. Here there were trees again – little innocent new-planted firs, which flourished ill. Some large plane trees grew near the house, and there were thickets upon thickets of the ugly elderberry. Even in the half darkness I could see that the lawns were trim and the flower beds respectable for the season; doubtless Sibyl looked after the gardeners. The oblong whitewashed house, more like a barrack than ever, opened suddenly on my sight, and I experienced my first sense of comfort since I left Glenaicill. Here I should find warmth and company; and sure enough, the hall door was wide open, and in the great flood of light which poured from it Sibyl stood to welcome me.

She ran down the steps as I dismounted, and, with a word to the groom, caught my arm and drew me into the shadow. 'Oh, Henry, it was so good of you to come. You mustn't let Bob think that you know he is ill. We don't talk about it. I'll tell you afterwards. I want you to cheer him up. Now we must go in, for he is in the hall expecting you.'

While I stood blinking in the light, Ladlaw came forward with outstretched hand and his usual cheery greeting. I looked at him and saw nothing unusual in his appearance; a little drawn at the lips, perhaps, and heavy below the eyes, but still fresh-coloured and healthy. It was Sibyl who showed change. She was very pale, her pretty eyes were deplorably mournful, and in place of her delightful shyness there were the self-confidence and composure of pain. I was honestly shocked, and as I dressed my heart was full of hard thoughts about Ladlaw. What could his illness mean? He seemed well and cheerful, while Sibyl was pale; and yet it was Sibyl who had written the postscript. As I warmed myself by the fire, I resolved that this particular family difficulty was my proper business.

The Ladlaws were waiting for me in the drawing-room. I noticed something new and strange in Sibyl's demeanor. She looked to her husband with a motherly, protective air, while Ladlaw, who had been the extreme of masculine independence, seemed to cling to his wife with a curious appealing fidelity. In conversation he did little more than echo her words. Till dinner was announced he spoke of the weather, the shooting, and Mabel Clanroyden. Then he did a queer thing; for when I was about to offer my arm to Sibyl he forestalled me, and clutching her right arm with his left hand led the way to the dining room, leaving me to follow in some bewilderment.

I have rarely taken part in a more dismal meal. The House of More has a pretty Georgian paneling through most of the rooms, but in the dining room the walls are level and painted a dull stone colour. Abraham offered up Isaac in a ghastly picture in front of me. Some photographs of the Quorn hung over the mantelpiece, and five or six drab ancestors filled up the remaining space. But one thing was new and startling. A great marble bust, a genuine antique, frowned on me from a pedestal. The head was in the late Roman style, clearly of some emperor, and in its commonplace environment the great brows, the massive neck, and the mysterious solemn lips had a surprising effect. I nodded toward the thing, and asked what it represented.

Ladlaw grunted something which I took for 'Justinian,' but he never raised his eyes from his plate. By accident I caught Sibyl's glance. She looked toward the bust, and laid a finger on her lips.

The meal grew more doleful as it advanced. Sibyl scarcely touched a dish, but her husband ate ravenously of everything. He was a strong, thickset man, with a square kindly face burned brown by the sun. Now he seemed to have suddenly coarsened. He gobbled with undignified haste, and his eye was extraordinarily vacant. A question made him start, and he would turn on me a face so strange and inert that I repented the interruption.

I asked him about the autumn's sport. He collected his wits with difficulty. He thought it had been good, on the whole, but he had shot badly. He had not been quite so fit as usual. No, he had had nobody staying with him. Sibyl had wanted to be alone. He was afraid the moor might have been undershot, but he would make a big day with keepers and farmers before the winter.

'Bob has done pretty well,' Sibyl said. 'He hasn't been out

often, for the weather has been very bad here. You can have no idea, Henry, how horrible this moorland place of ours can be when it tries. It is one great sponge sometimes, with ugly red burns and mud to the ankles.'

'I don't think it's healthy,' said I.

Ladlaw lifted his face. 'Nor do I. I think it's intolerable, but I am so busy I can't get away.'

Once again I caught Sibyl's warning eye as I was about to question him on his business.

Clearly the man's brain had received a shock, and he was beginning to suffer from hallucinations. This could be the only explanation, for he had always led a temperate life. The distrait, wandering manner was the only sign of his malady, for otherwise he seemed normal and mediocre as ever. My heart grieved for Sibyl, alone with him in this wilderness.

Then he broke the silence. He lifted his head and looked nervously around till his eye fell on the Roman bust.

'Do you know that this countryside is the old Manann?' he said.

It was an odd turn to the conversation, but I was glad of a sign of intelligence. I answered that I had heard so.

'It's a queer name,' he said oracularly, 'but the thing it stood for was queerer, Manann, Manaw,' he repeated, rolling the words on his tongue. As he spoke, he glanced sharply, and, as it seemed to me, fearfully, at his left side.

The movement of his body made his napkin slip from his left knee and fall on the floor. It leaned against his leg, and he started from its touch as if he had been bitten by a snake. I have never seen a more sheer and transparent terror on a man's face. He got to his feet, his strong frame shaking like a rush. Sibyl ran round to his side, picked up the napkin and flung it on a side-board. Then she stroked his hair as one would stroke a frightened horse. She called him by his old boy's name of Robin, and at her touch and voice he became quiet. But the particular course then in progress was removed, untasted.

In a few minutes he seemed to have forgotten his behaviour, for he took up the former conversation. For a time he spoke well and briskly. 'You lawyers,' he said, 'understand only the dry framework of the past. You cannot conceive the rapture, which only the antiquary can feel, of constructing in every detail an old culture. Take this Manann. If I could explore the secret of these moors, I would write the world's greatest book. I would write of that prehistoric life when man was knit close to nature. I would describe the people who were brothers of the red earth and the red rock and the red streams of the hills. Oh, it would be horrible, but superb, tremendous! It would be more than a piece of history; it would be a new gospel, a new theory of life. It would kill materialism once and for all. Why, man, all the poets who have deified and personified nature would not do an eighth part of my work. I would show you the unknown, the hideous, shrieking mystery at the back of this simple nature. Men would see the profundity of the old crude faiths which they affect to despise. I would make a picture of our shaggy, sombre-eyed forefather, who heard strange things in the hill silences. I would show him brutal and terror-stricken, but wise, wise, God alone knows how wise! The Romans knew it, and they learned what they could from him, though he did not tell them much. But we have some of his blood in us, and we may go deeper. Manann! A queer land nowadays! I sometimes love it and sometimes hate it, but I always fear it. It is like that statue, inscrutable.'

I would have told him that he was talking mystical nonsense, but I had looked toward the bust, and my rudeness was checked on my lips. The moor might be a common piece of ugly waste land, but the statue was inscrutable, – of that there was no doubt. I hate your cruel heavy-mouthed Roman busts; to me they have none of the beauty of life, and little of the interest of art. But my eyes were fastened on this as they had never before looked on marble. The oppression of the heavy woodlands, the mystery of the silent moor, seemed to be caught and held in this face. It was the intangible mystery of culture on the verge of savagery – a cruel, lustful wisdom, and yet a kind of bitter austerity which laughed at the game of life and stood aloof. There was no weakness in the heavy-veined brow and slumbrous eyelids. It was the face of one who had conquered the world, and found it dust and ashes; one who had eaten of the tree of the knowledge of good and evil, and scorned human wisdom. And at the same time, it was the face of one who knew uncanny things, a man who was the intimate of the half-world and the dim background of life. Why on earth I should connect the Roman grandee* with the moorland parish of More I cannot say, but the fact remains that there was that in the face which I knew had haunted me through the woodlands and bogs of the place – a sleepless, dismal, incoherent melancholy.

'I bought that at Colenzo's,' Ladlaw said, 'because it took my fancy. It matches well with this place?'

I thought it matched very ill with his drab walls and Quorn photographs, but I held my peace.

'Do you know who it is?' he asked. 'It is the head of the greatest man the world has ever seen. You are a lawyer and know your Justinian.'

The Pandects are scarcely part of the daily work of a common-law barrister. I had not looked into them since I left college.

'I know that he married an actress,' I said, 'and was a sort of all-round genius. He made law, and fought battles, and had rows with the Church. A curious man! And wasn't there some story about his selling his soul to the devil, and getting law in exchange? Rather a poor bargain!'

I chattered away, sillily enough, to dispel the gloom of that dinner table. The result of my words was unhappy. Ladlaw gasped and caught at his left side, as if in pain. Sibyl, with tragic eyes, had been making signs to me to hold my peace. Now she ran round to her husband's side and comforted him like a child. As she passed me, she managed to whisper in my ear to talk to her only, and let her husband alone.

---

* I have identified the bust, which, when seen under other circumstances, had little power to affect me. It was a copy of the head of Justinian in the Tesci Museum at Venice, and several duplicates exist, dating apparently from the seventh century, and showing traces of Byzantine decadence in the scroll work on the hair. It is engraved in M. Delacroix's Byzantium, and, I think, in Windscheid's Pandektenlehrbuch.

For the rest of dinner I obeyed my orders to the letter. Ladlaw ate his food in gloomy silence, while I spoke to Sibyl of our relatives and friends, of London, Glenaicill, and any random subject. The poor girl was dismally forgetful, and her eye would wander to her husband with wifely anxiety. I remember being suddenly overcome by the comic aspect of it all. Here were we three fools alone in the dank upland: one of us sick and nervous, talking out-of-the-way nonsense about Manann and Justinian, gobbling his food and getting scared at his napkin; another gravely anxious; and myself at my wits' end for a solution. It was a Mad Tea-Party with a vengeance: Sibyl the melancholy little Dormouse, and Ladlaw the incomprehensible Hatter. I laughed aloud, but checked myself when I caught my cousin's eye. It was really no case for finding humour. Ladlaw was very ill, and Sibyl's face was getting deplorably thin.

I welcomed the end of that meal with unmannerly joy, for I wanted to speak seriously with my host. Sibyl told the butler to have the lamps lighted in the library. Then she leaned over toward me and spoke low and rapidly: 'I want you to talk with Bob. I'm sure you can do him good. You'll have to be very patient with him, and very gentle. Oh, please try to find out what is wrong with him. He won't tell me, and I can only guess.'

The butler returned with word that the library was ready to receive us, and Sibyl rose to go. Ladlaw half rose, protesting, making the most curious feeble clutches to his side. His wife quieted him. 'Henry will look after you, dear,' she said. 'You are going into the library to smoke.' Then she slipped from the room, and we were left alone.

He caught my arm fiercely with his left hand, and his grip nearly made me cry out. As we walked down the hall, I could feel his arm twitching from the elbow to the shoulder. Clearly he was in pain, and I set it down to some form of cardiac affection, which might possibly issue in paralysis.

I settled him in the biggest armchair, and took one of his cigars. The library is the pleasantest room in the house, and at night, when a peat fire burned on the old hearth and the great red curtains were drawn, it used to be the place for comfort and good talk. Now I noticed changes. Ladlaw's bookshelves had been filled with the Proceedings of antiquarian societies and many light-hearted works on sport. But now the Badminton library had been cleared out of a shelf where it stood most convenient to the hand, and its place taken by an old Leyden reprint of Justinian. There were books on Byzantine subjects of which I never dreamed he had heard the names; there were volumes of history and speculation, all of a slightly bizarre kind; and to crown everything, there were several bulky medical works with gaudily coloured plates. The old atmosphere of sport and travel had gone from the room with the medley of rods, whips, and gun cases which used to cumber the tables. Now the place was moderately tidy and somewhat learned, and I did not like it.

Ladlaw refused to smoke, and sat for a little while in silence. Then of his own accord he broke the tension.

'It was devilish good of you to come, Harry. This is a lonely place for a man who is a bit seedy.'

'I thought you might be alone,' I said, 'so I looked you up on my way down from Glenaicill. I'm sorry to find you feeling ill.'

'Do you notice it?' he asked sharply.

'It's tolerably patent,' I said. 'Have you seen a doctor?'

He said something uncomplimentary about doctors, and kept looking at me with his curious dull eyes.

I remarked the strange posture in which he sat, his head screwed round to his right shoulder, and his whole body a protest against something at his left hand.

'It looks like a heart,' I said. 'You seem to have pains in your left side.'

Again a spasm of fear. I went over to him and stood at the back of his chair.

'Now for goodness' sake, my dear fellow, tell me what is wrong. You're scaring Sibyl to death. It's lonely work for the poor girl, and I wish you would let me help you.'

He was lying back in his chair now, with his eyes half shut, and shivering like a frightened colt. The extraordinary change in one who had been the strongest of the strong kept me from realizing his gravity. I put a hand on his shoulder, but he flung it off.

'For God's sake, sit down!' he said hoarsely. 'I'm going to tell you, but I'll never make you understand.'

I sat down promptly opposite him.

'It's the devil,' he said very solemnly.

I am afraid that I was rude enough to laugh. He took no notice, but sat, with the same tense, miserable air, staring over my head.

'Right,' said I. 'Then it is the devil. It's a new complaint, so it's as well I did not bring a doctor. How does it affect you?'

He made the old impotent clutch at the air with his left hand. I had the sense to become grave at once. Clearly this was some serious mental affection, some hallucination born of physical pain.

Then he began to talk in a low voice, very rapidly, with his head bent forward like a hunted animal's. I am not going to set down what he told me in his own words, for they were incoherent often, and there was much repetition. But I am going to write the gist of the odd story which took my sleep away on that autumn night, with such explanations and additions I think needful. The fire died down, the wind arose, the hour grew late, and still he went on in his mumbling recitative. I forgot to smoke, forgot my comfort – everything but the odd figure of my friend and his inconceivable romance. And the night before I had been in cheerful Glenaicill!

He had returned to the House of More, he said, in the latter part of May, and shortly after he fell ill. It was a trifling sickness, – influenza or something, – but he had never quite recovered. The rainy weather of June depressed him, and the extreme heat of July made him listless and weary. A kind of insistent sleepiness hung over him, and he suffered much from nightmare. Toward the end of July his former health returned, but he was haunted with a curious oppression. He seemed to himself to have lost the art of being alone. There was a perpetual sound in his left ear, a kind of moving and rustling at his left side, which never left him by night or day. In addition, he had become the prey of nerves and an insensate dread of the unknown.

Ladlaw, as I have explained, was a commonplace man, with fair talents, a mediocre culture, honest instincts, and the beliefs and incredulities of his class. On abstract grounds, I should have declared him an unlikely man to be the victim of an hallucination. He had a kind of dull bourgeois rationalism, which used to find reasons for all things in heaven and earth. At first he controlled his dread with proverbs. He told himself it was the sequel of his illness or the light-headedness of summer heat on the moors. But it soon outgrew his comfort. It became a living second presence, an *alter ego* which dogged his footsteps. He grew acutely afraid of it. He dared not be alone for a moment, and clung to Sibyl's company despairingly. She went off for a week's visit in the beginning of August, and he endured for seven days the tortures of the lost. The malady advanced upon him with swift steps. The presence became more real daily. In the early dawning, in the twilight, and in the first hour of the morning it seemed at times to take a visible bodily form. A kind of amorphous featureless shadow would run from his side into the darkness, and he would sit palsied with terror. Sometimes, in lonely places, his footsteps sounded double, and something would brush elbows with him. Human society alone exorcised it. With Sibyl at his side he was happy; but as soon as she left him, the thing came slinking back from the unknown to watch by him. Company might have saved him, but joined to his affliction was a crazy dread of his fellows. He would not leave his moorland home, but must bear his burden alone among the wild streams and mosses of that dismal place.

The 12th came, and he shot wretchedly, for his nerve had gone to pieces. He stood exhaustion badly, and became a dweller about the doors. But with this bodily inertness came an extraordinary intellectual revival. He read widely in a blundering way, and he speculated unceasingly. It was characteristic of the man that as soon as he left the paths of the prosaic he should seek his supernatural in a very concrete form. He assumed that he was haunted by the devil – the visible personal devil in whom our fathers believed. He waited hourly for the shape at his side to speak, but no words came. The Accuser of the Brethren in all but tangible form was his ever present companion. He felt, he declared, the spirit of old evil entering subtly into his blood. He sold his soul many times over, and yet there was no possibility of resistance. It was a Visitation more undeserved than Job's, and a thousandfold more awful.

For a week or more he was tortured with a kind of religious mania. When a man of a healthy secular mind finds himself adrift on the terrible ocean of religious troubles he is peculiarly helpless, for he has not the most rudimentary knowledge of the winds and tides. It was useless to call up his old carelessness; he had suddenly dropped into a new world where old proverbs did not apply. And all the while, mind you, there was the shrinking terror of it – an intellect all alive to the torture and the most unceasing physical fear. For a little he was on the far edge of idiocy.

Then by accident it took a new form. While sitting with Sibyl one day in the library, he began listlessly to turn over the leaves of an old book. He read a few pages, and found the hint to a story like his own. It was some French Life of Justinian, one of the unscholarly productions of last century, made up of stories from Procopius and tags of Roman law. Here was his own case written down in black and white; and the man had been a king of kings. This was a new comfort, and for a little – strange though it may seem – he took a sort of pride in his affliction. He worshipped the great Emperor, and read every scrap he could find on him, not excepting the Pandects and the Digest. He sent for the bust in the dining room, paying a fabulous price. Then he settled himself to study his imperial prototype, and the study became an idolatry. As I have said, Ladlaw was a man of ordinary talents, and certainly of meagre imaginative power. And yet from the lies of the Secret History and the crudities of German legalists he had constructed a marvellous portrait of a man. Sitting there in the half-lighted room, he drew the picture: the quiet cold man with his inheritance of Dacian mysticism, holding the great world in fee, giving it law and religion, fighting its wars, building its churches, and yet all the while intent upon his own private work of making his peace with his soul – the churchman and warrior whom all the world worshipped, and yet one going through life with his lip quivering. He Watched by the Threshold ever at the left side. Sometimes at night, in the great Brazen Palace, warders heard the Emperor walking in the dark corridors, alone, and yet not alone; for once, when a servant entered with a lamp, he saw his master with a face as of another world, and something beside him which had no face or shape, but which he knew to be that hoary Evil which is older than the stars.

Crazy nonsense! I had to rub my eyes to assure myself that I was not sleeping. No! There was my friend with his suffering face, and it was the library of More.

And then he spoke of Theodora, – actress, harlot, *dévote,* empress. For him the lady was but another part of the uttermost horror, a form of the shapeless thing at his side. I felt myself falling under the fascination. I have no nerves and little imagination, but in a flash I seemed to realize something of that awful featureless face, crouching ever at a man's hand, till darkness and loneliness come, and it rises to its mastery. I shivered as I looked at the man in the chair before me. These dull eyes of his were looking upon things I could not see, and I saw their terror. I realized that it was grim earnest for him. Nonsense or no, some devilish fancy had usurped the place of his sanity, and he was being slowly broken upon the wheel. And then, when his left hand twitched, I almost cried out. I had thought it comic before; now it seemed the last proof of tragedy.

He stopped, and I got up with loose knees and went to the window. Better the black night than the intangible horror within. I flung up the sash and looked out across the moor. There was no light; nothing but an inky darkness and the uncanny rustle of elder bushes. The sound chilled me, and I closed the window.

'The land is the old Manann,' Ladlaw was saying. 'We are beyond the pale here. Do you hear the wind?'

I forced myself back into sanity and looked at my watch. It was nearly one o'clock.

'What ghastly idiots we are!' I said. 'I am off to bed.'

Ladlaw looked at me helplessly. 'For God's sake, don't leave me alone!' he moaned. 'Get Sibyl.'

We went together back to the hall, while he kept the same feverish grasp on my arm. Someone was sleeping in a chair by the hall fire, and to my distress I recognized my hostess. The poor child must have been sadly wearied. She came forward with her anxious face.

'I'm afraid Bob has kept you very late, Henry,' she said. 'I hope you will sleep well. Breakfast at nine, you know.' And then I left them.

Over my bed there was a little picture, a reproduction of some Italian work, of Christ and the Demoniac. Some impulse made me hold my candle up to it. The madman's face was torn with passion and suffering, and his eye had the pained furtive expression which I had come to know. And by his left side there was a dim shape crouching.

I got into bed hastily, but not to sleep. I felt that my reason must be going. I had been pitchforked from our clear and cheerful modern life into the mists of old superstition. Old tragic stories of my Calvinist upbringing returned to haunt me. The man dwelt in by a devil was no new fancy, but I believed that science had docketed and analyzed and explained the devil out of the world. I remembered my dabblings in the occult before I settled down to law – the story of Donisarius, the monk of Padua, the unholy legend of the Face of Proserpine, the tales of *succubi* and *incubi,* the Leannain Sith and the Hidden Presence. But here was something stranger still. I had stumbled upon that very possession which fifteen hundred years ago had made the monks of New Rome tremble and cross themselves. Some devilish occult force, lingering through the ages, had come to life after a long sleep. God knows what earthly connection there was between the splendid Emperor of the World and my prosaic friend, or between the glittering shores of the Bosporus and this moorland parish! But the land was the old Manann! The spirit may have lingered in the earth and air, a deadly legacy from Piet and Roman. I had felt the uncanniness of the place; I had augured ill of it from the first. And then in sheer disgust I rose and splashed my face with cold water.

I lay down again, laughing miserably at my credulity. That I, the sober and rational, should believe in this crazy fable was too palpably absurd. I would steel my mind resolutely against such harebrained theories. It was a mere bodily ailment – liver out of order, weak heart, bad circulation, or something of that sort. At the worst it might be some affection of the brain, to be treated by a specialist. I vowed to myself that next morning the best doctor in Edinburgh should be brought to More.

The worst of it was that my duty compelled me to stand my ground. I foresaw the few remaining weeks of my holiday blighted. I should be tied to this moorland prison, a sort of keeper and nurse in one, tormented by silly fancies. It was a charming prospect, and the thought of Glenaicill and the woodcock made me bitter against Ladlaw. But there was no way out of it. I might do Ladlaw good, and I could not have Sibyl worn to death by his vagaries.

My ill nature comforted me, and I forgot the horror of the thing in its vexation. After that I think I fell asleep and dozed uneasily till morning. When I woke I was in a better frame of mind. The early sun had worked wonders with the moorland. The low hills stood out fresh-coloured and clear against a pale October sky; the elders sparkled with frost; the raw film of morn was rising from the little loch in tiny clouds. It was a cold, rousing day, and I dressed in good spirits and went down to breakfast.

I found Ladlaw looking ruddy and well; very different from the broken man I remembered of the night before. We were alone, for Sibyl was breakfasting in bed. I remarked on his ravenous appetite, and he smiled cheerily. He made two jokes during the meal; he laughed often, and I began to forget the events of the previous day. It seemed to me that I might still flee from More with a clear conscience. He had forgotten about his illness. When I touched distantly upon the matter he showed a blank face.

It might be that the affection had passed; on the other hand, it might return to him at the darkening. I had no means to decide. His manner was still a trifle distrait and peculiar, and I did not like the dullness in his eye. At any rate, I should spend the day in his company, and the evening would decide the question.

I proposed shooting, which he promptly vetoed. He was no good at walking, he said, and the birds were wild. This seriously limited the possible occupations. Fishing there was none, and hill-climbing was out of the question. He proposed a game at billiards, and I pointed to the glory of the morning. It would have been sacrilege to waste such sunshine in knocking balls about. Finally we agreed to drive somewhere and have lunch, and he ordered the dogcart.

In spite of all forebodings I enjoyed the day. We drove in the opposite direction from the woodland parts, right away across the moor to the coal country beyond. We lunched at the little mining town of Borrowmuir, in a small and noisy public house. The roads made bad going, the country was far from pretty, and yet the drive did not bore me. Ladlaw talked incessantly – talked as I had never heard man talk before. There was something indescribable in all he said, a different point of view, a lost groove of thought, a kind of innocence and archaic shrewdness in one. I can only give you a hint of it, by saying that it was like the mind of an early ancestor placed suddenly among modern surroundings. It was wise with a remote wisdom, and silly (now and then) with a quite antique and distant silliness.

I will give instances of both. He provided me with a theory of certain early fortifications, which must be true, which commends itself to the mind with overwhelming conviction, and yet which is so out of the way of common speculation that no man could have guessed it. I do not propose to set down the details, for I am working at it on my own account. Again, he told me the story of an old marriage custom, which till recently survived in this district – told it with full circumstantial detail and constant allusions to other customs which he could not possibly have known of. Now for the other side. He explained why well water is in winter warmer than a running stream, and this was his explanation: at the antipodes our winter is summer, consequently, the water of a well which comes through from the other side of the earth must be warm in winter and cold in summer, since in our summer it is winter there. You perceive what this is. It is no mere silliness, but a genuine effort of an early mind, which had just grasped the fact of the antipodes, to use it in explanation.

Gradually I was forced to the belief that it was not Ladlaw who was talking to me, but something speaking through him, something at once wiser and simpler. My old fear of the devil began to depart. This spirit, the exhalation, whatever it was, was ingenuous in its way, at least in its daylight aspect. For a moment I had an idea that it was a real reflex of Byzantine thought, and that by cross-examining I might make marvellous discoveries. The ardor of the scholar began to rise in me, and I asked a question about that much-debated point, the legal status of the *apocrisiarii*. To my vexation he gave no response. Clearly the intelligence of this familiar had its limits.

It was about three in the afternoon, and we had gone half of our homeward journey, when signs of the old terror began to appear. I was driving, and Ladlaw sat on my left. I noticed him growing nervous and silent, shivering at the flick of the whip, and turning halfway round toward me. Then he asked me to change places, and I had the unpleasant work of driving from the wrong side. After that I do not think he spoke once till we arrived at More, but sat huddled together, with the driving rug almost up to his chin – an eccentric figure of a man.

I foresaw another such night as the last, and I confess my heart sank. I had no stomach for more mysteries, and somehow with the approach of twilight the confidence of the day departed. The thing appeared in darker colours, and I found it in my mind to turn coward. Sibyl alone deterred me. I could not bear to think of her alone with this demented being. I remembered her shy timidity, her innocence. It was monstrous that the poor thing should be called on thus to fight alone with phantoms.

When we came to the House it was almost sunset. Ladlaw got out very carefully on the right side, and for a second stood by the horse. The sun was making our shadows long, and as I stood beyond him it seemed for a moment that his shadow was double. It may have been mere fancy, for I had not time to look twice. He was standing, as I have said, with his left side next the horse. Suddenly the harmless elderly cob fell into a very panic of fright, reared upright, and all but succeeded in killing its master. I was in time to pluck Ladlaw from under its feet, but the beast had become perfectly unmanageable, and we left a groom struggling to quiet it.

In the hall the butler gave me a telegram. It was from my clerk, summoning me back at once to an important consultation.

Here was a prompt removal of my scruples. There could be no question of my remaining, for the case was one of the first importance, which I had feared might break off my holiday. The consultation fell in vacation time to meet the convenience of certain people who were going abroad, and there was the most instant demand for my presence. I must go, and at once; and, as I hunted in the time-table, I found that in three hours' time a night train for the south would pass Borrowmuir which might be stopped by special wire.

But I had no pleasure in my freedom. I was in despair about Sibyl, and I hated myself for my cowardly relief. The dreary dining room, the sinister bust, and Ladlaw crouching and quivering – the recollection, now that escape was before me, came back on my mind with the terror of a nightmare. My first thought was to persuade the Ladlaws to come away with me. I found them both in the drawing-room – Sibyl very fragile and pale, and her husband sitting as usual like a frightened child in the shadow of her skirts. A sight of him was enough to dispel my hope. The man was fatally ill, mentally, bodily; and who was I to attempt to minister to a mind diseased?

But Sibyl – she might be saved from the martyrdom. The servants would take care of him, and, if need be, a doctor might be got from Edinburgh to live in the house. So while he sat with vacant eyes staring into the twilight, I tried to persuade Sibyl to think of herself. I am frankly a sun worshiper. I have no taste for arduous duty, and the quixotic is my abhorrence. I laboured to bring my cousin to this frame of mind. I told her that her first duty was to herself, and that this vigil of hers was beyond human endurance. But she had no ears for my arguments.

'While Bob is ill I must stay with him,' she said always in answer, and then she thanked me for my visit, till I felt a brute and a coward. I strove to quiet my conscience, but it told me always that I was fleeing from my duty; and then, when I was on the brink of a nobler resolution, a sudden overmastering terror would take hold of me, and I would listen hysterically for the sound of the dogcart on the gravel.

At last it came, and in a sort of fever I tried to say the conventional farewells. I shook hands with Ladlaw, and when I dropped his hand it fell numbly on his knee. Then I took my leave, muttering hoarse nonsense about having had a 'charming visit,' and 'hoping soon to see them both in town.' As I backed to the door, I knocked over a lamp on a small table. It crashed on the floor and went out, and at the sound Ladlaw gave a curious childish cry. I turned like a coward, and ran across the hall to the front door, and scrambled into the dogcart.

The groom would have driven me sedately through the park, but I must have speed or go mad. I took the reins from him and put the horse into a canter. We swung through the gates and out into the moor road, for I could have no peace till the ghoulish elder world was exchanged for the homely ugliness of civilization. Once only I looked back, and there against the sky line, with a solitary lit window, the House of More stood lonely in the red desert.

Nevil Shute

TUDOR WINDOWS

NEVIL SHUTE NORWAY (1899-1960), *who wrote under the name Nevil Shute in order to keep his career as an aeronautical engineer separate from his novel writing, was one of the most popular and beloved English novelists of the 20th century. More than fifty years after his death virtually all his work remains in print and widely read. Reflecting his own experience and interests, many of his novels featured aviation themes, including two republished by Valancourt,* Landfall *(1940), the story of an RAF pilot accused of accidentally sinking an English submarine, and* An Old Captivity *(1940), concerning an aerial expedition to Greenland with unexpected consequences. At first glance, Shute might seem the most surprising contributor to this anthology, since his down-to-earth, realistic novels, often loaded with technical detail, are the very opposite of speculative or fantastic fiction. Yet Shute was no stranger to imaginative fiction.* An Old Captivity, *for example, features a fascinating subplot involving reincarnation, while* On the Beach *(1957) recounts the extinction of the human race following a nuclear war, with the last group of survivors waiting in Australia for the arrival of the nuclear fallout that will kill them. 'Tudor Windows', published for the first time here, was found among Shute's papers after his death. The address on the cover page of the typescript, held at the National Library of Australia, is one at which Shute lived from 1931-33, making it possible to date the story to this early period of his career. A young Shute's experiment in writing a ghost story, it is an intriguing piece of work that reveals a previously unseen side to this popular writer.*

THE CLUB WAITER CAME and cleared the glasses from our table, and placed the ebony cigar cutter to hand.

'You say that the house is on your land?' I repeated.

'I told you so,' he said, a little testily. 'The house is the timbered one – next to Horter's. On the right as you come up from the Square. You must have passed it a dozen times. I've got all that side of the street.'

I have heard it said that eccentricity grows more pronounced with age; at the time I thought that Jonas must be ageing rather quickly. I turned again to the reproduction of the portrait of Mrs Lyell.

'Where is the original of this?' I asked.

'In America,' said Jonas. 'I have never seen it. But from that photograph the resemblance would be exact.'

There is a note in Halley's 'Modes' to the effect that one of the fashions of the period was to crop the hair somewhat in the modern manner. It gave an air of realism to the portrait. Curiously, I laid my hand over the reproduction to hide the eighteenth century costume; the head that I saw then was one that might have been pressed against my shoulder that morning in the bustle of the Tube. I still stand a head and shoulders above most women.

'Pleasant, isn't it?' said Jonas. 'They all are.'

The face was oval, the hair dark, short, and fluffed out from the head, the features a little finely drawn, the eyes bright and sparkling even in the photograph. Certainly it was a pleasant portrait.

'You say that this was painted four years before her death?' I asked.

'It was painted in June,' he replied concisely. I remember that I was struck by the realism of his statement; it was as if he had been speaking of his cousin. 'She was thirty nine when that was painted. That was in 1763. She died in October 1767 – forty-three years old.'

'Damme,' I said irritably. 'It's the most utter nonsense I have ever heard.'

He made no answer and I closed the book and laid it beside my chair, a little ashamed of my temper. Jonas has been my solicitor since we both came down from Oxford. With the passing of the swift years his historical interests have grown into a regular obsession; I can think of nobody else who would have had the patience to dig into the county records as he had done. Still, what he said was ludicrous. If one accepted it as a fact that he had found a certain run of ages in the registers, it seemed to me that the conclusions he had built upon that flimsy evidence were quite unsound.

'Dates meant very little in the eighteenth century,' I said. 'Much less than nowadays. You should know that. I don't suppose one of those women could have told you how old they were.'

'Eh?' he replied. 'What's that you say? How old? I told you how old she was. Forty-three. They were all forty-three years old – all that are in the registers. From Ann Farrar onwards.'

There was a minute's silence.

'You surely don't believe in it yourself?' I asked. 'This . . .' I boggled at the word, '. . . reincarnation stuff?'

In a few moments I was wishing that I had put that question differently. And yet perhaps it is as well that I came to the root of the matter at once, because if I had not come to realise that he trusted in his own story with an almost childlike faith I should never have gone down to see the place. It takes a good deal to move Jonas. So many title deeds, so many settlements and windings up have made him very dry. Even at the Varsity I remember him as elderly. It came as a great shock to me to find him so upset.

'I came very near to taking the house myself once,' he said at last. 'I had a great mind to set up in practice there. Forty years ago – just after my marriage. I did not know about this then. I should certainly have lived there . . . But I came to Town.'

'That was fortunate,' I said gravely.

He turned to me. 'You must not think of it like that. It has been a happy house. I do not know of any place where people live more pleasantly.'

I suppose I looked doubtful.

'You must come down to us,' he said. 'I should like to show it to you. Now that you know something of what goes on.'

I daresay I went because I was curious. It may have been because I have known Jonas for so many years, because he has been so much a part of the business of my domestic life, because I was startled and concerned to find him so much affected by his own fantasy. That may have shaken me, myself. One grows old unknowingly. One accepts the passing of years as a phenomenon that has little bearing on one's personality. And then, quite suddenly, one comes to the realisation that one's contemporaries are growing a little old, falling off a little. One realises that one's hair is white.

I knew the house, of course. Jonas had pointed it out to me before, the oldest in the little town. That I could well believe. It is a timbered house, two storied, the roof tree running parallel with the street. It stands on the pavement of the main street surrounded by minor shops, but the house has never been a shop itself. I am quite sure of that. I am quite sure that it will never be one.

'I've let it to a man called Elroy,' said Jonas. 'A writer, a poet in a small way, they say. It isn't everybody's house.'

'Martin Elroy?' I enquired.

'M.C. Elroy. I believe his name is Martin. D'you know him?'

'I know his work,' I said.

'I want you to come and have a look at Mrs Elroy,' said Jonas, fussing a little with his gloves and muffler in the hall.

I might have answered shortly. I should have done so if I had been myself, I suppose, but something made me gentle. I thought as we walked through the town towards the house that the time for that was past, that we should be generous to our old age, that what Jonas had lost in delicacy I had lost in self control. The house could mean nothing for us now.

'John Lyell, the painter, lived here once,' said Jonas. 'In this house. Did I tell you that?'

'You showed me the portrait of his wife,' I replied. As a musician John Lyell was never more than a gifted amateur; I think that that is generally admitted now. As a portrait painter, of course, he was unique within the limits that he laid down for himself. Till Jonas told me I had not realised that it was in this little town that he had lived and worked for the greater part of his painting career – in fact, until the death of his wife. That

makes a great break in a man's life. Beau Alleyne has a reference to it in his memoirs, though that, indeed, is little enough
to guarantee the authenticity of any tale. But as he tells it,

'It is come to an End,' he said, 'as it has used to do all through
the ages,' and though I diligently enquired of him his
meaning he would say no more, but thereafter he laid aside
his Painting Gear and wholly gave himself to Musick, thus
transferring his Devotions from Melpomene to Euterpe.

That morning we came through the town to the main street
and saw the house before us, timbered and friendly in the
sunlight, with the bustle of the town all around it. I say that
it looked friendly. There are houses that I would not live in if
it were to be avoided. But of this house what Jonas said was
true; it was a happy house. I knew that when I saw it for the first
time.

'Everybody thinks well of it,' said Jonas. 'But it isn't everybody's house to live in.'

The door was opened for us by Mrs Elroy. Jonas went in first
to greet her; for myself, I hung back for a moment in amazement before I followed him into the long room that ran across
the front part of the ground floor, half hall, half living room.
Jonas was talking to the woman in the middle of the room,
asking her for leave to show me the house. He was telling her
about my books. That gave me a little time in which to steady
myself, in which to study her features, in which to compare her
with my memory, in which to brace myself to meet her and to
hear her speak to me. She turned to me.

'I'm always glad to show anybody the house,' she said,
' – anybody who knows about these old houses. With a house
like this, one wants to treat it properly. You really ought to know
its history – what it's been before. I don't know very much about
it, I'm afraid.' From the Lyell portrait I could have sworn to that
turn of the head, that half smile. 'That's why I like showing the
house to people – people who really know. I pick up bits about
it.' The candour was in the portrait. It was all there.

She led the way upstairs – broad, shallow stairs in a box-like well beside the central chimney of the house, entered by an arch from the kitchen premises.

I pressed by Jonas. 'The resemblance is extraordinary,' I muttered. 'I should certainly have taken her for the original.'

The house was built of ships' timbers; I put the date of it between 1540 and 1580. Probably they got the wood from Poole. There was very little evidence of restoration, and such alterations as were necessary had been well carried out. The majority of the doors were as old as the house, opening with strings and latches. It was kept in the manner that I like to see such houses, not with meticulous care for the preservation of the fabric at the expense of the comfort of the occupants. It was a house to live in.

She took us through the rooms. A child came out from somewhere – it was dark in the passages – and followed after us: a girl perhaps ten or twelve years old, with straight bobbed hair and with a merry little face. Elroy himself was away from home, I think. At the last we come down from the attics, waiting in a passage on the first floor while Mrs Elroy latched a door above us. For a moment we waited.

'We must have seen the greater part of it,' I muttered. There are generally one or two rooms that the tenant does not offer to display.

The little girl interposed herself between Jonas and myself. 'You haven't been in Mummy's room,' she said gravely.

I am awkward with children. Jonas had several, and knows better than I how they should be answered. He coughed.

'We'll see your mother's room some other time, my dear,' he said heavily.

There was a quick step down the stairs, and our hostess was beside us in the gloom of the passage. The child moved past me; I remember that her short hair brushed my hand.

'They haven't seen your room, Mummy,' she said.

Mrs Elroy laughed quietly. 'You funny thing. All right, take them and show them my room.' She turned to us, the laughter still bright in her eyes. 'I didn't think it was worth showing you . . .'

The child moved down the passage and paused before a closed door.

'This is Mummy's room,' she said gravely. She turned the handle and I followed her over the threshold. It was the box room. It was a fair sized room lit only by one small window high up in the wall opposite the door, and it was filled with old portmanteaus, trunks, curtain poles, sugar boxes, and dust.

'We don't use it,' said Mrs Elroy. 'The light's so bad. It seems so funny to have made a room like this with only that one window.' For some reason I did not speak. 'The children always call this Mummy's room.' She dropped an arm round the child's shoulders. 'Don't you?'

I took one more long look at the west wall, noticing every discolouration of the plaster, and then turned away. It reminded me of a house that I saw in Warwickshire once, when I was a young man. It was just like that.

We took our leave in the big front room. I had to brace afresh to face that amazing likeness, and to thank her for her trouble. 'You have a most delightful house,' I said.

She nodded. 'It's like one likes to have it,' she said, a little incoherently. 'Almost like a house one builds oneself, if you know what I mean.'

We went out into the street.

'That room,' I said, and paused.

'Eh?' said Jonas. 'What's that? The box room?'

I nodded. 'It's the best situation in the house. The builder must have meant it for the best bedroom.'

He made no answer, and we walked on in silence. It was not till that evening after dinner that he mentioned it again.

'It's in the west wall, isn't it?' he asked.

I laid down my glass. In the candle light the room was very dim; in the corners the heavy Victorian furniture loomed black and shadowy. 'There was an alcove in the west wall,' I said. 'About six feet deep, I suppose. With a window. That was before the barn was built against that wall. The barn may have been put there on purpose.'

I paused. 'You can see the space if you know where to look,'

I said. 'Or you can measure up. But the shape of the room is wrong for that period. That tells you straight away.'

He dropped a walnut with a tiny clatter among the litter of the shells upon his plate.

'I knew it was that room,' he muttered. 'I slept in the house once.'

There was a long silence. 'What will you do?' I said at last.

He roused himself. 'Do? I don't want to do anything.' He fingered the table things irresolutely. 'Do you want to open up the wall?'

'Yes,' I said frankly. 'I want to see if there is anything there.'

He rose heavily from the table. 'I will not allow it.'

'Why not?'

'Not while the house is occupied.'

'The room is only used for a box room,' I said. 'We could take out a few bricks without disturbing the remainder of the house.'

He moved towards the fireplace. As he came forward into the strong light I saw his face, and I knew that I must yield that point.

'I think that it would be the death of her,' he said simply.

II

From time to time I met Jonas at the Club, perhaps once in two months. I do not think that either of us changed very much during the next three years. I saw him sometimes at the Club, as I say, but we never did much more than pass the time of day together. For my part, I was unwilling to bring up a subject on which I knew him to be queer; for his, I suppose he was reticent. I know now that there is a streak of heavy idealism in him; throughout the strain of that incredible three years Jonas remained unchanged, phlegmatic.

He crossed the room to me. 'The house is empty now,' he said.

I knew what he was speaking of. For three years now I had never thought of Jonas but I had thought immediately of that old house, and of his extraordinary fancy.

'The Elroys have left it?'

'Elroy took the children away,' said Jonas. 'Mrs Elroy died last June.'

I was silent.

'I want you to come down,' he said. 'That wall. I am having it opened up. You see, the house is not now tenanted.'

He had taken considerable precautions. He had brought up an old mason from Devonshire to do the work; the man was under some obligation to him. He guarded the reputation of that house most jealously. I went down to stay with him the evening before the work was to begin, and dined in his house that night.

He left me next morning, standing in the main street before the house, while he went to fetch the key from some caretaker that he had appointed. The house was empty, and yet it was not desolate. I moved up the pavement idly till I was opposite the shop next door. Horter, the butcher, was a tenant of Jonas'; he knew me by sight.

'Sad business for Mr Elroy, sir,' he remarked, wiping his hands on his apron.

I nodded. 'Was she ill long?'

'Just a week. Yes, it come very sudden, that did. Not as if she was an old lady, neither. Only forty-three.'

I pulled myself together. 'I didn't know them well,' I muttered. 'I met her once, she showed me the house – three years ago.'

'Aye,' he said, 'it's a fine house. One of the real old ones. I lived there one time, you know.'

'You lived there?' I exclaimed.

'Aye – before Mr Elroy come here. That was when I took over this business. Near twenty years ago now – nineteen year last December. I thought as it 'ld be handy for the shop, you see – running in and out. But the wife took a fancy against it, and we only stayed six months. Seemed like it wasn't the house for us, and we moved up to the top o' the hill.' He jerked his hand towards the little villas on the rising ground.

'There's a good number only stays a short time,' he said. 'There was two or three afore us that didn't stay long. Mrs Elroy, she lived there twenty year. Then there was Dr and Mrs Weyman when I was a lad – they must have had it longer nor that. Very like Mrs Weyman was to Mrs Elroy. Very sim'lar to look at.'

He regarded the house thoughtfully, sucking his teeth. 'It's a lady's house,' he said at last.

He laughed, and went back into the shop.

We went into the house. Within an hour the mason had withdrawn the first brick from the box room wall. Jonas peered in through the aperture.

'What is there in there?' I asked.

He drew back from the wall. 'See for yourself,' he said.

I knelt down in the litter beside the hole. The alcove was there as I had supposed, about six feet deep. In the far wall, facing me, was the window, bricked over on the outside, with the tattered linen still hanging from the frames in shreds. I have never seen a Tudor window so complete. In front of the window stood a table, a plain oak table measuring perhaps three feet by two feet. There were several articles upon it. That was all.

'Go on,' said Jonas to the mason. 'Be very careful. I am particularly anxious that nothing should be disturbed.'

He glanced at me curiously. 'Are you all right?'

I nodded. 'I did not expect that we should find anything at all,' I said at last. 'I did not believe in it. I am not sure that I believe in it now.'

'There has been proof enough,' he said. 'But I have known this house for the whole of my life. I hope to God that we are doing nothing wrong.'

He bent again to the hole. 'What are those things on the table?' he asked. 'What is that thing like a blotting book?'

I stooped beside him. 'I think it is a dressing table,' I said. 'A lady's table. By those little earthenware pots. I don't think the blotting book has anything to do with the table.'

'It would be reasonable to find that here,' he muttered. 'But it is not what I expected.'

That was all there was. We opened up the hole till it was sufficiently wide to enable a man to pass through. The alcove was in a very perfect state of preservation; whoever had bricked it up had done his work most carefully. There was little decay.

'Why was it left like this?' I asked.

He shook his head. 'Who knows?'

We passed through the hole, Jonas and I, and stood beside the table. It was a lady's dressing table, as I have said; the period I put at some time in the sixteenth century. There were two little earthenware pots with lids that might once have held cosmetics, enamelled blue and white. There was a flat earthenware bowl about eighteen inches in diameter, and in this there was a smaller wooden bowl with a black residue of soap caked in the bottom of it. There was a little wooden bottle with a glass stopper. I do not know what that was for. There was a comb made of some hard black wood, with thick teeth and a long handle. There was a convex mirror, much corroded, set in a round wooden frame without a handle, about six inches in diameter. There was a little flat wooden tray and in this lay two silver rings, both rather massive and clumsy in design, and a little piece of green jade with a silver ring through it. There was a little knife with a horn handle. In the centre of the table was the leather portfolio that we had noticed.

Jonas lifted each of the rings in turn. One was a garnet, the other an emerald surrounded by seed pearls. Both were set in silver, black with age. Very carefully he replaced them exactly where he had found them.

'We did wrong to come here,' he muttered. 'If I had known that it was only this I would not have broken in.'

He laid his hand on the portfolio and lifted it carefully from the table. 'This will tell us who she is.'

It was fastened with three leather thongs. They were stiff with age, but we untied them without great difficulty. Very carefully Jonas opened the covers. There was a portrait there.

I suppose we knew what we should find. I suppose we were

both ready for it, so far as one could ever be prepared to meet
that amazing likeness. I was not myself that day. I know that I
stood staring dumbly at the portrait and it seemed to me that
I had slipped back three years, that I was still standing in the
doorway of the room behind me, that I was listening to her
voice.

> 'It seems so funny to have made a room like this with only
> that one window,' she was saying. 'The children always call
> this Mummy's room . . .'

I do not know how long it was before Jonas touched me on
the arm to draw my attention to the portrait again. I must have
been staring at the empty doorway, for I can remember that I
had to turn to him.

'Ann Farrar,' he said. 'I should have known. The house was
built for her.'

I nodded. 'I see,' I said. 'You mean that this – all this is hers?'

'This is her house,' he said simply.

I turned again to the portrait and saw that the name was
printed carefully at the foot. And then I suppose the collector
in me awoke because on the instant I had forgotten everything
else, the things that should have mattered more than drawing.

'My goodness,' I exclaimed. 'That's a Holbein!'

Jonas glanced at it indifferently. 'It is very like a Holbein,' he
replied. 'It may be the work of a pupil. That was the period.'

I fumbled a little with my glasses and peered at the drawing. 'I should be very much surprised if that was the work of a
pupil,' I said. 'Bring it out into the light.'

He turned and moved towards the hole. I saw him hesitate,
and then he stopped.

'No,' he said. 'We ought not to do that. It must stay in here.'

I protested with some vigour. I remember that I watched
him retie the folio with great deliberation and lay it on the
table. I was half afraid to interfere, but at last,

'Damme!' I said. 'You do not intend to leave it in there like
that? It's a Holbein!'

He turned and looked at me, and in the heat of my irritation I was ashamed.

'If it were forty times a Holbein,' he said quietly, 'I would leave it there.'

He motioned me away, and I stepped out through the hole into the room beyond. Jonas remained inside; he had his back turned to the hole so that I could not see what he was doing. Then he stepped clumsily backwards into the room. For a moment he paused, looking in at that table and at that Tudor window.

Then he turned to the mason. 'Go on,' he said. 'Put it all back again. Be careful that no dust or brick remains inside. I want it all to be quite clean.'

I inclined my head towards the table. 'You are leaving it like that?' I asked. 'That will not help you with this – this trouble.'

There was a rustle of footsteps in the room. I could declare on oath that at that moment there were four of us together, and I looked at Jonas, and he looked at me, and we were silent. And presently she went.

He eyed me steadily. 'You mean this haunting,' he said at last. 'You are right. I have known this place all my life. I have known since I was twenty years old that this house was haunted – haunted with the remains of some old happiness.' He broke off.

'I am seventy years old,' he muttered. 'I wish to God that I had come here as a young man.'

It took the mason the remainder of the day to replace the brickwork of the wall, and all that time Jonas never left the room. The next day the man peeled the plaster from the remainder of the wall and commenced to plaster up the whole afresh. When that was dry a coat of colour wash would do the rest.

That is the last time that I was in the house. I am not very sure in my own mind that I should care to revisit it, now. As we passed out into the street I remember that I spoke of it to him.

'You have reached an impasse,' I said. 'What are you going to do?'

We walked a little way before he spoke.

'I shall let it again,' he said at last. 'A tenant will arrive.'

John Metcalfe

NO SIN

JOHN METCALFE (1891-1965) *is a name probably known only to connoisseurs and collectors of rare horror and weird fiction, since most of his work has been long out of print and unavailable to readers with more modest budgets. Most of his horror fiction is collected in the volumes* The Smoking Leg and Other Stories *(1925) and* Judas and Other Stories *(1931), neither of which has ever been reprinted, although Ash-Tree Press released a volume collecting some of Metcalfe's fiction in 1998. Perhaps his strangest and most interesting work is the novella* The Feasting Dead *(1954), originally published by Arkham House in 1954 and republished by Valancourt in 2014. The story of a young English boy who falls under the corrupting influence of a vampiric being from medieval French folklore, it bears comparison with the best works of British supernatural fiction. 'No Sin', a strange and very Gothic tale, first appeared in* Judas and Other Stories *and has never been reprinted.*

i. The Widower

THE HOUSE OF PROTOPART had raised its conscious head above the nether haze of Norwood and now seemed to sail and swim upon that lower sea of sun-fraught mist and multitudinous dwelling with the dignified precision of a swan. The square tower of white and lemon brick which Protopart had built led the way and the house streamed out behind it. Inside that tower Protopart himself rallied his forces and set the course, for it was now more than a month since Charlotte had been buried, and it was time the turret room should be got ready.

He was a small man and broad-shouldered, with something of the bull about his head. His eyes were brown and liquid and his infrequent voice soft and low. A dull, angry patch, almost resembling a bruise, marked either cheek-bone, and the apple of his neck showed red where his collar chafed it. Some little, light-brown hairs curled, shining, in his ears, and about his whole body there hung a peculiar and odorous sweetness like the breath of cows.

For the first time since his wife's death he had got out of the fine black cashmere suit that irked his limbs and into the shabby old jacket and trousers that he loved. He had, too, an idea that the change of clothes might help him to forget, but he was wrong. Incessantly, with the minute agility of an ant, his mind would still be running back and forth within the limits of the single week that had included, first, the whispered preparations for Charlotte's imminent demise, then the unexpected rallying and emergence from the trance-like coma of two years, next the astounding scene by the bedside, followed immediately by her relapse into the old stupor, and finally her quiet passing and her burial.

After all, what had been the words with which that dark-browed woman had broken her long silence? As Protopart moved softly about the turret room, shifting chairs and table and rolling back the carpet from the inner, or windowless, wall, he repeated to himself for the thousandth time the few short sentences he knew so well.

'Flora,' she had said, 'Flora had better go over to the Vicarage for a time. The Cowans would be glad, and you could hardly wish her to remain, as things will be. She can spend her time here when she wants to, but all her things had better be taken out of the turret room. You will understand why when you open the first of the two letters. Give her my love ... And remember, Jasper, closely as you have watched me for the last two years, I have watched you as closely. I shall go on watching you after I have gone ...'

The queer phrasing of those final sentences had struck upon him strangely. When his half-blind ward, Flora, had asked him what Charlotte had said he had even thought it wise to make a slight alteration. For 'watching' he had substituted 'watching over' – 'shall go on watching over you after I have gone.' That was so much better. It must have been what she had meant to say.

Yet even with this emendation his wife's last words possessed, in retrospect, a curiously unfamiliar ring. It almost was as though, during those two years of living death, her voice had caught a different accent and her brain a different idiom.

The two letters of which she had spoken had been written and deposited with the lawyer just before, and in hourly expectation of, the seizure which preceded her paralysis. One, Protopart was not to open till three months after her decease, but the other he had already read, and the strangeness of its contents baffled him again with the vision of an alien, an unknown, Charlotte.

It was in compliance with the terms of this first letter that he now removed from the turret room the last signs of his ward's occupancy. The place would be Flora's oratory no longer. Shrine, ornaments, kneeling-desk and lamp, all had followed her to the Cowans' three weeks back. Only the heavy books in braille remained, and these he had stacked carefully on one side ready to take over in the morning.

Presently the northern wall stood bare and white before him, and with a pang of misgiving he saw that the work was finished and the room waiting for that extraordinary and now imminent fulfilment of a dead wife's whim.

As he stood considering, he heard through the open window the heavy crunching of gravel in the drive and then a knocking. Protopart hesitated a second, then flung wide the door, moistened his dry lips, and descended in the direction of the sounds.

ii. '——*but not forgotten*'

The image which Charlotte had ordained hung sleek and glistering upon the wall. Life-size, life-like, it towered with a fatal authenticity. He took a backward step. Kreubler had done his work – too well. The hair, the powerful forehead and the resolute jaw, the bitter lines about the eyes and mouth, even the tiny scar below an ear . . . The thing was horrible.

Two hours had passed since he let in the men. They had come and gone. The turret room which they had filled with muffled batterings was silent once again. Only upon that northern wall which had been bare their handiwork remained.

Whilst they had toiled in haste Protopart had withdrawn into the room below to wait. First he had stuffed the door to dull the sounds. In vain. He could not stifle that appalling din.

He had paced feverishly up and down, pausing at intervals to listen. What if the maids should suddenly return? It had been difficult to clear the house of them, to get them out together. All sorts of pretexts, subterfuge – for this! Suppose someone were watching from the road? No, that was safe enough; the blinds were drawn that side. His daughters – they at least would have to know, – and see . . . A nauseous phrase occurred to him, 'the private view.' Hilda and Joyce were present at the reading of the will, but not, he recollected, at the taking of the mask. They didn't know the worst, the full enormity . . .

And now once more he was alone. The workmen, clumping down the winding stair, had stopped outside his door. Would he go up to see? 'No' – he had shaken his head casually, had tipped them handsomely, received their heavy-breathing thanks. His gaze had shrunk before their curious stare. Not till he'd watched them go, shouldering the wooden litter with its trailing sheet, clanking a metal bucket with unnecessary violence, would he go up to look.

Only a moment had he paused before the turret door. Then he had turned the handle softly and gone in.

A curious, plastery odour, mingled with the smell of the distemper which the workmen had employed to cover up the traces of their labour, had struck faint upon his nostrils. His foot had overturned an empty bottle left upon the floor.

Walking across the room, he had pulled up the blind, then, trembling, turned to gaze.

Now, having looked, he stifled a half-cry and, shrinking sidewise from the effigy, leaned his right arm upon the wall. For a time he thought that he was going to faint. After a while, however, the seizure passed, and then he stared again.

Here, in this ponderous mass of gleaming stone, was Charlotte's last authority upheld, her final mandate from the tomb obeyed, her ghastly whim indulged. There had been no escaping the provisions of the will nor the minute instructions of the letter he had opened at her death. In every detail they had been complied with. Kreubler, the sculptor, had been summoned hastily to take the mask. With that, and with the favourite photograph of the deceased, he had returned to Kensington. There, in his studio, he had been chiselling back and back, working nine hours a day, so he had said, using the death-mask only as a starting-point from which to reconstruct the Charlotte of five years ago – the vital, stormy Charlotte of the photograph, yet unapprised of the first dread oncomings of disease.

And beyond expectation, beyond fear, he had succeeded. He had been paid extravagantly; but not for this.

Protopart backed away a step or two. The aspect of the effigy was faintly minatory. He realised that the thing was wonderful, a masterpiece. And yet, beneath those features that he knew lay something which at first seemed alien and unfamiliar. Only at first. His memory swept back. Yes, it was true; sometimes she had that look. But Kreubler – how could he have guessed? How caught it, prisoned it? It wasn't fair to her.

He shivered, in a superstitious awe, and turned his head away. It was as though he feared that, if he looked too long, Charlotte herself might stir and quicken in the stone – as though, before his fascinated gaze, that hair might bristle and those eyes revolve.

A tear ran down his cheek; but it was not for Charlotte that he wept. Resentment and a sense of cruel injury had long replaced the proper grief he would have felt but for this monstrous act. Why had she done it – why? A wife could surely leave her photograph, a lock of hair, even a bust perhaps – but this . . . This was beyond all precedent, outrageous, morbid, ghoulish affronting decency itself . . .

That was the worst. The figure was undraped.

Close at his side and reaching almost to the window-ledge were stacked the ponderous tomes in braille which must next morning follow Flora to the Vicarage. They had been covered with a tablecloth to save them from the dust.

He seized the cloth and, standing upon tiptoe, secured it about the shoulders of the effigy.

Once more he had retreated to the window. His pulses raced, but for a moment he no longer felt afraid. His draping of the figure had increased his boldness. He would do more! Why shouldn't he? Lock up the room, not let his daughters see. Cover the thing entirely. Even – By God, he would! – even——

But there he stopped. His courage ebbed away. The wording of the will was too precise. Charlotte had made so sure. Three pounds a year were even set apart for 'maintenance'!

For some time he stood motionless. The afternoon sun had fallen on the effigy's left hand. The other, pressed against a breast, was hidden by the cloth.

Protopart gave a sudden start. He almost had forgotten . . . One thing there yet remained which he must do, one last and grim command was still to be obeyed. A tremor of repugnance made him shiver as he approached the image. From his pocket he took out a small morocco case. Some seconds passed before he pressed its spring. Within there lay a circle of plain gold. Shuddering, he made to place it on the wedding-finger of the effigy.

He was so intent upon his task that he did not hear the soft ascent of footsteps up the turret stair. The ring was difficult to fit. He had to strain and press. Not till at last he forced it home beyond the stony knuckle did he swing terrified around.

Before him, with one groping hand upon the window-ledge, stood Flora, his blind ward.

iii. *Maiden*

'Jasper!'

For some seconds he was too taken by surprise to realise the disaster. She had even crossed the room without his hearing her.

'Jasper!' she repeated.

He had started violently already, and the tones of her voice, sweet, clear and searching, always like their own bell-echo, made him start yet again.

'Flora – how – how did you manage to come up, all by yourself?'

'Oh . . . Mr Cowan brought me to the gate, and the side-door was open. It was easy, but . . . where's everybody gone? What are you doing here alone? And——'

Protopart regarded her with dismay. He must tell her. It would be more dignified to tell her before she could find out. In a sort of nightmare infatuation he watched her as she moved slowly toward a corner of the room where there was, ordinarily, a chair.

'It's gone. It isn't there!' It was he who uttered the words, warningly. Flora stopped abruptly, turning her face to his. Yes, he *must* tell her. All at once he recollected, as if this were a suddenly-remembered fact which crushed out hope, that she was not entirely blind. She could at least distinguish light from shade.

'Jasper – there's something different, Jasper. Whitewash – I smell it. And – I – I can see something – on that wall!'

He was too late. By intuition if not actually by sight she had forestalled the revelation he had been too cowardly to make. She was already moving toward the effigy. Before he could prevent her she had reached it. Fascinated, he stared at her as her hands explored its contours underneath the cloth.

'Jasper – why – it's a statue! Of . . . why, I believe . . . of – Charlotte!'

Protopart licked dry lips. A reflection, charged with an inexplicable despair and menace, came to him. How *small* Flora looked! He and his ward were both short people – in comparison with Charlotte.

'Yes,' he said hoarsely. 'It's – her statue. She – she wanted it. It was her wish; not mine.'

Flora's face, flushed delicately to a coral pink, amazed him by its smile.

'But why – why didn't you tell me? It's – why, it's lovely, beautiful, I think . . . I think it's beautiful . . .'

iv. *The Bride of Christ*

Flora's thoughts, an hour later, went weaving, weaving over what had come to pass. The hot afternoon, she knew, drooped all about her, round the Cowans' house, but its stale languor did not penetrate. Through the most torrid of South London dog-days she could carry her own coolness. It was a faculty of which she was herself half-conscious. Down its own private dream her mind tripped nimbly, with a stag-footed lightness, veering in shy assault, in mimic delicate affray, in instant and fastidious withdrawal. Charlotte's statue had been beautiful, but Jasper when he had walked back with her to the Vicarage had been so tired and so miserable . . .

Mr Cowan, to whom she had spoken of the effigy, had expressed no direct surprise. The notion, he had told her, was not *so* unusual, not so very. The Cowans had been very good to her since Charlotte's death, but she could never be so fond of Mr Cowan as of Jasper.

Now, after tea, she set out for St Agatha's, which stood, secluded in a small, tree-sprinkled park, no more than a long stone's-throw from the Vicarage. At her side, occasionally grunting a perfunctory admonition, walked a dun-coloured boy, known as William, who carried soap, two nail-brushes, a tin of Vim, and a large pail of water. Flora was periodically of opinion that she could see quite well enough to clean the reredos, and from this innocent and pious exercise no one had the unkindness to dissuade her.

In the grateful coolness of the church they worked together for an hour. Flora, wrinkling her small nose in wry affectation of disdain, was deciding that the building smelled a little 'mousy,' but, simultaneously, she was in the turret room once more with

Jasper Protopart, hearing his pained, grief-laden voice go on 'explaining,' wondering why he sounded so exhausted and so hurt. Over these things her mind played like a darting, intermittent flame, seizing ideas and dropping them dismayed, daintily reaching forth for them again, and shrinking back.

To have his dead wife's statue fixed up there was evidently 'funny.' Mr Cowan, in denying it, had now implied as much. It was all in the will . . . And there was yet another letter to be opened soon. She, Flora, would have still remained in ignorance if she had not encountered Lizzie Turnbull just before. Lizzie had told her of sepulchral happenings in Jasper's house, of something on a shutter, 'going in' . . .

Jasper's image rose, fragrantly, in Flora's brain, the image of something warm and reassuring, like an old shabby frock, a sort of hot, protecting duskiness . . . He said so very little. All his confidences had got to be wooed from him. Naturally, he had been prostrated by the simple *shock* of Charlotte's death. And yet – it must have been in some sense a relief – release . . .

Suddenly one of those ideas which she had fingered gingerly and then let fall so many times flashed up once more. She had never really liked Charlotte very much – even before the paralysis – and Charlotte, she was sure, *had not liked her.* A cold, obstinate word precipitated itself finally, stayed with her tinglingly. Could *that* be possible . . . ?

The dun-coloured boy, breathing stertorously over St James the Less, did not notice that his companion dropped her brush and, after gropingly retrieving it, knelt motionless and idle for a full minute with her lips parted and a slow colour mounting to her cheeks.

She could feel her own heart fluttering. As if to regain some departed warmth she was hugging herself in a curious, secret chill which, she recalled, had come upon her once or twice before. Was that when she was just a little girl, one night in Charlotte's room, and sickening, as afterwards appeared, for chickenpox? No, it was much more recent. Yet it *was* like a fever too, the strange, half-pleasurable onset of some slow, mysterious and destructive change – the dim, almost delicious herald

and forerunner of disease. And 'Plaster of Paris,' she was thinking. 'That was how it was done . . . All those years and years . . .
she must . . . have thought – she must have been – *jealous* . . .'

High, far above her, streaming on an eastern pane (though
she could not observe it save as a vague patch of light) the
remote, languid figure of the Christ fled upward in a lambent
glow of colour.

In what she thought was its direction she bestowed an apologetic glance, and on the next apostle a conciliatory rub.

v. *Communion*

Up in his turret room one morning in the following week,
Protopart shrinkingly stared out, in forced serenity, on the
tranced London panorama that he knew. Through the half-
open windows a low, echoing murmur stole, a hoarse and
languid composite of sound came rising in. Far away, beyond
Streatham, toy trains went brightly pointing in a grey-golden
haze, leaving doll trails of smoke. He gazed at them unseeingly,
his mind lapped in painful recollection. This day, with its queer,
muted quality of omen – of some disquiet message going on
and on for him, continually uncaught, in teeming distant streets
– oppressed him with the flavour of a dream. Faint on the skyline he could make out blurred yet beckoning shapes. Faint to
his ears there crept an intimated cadence, always promised,
constantly withheld. Over there, where the sun's rays shot
fanwise on remote, leaden-glittering points, something was
dumbly striving, being said to him in vain. His brain was numb,
lost in a waking swoon. Yes, this was like that other day, he
thought, just after Charlotte died. Then, too, there was some
whisper that eluded him; then, too, some patient undertone
of meaning had informed the storied cliffs of brick and toss-
ing masonry, swum in the weltering human gulf of Penge and
Southern Anerley, ungrasped.

He had stood on that day, as now, in his high white-and-
lemon watch-tower, listening to this slow surge that beat up to

the windows from reverberating depths beneath. Even in the
midst of his distress he had wondered about it. That sound, to
which a million irretrievable, unreckoned sounds contributed,
bore on him with a sense of anguished impotence. Refined to a
vast, level melancholy, it was the distillation of all vainer cries,
charged with a curious, filtered sorrow he could recognise but
not interpret. Sensible of some pathos not mundane, he was
unable to accept its burden or extract its essence. He had looked
down into swarming, heat-vague streets and steeled his heart.
Once and again amidst that arid, far-flung waste of drab and
burnished grey he had picked out in fearful intuition some
barely moving, distant dot of black, marked it wend slowly
nearer and resolve as slowly into brougham or landau, turn up
restrainedly along his gravel drive, disgorge its callers and its
sympathy in a decorous hush. He had seen none of them. Their
cards alone were left.

All that was over now, but he was harassed yet. His mind
was cluttered with the undigested shapes of grief he could not
feel. Deplorable words and phrases seethed, with a nauseous,
iterated inappropriateness, in his brain. 'Manfully,' 'bearing
up,' 'irreparable loss,' 'Time, the great healer,' 'Resurrection
morn'...

Behind him, Charlotte beetled on the wall. It was on Sunday
that he had been forced at last to let his daughters see. Even in
imagination he shrank sickly from that picture. He could still
feel the trembling of his knees as he had headed the inevitable,
shamed procession up the stairs to the locked room. Then,
when the key was turned, had come the necessary raising of the
blinds, the spellbound stares, the shocked and stifled wonder of
the girls...

Now, wheeling from the window, Protopart faced the effigy,
at first indignantly, shambled before it in a growing nervousness
for half a minute, and then dropped his glance. He sat down at
a table and began to write. His pen scratched only a few lines
beneath the letter-head, and ceased. He struck a match and lit
a pipe.

Presently he altered his position somewhat so that his gaze

once more swept the dim, sweltering London sea. His pipe went out, and in the action of relighting it he turned slightly inwards to the room. The white face of the statue moved into the circle of his vision and he stopped, abruptly, to regard it.

The eyes crept.

A curious rage came upon him, with it a sudden apprehension. Panic-stricken, he leaped to his feet and hurriedly drew down the blinds.

Then, in a mute despair, he tiptoed to the door, opened it softly, left the turret room, and turned the key behind him. He could stay there no longer. It was quite impossible. The place was haunted, had the charnel fragrance of a mausoleum.

For an hour or more he wandered in suburban streets that like himself were pale and somnolent. The heat-drooped air had become tense and stale, unnaturally still. Probably a storm was brewing. In an effort to distract his thoughts he tried to fix attention on the multiplying signs of its approach. It was of no avail. Eternally, his mind harked back to Charlotte. Could she be seen, he wondered, from the road – from any road? Perhaps, if someone quite a long way off had got a telescope, and if the blinds were up . . . He *must* not think. Now, until rain fell, he would cease to brood, tire himself by rapid walking around Gipsy Hill, forget, if possible, the turret room and what it held.

It brought him back.

As he passed inwards, toward the dining-room, his youngest daughter, Mabel, met him in the hall. 'Oh, so you're home . . . It's just begun to rain. Flora's here, too. She came to get a book.'

Flora herself appeared, smiling. 'It's the "Imitation." I've got all my brailles except that one. You must have left it up there by mistake.' On Mabel's face as well, for no too-obvious reason, was a smile.

Protopart demurred. 'I'm sure it isn't there. All of your books went over days ago.'

Flora insisted. 'Do you mind just looking? I'm coming with you too . . .'

Together they ascended, silently. The key turned in the lock; the blinds flew up. For some seconds they remained, motionless and hardly breathing, too awe-struck by the instant impact of some formidable and conscious presence to make sound or stir.

Above their heads, Charlotte stared past and over them toward the gathering storm with a remote and enigmatic frown.

vi. *Thunderclap*

Within another quarter of an hour the tempest broke. The rain, at first descending in sparse, sullen drops, burst suddenly in a cold, lashing fury. A livid throat of deepest indigo, stretching its vault from Upper Norwood over Thornton Heath, was seamed and wrinkled into reeling cliffs, stitched intermittently with lightning. The bumping hubbub of the thunder was augmented periodically by fresh entries from the outer suburbs. Catford announced itself in one terrific roar, and Anerley came in next moment with a stupendous series of crescendo crashes like the disruption of Plutonic arsenals. Under the heady chaos of the sky, now gushing with pale fire, the earth appeared upended, tossed this way and that. Protopart, staring through the streaming windows of the turret room, saw his lawn littered instantaneously with sodden leaves, branches, and even boughs, torn from the writhing trees. He had to shout to render his voice audible.

'What a storm! It'll clear the air, though . . .'

Flora's face, lit by a flash, had a queer expression. The fruitless search for the missing book had been perfunctory, and she was now standing close behind him, near the statue. Her lips moved, but to hear her he had to bend an ear beside her mouth.

'Jasper – why did she do it? Tell me . . .'

He drew back, startled. After a moment's pause he answered her, defensively:

'It isn't so peculiar as you think. Poor Charlie! She didn't want us to forget.'

Flora, he fancied, had not caught his answer. The racket

of the storm, though lessening somewhat, was an effectual obstacle to conversation, particularly upon such a subject. For several minutes they abandoned the attempt to speak.

Presently, however, at the commencement of what proved to be a longer lull, Flora resumed: 'It wasn't *usual*, was it?'

Protopart looked at her in consternation. What had come over her to make her talk like this? A conviction that she must be ill, or frightened by the storm, restrained him from rebuking her. Instead, he forced himself to reply steadily:

'Poor Charlotte. One mustn't judge by ordinary standards. In her condition . . .'

Flora interrupted him. 'You mean that, at the end, when she – came to, and spoke, she wasn't quite – quite normal. Jasper, you're wrong. Just listen. When Charlotte died she was – all there! Oh yes, she was all there!'

' "All there" . . . !'

'Oh yes, I know . . . You know as well as I. That thing up there – you feel it like I do. Don't you feel Charlotte herself looking at you and . . . remembering things?'

Protopart was about to answer, but a louder clap than usual silenced him. While he was waiting for another lull he scanned Flora's face anxiously, yet with a sense of unreality that made this whole preposterous argument a dream. Why had she started it – got him up here on the pretence of looking for a book?

'Flora,' he said, when the weird, pealing uproar had died down, 'Flora, you – you exaggerate. You'll see things differently . . . Wait a bit . . .'

'No, I shan't wait. You've never told me all that Charlie said – but I can guess without. The watching wasn't only on *her* side those last six months. The watching – and – and the listening!'

' "Listening"!'

'Yes, listening! I've heard her talking – when you thought she couldn't talk. Talking to herself about us. Talking——'

He made a desperate waving motion, but she went on remorselessly:

'Of course . . . of *course*! I expect she made her mind up about *that* – the statue – months before. Even left money for it in her will . . .'

'Flora . . . don't!' How could he silence her, forget what she had said? With some notion of dragging her by main force from the room he had laid a hand upon her shoulder when a voice rose abruptly up the stairs. 'Dad-*dy*! Flor-*a* . . . !' It was Mabel calling to them to come down.

'Yes, very well . . . I'm coming . . .' Flora's tones were choked. 'Yes, let's go down . . .' Suddenly, as they were moving toward the door, she threw one arm around his neck and kissed his cheek. 'Forgive me, oh, forgive me! Jasper, *please* . . . !'

II

i. Marriage—

Three months – exactly thirteen weeks since Charlotte's burial – had elapsed, and Protopart was bowling homewards from his lawyer's office in a hired brougham. As for forgiving Flora – he had done that long ago, yet, as it happened, he was thinking at this very moment of her strange behaviour on that stormy August afternoon. What she had said then he had managed to excuse, but not forget. How would she be affected by the news that he was bringing to her now – the news, so unexpected and perturbing, which his dead wife's second letter held for both of them?

Reclining in the dark-blue cloth upholstery of the old-fashioned vehicle, he put a hand into the breast-pocket of his jacket, then timorously withdrew it. No, he would not take out the letter now. He knew the whole of it by heart. Later, when he got home, he'd have a drink of wine. How strange – how very strange! What would his daughters think? For this visit to the lawyer's he had somehow felt constrained to put on, once again, the cashmere suit which he had worn in mourning. It had seemed appropriate. Now, in the rather stuffy confines of the brougham, he sniffed repugnantly. The suit, he fancied, drew from him a sourish smell which he found faintly disagreeable. Although the day, for mid-November, was quite mild and sunny, it was not warm enough to let down either of the windows.

Flora! His thoughts returned to her unceasingly, revolved disquietly about her face, her voice, her gestures and her conduct. If only – if only Flora would stop acting as she did about the statue! It was quite bad and horrible enough without her going on in that peculiar way . . .

However, he refused to take her attitude too seriously. Flora had always been extremely highly-strung, and her half-blindness might account for much. Cowan had told him that she was increasingly devout, perhaps *too* zealous since she had been made a deaconess, and wearing herself out with fastings, vigils and long hours of prayer. Even on one occasion, she had said something about entering a convent . . .

The vehicle drew up before his door. Protopart alighted heavily, went in. The dining-room was deserted, and he refreshed himself with a glass of claret. Then he ascended to the turret room.

For several minutes he stood looking at the statue. He could remember, but too plainly, how, during these three months, he had resented its insistent, frowning presence on the wall – felt injured, mortified, enraged and terrified by turns. And – he had been unable to prevent the story's leaking out. Whispers, inevitably, had got about. His grief, throughout, had been confused and complicated by a faint, unpleasant shadow of absurdity. He, also, had been forced to seem eccentric, odd . . .

But now he could relent and comprehend at last. Poor Charlie – she was kinder, far more understanding than he guessed. He had misjudged her cruelly. And Flora, *Flora* . . . ! To-morrow, possibly to-day, he would tell Flora.

ii.   —*is honourable*

However, it was not until the middle of the following week that he had any opportunity to speak with her. His ward had been confined to bed for two days with a chill, and when at length she was escorted, against protest, from the Vicarage by Miss Turnbull her cheeks were flushed and her eyes feverishly bright. 'She really oughtn't to have come . . . I'll call for her and take her back with me at five – five sharp.'

To Jasper Protopart himself meanwhile had come a change of mind if not of heart. He was the prey of anguished doubts and dark misgivings. A degree of trepidation might be natural and seemly, but, beyond that, he knew a keener apprehension. He must think very seriously about this step . . . The elation which he had experienced after he had left the lawyer's office and opened Charlotte's letter had entirely ebbed away, leaving him flat and stale.

For the first time that month he had spent one whole morning in the turret room, where a low fire had been kindled on the tiny hearth. He had looked long and earnestly at Charlotte. Had she been really kind? He could not say. At all events, her imputation to him of a frailty which, if it had existed, she should not have seemed to guess was scarcely kind . . . Suddenly, as he stared, he had imagined that the statue's face had changed, had undergone some strange disfigurement. One corner of the lips had tilted upwards in a sort of sneer. With his scalp prickling he had started back in horror. Not for some moments did he realise that a fly, resuscitated by the fire's warmth, had settled on the stony mouth, was slowly crawling . . . Beating it hurriedly away, he had observed, as well, that the great metal pins which held the mass of marble to the wall were working loose. That, he supposed with nausea, must be attended to . . . Overcome by revulsion, he turned, in sick abhorrence, from the effigy, looked out again across that sombre wilderness that fled and streamed, rocking and heaving in vast neutral-tinted billows to the sighing, fog-dimmed bounds of the horizon. No, it was useless; he could never bring himself to do as Charlotte had suggested. He was old – worse than old, was elderly. In his own nostrils the 'body of this death' was rank and mortified.

Now, as he welcomed Flora in the hall, he was ashamed and chagrined. He had resolved to tell her nothing for the present about Charlotte's letter. Somewhere at the back of the house the maids were singing. Yes, it was 'Jesu, Lover of my Soul' – one of the hymns, it chanced, that had been sung at Charlotte's funeral. Flora, inclining her head to listen, touched his arm, then nodded, but in what kind of meaning he could not determine. Her friend, Miss Turnbull, already had departed. Mabel, joined presently by Jasper's second daughter, Hilda, came in through a side-door that led out to the shrubbery, her hands encased in gardening-gloves and bearing a large bouquet of chrysanthemums. 'Hello ... Flora! It's too cold to stay out any more ... Shall we try over those new parts for Stainer's anthem? I've muffed my entries every time so far ...'

'Directly,' answered Flora, 'yes, directly.' Protopart's heart sank in a foreboding too well founded. 'Jasper, I want to talk. Can we go up a while – up there?'

It appeared useless to resist. His ears still ringing with the hard chanting of the hymn, he accompanied her reluctantly to the turret room. Mabel and Hilda, with a swift interchange of glances, retired to the drawing-room to play bezique.

iii.   Guiltless

'I talked it out again with Mr Cowan yesterday. Of course, he told me what a serious step it was to take, and that I ought to speak to you about it first.'

Protopart had lit the fire. Its pale commencing glow played timidly about the upturned features of his ward. Almost without preamble she had launched into this one-sided discussion of her plans, sounding, it seemed to him, the death-knell of his hopes.

'Cowan was right. After all, you're only how old? Just nineteen. There's lots of time ...'

'It isn't years that count, but how you feel. I've thought it out. I should be – safer, in St Sepulchre's. It's a lot wiser I should realise that, and go, at once. And *she* – if she were here she would be glad ...'

Beneath her strained composure he could recognise a growing agitation. Outside, though it was barely three o'clock, a
foggy dusk was settling. His own tones as he answered her were
husky.

'How do you know that you have a – vocation? You should
be very sure that you aren't doing something you'll regret. I –
I'm your guardian, Flora, and, as for Charlie, if she were with us
now she'd say the same. I——'

'Don't! Jasper, please, don't talk like that! Don't let's *pre-
tend*!' Rising from her chair, she now stood facing him. Not
comprehending her emotion, he was, no less, excited and
alarmed. What did she mean? This inexplicable and openly
expressed hostility to his dead wife argued not only a strange
lack of delicacy toward himself but gross ingratitude as well.
And her unjustified assumption that he shared in it – was, as it
were, her ally and accomplice – her implication of some tacit
understanding, mutual agreement, against Charlotte, seemed
a most shocking, painful and extraordinary idea, of which he
had attempted vainly many times to disabuse her. Looking at
her, as her fingers clenched and unclenched nervously upon her
rosary, he was struck by her too-evident fragility. Phrases ran
pitifully, excusingly, across his brain – 'the earthly tenement,'
'purged of all dross,' 'the spirit's flame.' He felt old, very old
and cumbrous, stricken with something that was making him
pathetically incapable of bridging a profound and ever widen-
ing gulf, of coming near to her.

'Jasp, let's be honest about everything this once. You know,
as well as I do, why she hated me . . . Do let's play fair. Don't
make it harder for me than it is. I've got to go because – because
I'm weaker than I thought I was, that's all.' Her voice was
choked. After a pause she took a deep breath and continued,
while he stared at her, spellbound in dismay. 'It was all right
until about three years ago. That time you kissed me, in the
summer-house, do you remember? Ever since then I knew . . .
and Charlotte knew, at once. Ever since then she knew, still
knows. Even at this moment, while we're——'

'Stop! Flora . . . !' Without the recollection of having moved toward her he found his arms enfolding her. She lay on his breast, panting, her body shuddering, and her eyes, upturned to his, convulsed. More loudly now, beyond his power to silence or restrain, her voice raced on:

'Even at this moment we're – we're sinning, playing with fire, while she's watching us... I've got to go. It's sacrifice, renunciation, for you, too, for both of us... It's sin! I never knew what sin was like till then, how – yes, how wonderful! Like a black light. I can't resist. We're both of us too weak. I've——'

'Flora, darling Flora, I beg you, I entreat you, listen...!'

She had slid from him to the floor and, still upon her knees, approached the statue. Her hands, upraised, were clasped, as if in supplication, round the stony feet. From that repellent picture, which too instantly suggested some capricious act of worship, he might recoil and turn his eyes away, but could not stop his ears to what he heard.

'I was afraid of you at first – and so was Jasp, but now – we're *proud*! Living in sin, for months and months, under your eyes! It's been our meat and drink... And now you've gone it's just as much a sin. He's still your husband, and you're watching us, the pair of us, in *sin*!'

'Flora, *Flora*...!' Had she gone mad? He must do something, stop her raving, get her out of here, or else——

She had half-raised herself. Her hands, exploring first the statue's breast, stole, with fierce delicacy, over it and downwards, so that she finally was forced to crouch. In this performance she was so engrossed that, when he sprang to her at last, she did not turn her head or seem to notice him.

'Flora, listen! You *must* listen! And believe what I'm going to tell you is the truth. There was no sin. And there is no sin now. It's only – only because you're ill that you imagine it. Charlotte was never like you think. I know it. I can prove it!'

He had seized her hands, but she wrenched them violently from his grasp and raised them once again toward the image. On her face, however, was a peculiar, arrested expression, of mute expectancy, crossed with misgiving.

Protopart continued, slowly and convincingly, throwing

his every ounce of energy behind the measured words so as to capture and retain her wandering attention. 'Charlie was not like that, *not* jealous. She wanted us to marry. And I want it, too. It's in this letter, *here,* this letter. She wanted us to marry after she was gone.'

He waited.

'Do you hear, Flora?'

Her fingers still ran busily about the marble thighs, from which the screening cloth had long since fallen to the floor. Without ceasing her uneasy motion she replied in a low voice:

'You – you mean that? You swear it?'

'About Charlotte? Yes, I tell you that I have the letter *here,* here now. You can show it to whom you like and they can read it to you. I got it from the lawyer a few days ago. It was written before her last stroke. You see, she had – thought of that, even then. If she were with us now she would be *pleased,* not jealous – *pleased* . . . I know that if——' He broke off, all at once, aghast. 'Flora, what are you doing? Flora, the——'

Too late! She was indeed convinced. A spasm, as of appalled comprehension, veiled her eyes, then, passing, left her face abashed and desolate. Her mouth dropped open, but her hands tore frenziedly at Charlotte's knees.

'*Flora,* the——'

With a slow, grinding sound, the upper iron pins began to leave their sockets, and for an instant the great white image seemed to hover, poised in space, above them. Then, as the pattering rain of brick and powdered masonry increased, it lurched. Charlotte's brute weight sped downwards on them both, mangling their limbs, their dreams, involving them in chaos of disintegrated plaster, fractured stone, and drowning out their screams in one colossal and reverberating crash.

iv. *Impromptu Fib*

The air was thick with dust. Protopart's daughters – now including Joyce, the eldest sister – made him out, in the firelight, through a choking, gritty cloud. His face was bloody, but, although prostrate, he apparently had come off far more lightly than his ward. The floor was strewn with rubble and with some broken fragments of the statue – feet and arms. The major mass, however, had remained intact, pinning the wretched Flora to the ground.

Even to the three panic-stricken girls it was quite evident that she had not long to live. Her body, under Charlotte's torso, was grotesquely twisted, and, on the boards nearby, an ominous dark stain was oozing out. As they gazed at her, powerless for several seconds to take any action, her eyes, now glazing, turned in the direction of her guardian. Summoning all her strength, she raised her head. Her lips moved, and the dreadful moaning ceased. They caught her words:

'I – I pulled it down on purpose. He was trying to – Jasper attacked me. He was trying to——'

Mabel, recovering the first, sprang forward suddenly. 'Don't listen to her! Let's try and move this off her chest. Don't listen to her! Fetch a doctor, quick!'

But Flora said no more. Her final and surprising accusation had been made. By the time Protopart had crawled to her, across the wreck, she had already breathed her last.

Thomas De Quincey

THE DICE

THOMAS DE QUINCEY (1785-1859) *is probably best known today for* Confessions of an English Opium Eater (1821), *an autobiographical account of his experiences – first positive and later horrific – with the use of opium. His essay 'On Murder Considered as one of the Fine Arts', a satirical discussion of the aesthetic aspects of murder, influenced many 19th and 20th century authors and was reputedly deemed 'delightful' by Alfred Hitchcock. De Quincey did not write a great deal of fiction; however his* Klosterheim; or, The Masque (1832), *a Gothic novel inspired by the works of Walpole and Radcliffe and probably an influence on Edgar Allan Poe's 'The Masque of the Red Death', is well worth reading and has been reissued by Valancourt. 'The Dice', purportedly a translation from a German original, first appeared in* London Magazine *in August 1823. Featuring a mysterious book bound in black velvet, a demonic bargain, and a pair of haunted dice, it reflects De Quincey's lifelong interest in the Gothic and supernatural.*

FOR MORE THAN 150 YEARS had the family of Schroll been settled at Taubendorf, and generally respected for knowledge and refinement of manners superior to its station. Its present representative, the bailiff Elias Schroll, had in his youth attached himself to literature, but, later in life, from love to the country, he had returned to his native village, and lived there in great credit and esteem.

During this whole period of 150 years, tradition had recorded only one single Schroll as having borne a doubtful character; he, indeed, as many persons affirmed, had dealt with the devil. Certain it is that there was still preserved in the house a scrutoire fixed in the wall, and containing some mysterious manuscripts attributed to him, and the date of the year, 1630, which was carved upon the front, tallied with his era. The key

to this scrutoire had been constantly handed down to the eldest
son through five generations, with a solemn charge to take care
that no other eye or ear should ever become acquainted with
its contents. Every precaution had been taken to guard against
accidents or oversights; the lock was so constructed, that even
with the right key it could not be opened without special
instructions; and for still greater security the present proprietor
had added a padlock of most elaborate workmanship, which
presented a sufficient obstacle before the main lock could be
approached.

In vain did the curiosity of the whole family direct itself to
this scrutoire. Nobody had succeeded in discovering any part of
its contents, except Rudolph, the only son of the bailiff; he *had*
succeeded; at least his own belief was, that the old folio with
gilt edges, and bound in black velvet, which he had one day
surprised his father anxiously reading, belonged to the mysterious scrutoire; for the door of the scrutoire, though not open,
was unlocked, and Elias had hastily closed the book with great
agitation, at the same time ordering his son out of the room in
no very gentle tone. At the time of this incident Rudolph was
about twelve years of age.

Since that time the young man had sustained two great
losses in the deaths of his excellent mother and a sister ten-
derly beloved. His father also had suffered deeply in health
and spirits under these afflictions. Every day he grew more
fretful and humoursome; and Rudolph, upon his final return
home from school in his eighteenth year, was shocked to find
him greatly altered in mind as well as in person. His flesh had
fallen away, and he seemed to be consumed by some internal
strife of thought. It was evidently his own opinion that he was
standing on the edge of the grave, and he employed himself
unceasingly in arranging his affairs, and in making his succes-
sor acquainted with all such arrangements as regarded his more
peculiar interests. One evening as Rudolph came in suddenly
from a neighbor's house, and happened to pass the scrutoire,
he found the door wide open, and the inside obviously empty.
Looking round he observed his father standing on the hearth

close to a great fire, in the midst of which was consuming the old black book.

Elias entreated his son earnestly to withdraw, but Rudolph could not command himself; and he exclaimed, 'I doubt, I doubt, sir, that this is the book which belongs to the scrutoire.'

His father assented with visible confusion.

'Well, then, allow me to say that I am greatly surprised at your treating in this way an heirloom that for a century and more has always been transmitted to the eldest son.'

'You are in the right, my son,' said the father affectionately, taking him by the hand. 'You are partly in the right; it is not quite defensible, I admit; and I myself have had many scruples about the course I have taken. Yet still I feel myself glad upon the whole that I have destroyed this accursed book. He that wrote it never prospered, – all traditions agree in that; why then leave to one's descendants a miserable legacy of unhallowed mysteries?'

This excuse, however, did not satisfy Rudolph. He maintained that his father had made an aggression upon his rights of inheritance; and he argued the point so well, that Elias himself began to see that his son's complaint was not altogether groundless. The whole of the next day they behaved to each other, not unkindly, but yet with some coolness. At night Elias could bear this no longer, and he said, 'Dear Rudolph, we have lived long together in harmony and love; let us not begin to show an altered countenance to each other during the few days that I have yet to live.'

Rudolph pressed his father's offered hand with a filial warmth; and the latter went on to say, 'I purpose now to communicate to you by word of mouth the contents of the book which I have destroyed. I will do this with good faith and without reserve, unless you yourself can be persuaded to forego your own right to such a communication.'

Elias paused, flattering himself as it seemed that his son *would* forego his right. But in this he was mistaken; Rudolph was far too eager for the disclosure, and earnestly pressed his father to proceed.

Again Elias hesitated, and threw a glance of profound love and pity upon his son, – a glance that conjured him to think better, and to waive his claim, but this being at length obviously hopeless, he spoke as follows: 'The book relates chiefly to yourself; it points to you as *to the last of our race*. You turn pale. Surely, Rudolph, it would have been better that you had resolved to trouble yourself no further about it?'

'No,' said Rudolph, recovering his self-possession. 'No; for it still remains a question whether this prophecy be true.'

'It does so; it does, no doubt.'

'And is this all that the book says in regard to me?'

'No, it is *not* all; there is something more. But possibly you will only laugh when you hear it; for at this day nobody believes in such strange stories. However, be *that* as it may, the book goes on to say plainly and positively, that the Evil One (Heaven protect us!) will make you an offer tending greatly to your worldly advantage.'

Rudolph laughed outright, and replied, that, judging by the grave exterior of the book, he had looked to hear of more serious contents.

'Well, well, my son,' said the old man, 'I know not that I myself am disposed to place much confidence in these tales of contracts with the devil. But, true or not, we ought not to laugh at them. Enough for me that under any circumstances I am satisfied you have so much natural piety, that you would reject all worldly good fortune that could meet you upon unhallowed paths.'

Here Elias would have broken off, but Rudolph said, 'One thing more I wish to know: what is to be the nature of the good fortune offered to me? and did the book say whether I should accept it or not?'

'Upon the nature of the good fortune the writer has not explained himself; all that he says is, that by a discreet use of it, it is in your power to become a very great man. Whether you will accept it – but God preserve thee, my child, from any thought so criminal – upon this question there is a profound silence. Nay, it seems even as if this trader in black arts had at that very point been overtaken by death, for he had broken off in the very middle of the word. The Lord have mercy upon his soul!'

Little as Rudolph's faith was in the possibility of such a proposal, yet he was uneasy at his father's communication and visibly disturbed; so that the latter said to him, 'Had it not been better, Rudolph, that you had left the mystery to be buried with me in the grave?'

Rudolph said, 'No:' but his restless eye and his agitated air too evidently approved the accuracy of his father's solicitude.

The deep impression upon Rudolph's mind from this conversation – the last he was ever to hold with his father – was rendered still deeper by the solemn event which followed. About the middle of that same night he was awakened suddenly by a summons to his father's bedside; his father was dying, and earnestly asking for him.

'My son!' he exclaimed with an expression of the bitterest anguish; stretched out both his arms in supplication towards him; and in the anguish of the effort he expired.

The levity of youthful spirits soon dispersed the gloom which at first hung over Rudolph's mind. Surrounded by jovial companions at the university which he now visited, he found no room left in his bosom for sorrow or care: and his heaviest affliction was the refusal of his guardian at times to comply with his too frequent importunities for money.

After a residence of one year at the university, some youthful irregularities in which Rudolph was concerned subjected him, jointly with three others, to expulsion. Just at that time the Seven Years' War happened to break out; two of the party, named Theiler and Werl, entered the military service together with Rudolph; the last very much against the will of a young woman to whom he was engaged. Charlotte herself, however, became reconciled to this arrangement, when she saw that her objections availed nothing against Rudolph's resolution, and heard her lover describe in the most flattering colours his own return to her arms in the uniform of an officer; for that his distinguished courage must carry him in the very first campaign to the rank of lieutenant, was as evident to his own mind as that he could not possibly fall on the field of battle.

The three friends were fortunate enough to be placed in the same company. But, in the first battle, Werl and Theiler were stretched lifeless by Rudolph's side; Werl by a musket-ball through his heart, and Theiler by a cannon-shot which took off his head.

Soon after this event, Rudolph himself returned home; but how? Not, as he had fondly anticipated, in the brilliant decorations of a distinguished officer, but as a prisoner in close custody: in a transport of youthful anger he had been guilty, in company with two others, of insubordination and mutiny.

The court-martial sentenced them to death. The judges, however, were so favorably impressed by their good conduct while under confinement, that they would certainly have recommended them unconditionally to the royal mercy, if it had not been deemed necessary to make an example. However, the sentence was so far mitigated, that only one of the three was to be shot. And which was he? That point was reserved in suspense until the day of execution, when it was to be decided by the cast of the dice.

As the fatal day drew near, a tempest of passionate grief assailed the three prisoners. One of them was agitated by the tears of his father; the second, by the sad situation of a sickly wife and two children. The third, Rudolph, in case the lot fell upon him, would be summoned to part not only with his life, but also with a young and blooming bride, that lay nearer to his heart than anything else in the world. 'Ah!' said he on the evening before the day of final decision, 'Ah! if but this once I could secure a lucky throw of the dice!' And scarce was the wish uttered, when his comrade Werl, whom he had seen fall by his side in the field of battle, stepped into his cell.

'So, brother Schroll, I suppose you didn't much expect to see me?'

'No, indeed, did I not,' exclaimed Rudolph in consternation; for, in fact, on the next day after the battle he had seen with his own eyes this very Werl committed to the grave.

'Ay, ay, it's strange enough, I allow; but there are not many such surgeons as he is that belongs to our regiment; he had me dug up, and brought me round again, I'll assure you. One would think the man was a conjurer. Indeed, there are many things he can do which I defy any man to explain; and to say the truth, I'm convinced he can execute impossibilities.'

'Well, so let him, for aught that I care; all his art will scarcely do me any good.'

'Who knows, brother? who knows? The man is in this town at this very time; and for old friendship's sake I've just spoken to him about you; and he has promised me a lucky throw of the dice, that shall deliver you from all danger.'

'Ah!' said the dejected Rudolph, 'but even this would be of little service to me.'

'Why, how so?' asked the other.

'How so? Why, because – even if there were such dice (a matter I very much dispute) – yet I could never allow myself to turn aside, by black arts, any bad luck designed for myself upon the heads of either of my comrades.'

'Now this, I suppose, is what you call being noble? But excuse me, if I think that in such cases one's first duty is to one's self.'

'Ah, but just consider; one of my comrades has an old father to maintain, the other a sick wife with two children.'

'Schroll, Schroll, if your young bride were to hear you, I fancy she wouldn't think herself much flattered. Does poor Charlotte deserve that you should not bestow a thought on her and her fate? A dear young creature, that places her whole happiness in you, has nearer claims (I think) upon your consideration than an old dotard with one foot in the grave, or a wife and two children that are nothing at all to you. Ah! what a deal of good might you do in the course of a long life with your Charlotte! So then, you really are determined to reject the course which I point out to you? Take care, Schroll! If you disdain my offer, and the lot should chance to fall upon you, – take care lest the thought of a young bride whom you have betrayed, take care I say, lest this thought should add to the bitterness of death when you come to kneel down on the sand-hill. However, I've given you advice sufficient, and have discharged my conscience. Look to it yourself: and farewell!'

'Stay, brother, a word or two,' said Rudolph, who was powerfully impressed by the last speech, and the picture of domestic happiness held up before him, which he had often dallied with in thought, both when alone and in company with Charlotte. 'Stay a moment. Undoubtedly, I do not deny that I wish for life, if I could receive it a gift from Heaven; and *that* is not impossible. Only I would not willingly have the guilt upon my conscience of being the cause of misery to another. However, if the man you speak of can tell, I should be glad that you would ask him upon which of us three the lot of death will fall. Or – stay; don't ask him,' said Rudolph, sighing deeply.

'I have already asked him,' was the answer.

'Ah! have you so? *And it is after his reply that you come to me with this counsel?*'

The foretaste of death overspread the blooming face of Rudolph with a livid paleness; thick drops of sweat gathered upon his forehead; and the other exclaimed with a sneer: 'I'm going; you take too much time for consideration. Maybe you will see and recognize me at the place of execution; and, if so, I shall have the dice with me; and it will not be too late even then to give me a sign; but, take notice, I can't promise to attend.'

Rudolph raised his forehead from the palm of his hand, in which he had buried it during the last moments of his perturbation, and would have spoken something in reply; but his counsellor was already gone. He felt glad, and yet at the same time sorry. The more he considered the man and his appearance, so much the less seemed his resemblance to his friend whom he had left buried on the field of battle. This friend had been the very soul of affectionate cordiality, – a temper that was altogether wanting to his present counsellor. No! the scornful and insulting tone with which he treated the unhappy prisoner, and the unkind manner with which he had left him, convinced Schroll that he and Werl must be two different persons. Just at this moment a thought struck him, like a blast of lightning, of the black book which had perished in the fire and its ominous contents. A lucky cast of the dice! Ay; *that* then was the shape in which the tempter had presented himself; and heartily glad he felt that he had not availed himself of his suggestions.

But this temper of mind was speedily changed by his young bride, who hurried in soon after, sobbing, and flung her arms about his neck. He told her of the proposal which had been made to him; and she was shocked that he had not immediately accepted it.

With a bleeding heart, Rudolph objected that so charming and lovely a creature could not miss of a happy fate, even if he should be forced to quit her. But she protested vehemently that he or nobody should enjoy her love.

The clergyman, who visited the prisoner immediately after her departure, restored some composure to his mind, which had been altogether banished by the presence of his bride. 'Blessed are they who die in the Lord!' said the gray-haired divine; and with so much earnestness and devotion, that this single speech had the happiest effect upon the prisoner's mind.

On the morning after this night of agitation, the morning of the fatal day, the three criminals saw each other for the first time since their arrest. Community of fate, and long separation from each other, contributed to draw still closer the bond of friendship that had been first knit on the field of battle. Each of the three testified a lively abhorrence for the wretched necessity of throwing death to some one of his comrades, by any cast of the dice which should bring life to himself. Dear as their several friends were to all, yet at this moment the brotherly league, which had been tried and proved in the furnace of battle, was triumphant over all opposing considerations. Each would have preferred death himself, rather than escape it at the expense of his comrade.

The worthy clergyman, who possessed their entire confidence, found them loudly giving utterance to this heroic determination. Shaking his head, he pointed their attention to those who had claims upon them whilst living, and for whom it was their duty to wish to live as long as possible. 'Place your trust in God!' said he: 'resign yourselves to him! He it is that will bring about the decision through your hands; and think not of ascribing that power to yourselves, or to his lifeless instruments – the dice. He, without whose permission no sparrow falls to the ground, and who has numbered every hair upon your head – He it is that knows best what is good for you; and He only.'

The prisoners assented by squeezing his hand, embraced each other, and received the sacrament in the best disposition of mind. After this ceremony they breakfasted together, in as resigned, nay, almost in as joyous a mood as if the gloomy and bloody morning which lay before them were ushering in some gladsome festival.

When, however, the procession was marshalled from the outer gate, and their beloved friends were admitted to utter their last farewells, then again the sternness of their courage sank beneath the burden of their melancholy fate. 'Rudolph!' whispered amongst the rest his despairing bride, 'Rudolph! why did you reject the help that was offered to you?' He adjured her not to add to the bitterness of parting; and she in turn adjured him, a little before the word of command was given to march, – which robbed her of all consciousness, – to make a sign to the stranger who had volunteered his offer of deliverance, provided he should anywhere observe him in the crowd.

The streets and the windows were lined with spectators. Vainly did each of the criminals seek, by accompanying the clergyman in his prayers, to shelter himself from the thought, that all return, perhaps, was cut off from him. The large house of his bride's father reminded Schroll of a happiness that was now lost to him forever, if any faith were to be put in the words of his yesterday's monitor; and a very remarkable faintness came over him. The clergyman, who was acquainted with the circumstances of his case, and therefore guessed the occasion of his sudden agitation, laid hold of his arm, and said, with a powerful voice, that he who trusted in God would assuredly see all his *righteous* hopes accomplished – in this world, if it were God's pleasure; but, if not, in a better.

These were words of comfort: but their effect lasted only for a few moments. Outside the city gate his eyes were met by the sand-hill already thrown up; a spectacle which renewed his earthly hopes and fears. He threw a hurried glance about him: but nowhere could he see his last night's visitor.

Every moment the decision came nearer and nearer. It has begun. One of the three has already shaken the box: the die is cast; he has thrown a six. This throw was now registered amidst the solemn silence of the crowd. The by-standers regarded him with solemn congratulations in their eyes; for this man and Rudolph were the two special objects of the general compassion: this man, as the husband and father; Rudolph, as the youngest and handsomest, and because some report had gone abroad of his superior education and attainments.

Rudolph was youngest in a double sense; youngest in years, and youngest in the service: for both reasons he was to throw last. It may be supposed, therefore, how much all present trembled for the poor delinquent, when the second of his comrades likewise flung a six.

Prostrated in spirit, Rudolph stared at the unpropitious die. Then a second time he threw a horrid glance around him, and that so full of despair, that from horrid sympathy a violent shuddering ran through the by-standers. 'Here is no deliverer,' thought Rudolph; 'none to see me or to hear me! And if there were, it is now too late; for no change of the die is any longer possible.' So saying, he seized the fatal die, convulsively his hand clutches it, and before the throw is made he feels that the die is broken in two.

During the universal thrill of astonishment which succeeded to this strange accident, he looked round again. A sudden shock and a sudden joy fled through his countenance. Not far from him, in the dress of a pedler, stands Theiler without a wound, the comrade whose head had been carried off on the field of battle by a cannon-ball. Rudolph made an under-sign to him with his eye; for clear as it now was to his mind with whom he was dealing, yet the dreadful trial of the moment overpowered his better resolutions.

The military commission were in some confusion. No provision having been thought of against so strange an accident, there was no second die at hand. They were just on the point of despatching a messenger to fetch one, when the pedler presented himself with the offer of supplying the loss. The new die is examined by the auditor, and delivered to the unfortunate Rudolph. He throws; the die is lying on the drum, and again it is a six! The amazement is universal; nothing is decided; the throws must be repeated. They *are*; and Weber, the husband of the sick wife, the father of the two half-naked children, flings the lowest throw.

Immediately the officer's voice was heard wheeling his men into their position. On the part of Weber there was as little delay. The overwhelming injury to his wife and children, indicted by his own act, was too mighty to contemplate. He shook hands rapidly with his two comrades; stept nimbly into his place; kneeled down. The word of command was heard, 'Lower your muskets;' instantly he dropped the fatal handkerchief with the gesture of one who prays for some incalculable blessing, and, in the twinkling of an eye, sixteen bullets had lightened the heart of the poor mutineer from its whole immeasurable freight of anguish.

All the congratulations with which they were welcomed on their return into the city, fell powerless on Rudolph's ear. Scarcely could even Charlotte's caresses affect with any pleasure the man who believed himself to have sacrificed his comrade through collusion with a fiend.

The importunities of Charlotte prevailed over all objections which the pride of her aged father suggested against a son-in-law who had been capitally convicted. The marriage was solemnized; but at the wedding-festival, amidst the uproar of merriment, the parties chiefly concerned were not happy or tranquil. In no long time the father-in-law died, and by his death placed the young couple in a state of complete independence; but Charlotte's fortune, and the remainder of what Rudolph had inherited from his father, were speedily swallowed up by an idle and luxurious mode of living. Rudolph now began to ill-use his wife. To escape from his own conscience, he plunged into all sorts of dissolute courses; and very remarkable it was, that, from manifesting the most violent abhorrence for everything which could lead his thoughts to his own fortunate cast of the die, he gradually came to entertain so uncontrollable a passion for playing at dice, that he spent all his time in the company of those with whom he could turn this passion to account. His house had long since passed out of his own hands; not a soul could be found anywhere to lend him a shilling. The sickly widow of Weber, and her two children, whom he had hitherto supported, lost their home and means of livelihood, and in no long space of time the same fate fell upon himself, his wife, and his child.

Too little used to labour to have any hope of improving his condition in that way, one day he bethought himself that the Medical Institute was in the habit of purchasing from poor people, during their lifetime, the reversion of their bodies. To this establishment he addressed himself; and the ravages in his personal appearance and health, caused by his dissolute life, induced them the more readily to lend an ear to his proposal.

But the money thus obtained, which had been designed for the support of his wife and half-famished children, was squandered at the gaming-table. As the last dollar vanished, Schroll bit one of the dice furiously between his teeth. Just then he heard these words whispered at his ear, – 'Gently, brother, gently; all dice do not split in two like that on the sand-hill.' He looked round in agitation, but saw no trace of any one who could have uttered the words.

With dreadful imprecations on himself and those with whom he had played, he flung out of the gaming-house home-wards on his road to the wretched garret, where his wife and children were awaiting his return and his succor; but here the poor creatures, tormented by hunger and cold, pressed upon him so importunately, that he had no way to deliver himself from misery but by flying from the spectacle. But whither could he go thus late at night, when his utter poverty was known in every alehouse? Roaming he knew not whither, he found himself at length in the churchyard. The moon was shining solemnly upon the quiet gravestones, though obscured at intervals by piles of stormy clouds. Rudolph shuddered at nothing but at himself and his own existence. He strode with bursts of laughter over the dwellings of the departed, and entered a vault which gave him shelter from the icy blasts of wind which now began to bluster more loudly than before. The moon threw her rays into the vault full upon the golden legend inscribed in the wall, – *'Blessed are the dead that die in the Lord!'* Schroll took up a spade that was sticking in the ground, and struck with it furiously against the gilt letters on the wall, but they seemed indestructible; and he was going to assault them with a mattock, when suddenly a hand touched him on the shoulder, and said to him, 'Gently, comrade; thy pains are all thrown away.' Schroll uttered a loud exclamation of terror, for in these words he heard the voice of Weber, and, on turning round, recognized his whole person.

'What wouldst thou have?' asked Rudolph. 'What art thou come for?'

'To comfort thee,' replied the figure, which now suddenly assumed the form and voice of the pedler to whom Schroll was indebted for the fortunate die. 'Thou hast forgotten me; and thence it is that thou art fallen into misfortune. Look up and acknowledge thy friend in need, that comes only to make thee happy again.'

'If *that* be thy purpose, wherefore is it that thou wearest a shape, before which, of all others that have been on earth, I have most reason to shudder?'

'The reason is, because I must not allow to any man my help or my converse on too easy terms. Before ever my die was allowed to turn thy fate, I was compelled to give thee certain intimations from which thou knewest with whom it was that thou wert dealing.'

'With whom, then, was it that I was dealing?' cried Schroll, staring with his eyes wide open, and his hair standing erect.

'Thou knewest, comrade, at that time, thou knewest at this moment,' said the pedler laughing, and tapping him on the shoulder. 'But what is it that thou desirest?'

Schroll struggled internally; but, overcome by his desolate

condition, he said immediately, 'Dice: I would have dice that shall win whenever I wish.'

'Very well; but first of all stand out of the blaze of this golden writing on the wall; it is a writing that has nothing to do with thee. Here are dice; never allow them to go out of thy own possession; for *that* might bring thee into great trouble. When thou needest me, light a fire at the last stroke of the midnight hour; throw in my dice and with loud laughter. They will crack once or twice, and then split. At that moment catch at them in the flames; but let not the moment slip, or thou art lost. And let not thy courage be daunted by the sights that I cannot but send before me whensoever I appear. Lastly, avoid choosing any holy day for this work; and beware of the priest's benediction. Here, take the dice.'

Schroll caught at the dice with one hand, whilst with the other he covered his eyes. When he next looked up, he was standing alone.

He now quitted the burying-ground to return as hastily as possible to the gaming-house, where the light of candles was still visible. But it was with the greatest difficulty that he obtained money enough from a 'friend' to enable him to make the lowest stake which the rules allowed. He found it a much easier task to persuade the company to use the dice which he had brought with him. They saw in this nothing but a very common superstition, and no possibility of any imposture, as they and he should naturally have benefited alike by the good luck supposed to accompany the dice. But the nature of the charm was, that only the possessor of the dice enjoyed their supernatural powers; and hence it was, that, towards morning, Schroll reeled home intoxicated with wine and pleasure, and laden with the money of all present, to the garret where his family were lying, half frozen and famished.

Their outward condition was immediately improved. The money which Schroll had won was sufficient not only for their immediate and most pressing wants: it was enough also to pay for a front apartment, and to leave a sum sufficient for a very considerable stake.

With this sum, and in better attire, Rudolph repaired to a gaming-house of more fashionable resort, and came home in the evening laden with gold.

He now opened a gaming establishment himself; and so much did his family improve in external appearances within a very few weeks, that the police began to keep a watchful eye over him.

This induced him to quit the city, and to change his residence continually. All the different baths of Germany he resorted to beyond other towns: but, though his dice perseveringly maintained their luck, he yet never accumulated any money. Everything was squandered upon the dissipated life which he and his family pursued.

At length, at the Baths of ——, the matter began to take an unfortunate turn. A violent passion for a beautiful young lady whom Rudolph had attached himself to in vain at balls, concerts, and even at church, suddenly bereft him of all sense and discretion. One night when Schroll (who now styled himself Captain von Schrollshausen) was anticipating a master-stroke from his dice, probably for the purpose of winning the lady by the display of overflowing wealth and splendour, suddenly they lost their virtue, and failed him without warning. Hitherto they had lost only when he willed them to lose: but, on this occasion, they failed at so critical a moment, as to lose him not only all his own money, but a good deal beside that he had borrowed.

Foaming with rage, he came home. He asked furiously after his wife: she was from home. He examined the dice attentively; and it appeared to him that they were not his own. A powerful suspicion seized upon him. Madame von Schrollshausen had her own gaming circle as well as himself. Without betraying its origin, he had occasionally given her a few specimens of the privilege attached to his dice: and she had pressed him earnestly to allow her the use of them for a single evening. It was true he never parted with them even on going to bed: but it was possible that they might have been changed whilst he was sleeping. The more he brooded upon this suspicion, the more it strengthened: from being barely possible, it became probable: from a probability it ripened into a certainty; and this certainty received the fullest confirmation at this moment, when she returned home in the gayest temper, and announced to him that she had been this night overwhelmed with good luck; in proof of which, she poured out upon the table a considerable sum in gold coin. 'And now,' she added laughingly, 'I care no longer for your dice; nay, to tell you the truth, I would not exchange my own for them.'

Rudolph, now confirmed in his suspicions, demanded the dice, as his property that had been purloined from him. She laughed and refused. He insisted with more vehemence; she retorted with warmth; both parties were irritated: and, at length, in the extremity of his wrath, Rudolph snatched up a knife and stabbed her; the knife pierced her heart; she uttered a single sob, was convulsed for a moment, and expired. 'Cursed accident!' he exclaimed, when it clearly appeared, on examination, that the dice which she had in her purse were not those which he suspected himself to have lost.

No eye but Rudolph's had witnessed the murder: the child had slept on undisturbed: but circumstances betrayed it to the knowledge of the landlord; and, in the morning, he was preparing to make it public. By great offers, however, Rudolph succeeded in purchasing the man's silence: he engaged in substance to make over to the landlord a large sum of money, and to marry his daughter, with whom he had long pursued a clandestine intrigue. Agreeably to this arrangement, it was publicly notified that Madame von Schrollshausen had destroyed herself under a sudden attack of hypochondriasis, to which she had been long subject. Some there were undoubtedly who chose to be sceptics on this matter: but nobody had an interest sufficiently deep in the murdered person to prompt him to a legal inquiry.

A fact, which at this time gave Rudolph far more disturbance of mind than the murder of his once beloved wife, was the full confirmation, upon repeated experience, that his dice had forfeited their power. For he had now been a loser for two days running to so great an extent, that he was obliged to abscond on a misty night. His child, towards whom his affection increased daily, he was under the necessity of leaving with his host, as a pledge for his return and fulfilment of his promises. He would not have absconded, if it had been in his power to summon his dark counsellor forthwith; but on account of the great festival of Pentecost, which fell on the very next day, this summons was necessarily delayed for a short time. By staying, he would have reduced himself to the necessity of inventing various pretexts for delay, in order to keep up his character with his creditors; whereas, when he returned with a sum of money sufficient to meet his debts, all suspicions would be silenced at once.

In the metropolis of an adjacent territory, to which he resorted so often that he kept lodgings there constantly, he passed Whitsunday with impatience, and resolved on the succeeding night to summon and converse with his counsellor. Impatient, however, as he was of any delay, he did not on that account feel the less anxiety as the hour of midnight approached. Though he was quite alone in his apartments, and had left his servant behind at the baths, yet long before midnight he fancied that he heard footsteps and whisperings round about him. The purpose he was meditating, that he had regarded till now as a matter of indifference, now displayed itself in its whole monstrous shape. Moreover, he remembered that his wicked counsellor had himself thought it necessary to exhort him to courage, which at present he felt greatly shaken. However, he had no choice. As he was enjoined, therefore, with the last stroke of twelve, he set on fire the wood which lay ready split upon the hearth, and threw the dice into the flames, with a loud laughter that echoed frightfully from the empty hall and staircases. Confused and half stifled by the smoke which accompanied the roaring flames, he stood still for a few minutes, when suddenly all the surrounding objects seemed changed, and he found himself transported to his father's house. His father was lying on his death-bed just as he had actually beheld him. He had upon his lips the very same expression of supplication and anguish with which he had at that time striven to address him. Once again he stretched out his arms in love and pity to his son; and once again he seemed to expire in the act.

Schroll was agitated by the picture, which called up and re-animated in his memory, with the power of a mighty tormentor, all his honourable plans and prospects from that innocent period of his life. At this moment the dice cracked for the first time; and Schroll turned his face towards the flames. A second time the smoke stifled the light in order to reveal a second picture. He saw himself on the day before the scene of the sand-hill, sitting in his dungeon. The clergyman was with him. From the expression of his countenance, he appeared to be just saying: 'Blessed are the dead that die in the Lord.' Rudolph thought of the disposition in which he then was, of the hopes which the clergyman had raised in him, and of the feeling which he then had, that he was still worthy to be reunited to his father, or had become worthy by bitter penitence. The next fracture of the die disturbed the scene, – but to substitute one that was not at all more consolatory. For now appeared a den of thieves, in which the unhappy widow of Weber was cursing her children, who – left without support, without counsel, without protection – had taken to evil courses. In the background stood the bleeding father of these ruined children, one hand stretched out towards Schroll with a menacing gesture, and the other lifted towards heaven with a record of impeachment against him.

At the third splitting of the dice, out of the bosom of the smoke arose the figure of his murdered wife, who seemed to chase him from one corner of the room to another, until at length she came and took a seat at the fire-place; by the side of which, as Rudolph now observed with horror, his buried father and the unhappy Weber had stretched themselves; and they carried on together a low and noiseless whispering and moaning, that agitated him with a mysterious horror.

After long and hideous visions, Rudolph beheld the flames grow weaker and weaker. He approached. The figures that stood round about held up their hands in a threatening attitude. A moment later, and the time was gone for ever; and Rudolph, as his false friend had asserted, was a lost man. With the courage of despair he plunged through the midst of the threatening figures, and snatched at the glowing dice, – which were no sooner touched than they split asunder with a dreadful sound, before which the apparitions vanished in a body.

The evil counsellor appeared on this occasion in the dress of a grave-digger, and asked, with a snorting sound, 'What wouldst thou from me?'

'I would remind you of your promise,' answered Schroll, stepping back with awe; 'your dice have lost their power.'

'Through whose fault?'

Rudolph was silent, and covered his eyes from the withering glances of the fiendish being who was gazing upon him.

'Thy foolish desires led thee in chase of the beautiful maiden into the church; my words were forgotten; and the benediction, against which I warned thee, disarmed the dice of their power. In future observe my directions better.'

So saying he vanished; and Schroll found three new dice upon the hearth.

After such scenes sleep was not to be thought of; and Rudolph resolved, if possible, to make trial of his dice this very night. The ball at the hotel over the way, to which he had been invited, and from which the steps of the waltzers were still audible, appeared to present a fair opportunity. Thither he repaired; but not without some anxiety, lest some of the noises in his own lodgings should have reached the houses over the way. He was happy to find this fear unfounded. Everything appeared as if calculated only for *his* senses; for when he inquired, with assumed carelessness, what great explosion *that* was which occurred about midnight, nobody acknowledged to having heard it.

The dice also, he was happy to find, answered his expectations. He found a company engaged at play, and, by the break of day, he had met with so much luck, that he was immediately able to travel back to the baths, and to redeem his child and his word of honour.

In the baths he now made as many new acquaintances as the losses were important which he had lately sustained. He was reputed one of the wealthiest cavaliers in the place; and many who had designs upon him in consequence of this reputed wealth, willingly lost money to him to favor their own schemes; so that in a single month he gained sums which would have established him as a man of fortune. Under countenance of this repute, and as a widower, no doubt he might now have made successful advances to the young lady whom he had formerly pursued, for her father had an exclusive regard to property, and would have overlooked morals and respectability of that sort in any candidate for his daughter's hand; but with the largest offers of money, he could not purchase his freedom from the contract made with his landlord's daughter, – a woman of very disreputable character. In fact, six months after the death of his first wife, he was married to her.

By the unlimited profusion of money with which his second wife sought to wash out the stains upon her honour, Rudolph's new-raised property was as speedily squandered. To part from her, was one of the wishes which lay nearest his heart. He had, however, never ventured to express it a second time before his father-in-law, for, on the single occasion when he had hinted at such an intention, that person had immediately broken out into the most dreadful threats. The murder of his first wife was the chain which bound him to his second. The boy whom his first wife had left him, closely as he resembled her in features and in the bad traits of her character, was his only comfort, if indeed his gloomy and perturbed mind would allow him at any time to taste of comfort.

To preserve this boy from the evil influences of the many bad examples about him, he had already made an agreement with a man of distinguished abilities, who was to have superintended his education in his own family. But all was frustrated. Madame von Schrollshausen, whose love of pomp and display led her eagerly to catch at every pretext for creating a *fête*, had invited a party on the evening before the young boy's intended departure. The time which was not occupied in the eating-room was spent at the gaming-table, and dedicated to the dice, of whose extraordinary powers the owner was at this time availing himself with more zeal than usual, having just invested all his dis-

posable money in the purchase of a landed estate. One of the
guests having lost very considerable sums in an uninterrupted
train of ill-luck, threw the dice, in his vexation, with such force
upon the table, that one of them fell down. The attendants
searched for it on the floor, and the child also crept about in
quest of it. Not finding it, he rose, and in rising stept upon it,
lost his balance, and fell with such violence against the edge of
the stove, that he died in a few hours of the injury inflicted on
the head.

This accident made the most powerful impression upon
the father. He recapitulated the whole of his life from the first
trial he had made of the dice; from them had arisen all his
misfortunes; in what way could he liberate himself from their
accursed influence? Revolving this point, and in the deepest
distress of mind, Schroll wandered out towards nightfall, and
strolled through the town. Coming to a solitary bridge in the
outskirts, he looked down from the battlements upon the
gloomy depths of the waters below, which seemed to regard
him with looks of sympathy and strong fascination. 'So be it
then!' he exclaimed, and sprang over the railing; but instead
of finding his grave in the waters, he felt himself below seized
powerfully by the grasp of a man, whom, from his scornful
laugh, he recognized as his evil counsellor. The man bore him
to the shore, and said, 'No, no! my good friend; he that once
enters into a league with me, him I shall deliver from death
even in his own despite.'

Half crazy with despair, the next morning Schroll crept out
of the town with a loaded pistol. Spring was abroad; spring
flowers, spring breezes, and nightingales. They were all abroad,
but not for *him* or *his* delight. A crowd of itinerant trades-
men passed him, who were on the road to a neighboring fair.
One of them, observing his dejected countenance with pity,
attached himself to his side, and asked in a tone of sympathy
what was the matter. Two others of the passers-by Schroll
heard distinctly saying, 'Faith, I should not like, for my part, to
walk alone with such an ill-looking fellow.' He darted a furious
glance at the men, separated from his pitying companion with

a fervent pressure of his hand, and struck off into a solitary track of the forest. In the first retired spot he fired the pistol, and behold the man who had spoken to him with so much kindness lies stretched in his blood, and he himself is without a wound. At this moment, while staring half unconsciously at the face of the murdered man, he feels himself seized from behind. Already he seems to himself in the hands of the public executioner. Turning round, however, he hardly knows whether to feel pleasure or pain on seeing his evil suggester in the dress of a grave-digger. 'My friend,' said the grave-digger, 'if you cannot be content to wait for death until I send it, I must be forced to end with dragging you to *that* from which I began by saving you, – a public execution. But think not thus, or by any other way, to escape me. After death, thou wilt assuredly be mine again.'

'Who, then,' said the unhappy man, 'who is the murderer of the poor traveller?'

'Who? why, who but yourself? Was it not yourself that fired the pistol?'

'Ay, but at my own head.'

The fiend laughed in a way that made Schroll's flesh creep on his bones. 'Understand this, friend, that he whose fate I hold in my hands cannot anticipate it by his own act. For the present, begone, if you would escape the scaffold. To oblige you once more, I shall throw a veil over this murder.'

Thereupon the grave-digger set about making a grave for the corpse, whilst Schroll wandered away, – more for the sake of escaping the hideous presence in which he stood, than with any view to his own security from punishment.

Seeing by accident a prisoner under arrest at the guardhouse, Schroll's thoughts reverted to his own confinement. 'How happy,' said he, 'for me and for Charlotte, had I then refused to purchase life on such terms, and had better laid to heart the counsel of my good spiritual adviser!' Upon this a sudden thought struck him, that he would go and find out the old clergyman, and would unfold to him his wretched history and situation. He told his wife that some private affairs required his attendance for a few days at the town of ——. But, say what he would, he could not prevail on her to desist from accompanying him.

On the journey his chief anxiety was lest the clergyman, who was already advanced in years at the memorable scene of the sand-hill, might now be dead. But at the very entrance of the town he saw him walking in the street, and immediately felt himself more composed in mind than he had done for years. The venerable appearance of the old man confirmed him still more in his resolution of making a full disclosure to him of his whole past life: one only transaction, the murder of his first wife, he thought himself justified in concealing; since, with all his penitence for it, that act was now beyond the possibility of reparation.

For a long time the pious clergyman refused all belief to Schroll's narrative; but being at length convinced that he had a wounded spirit to deal with, and not a disordered intellect, he exerted himself to present all those views of religious consolation which his philanthropic character and his long experience suggested to him as likely to be effectual. Eight days' conversation with the clergyman restored Schroll to the hopes of a less miserable future. But the good man admonished him at parting to put away from himself whatsoever could in any way tend to support his unhallowed connection.

In this direction Schroll was aware that the dice were included: and he resolved firmly that his first measure on returning home should be to bury in an inaccessible place these accursed implements, that could not but bring mischief to every possessor. On entering the inn, he was met by his wife, who was in the highest spirits, and laughing profusely. He inquired the cause. 'No,' said she: 'you refused to communicate your motive for coming hither, and the nature of your business for the last week: I, too, shall have my mysteries. As to your leaving me in solitude at an inn, *that* is a sort of courtesy which marriage naturally brings with it; but that you should have travelled hither for no other purpose than that of trifling away your time in the company of an old tedious parson, *that* (you will

allow me to say) is a caprice which seems scarcely worth the
money it will cost.'

'Who, then, has told you that I have passed my time with an
old parson?' said the astonished Schroll.

'Who told me? Why, just let me know what your business
was with the parson, and I'll let you know in turn who it was
that told me. So much I will assure you, however, now, – that
the cavalier, who was my informant, is a thousand times hand-
somer, and a more interesting companion, than an old dotard
who is standing at the edge of the grave.'

All the efforts of Madame von Schrollshausen to irritate
the curiosity of her husband proved ineffectual to draw from
him his secret. The next day, on their return homewards, she
repeated her attempts. But he parried them all with firmness.
A more severe trial to his firmness was prepared for him in the
heavy bills which his wife presented to him on his reaching
home. Her expenses in clothes and in jewels had been so pro-
fuse, that no expedient remained to Schroll but that of selling
without delay the landed estate he had so lately purchased. A
declaration to this effect was very ill received by his wife. 'Sell
the estate?' said she; 'what, sell the sole resource I shall have to
rely on when you are dead? And for what reason, I should be
glad to know; when a very little of the customary luck of your
dice will enable you to pay off these trifles? And whether the
bills be paid to-day or to-morrow cannot be of any very great
importance.' Upon this, Schroll declared with firmness that he
never meant to play again. 'Not play again!' exclaimed his wife,
'pooh! pooh! you make me blush for you! So, then, I suppose
it's all true, as was said, that scruples of conscience drove you to
the old rusty parson; and that he enjoined as a penance that you
should abstain from gaming? I was told as much: but I refused
to believe it; for in your circumstances the thing seemed too
senseless and irrational.'

'My dear girl,' said Schroll, 'consider – '

'Consider! what's the use of considering? what is there to
consider about?' interrupted Madame von Schrollshausen:
and, recollecting the gay cavalier whom she had met at the inn,

she now, for the first time, proposed a separation herself. 'Very well,' said her husband, 'I am content.' 'So am I,' said his father-in-law, who joined them at that moment. 'But take notice that first of all I must have paid over to me an adequate sum of money for the creditable support of my daughter: else – '

Here he took Schroll aside, and the old threat of revealing the murder so utterly disheartened him, that at length in despair he consented to his terms.

Once more, therefore, the dice were to be tried; but only for the purpose of accomplishing the separation: *that* over, Schroll resolved to seek a livelihood in any other way, even if it were as a day-labourer. The stipulated sum was at length all collected within a few hundred dollars; and Schroll was already looking out for some old disused well into which he might throw the dice, and then have it filled up; for even a river seemed to him a hiding-place not sufficiently secure for such instruments of misery.

Remarkable it was on the very night when the last arrears were to be obtained of his father-in-law's demand – a night which Schroll had anticipated with so much bitter anxiety – that he became unusually gloomy and dejected. He was particularly disturbed by the countenance of a stranger, who for several days running had lost considerable sums. The man called himself Stutz; but he had a most striking resemblance to his old comrade Weber, who had been shot at the sand-hill; and differed indeed in nothing but in the advantage of blooming youth. Scarce had he leisure to recover from the shock which this spectacle occasioned, when a second occurred. About midnight another man, whom nobody knew, came up to the gaming-table, and interrupted the play by recounting an event which he represented as having just happened. A certain man, he said, had made a covenant with some person or other that they call the Evil One, – or what is it you call him? – and by means of this covenant he had obtained a steady run of good luck at play. 'Well, sir,' he went on, 'and would you believe it, the other day he began to repent of this covenant; my gentleman wanted to rat, he wanted to rat, sir. Only, first of all, he resolved privately to make up a certain sum of money. Ah, the poor idiot! he little knew whom he had to deal with: the Evil One, as they choose to call him, was not a man to let himself be swindled in that manner. No, no, my good friend. I saw – I mean, the Evil One saw – what was going on betimes; and he secured the swindler just as he fancied himself on the point of pocketing the last arrears of the sum wanted.'

The company began to laugh so loudly at this pleasant fiction, as they conceived it, that Madame von Schrollshausen was attracted from the adjoining room. The story was repeated to her; and she was the more delighted with it, because in the relater she recognized the gay cavalier whom she had met at the inn. Everybody laughed again, except two persons, – Stutz and Schroll. The first had again lost all the money in his purse; and the second was so confounded by the story, that he could not forbear staring with fixed eyes on the stranger, who stood over against him. His consternation increased when he perceived that the stranger's countenance seemed to alter at every moment; and that nothing remained unchanged in it, except the cold expression of inhuman scorn with which he perseveringly regarded himself.

At length he could endure this no longer: and he remarked, therefore, upon Stutz again losing a bet, that it was now late; that Mr Stutz was too much in a run of bad luck; and that on these accounts he would defer the further pursuit of their play until another day. And thereupon he put the dice into his pocket.

'Stop!' said the strange cavalier; and the voice froze Schroll with horror; for he knew too well to whom that dreadful tone and those fiery eyes belonged.

'Stop!' he said again; 'produce your dice!' And tremblingly Schroll threw them upon the table.

'Ah! I thought as much,' said the stranger; 'they are loaded dice!' So saying, he called for a hammer, and struck one of them in two. 'See!' said he to Stutz, holding out to him the broken dice, which in fact seemed loaded with lead. 'Stop! vile impostor!' exclaimed the young man, as Schroll was preparing to quit the room in the greatest confusion; and he threw the dice at him, one of which lodged in his right eye. The tumult increased; the police came in; and Stutz was apprehended, as Schroll's wound assumed a very dangerous appearance.

Next day Schroll was in a violent fever. He asked repeatedly for Stutz. But Stutz had been committed to close confinement; it having been found that he had travelled with false passes. He now confessed that he was one of the sons of the mutineer Weber; that his sickly mother had died soon after his father's execution; and that himself and his brother, left without the control of guardians, and without support, had taken to bad courses.

On hearing this report, Schroll rapidly worsened; and he unfolded to a young clergyman his whole unfortunate history. About midnight, he sent again in great haste for the clergyman. He came. But at sight of him Schroll stretched out his hands in extremity of horror, and waved him away from his presence; but before his signals were complied with, the wretched man had expired in convulsions.

From his horror at the sight of the young clergyman, and from the astonishment of the clergyman himself, on arriving and hearing that he had already been seen in the sick-room, it was inferred that his figure had been assumed for fiendish purposes. The dice and the strange cavalier disappeared at the same time with their wretched victim, and were seen no more.

Basil Copper

CAMERA OBSCURA

BASIL COPPER (1924-2013) *was a prolific writer of novels and short stories, including the series of hard-boiled thrillers featuring Los Angeles detective Mike Faraday and several works featuring the character Solar Pons, a pastiche of Sherlock Holmes. Three of his novels – the Lovecraftian gem* The Great White Space (1974), *the Victorian gaslight Gothic* Necropolis (1980), *and the old-fashioned werewolf novel* The House of the Wolf (1983) – *have been reissued by Valancourt Books. His horror stories in particular were highly regarded, with Colin Wilson calling him 'one of the last great traditionalists of English fiction' and Michael and Mollie Hardwick declaring him to be 'in the same class as M. R. James and Algernon Blackwood'. 'Camera Obscura', one of his earliest tales, first appeared in the sixth volume of Herbert Van Thal's legendary* Pan Book of Horror Stories *series and is perhaps one of the most outright chilling tales in this volume.*

A S MR SHARSTED PUSHED HIS WAY up the narrow, fussily conceived lanes that led to the older part of the town, he was increasingly aware that there was something about Mr Gingold he didn't like. It was not only the old-fashioned, outdated air of courtesy that irritated the moneylender but the gentle, absent-minded way in which he continually put off settlement. Almost as if money were of no importance.

The moneylender hesitated even to say this to himself; the thought was a blasphemy that rocked the very foundations of his world. He pursed his lips grimly and set himself to mount the ill-paved and flinty roadway that bisected the hilly terrain of this remote part of the town.

The moneylender's narrow, lopsided face was perspiring under his hard hat; lank hair started from beneath the brim, which lent him a curious aspect. This, combined with the green-tinted spectacles he wore, gave him a sinister, decayed look, like someone long dead. The thought may have occurred to the few, scattered passers-by he met in the course of his ascent, for almost to a person they gave one cautious glance and then hurried on as though eager to be rid of his presence.

He turned in at a small courtyard and stood in the shelter of a great old ruined church to catch his breath; his heart was thumping uncomfortably in the confines of his narrow chest and his breath rasped in his throat. Assuredly, he was out of condition, he told himself. Long hours of sedentary work huddled over his accounts were taking their toll; he really must get out more and take some exercise.

The moneylender's sallow face brightened momentarily as he thought of his increasing prosperity, but then he frowned again as he remembered the purpose of his errand. Gingold must be made to toe the line, he told himself, as he set out over the last half-mile of his journey.

If he couldn't raise the necessary cash, there must be many valuables in that rambling old house of his which he could sell and realize on. As Mr Sharsted forged his way deeper into this forgotten corner of the town, the sun, which was already low in the sky, seemed to have already set, the light was so constricted by the maze of small courts and alleys into which he had plunged. He was panting again when he came at last, abruptly, to a large green door, set crookedly at the top of a flight of time-worn steps.

He stood arrested for a moment or two, one hand grasping the old balustrade, even his mean soul uplifted momentarily by the sight of the smoky haze of the town below, tilted beneath the yellow sky. Everything seemed to be set awry upon this hill, so that the very horizon rushed slanting across the far distance, giving the spectator a feeling of vertigo. A bell pealed faintly as he seized an iron scrollwork pull set into a metal rose alongside the front door. The moneylender's thoughts were turned to irritation again; everything about Mr Gingold was peculiar, he felt. Even the fittings of his household were things one never saw elsewhere.

Though this might be an advantage if he ever gained control of Mr Gingold's assets and had need to sell the property; there must be a lot of valuable stuff in this old house he had never seen, he mused. Which was another reason he felt it strange that the old man was unable to pay his dues; he must have a great deal of money, if not in cash, in property, one way or another.

He found it difficult to realize why Mr Gingold kept hedging over a matter of three hundred pounds; he could easily sell the old place and go to live in a more attractive part of town in a modern, well-appointed villa and still keep his antiquarian interests. Mr Sharsted sighed. Still, it was none of his business. All he was concerned with was the matter of the money; he had been kept waiting long enough, and he wouldn't be fobbed off any longer. Gingold had got to settle by Monday, or he'd make things unpleasant for him.

Mr Sharsted's thin lips tightened in an ugly manner as he mused on, oblivious of the sunset staining the upper storeys of the old houses and dyeing the mean streets below the hill a rich carmine. He pulled the bell again impatiently, and this time the door was opened almost immediately.

Mr Gingold was a very tall, white-haired man with a gentle, almost apologetic manner. He stood slightly stooping in the doorway, blinking as though astonished at the sunlight, half afraid it would fade him if he allowed too much of it to absorb him.

His clothes, which were of good quality and cut, were untidy and sagged loosely on his big frame; they seemed washed out in the bright light of the sun and appeared to Mr Sharsted to be all of a part with the man himself; indeed, Mr Gingold was rinsed to a pale, insipid shade by the sunshine, so that his white hair and face and clothing ran into one another and, somehow, the different aspects of the picture became blurred and indeterminate.

To Mr Sharsted he bore the aspect of an old photograph which had never been properly fixed and had turned brown and faded with time. Mr Sharsted thought he might blow away with the breeze that had started up, but Mr Gingold merely smiled shyly and said, 'Oh, there you are, Sharsted. Come on in,' as though he had been expecting him all the time.

Surprisingly, Mr Gingold's eyes were of a marvellous shade of blue and they made his whole face come vividly alive, fighting and challenging the overall neutral tints of his clothing and features. He led the way into a cavernous hall. Mr Sharsted followed cautiously, his eyes adjusting with difficulty to the cool gloom of the interior. With courteous, old-world motions Mr Gingold beckoned him forward.

The two men ascended a finely carved staircase, whose balustrades, convoluted and serpentine, seemed to writhe sinuously upwards into the darkness.

'My business will only take a moment,' protested Sharsted, anxious to present his ultimatum and depart. But Mr Gingold merely continued to ascend the staircase.

'Come along, come along,' he said gently, as though he hadn't heard Mr Sharsted's expostulation. 'You must take a glass of wine with me. I have so few visitors . . .'

Mr Sharsted looked about him curiously; he had never been in this part of the house. Usually, Mr Gingold received occasional callers in a big, cluttered room on the ground floor. This afternoon, for some reason known only to himself, he had chosen to show Mr Sharsted another part of his domain. Mr Sharsted thought that perhaps Mr Gingold intended to settle the matter of his repayments. This might be where he transacted business, perhaps kept his money. His thin fingers twitched with nervous excitement.

They continued to ascend what seemed to the moneylender to be enormous distances. The staircase still unwound in front of their measured progress. From the little light which filtered in through rounded windows, Sharsted caught occasional glimpses of objects that aroused his professional curiosity and acquisitive sense. Here a large oil painting swung into view round the bend of the stair; in the necessarily brief glance that Mr Sharsted caught, he could have sworn it was a Poussin.

A moment later, a large sideboard laden with porcelain slid by the corner of his eye. He stumbled on the stair as he glanced back over his shoulder and in so doing, almost missed a rare suit of Genoese armour which stood concealed in a niche set back from the staircase. The moneylender had reached a state of confused bewilderment when at length Mr Gingold flung aside a large mahogany door, high up in the house, and motioned him forward.

Mr Gingold must be a wealthy man and could easily realise enormous amounts on any one of the *objets d'art* Sharsted had seen; why then, thought the latter, did he find it necessary to borrow so frequently, and why was it so difficult to obtain repayment? With interest, the sum owed Sharsted had now risen to a considerable figure; Mr Gingold must be a compulsive buyer of rare items. Allied to the general shabbiness of the house as seen by the casual visitor, it must mean that his collector's instinct would refuse to allow him to part with anything once bought, which had made him run himself into debt. The moneylender's lips tightened again; well, he must be made to settle his debts, like anyone else.

If not, perhaps Sharsted could force him to part with something – porcelain, a picture – that could be made to realise a handsome profit on the deal. Business was business, and Gingold could not expect him to wait for ever. His musings were interrupted by a query from his host and Sharsted muttered an apology as he saw that Mr Gingold was waiting, one hand on the neck of a heavy silver and crystal decanter.

'Yes, yes, a sherry, thank you,' he murmured in confusion, moving awkwardly. The light was so bad in this place that he felt it difficult to focus his eyes, and objects had a habit of shifting and billowing as though seen under water. Mr Sharsted was forced to wear tinted spectacles, as his eyes had been weak from childhood. They made these apartments seem twice as dark as they might be. But though Mr Sharsted squinted over the top of his lenses as Mr Gingold poured the sherry, he still could not make out objects clearly. He really would have to consult his oculist soon, if this trouble continued.

His voice sounded hollow to his own ears as he ventured a commonplace when Mr Gingold handed him the glass. He sat down gingerly on a ladderback chair indicated to him by Mr Gingold, and sipped at the amber liquid in a hesitant fashion. It tasted uncommonly good, but this unexpected hospitality was putting him on a wrong footing with Gingold. He must assert himself and broach the subject of his business. But he felt a curious reluctance and merely sat on in embarrassed silence, one hand round the stem of his goblet, listening to the soothing tick of an old clock, which was the only thing which broke the silence.

He saw now that he was in a large apartment, expensively furnished, which must be high up in the house, under the eaves. Hardly a sound from outside penetrated the windows, which were hung with thick blue-velvet curtains; the parquet floor was covered with exquisitely worked Chinese rugs and the room was apparently divided in half by heavy velvet curtaining to match those which masked the windows.

Mr Gingold said little, but sat at a large mahogany table, tapping his sherry glass with his long fingers; his bright blue eyes looked with mild interest at Mr Sharsted as they spoke of everyday matters. At last Mr Sharsted was moved to broach the object of his visit. He spoke of the long-outstanding sum which he had advanced to Mr Gingold, of the continued applications for settlement and of the necessity of securing early payment. Strangely, as Mr Sharsted progressed, his voice began to stammer and eventually he was at a loss for words; normally, as working-class people in the town had reason to know, he was brusque, businesslike, and ruthless. He never hesitated to distrain on debtor's goods, or to evict if necessary and that he was the object of universal hatred in the outside world, bothered him not in the slightest.

In fact, he felt it to be an asset; his reputation in business affairs preceded him, as it were, and acted as an incentive to prompt repayment. If people were fool enough to be poor or to run into debt and couldn't meet their dues, well then, let them; it was all grist to his mill and he could not be expected to run his business on a lot of sentimental nonsense. He felt more irritated with Mr Gingold than he need have been, for his money was obviously safe; but what continued to baffle him was the man's gentle docility, his obvious wealth, and his reluctance to settle his debts.

Something of this must have eventually permeated his conversation, for Mr Gingold shifted in his seat, made no comment whatever on Mr Sharsted's pressing demands and only said, in another of his softly spoken sentences, 'Do have another sherry, Mr Sharsted.'

The moneylender felt all the strength going out of him as he weakly assented. He leaned back on his comfortable chair with a swimming head and allowed the second glass to be pressed into his hand, the thread of his discourse completely lost. He mentally cursed himself for a dithering fool and tried to concentrate, but Mr Gingold's benevolent smile, the curious way the objects in the room shifted and wavered in the heat haze; the general gloom and the discreet curtaining, came more and more to weigh on and oppress his spirits.

So it was with something like relief that Sharsted saw his host rise from the table. He had not changed the topic, but continued to speak as though Mr Sharsted had never mentioned money to him at all; he merely ignored the whole situation and with an enthusiasm Sharsted found difficult to share, murmured soothingly on about Chinese wall paintings, a subject of which Mr Sharsted knew nothing.

He found his eyes closing and with an effort opened them again. Mr Gingold was saying, 'I think this will interest you, Mr Sharsted. Come along . . .'

His host had moved forward and the moneylender, following him down the room, saw that the large expanse of velvet curtaining was in motion. The two men walked through the parted curtains, which closed behind them, and Mr Sharsted then saw that they were in a semicircular chamber.

This room was, if anything, even dimmer than the one they had just left. But the moneylender's interest began to revive; his head felt clearer and he took in a large circular table, some brass wheels and levers which winked in the gloom, and a long shaft which went up to the ceiling.

'This has almost become an obsession with me,' murmured Mr Gingold, as though apologizing to his guest. 'You are aware of the principles of the camera obscura, Mr Sharsted?'

The moneylender pondered slowly, reaching back into memory. 'Some sort of Victorian toy, isn't it?' he said at length. Mr Gingold looked pained, but the expression of his voice did not change.

'Hardly that, Mr Sharsted,' he rejoined. 'A most fascinating pursuit. Few people of my acquaintance have been here and seen what you are going to see.'

He motioned to the shafting, which passed up through a louvre in the ceiling.

'These controls are coupled to the system of lenses and prisms on the roof. As you will see, the hidden camera, as the Victorian scientists came to call it, gathers a panorama of the town below and transmits it here on to the viewing table. An absorbing study, one's fellow man, don't you think? I spend many hours up here.'

Mr Sharsted had never heard Mr Gingold in such a talkative mood and now that the wretchedness which had assailed him earlier had disappeared, he felt more suited to tackle him about his debts. First, he would humour him by feigning interest in his stupid toy. But Mr Sharsted had to admit, almost with a gasp of surprise, that Mr Gingold's obsession had a valid cause.

For suddenly, as Mr Gingold moved his hand upon the lever, the room was flooded with light of a blinding clarity and the moneylender saw why gloom was a necessity in this chamber. Presumably, a shutter over the camera obscura slid away upon the rooftop and almost at the same moment, a panel in the ceiling opened to admit a shaft of light directed upon the table before them.

In a second of God-like vision, Mr Sharsted saw a panorama of part of the old town spread out before him in superbly natural colour. Here were the quaint, cobbled streets dropping to the valley, with the blue hills beyond; factory chimneys smoked in the early evening air; people went about their business in half a hundred roads; distant traffic went noiselessly on its way;

once, even, a great white bird soared across the field of vision, so apparently close that Mr Sharsted started back from the table.

Mr Gingold gave a dry chuckle and moved a brass wheel at his elbow. The viewpoint abruptly shifted and Mr Sharsted saw with another gasp, a sparkling vista of the estuary with a big coaling ship moving slowly out to sea. Gulls soared in the foreground and the sullen wash of the tide ringed the shore. Mr Sharsted, his errand quite forgotten, was fascinated. Half an hour must have passed, each view more enchanting than the last; from this height, the squalor of the town was quite transformed.

He was abruptly recalled to the present, however, by the latest of the views; Mr Gingold spun the control for the last time and a huddle of crumbling tenements wheeled into view. 'The former home of Mrs Thwaites, I believe,' said Mr Gingold mildly.

Mr Sharsted flushed and bit his lip in anger. The Thwaites business had aroused more notoriety than he had intended; the woman had borrowed a greater sum than she could afford, the interest mounted, she borrowed again; could he help it if she had a tubercular husband and three children? He had to make an example of her in order to keep his other clients in line; now there was a distraint on the furniture and the Thwaiteses were being turned on to the street. Could he help this? If only people would repay their debts all would be well; he wasn't a philanthropic institution, he told himself angrily.

And at this reference to what was rapidly becoming a scandal in the town, all his smouldering resentment against Mr Gingold broke out afresh; enough of all these views and childish playthings. Camera obscura, indeed; if Mr Gingold did not meet his obligations like a gentleman he could sell this pretty toy to meet his debt.

He controlled himself with an effort as he turned to meet Mr Gingold's gently ironic gaze.

'Ah, yes,' said Mr Sharsted. 'The Thwaites business is my affair, Mr Gingold. Will you please confine yourself to the matter in hand. I have had to come here again at great inconvenience; I must tell you that if the £300, representing the current instalment on our loan is not forthcoming by Monday, I shall be obliged to take legal action.'

Mr Sharsted's cheeks were burning and his voice trembled as he pronounced these words; if he expected a violent reaction from Mr Gingold, he was disappointed. The latter merely gazed at him in mute reproach.

'This is your last word?' he said regretfully. 'You will not reconsider?'

'Certainly not,' snapped Mr Sharsted. 'I must have the money by Monday.'

'You misunderstand me, Mr Sharsted,' said Mr Gingold, still in that irritatingly mild voice. 'I was referring to Mrs Thwaites. Must you carry on with this unnecessary and somewhat inhuman action? I would . . .'

'Please mind your own business!' retorted Mr Sharsted, exasperated beyond measure. 'Mind what I say . . .'

He looked wildly round for the door through which he had entered.

'That is your last word?' said Mr Gingold again. One look at the moneylender's set, white face was his mute answer.

'Very well, then,' said Mr Gingold, with a heavy sigh. 'So be it. I will see you on your way.'

He moved forward again, pulling a heavy velvet cloth over the table of the camera obscura. The louvre in the ceiling closed with a barely audible rumble. To Mr Sharsted's surprise, he found himself following his host up yet another flight of stairs; these were of stone, fringed with an iron balustrade which was cold to the touch.

His anger was now subsiding as quickly as it had come; he was already regretting losing his temper over the Thwaites business and he hadn't intended to sound so crude and cold-blooded. What must Mr Gingold think of him? Strange how the story could have got to his ears; surprising how much information about the outside world a recluse could obtain just by sitting still.

Though, on this hill, he supposed Mr Gingold could be said to be at the centre of things. He shuddered suddenly, for the air seemed to have grown cold. Through a slit in the stone wall he could see the evening sky was already darkening. He really must be on his way; how did the old fool expect him to find his way out when they were still mounting to the very top of the house?

Mr Sharsted regretted, too, that in antagonizing Mr Gingold, he might have made it even more difficult to obtain his money; it was almost as though, in mentioning Mrs Thwaites and trying to take her part, he had been trying a form of subtle blackmail.

He would not have expected it of Gingold; it was not like him to meddle in other people's affairs. If he was so fond of the poor and needy he could well afford to advance the family some money themselves to tide them over their difficulties.

His brain seething with these confused and angry thoughts, Mr Sharsted, panting and dishevelled, now found himself on a worn stone platform where Mr Gingold was putting the key into an ancient wooden lock.

'My workshop,' he explained, with a shy smile to Mr Sharsted, who felt his tension eased away by this drop in the emotional atmosphere. Looking through an old, nearly triangular window in front of him, Mr Sharsted could see that they were in a small, turreted superstructure which towered a good twenty feet over the main roof of the house. There was a sprawl of unfamiliar alleys at the foot of the steep overhang of the building, as far as he could make out through the grimy panes.

'There is a staircase down the outside,' explained Mr Gingold, opening the door. 'It will lead you down the other side of the hill and cut over half a mile off your journey.'

The moneylender felt a sudden rush of relief at this. He had come almost to fear this deceptively mild and quiet old man who, though he said little and threatened not at all, had begun to exude a faint air of menace to Mr Sharsted's now overheated imagination.

'But first,' said Mr Gingold, taking the other man's arm in a surprisingly powerful grip, 'I want to show you something else – and this really has been seen by very few people indeed.'

Mr Sharsted looked at the other quickly, but could read nothing in Mr Gingold's enigmatic blue eyes.

He was surprised to find a similar, though smaller, chamber to the one they had just left. There was another table, another shaft ascending to a domed cupola in the ceiling, and a further arrangement of wheels and tubes.

'This camera obscura,' said Mr Gingold, 'is a very rare model, to be sure. In fact, I believe there are only three in existence today, and one of those is in Northern Italy.'

Mr Sharsted cleared his throat and made a non-committal reply.

'I felt sure you would like to see this before you leave,' said Mr Gingold softly. 'You are quite sure you won't change your mind?' he added, almost inaudibly, as he bent to the levers. 'About Mrs Thwaites, I mean.'

Sharsted felt another sudden spurt of anger, but kept his feelings under control.

'I'm sorry . . .' he began.

'No matter,' said Mr Gingold, regretfully. 'I only wanted to make sure, before we had a look at this.'

He laid his hand with infinite tenderness on Mr Sharsted's shoulder as he drew him forward.

He pressed the lever and Mr Sharsted almost cried out with the suddenness of the vision. He was God; the world was spread out before him in a crazy pattern, or at least the segment of it representing the part of the town surrounding the house in which he stood.

He viewed it from a great height, as a man might from an aeroplane; though nothing was quite in perspective.

The picture was of enormous clarity; it was like looking into an old cheval-glass which had a faint distorting quality. There was something oblique and elliptical about the sprawl of alleys and roads that spread about the foot of the hill.

The shadows were mauve and violet, and the extremes of

the picture were still tinged with the blood red of the dying sun.

It was an appalling, cataclysmic vision, and Mr Sharsted was shattered; he felt suspended in space, and almost cried out at the dizziness of the height.

When Mr Gingold twirled the wheel and the picture slowly began to revolve, Mr Sharsted did cry out and had to clutch at the back of a chair to prevent himself from falling.

He was perturbed, too, as he caught a glimpse of a big, white building in the foreground of the picture.

'I thought that was the old Corn Exchange,' he said in bewilderment. 'Surely that burned down before the last war?'

'Eh,' said Mr Gingold, as though he hadn't heard.

'It doesn't matter,' said Mr Sharsted, who now felt quite confused and ill. It must be the combination of the sherry and the enormous height at which he was viewing the vision in the camera obscura.

It was a demoniacal toy and he shrank away from the figure of Mr Gingold, which looked somewhat sinister in the blood-red and mauve light reflected from the image in the polished table surface.

'I thought you'd like to see this one,' said Mr Gingold, in the same maddening, insipid voice. 'It's really special, isn't it? Quite the best of the two ... you can see all sorts of things that are normally hidden.'

As he spoke there appeared on the screen two old buildings which Mr Sharsted was sure had been destroyed during the war; in fact, he was certain that a public garden and car park had now been erected on the site. His mouth suddenly became dry; he was not sure whether he had drunk too much sherry or the heat of the day had been too much for him.

He had been about to make a sharp remark that the sale of the camera obscura would liquidate Mr Gingold's current debt, but he felt this would not be a wise comment to make at this juncture. He felt faint, his brow went hot and cold and Mr Gingold was at his side in an instant.

Mr Sharsted became aware that the picture had faded from

the table and that the day was rapidly turning to dusk outside the dusty windows.

'I really must be going,' he said with feeble desperation, trying to free himself from Mr Gingold's quietly persistent grip.

'Certainly, Mr Sharsted,' said his host. 'This way.' He led him without ceremony over to a small oval doorway in a corner of the far wall.

'Just go down the stairs. It will bring you on to the street. Please slam the bottom door – it will lock itself.' As he spoke, he opened the door and Mr Sharsted saw a flight of clean, dry stone steps leading downwards. Light still flooded in from windows set in the circular walls.

Mr Gingold did not offer his hand and Mr Sharsted stood rather awkwardly, holding the door ajar.

'Until Monday, then,' he said.

Mr Gingold flatly ignored this.

'Goodnight, Mr Gingold,' said the moneylender with nervous haste, anxious to be gone.

'Goodbye, Mr Sharsted,' said Mr Gingold with kind finality.

Mr Sharsted almost thrust himself through the door and nervously fled down the staircase, mentally cursing himself for all sorts of a fool. His feet beat a rapid tattoo that echoed eerily up and down the old tower. Fortunately, there was still plenty of light; this would be a nasty place in the dark. He slowed his pace after a few moments and thought bitterly of the way he had allowed old Gingold to gain the ascendancy over him; and what an impertinence of the man to interfere in the matter of the Thwaites woman.

He would see what sort of man Mr Sharsted was when Monday came and the eviction went according to plan. Monday would also be a day of reckoning for Mr Gingold – it was a day they would both remember and Mr Sharsted felt himself quite looking forward to it.

He quickened his pace again, and presently found himself confronted by a thick oak door.

It gave beneath his hand as he lifted the big, well-oiled catch and the next moment he was in a high-walled alley leading to the street. The door slammed hollowly behind him and he breathed in the cool evening air with a sigh of relief. He jammed his hard hat back on his head and strode out over the cobbles, as though to affirm the solidity of the outside world.

Once in the street, which seemed somewhat unfamiliar to him, he hesitated which way to go and then set off to the right. He remembered that Mr Gingold had told him that this way took him over the other side of the hill; he had never been in this part of the town and the walk would do him good.

The sun had quite gone and a thin sliver of moon was showing in the early evening sky. There seemed few people about and when, ten minutes later, Mr Sharsted came out into a large square which had five or six roads leading off it, he determined to ask the correct way back down to his part of the town. With luck he could catch a tram, for he had now had enough of walking for one day.

There was a large, smoke-grimed chapel on a corner of this square and as Mr Sharsted passed it, he caught a glimpse of a board with gold-painted letters.

NINIAN'S REVIVALIST BROTHERHOOD, it said. The date, in flaked gold paint, was 1925.

Mr Sharsted walked on and selected the most important of the roads which faced him. It was getting quite dark and the lamps had not yet been lit on this part of the hill. As he went farther down, the buildings closed in about his head, and the lights of the town below disappeared. Mr Sharsted felt lost and a little forlorn. Due, no doubt, to the faintly incredible atmosphere of Mr Gingold's big house.

He determined to ask the next passer-by for the right direction, but for the moment he couldn't see anyone about; the absence of street lights also bothered him. The municipal authorities must have overlooked this section when they switched on at dusk, unless it came under the jurisdiction of another body.

Mr Sharsted was musing in this manner when he turned the corner of a narrow street and came out opposite a large, white building that looked familiar. For years Mr Sharsted had a picture of it on the yearly calendar sent by a local tradesman, which used to hang in his office. He gazed at its façade with mounting bewilderment as he approached. The title, CORN EXCHANGE, winked back dully in the moonlight as he got near enough to make out the lettering.

Mr Sharsted's bewilderment changed to distinct unease as he thought frantically that he had already seen this building once before this evening, in the image captured by the lens of Mr Gingold's second camera obscura. And he knew with numbing certainty that the old Corn Exchange had burned down in the late thirties.

He swallowed heavily, and hurried on; there was something devilishly wrong, unless he were the victim of an optical illusion engendered by the violence of his thoughts, the unaccustomed walking he had done that day, and the two glasses of sherry.

He had the uncomfortable feeling that Mr Gingold might be watching him at that very moment, on the table of his camera obscura, and at the thought a cold sweat burst out on his forehead.

He sent himself forward at a smart trot and had soon left the Corn Exchange far behind. In the distance he heard the sharp clopping and the grating rattle of a horse and cart, but as he gained the entrance of an alley he was disappointed to see its shadow disappear round the corner into the next road. He still could not see any people about and again had difficulty in fixing his position in relation to the town.

He set off once more, with a show of determination he was far from feeling, and five minutes later arrived in the middle of a square which was already familiar to him.

There was a chapel on the corner and Mr Sharsted read for the second time that evening the legend: NINIAN'S REVIVALIST BROTHERHOOD.

He stamped his foot in anger. He had walked quite three miles and had been fool enough to describe a complete circle; here he was, not five minutes from Gingold's house, where he had set out, nearly an hour before.

He pulled out his watch at this and was surprised to find it was only a quarter past six, though he could have sworn this was the time he had left Gingold.

Though it could have been a quarter past five; he hardly knew what he was doing this afternoon. He shook it to make sure it was still going and then replaced it in his pocket.

His feet beat the pavement in his fury as he ran down the length of the square. This time he wouldn't make the same silly mistake. He unhesitatingly chose a large, well-kept metalled road that ran fair and square in the direction he knew must take him back to the centre of the town. He found himself humming a little tune under his breath. As he turned the next corner, his confidence increased.

Lights burned brightly on every hand; the authorities must have realized their mistake and finally switched on. But again he was mistaken; there was a little cart parked at the side of the road, with a horse in the shafts. An old man mounted a ladder set against a lamp-post and Mr Sharsted saw the thin blue flame in the gloom and then the mellow blossoming of the gas lamp.

Now he felt irritated again; what an incredibly archaic part of the town old Gingold lived in. It would just suit him. Gas lamps! And what a system for lighting them; Sharsted thought this method had gone out with the Ark.

Nevertheless, he was most polite.

'Good evening,' he said, and the figure at the top of the lamp-post stirred uneasily. The face was in deep shadow.

'Good evening, sir,' the lamplighter said in a muffled voice. He started climbing down.

'Could you direct me to the town centre?' said Mr Sharsted with simulated confidence. He took a couple of paces forward and was then arrested with a shock.

There was a strange, sickly stench which reminded him of something he was unable to place. Really, the drains in this place were terrible; he certainly would have to write to the town hall about this backward part of the locality.

The lamplighter had descended to the ground now and he put something down in the back of his cart; the horse shifted uneasily and again Mr Sharsted caught the charnel stench, sickly sweet on the summer air.

'This is the town centre as far as I know, sir,' said the lamp-lighter. As he spoke he stepped forward and the pale lamplight fell on to his face, which had been in shadow before.

Mr Sharsted no longer waited to ask for any more directions but set off down the road at breakneck speed, not sure whether the green pallor of the man's face was due to a terrible suspicion or to the green-tinted glasses he wore.

What he was certain of was that something like a mass of writhing worms projected below the man's cap, where his hair would normally have been. Mr Sharsted hadn't waited to find out if this Medusa-like supposition were correct; beneath his hideous fear burned a savage anger at Gingold, whom some-how he suspected to be at the back of all these troubles.

Mr Sharsted fervently hoped that he might soon wake to find himself at home in bed, ready to begin the day that had ended so ignominiously at Gingold's, but even as he formulated the thought, he knew this was reality. This cold moonlight, the hard pavement, his frantic flight, and the breath rasping and sobbing in his throat.

As the mist cleared from in front of his eyes, he slowed to a walk and then found himself in the middle of the square; he knew where he was and he had to force his nerves into a ter-rible, unnatural calm, just this side of despair. He walked with controlled casualness past the legend, NINIAN'S REVIVALIST BROTHERHOOD, and this time chose the most unlikely road of all, little more than a narrow alley that appeared to lead in the wrong direction.

Mr Sharsted was willing to try anything which would lead him off this terrifying, accursed hill. There were no lights here and his feet stumbled on the rough stones and flints of the unmade roadway, but at least he was going downhill and the track gradually spiralled until he was in the right direction.

For some little while Mr Sharsted had heard faint, elusive stirrings in the darkness about him and once he was startled to hear, some way ahead of him, a muffled cough. At least there were other people about, at last, he thought and he was comforted, too, to see, far ahead of him, the dim lights of the town.

As he grew nearer, Mr Sharsted recovered his spirits and was relieved to see that they did not recede from him, as he had half suspected they might. The shapes about him, too, were solid enough. Their feet rang hollow on the roadway; evidently they were on their way to a meeting.

As Mr Sharsted came under the light of the first lamp, his earlier panic fear had abated. He still couldn't recognize exactly where he was, but the trim villas they were passing were reminiscent of the town proper.

Mr Sharsted stepped up on to the pavement when he reached the well-lit area and in so doing, cannoned into a large, well-built man who had just emerged from a gateway to join the throng in the roadway.

Mr Sharsted staggered under the impact and once again his nostrils caught the sickly sweet perfume of decay. The man caught him by the front of the coat to prevent him from falling.

'Evening, Mordecai,' he said in a thick voice. 'I thought you'd be coming, sooner or later.'

Mr Sharsted could not resist a cry of bubbling terror. It was not just the greenish pallor of the man's face or the rotted, leathery lips drawn back from the decayed teeth. He fell back against the fence as Abel Joyce passed on – Abel Joyce, a fellow moneylender and usurer who had died in the nineteen-twenties and whose funeral Mr Sharsted had attended.

Blackness was about him as he rushed away, a sobbing whistle in his throat. He was beginning to understand Mr Gingold and that devilish camera obscura; the lost and the damned. He began to babble to himself under his breath.

Now and again he cast a sidelong glimpse at his companions as he ran; there was old Mrs Sanderson who used to lay out corpses and rob her charges; there Grayson, the estate agent and undertaker; Amos, the war profiteer; Drucker, a swindler, all green of pallor and bearing with them the charnel stench.

All people Mr Sharsted had business with at one time or

another and all of whom had one thing in common. Without exception all had been dead for quite a number of years. Mr Sharsted stuffed his handkerchief over his mouth to blot out that unbearable odour and heard the mocking laughter as his racing feet carried him past.

'Evening, Mordecai,' they said. 'We thought you'd be joining us.' Mr Gingold equated him with these ghouls, he sobbed, as he ran on at headlong speed; if only he could make him understand. Sharsted didn't deserve such treatment. He was a businessman, not like these bloodsuckers on society; the lost and the damned. Now he knew why the Corn Exchange still stood and why the town was unfamiliar. It existed only in the eye of the camera obscura. Now he knew that Mr Gingold had been trying to give him a last chance and why he had said goodbye, instead of goodnight.

There was just one hope; if he could find the door back to Mr Gingold's perhaps he could make him change his mind. Mr Sharsted's feet flew over the cobbles as he thought this, his hat fell down and he scraped his hands against the wall. He left the walking corpses far behind, but though he was now looking for the familiar square he seemed to be finding his way back to the Corn Exchange.

He stopped for a moment to regain his breath. He must work this out logically. How had it happened before? Why, of course, by walking away from the desired destination. Mr Sharsted turned back and set himself to walk steadily towards the lights. Though terrified, he did not despair, now that he knew what he was up against. He felt himself a match for Mr Gingold. If only he could find the door!

As he reached the warm circle cast by the glow of the street lamps, Mr Sharsted breathed a sigh of relief. For as he turned a corner there was the big square, with the soot-grimed chapel on the corner. He hurried on. He must remember exactly the turnings he had taken; he couldn't afford to make a mistake.

So much depended on it. If only he could have another chance – he would let the Thwaites family keep their house, he would even be willing to forget Gingold's debt. He couldn't face the possibility of walking these endless streets – for how long? And with the creatures he had seen . . .

Mr Sharsted groaned as he remembered the face of one old woman he had seen earlier that evening – or what was left of that face, after years of wind and weather. He suddenly recalled that she had died before the 1914 war. The sweat burst out on his forehead and he tried not to think of it.

Once off the square, he plunged into the alley he remembered. Ah! there it was. Now all he had to do was to go to the left and there was the door. His heart beat higher and he began to hope, with a sick longing, for the security of his well-appointed house and his rows of friendly ledgers. Only one more corner. He ran on and turned up the road towards Mr Gingold's door. Another thirty yards to the peace of the ordinary world.

The moonlight winked on a wide, well-paved square. Shone, too, on a legend painted in gold leaf on a large board: NINIAN's REVIVALIST BROTHERHOOD. The date was 1925.

Mr Sharsted gave a hideous yell of fear and despair and fell to the pavement.

Mr Gingold sighed heavily and yawned. He glanced at the clock. It was time for bed. He went over once again and stared into the camera obscura. It had been a not altogether unsuccessful day. He put a black velvet cloth over the image in the lens and went off slowly to bed.

Under the cloth, in pitiless detail, was reflected the narrow tangle of streets round Mr Gingold's house, seen as through the eye of God; there went Mr Sharsted and his colleagues, the lost and the damned, trapped for eternity, stumbling, weeping, swearing, as they slipped and scrabbled along the alleys and squares of their own private hell, under the pale light of the stars.

Stephen Gregory

THE BOYS WHO WOULDN'T WAKE UP

This book opened with a tale set at Halloween, the holiday today most closely associated with horror stories, and it closes with one that takes place at Christmas, which in generations past was the time for telling spooky stories by firelight. Stephen Gregory *is the author of seven novels, the first three of which,* The Cormorant *(1986; winner of the Somerset Maugham Award and adapted for a film starring Ralph Fiennes),* The Woodwitch *(1988), and* The Blood of Angels *(1992) have been republished by Valancourt. Author Mark Morris has written that Gregory is 'one of the best and most underrated novelists in the world' and has noted the ways in which nature and the natural world play a prominent role in his fiction, particularly birds, which appear in Gregory's work as 'malign, destructive spirits or harbingers of doom'. 'The Boys Who Wouldn't Wake Up', published here for the first time, is a quiet ghost story that shows a different side to this fine horror author, who still awaits the broader recognition he deserves.*

I AN SAT ON HIS BED AND LOOKED OUT of the dormitory window, down to the drive in front of the school. One by one, all the other boys were collected by their parents or picked up in taxis and taken off to Salisbury station. A succession of cars swept up to the door, crunching on the gravel, and parked beneath the branches of the cedar; and then there were kisses and cries of joy as mothers and fathers greeted their sons. Leather-bound trunks were loaded into the boots of the cars or the waiting taxis. He saw Mr Hoddesdon down there, the head-master, shaking hands with the parents, ticking a name on his list as each boy left. Ian sat on his bed and watched. He was not going home. Soon there would be no one in the school except him and Mr Hoddesdon.

Ian Stott was seven years old. He was small and neat, like a vole, with glossy brown hair and wide, brown eyes. Although he was trying very hard not to cry, his cheeks shone with tears of unhappiness and fear. He wanted to be brave like his father, an army officer thousands of miles away in the Falkland Islands. But, when he thought of his mother, who had written to tell him she was skiing in Austria so he would have to stay in school over Christmas, the tears tingled and his heart seemed to rise into his throat.

Christmas ... Ian shuddered at the awfulness of it. He looked around the bare, cold, empty dormitory, at the eleven other beds all neatly made. He sniffed and shivered and he watched out of the window as the last of the cars drove away. He listened as the school fell silent.

It was four o'clock on a December afternoon. Dusk became a misty, whispering twilight. Not a sound, except the wind in the cedar tree ... Ian Stott was alone in Foxwood Manor with Mr Hoddesdon, the headmaster.

Foxwood Manor was in the Cranbourne Chase, an area of forest and downland in the triangle formed by Salisbury, Shaftesbury and Blandford Forum. A fine house with a single, high, square tower on the east wing, it stood in hundreds of acres of ancient oakwood and beechwood and bristling, black fir plantation. But the school was dwindling to the brink of closure. Years ago, it had had a reputation for academic excellence; but the numbers had shrunk and shrunk, so that Ian was one of only fifty pupils, supervised by five unqualified, uninspired teachers. There was a matron, a cook and a weary groundsman. The buildings were in cobwebby disrepair. The grass was long and untidy on the football pitches; the cobbled stable yard was a carpet of moss; jackdaws squabbled in the great, twiggy nests they had built in the crumbling chimneys. And the house itself was dark and dusty: the corridors and the oak-panelled halls were hung with yellowing photographs and gloomy paintings of long-dead headmasters.

Mr Hoddesdon was the headmaster. At last, when all the boys were ticked off and gone, he limped inside, shut and locked the front door and climbed stiffly up the spiral staircase to his room in the top of the tower. He stoked the smouldering fire, for he was aching and chilled from standing in the freezing dusk. He rumpled the heavy old head of Brutus, the black labrador, and he stared from his windows at the frosty twilight, at the dark, deep woods which stretched as far as the horizon.

Christmas ... Mr Hoddesdon snarled at the dread of it. Probably his last Christmas at Foxwood Manor, if the school was bound to close. He sat and stared at the fire and thought of the years gone by.

He had spent his life at Foxwood Manor; first of all as a boy evacuated to the country during the blitz, staying on to take Winchester scholarship; later, with a double first from Oxford which could have made him a brilliant young don or at least a master at Eton, he chose to return to Foxwood, to teach Latin and Greek to the brightest boys; and eventually, to become the headmaster, presiding over the school's dismal decline.

Alone ... always had been. Never married ... never would be. He never smiled ... probably he could not. He was seventy, a gaunt and solitary figure who stalked the classrooms and dormitories like a grizzled, grey wolf – hobbling with a stick and growling at the pain in his hips. Brutus was his only companion. For years, for decades, for a lifetime, he had lived in the high tower. Now, he stared into the fire, prodding it irritably until a reluctant, trembling flame stood up.

Another Christmas ... of waiting and hoping and inevitable disappointment. His last, probably. He glared around the books and photographs which lined his room, at the dust and cobwebs and useless clutter.

As evening became night, he suddenly remembered the boy, Stott, who was still in school. Cursing, he limped downstairs from his tower to the kitchen, rummaged for some milk and biscuits in the pantry and put them on a tray. The place was silent, deserted; only a few optimistic mice skittered in the skirting. Leaving the ground-floor in darkness, he stomped up the stairs and along the corridor to the boy's dormitory.

The little boy was sitting on his bed, staring from the window, although the world outside was black and still. He jumped when he heard the door open, when he saw the man come into the room.

'Stott,' the headmaster said.

'Yes, sir,' the boy said.

'Supper,' the headmaster said.

'Thank you, sir,' the boy said.

Shivering, Ian tried to eat and drink, but the biscuits and milk were a cold, thick paste in his throat. The man stood silently in the middle of the room and looked up and down the row of eleven empty beds. The walls were yellowed and bare and the floorboards were pocked with worm.

'Grim,' the headmaster said at last. 'Hardly changed since I was a boy at Foxwood, sixty years ago. This is my old dormitory, you know. That's my old bed you've got, right next to the window.'

The man snarled with regret and disappointment.

'Hurry up and eat your supper, boy, now that I've gone all the way down to the kitchen and back upstairs again to get it for you. If you're not going to eat it, get ready for bed.'

Then, seeing that Ian was shaking with cold and unhappiness, he added as gently as his growling voice could manage, 'We'll have to make the best of it this Christmas, the two of us. Perhaps we'll go out tomorrow, if the weather allows, walking with Brutus or out in the car. Come along now, stir yourself . . .'

While the old man waited, the boy changed into his red and white striped pyjamas, splashed his face and brushed his teeth at the wash basin and then climbed into bed. The headmaster moved to the door. But, as he lifted his hand to turn off the light, there was a rasping at the dormitory window as though someone outside were scratching his fingernails on the pane, and the man whirled round, suddenly startled. He stomped across the room again, stood at Ian's bedside and stared from the window, but all he could see was a glassy blackness.

'What the devil's that?' he exclaimed.

Ian said nothing, huddled in bed with the blankets to his chin, although he knew what had made the noise. It was a noise he was used to, every night in the big, bare room, but he was too frightened to say anything as the headmaster struggled to throw open the window and then leaned over the sill. Freezing air rushed into the freezing dormitory.

'By Jove,' the man said, muttering to himself as though the boy were not there. 'This old thing has grown a bit. I can reach it quite easily now. Here, let me just . . .'

And he stepped back into the room with a fistful of bristly needles from the cedar tree which stood on the lawn below, whose branches reached to the first floor and scratched the glass as they moved in the wind. He held the needles to his face, twitched his nostrils and inhaled the resinous scent.

'That smell,' he said to himself. 'After all these years, it still reminds me.'

Mumbling, growling, snuffling his face in the needles he rubbed in his fingers, he limped to the door again, flicked off the light and went stumping along the corridor . . . too distracted to say goodnight or to close the window he'd left wide open.

Ian waited until the footsteps had faded, until the house was in silence. Then he got out of bed to shut the window. For a moment he leaned out, as the headmaster had done, and he stroked the nearest branch of the cedar. The world was black and empty: no light in any direction, only the deep, dark forest for miles and miles around. Aching with cold, he tugged the window down and jumped back into bed.

There he lay, as the house creaked and whispered, as the needles scratched at the glass. Very lonely, very sad, Ian sobbed until he thought his chest might burst with sobbing, and at last he fell asleep.

*

But the following day was less horrid than he'd thought it might be.

Mr Hoddesdon woke him and hurried him downstairs, where they sat together and ate the breakfast that the head-master had cooked. The long refectory tables were empty and bare; the panelled hall was gloomy and chill. Mr Hoddesdon was gruff. Brutus sat beside him, lolling a huge, pink tongue, and was eventually rewarded with bacon rind and crusts of buttered toast.

'Coat!' the man said. 'Football socks inside your boots! Gloves! Hurry up and get ready, Stott – five minutes and we're off walking!'

They stepped into crisp, cold, glorious sunshine: Ian in gloves and scarf and Wellington boots; the headmaster with stick and pipe and binoculars and a curious little rucksack slung on his back; Brutus shambling beside him.

At the overgrown ha-ha, Mr Hoddesdon told Ian to leap down into the dilapidated bandstand and find owl-pellets in the dead nettles and the skeletons of willowherb; while the owl itself, blinking and bobbing like a demonic gnome, stared from the rafters at the man and the boy and the big, black dog. The headmaster broke the pellets in the palm of his hand and showed Ian the bones of mouse and shrew and the gleaming remains of beetles that the owl had eaten.

They walked slowly into the woodland. They saw a sparrow hawk, dashing between the trees with a thrush in its claws. They heard jays, shrieking like banshees. They saw deer and hare. The man smelled fox, and the boy sniffed it too, sharp and rank on the cold, dry leaves.

They pushed deep into the undergrowth, to the mounded earthworks of a Roman camp buried in brambles and bracken; and there, where the sunlight was warm, Mr Hoddesdon sat down and opened the mysterious rucksack: a picnic of pies and cakes and ginger beer – a pie for Brutus as well. Later, while the man smoked his pipe, Ian and the dog went burrowing in tunnels of thorn, exploring the ancient, long-lost site.

They walked back in the afternoon. The day grew quickly cold and dark. A grey mist drifted in the woods like smoke. Dusk fell. The forest was silent. Alarmed by the footfalls of man and boy, startled by the scent of dog, deer fled through the plantation and rabbits flashed their scuts. An owl hooted in the freezing twilight. As they broke from the trees, the headmaster and the boy saw the house in the distance, square and black like a huge gravestone.

'Chin up, Stott,' the old man said, seeing how despondent the boy had become. 'We've had a good day out, haven't we? We'll soon get warmed up when we get in. Ever been to the tower? Of course you haven't. No one has, except me and Brutus. Well, we're on our own this Christmas, the two of us. Got to make the best of things. Come on, before we catch our death.'

They crunched across the lawn in front of the house, under the looming cedar, and Mr Hoddesdon unlocked the front door. The hall was dark and very cold. They climbed up to the tower, the man and the dog both limping on the spiral stairs, the boy following, to the secret, private place at the top where the headmaster had lived for so long.

It was a tall, square room, cobwebby and cluttered and chill, with leaded windows on all four sides; a desk strewn with papers and books and photographs, a rumpled bed, threadbare furniture arranged by a little fireplace. While the boy stood and stared, sniffing the smell of tobacco and old man's clothes, Mr Hoddesdon knelt and lit the fire which was already laid in the grate. Soon, the windows gleamed with flamelight. The room was warmer. The man sat in his armchair and the boy sat on the rug, with hot toast and mugs of tea, with carols on the radio … scented wood-smoke, the headmaster's pipe, the smell of dead leaves and bracken on a weary old dog …

Ian and Mr Hoddesdon were weary too. They nodded asleep in front of the fire. Much later that evening, waking suddenly to find that the fire had gone out, the man shook the boy and led him down the stairs, along the corridor to the dormitory at the other end of the house and put him to bed. Ian fell asleep again, straightaway.

*

He thought he had a dream.

He dreamed that he sat up in bed and saw Mr Hoddesdon

in the moonlit dormitory. The headmaster was pacing from bed to bed, stopping at each one to shake at the pillow, tug at the sheets and rattle the bedstead. His face was contorted with panic and terror. He opened and closed his mouth as though he were shouting, but no sound came out. The only bed the man did not shake was Ian's. Again and again the headmaster shook the beds with terrible violence, although there was nobody in them. His face was more and more twisted, blanched by the moonlight, snarling with fear and despair. His throat bulged with silent screams. Until, with a shrug of utter hopelessness, he came to the window by Ian's bed, struggled and struggled to throw it open and then leaned so far out that Ian thought he must surely fall to the ground below ... only to pause, the panic on his face turning to surprise and bewilderment, to pluck a fistful of needles from the cedar and step back into the dormitory. Then, rubbing the needles between the palms of his hands, sniffing and sniffing them like a wolf, he walked slowly out of the room.

That was Ian's dream.

In the morning, the dormitory was very cold because the window was wide open. The other eleven beds were dreadfully rumpled. Puzzled by his dream, afraid that Mr Hoddesdon would be cross if he saw the untidiness, Ian made his own bed and all the others and went downstairs.

The headmaster looked tired and drawn, as though he had hardly slept at all. He had not shaved, so that his face was prickly with grey stubble. He grunted at the boy and then said nothing as they sat in the silent dining-hall and chewed their toast. At last, pushing back his chair and standing stiffly upright, he said, 'Wrap up warm, Stott, and wait for me in the stable yard. We're going out in the car,' before he shuffled upstairs. Brutus followed him. Ian took the dishes into the kitchen, washed them and put them away, and then he went through the corridors to the changing room, where all the rows and rows of hooks were empty except for his hook. He remembered the place in term-time, noisy and steamy, smelling of muddy boys and wet football boots; now it was bare and silent, swabbed with disinfectant. He put on his coat and scarf and gloves and went into the yard.

The headmaster was backing his car out of the stable. It was big and green and very old-looking. It rumbled and smoked tremendously. It had no roof. Brutus was sitting in the back, grinning.

'Alvis!' the headmaster barked to him. 'It's an Alvis! They don't make them anymore! I've had it for years, since I was your father's age, I suppose! Get in now. Hurry up!'

The boy slid onto the smooth red leather of the front seat, and the man eased the car down the gravel drive. They wound through the woods; they rumbled through Sixpenny Handley and Tollard Royal; they sped across the high, bare downs towards Shaftesbury. The town was lit for Christmas. The headmaster stopped the car beside a tinselled tree.

'Take the dog now, Stott,' the headmaster said. 'Go on, Brutus, take the boy for a walk! I've got things to do in town. Go on, off you go, the two of you.'

For the rest of the morning, long into the afternoon, Ian and the dog dragged one another about the cobbled lanes of Shaftesbury. They shared a pork pie in a leafless park. As the day grew misty and cold, the boy managed to haul the dog back to the headmaster's car in time to see Mr Hoddesdon and a shop assistant from a nearby store manhandling a wicker hamper into the boot of the Alvis.

'Had a good walk? You've eaten? Good, back to Foxwood now,' the headmaster said. 'Come on, Brutus, jump in! And you, Stott! Collars up, scarves and gloves on. We're off!'

It was a freezing dusk. The sky turned grey. The air crackled with frost. The car ran hot and loud up Zig-Zag Hill and left the town behind. They stopped at the top and let Brutus run for rabbits on the downs; there was a twinkling, twilit view of all England spread below them. The drive back, as darkness fell, was colder still, although the car smelled sweetly of warm leather and burning oil. In starlight, in moonlight, deer drifted like ghosts in the silvery fields. A badger shuffled across the narrow lane. Caught for a second in the headlamps, the fox was a quick, hot flame. The woods closed on either side, bristling and black, and at last there was the school, quite dead and silent and empty. Mr Hoddesdon stopped the car at the front door.

With difficulty, they lifted the hamper out of the boot and put it down inside the panelled dining-hall. Then, they went up the stairs to the old man's tower. This time, as Mr Hoddesdon seemed grey and worn and tired, Ian lit the fire and made tea for him. The dog collapsed on the rug. As the room grew warmer, the headmaster nodded in his armchair. His eyes closed, his chin dropped, his mouth fell open. He started to snore.

Ian waited until the man was soundly asleep. Then, holding his breath, afraid that the headmaster might wake up, he tip-toed around the room, turning over the cluttered knick-knacks, riffling the pages of dusty books, scanning the yellowed pho-tographs until at last he found the one he was looking for. He picked it up from the sideboard and studied the faces: a seven-year-old Mr Hoddesdon and the rest of his dormitory . . . a dozen tousled boys, some smiling, some serious, and, lean and tall and frowning, unmistakably the headmaster now snoring in front of the fire.

Ian picked up the photograph and turned back to the man, who was still sleeping: head on chest, feet outstretched so that one of his boots was steaming close to the fire, twitching one of his gnarled, brown-spotted hands. On a little table beside the armchair there was a saucer full of needles from the cedar tree. Kneeling with the photo, Ian took some of the needles and, without thinking, he threw them on the fire. The room was straightaway filled with a sharp, strong scent of resin.

At this, the headmaster woke up. He sprang to his feet. Sniff-ing, staring madly around him as though he were trapped in a nightmare, he lashed at the boy. He snatched the photograph, shouting so angrily that Ian recoiled from him and sat down on the rug with a thump. The dog fled to a corner.

'Damn you, you interfering boy!' the headmaster cried, his voice blurred, his eyes wild. 'Damn you! Why do you have to meddle? They're all gone! They're dead and gone! They wouldn't wake up! There's only me left!'

And he slumped into his armchair again, clutching the photograph to his heaving chest. Sitting on the rug, Ian stared at him. For a minute, the only sounds were the spit of the fire, the rustle of wind in the woods and the old man's tortured breathing. At last, seeing the hurt and loneliness on the boy's face, the headmaster grunted. He lit his pipe. He kicked at the fire until it flared alive. And then he started to talk, softly and gently, as though to make up for his outburst.

'Dead and gone,' he said. 'All of these boys in the photograph. Except for me. That's why I came back to teach at Foxwood, so many years ago ... Shall I tell you what happened? Well, this is the story, and it's all true.'

Ian sat close to the fire, on the rug, too startled and afraid to say anything at all, and he listened to the headmaster's story.

'It was wartime,' Mr Hoddesdon began, 'so the twelve of us stayed in school at Christmas instead of going home to the towns which might be bombed. Twelve of us boys, your age, with the headmaster and his wife. They tried to make it fun for us, Christmas Eve, with a bit of a turkey dinner in the dining-hall, with some carol singing, with a Christmas tree and candles. Then to bed, in the dormitory you're in. As I said before, I was in the bed you're using. We all fell asleep.'

The man was quiet for a moment, pulling on his pipe. It had gone out again. He applied another match to it and blew a plume of smoke from his mouth and nostrils.

'Smoke!' he said. 'The dormitory was full of smoke when I woke up. I woke up and sat up and the dorm was full of smoke. The place was on fire. It was a nightmare ... I still dream about it sometimes. I jumped out of bed and ran around the dorm, shaking and shaking my friends in their beds, tugging at their pillows. But they wouldn't wake up! It's a nightmare I still have, all these years later, haunting me. In a terrible panic, I went from bed to bed and shook it as hard as I could. There were flames too, from the dining-hall beneath the dorm, licking around the floorboards, licking at the door. At last, since it was impossible to rouse the other boys, I went choking and gagging to the window, struggled to get it open and stuck my head outside for some air. There was a bright moon and deep, gleaming snow. The cedar tree was smaller then, of course, and the branches didn't reach the building at all – this was sixty years ago – but I did the only thing I could to save myself. I stood on the window sill, took a huge breath and leapt towards the tree . . . just managed to scrabble at the nearest branch. Tearing at the needles, desperate for a grip, I fell through the branches and dropped to the ground. Even then, I shouted and shouted up at the window. No good! I must have been in shock, with fear and with choking and with the sudden icy cold, because they found me wandering in a kind of trance in the snowdrifts on the lawn, with my hands all ripped and flayed, with my feet and face all scratched.'

There was another long pause. Another cloud of smoke blew from the pipe. Mr Hoddesdon leaned suddenly forward and tossed the rest of the cedar needles onto the fire. They hissed into sweet, scented resin.

'That smell!' the old man said, frowning, shaking his grizzled head as though the memory were as cloying and sticky as the resin itself. 'That's the smell. It reminds me vividly of that terrible night and my leap from the dormitory window onto the cedar tree. By the time the fire brigade had come all the way from Shaftesbury, through the snowdrifts in the lanes, all my friends were dead, smothered by the smoke. All of them dead, because I couldn't wake them up. What more could I have done? It wasn't my fault. It wasn't!'

He was distraught. He steadied himself by gulping the air, like a man drowning. Then he went on, his voice shaking.

'The fire started in the Christmas tree in the dining-hall downstairs. I suppose the headmaster and his wife had had a drop to drink after they'd put us boys to bed, fallen asleep, and the candles set the tree alight. We'll never know. However it happened, I was the only boy who survived. To be haunted ever since.'

For a long time he looked at the photograph, thumbing the faces one by one, as though to impress them forever on his memory.

'What more could I have done?' he whispered. 'They wouldn't wake up.'

With a sigh, he handed the photograph to Ian and told him to put it back on the sideboard. Ian did so. When he turned round again, Mr Hoddesdon was staring into the fire.

'Christmas Eve tomorrow . . .' the old man said.

He leaned to the hearth, rubbing his hands together. He bent his face to the flames and sniffed.

'Christmas Eve again, and as usual, I've got everything ready, hoping and hoping and hoping. Perhaps this will be the last Christmas at Foxwood Manor . . .'

Then, suddenly embarrassed, as though he'd said more than he'd meant to say, he got creakily to his feet and ushered the boy to the door.

'In any case,' he muttered, 'at least there'll be the two of us. Come on now, Stott – it's time for bed. I've got a busy day tomorrow.'

Again, as the night before, he took the boy down the stairs and along the corridor to the dormitory. He waited while Ian changed into his red and white striped pyjamas, while the boy washed his face and brushed his teeth and then climbed into bed. The man looked up and down the other eleven empty beds, shaking his head sadly. He said goodnight, turned off the light and went out. His footsteps faded along the corridor and then there was silence.

Ian was alone in the big, old house, surrounded by the dense, dark, frozen woodland . . . alone, except for the headmaster, haunted in his firelit tower.

An owl hooted in the cedar. The branches scratched at the window. Ian fell asleep.

*

The next morning, Christmas Eve, Ian found Mr Hoddesdon as crusty as ever. Perhaps the man regretted that he'd taken the boy to his private tower and told him the story of the fatal fire. He had no time for the boy. His mind was on something else.

He gave Ian a quick breakfast in the chilly dining-hall and then packed him off with a few sandwiches and a flask to go walking with Brutus. Ian did as he was told. It was a steely, freezing day; the sky was heavy with snow. Ian and the dog stepped out as far as the Roman camp, they shared the picnic and they explored together; but it was a cold, lonely, desultory day out. Brutus stared in the direction of the house, whimpering pathetically, finally urging the boy back to the school.

The front door was locked. Ian knocked and knocked, frightened to knock too hard but so cold that he rapped until his knuckles were blue. At last Mr Hoddesdon opened up, with a turning of keys and a shooting of bolts. He peered out, blinking and staring as though he could hardly recognise the boy at all. Then, to Ian's amazement, he let the dog in and slammed the door again. The old man's voice rang behind the locked and bolted door.

'Not ready yet! Nowhere near! Go and clean the car, if you want something to do! Go on, boy! Not ready!'

In gathering dusk, in icy twilight, Ian trudged around to the stables. There, quite lost and utterly miserable, he slipped behind the steering wheel of the car and wept for his mother and father. He was seven years old, and this was Christmas: no friends, no family, no home. No cards, no presents. No love. He sobbed until his little heart ached with sobbing.

At last, conjuring the image of his father, he took a deep breath, gathered the shreds of his courage, slid out of the car and busied himself polishing the chrome on the bumpers and the grille. At least it was a bit warmer in the stable; lit by a hanging bulb, it was quite cosy with the smells of polish and leather and oil. Ian worked until the day outside was as dark as night. When at last he went into the yard and shut the stable doors, he was astonished to find that the world was covered in snow. The school buildings and all the fields and trees were covered by deep, soft, moonlit snow. The world was quite altered. Open-mouthed with astonishment, he went crunching to the front door again.

It was locked. The building was in darkness, apart from the

single, golden light high up in the tower. Knocking fearfully at the door, afraid that Mr Hoddesdon would be crabby and cross again, Ian peered through the windows into the dining-hall: pitch blackness. At last he heard the headmaster's slow, irregular footsteps and the door creaked open. Without saying anything, he let the boy inside.

It was very dark in the hall. At first, Ian could see nothing at all, although the smell of the man's smoky clothes was strong. He could smell Brutus too. But then, gleaming in the moon-light reflected from the snow outside, there were glasses and cutlery on one of the long refectory tables. It was set for a meal.

'Light the candles, boy,' the headmaster said softly, and Ian felt the man's horny hand pressing a box of matches at him. 'Light the candles on the table. My hands aren't so steady these days.'

So Ian struck a match. He went down the table on one side and up the other side, lighting all the candles; the whole table was set, six places on each side and one at the head – thirteen settings. As the candlelight flickered and then settled into a golden glow, Ian saw that there were cakes and pies, all kinds of jellies and fruit and syrupy drinks.

'The tree as well,' the man said, and Ian made out the bris-tling shape of a Christmas tree nearby. He lit the candles on it.

'And the fire.'

The huge fireplace was laid, ready with kindling and fir cones, with stacks of firewood on either side. Ian applied a match, and soon there was a crackling blaze. Mr Hoddesdon sat at the head of the table, and Ian sat next to him.

'Well, shall we start?' the headmaster said.

But they did not start. They simply sat, silent and still, and the feast was untouched.

Bemused, shivering although the hall was firelit and candle-lit, Ian sat by the old man. He waited for Mr Hoddesdon to do something, but there was only a long, long silence – not a sound except the crackle and hiss of the fire, the snow and wind in the forest. Ian looked up and down the table, at all the empty places. He looked up at the headmaster. The man had taken a yellowy brown photograph from his pocket and put it on his plate; himself and the other tousled seven-year-olds who had shared a dormitory so many years before. The man stared at it. Ian had never seen such a strange and terrible face in his short, young life.

Mr Hoddesdon was crying. A silvery tear ran down his cheek, into the corner of his mouth and down his chin. It dropped with a splash on the photograph.

The headmaster's voice was so hoarse that Ian could hardly hear what he was saying.

'I know I ought to go up and try again!' he was whispering, smearing the faces of the dead schoolboys with a tear-stained thumb. 'I know, I know! But I'm so tired. Every Christmas I go upstairs for them . . . and there they are. But they won't wake up! I shake them and shake them but they won't wake up! It's a horrible dream that's haunted me for years. So I leave them there and come downstairs again, on my own. Every Christmas for fifty years. Such a waste of a splendid feast!'

He tried a laugh, but it was an ugly sound, bitter with tears.

'Ha! No wonder they don't wake up, for a crusty, bad-tempered old fool like me! Why should they?'

He glanced down at Ian, who was staring incredulously to see this man, whom he had feared so much, blubbering like a baby. The headmaster controlled himself with a deep, gulping breath. He wiped his eyes with the backs of his hands. He leaned down to the boy, 'I don't suppose you'd go upstairs for me, would you? They might wake up for you! Please go for me!'

Too dumbfounded to refuse, and yet hardly understanding what the man had asked him to do, Ian stood up and left the hall; when he paused at the top of the stairs, he turned round to see the headmaster getting painfully to his feet, slipping the photograph into his pocket, limping to the front door with Brutus and going outside. The door clicked shut. Dazed, bewildered, Ian walked the long corridor towards his dormitory. It had never seemed so long, so long and cold and dark, like an endless tunnel. He walked and walked, seeing his dormitory door at the far end of the corridor . . . it hardly seemed to come any closer. He seemed to walk the tunnel for days and months and years. Until, at last, he was there. He pushed the door open and trod softly into the room.

It was bathed in moonlight. The air seemed to swirl with mist, an icy vapour which drifted like smoke. In every bed, a boy was asleep, lips and lashes as bright as the snow outside. No, not in every bed . . . his own bed was empty, the blankets and sheets tossed back. Beside it, the window was wide open. Ian crossed slowly to it, glancing from left to right at the faces of the sleeping boys, and he leaned out as far as he could. He could not reach the cedar tree. The nearest branch was a long way from the window sill. An avalanche of snow had fallen from it onto the ground below, as though . . .

Ian turned from the window. Not sure if he was awake or sleepwalking in a swirling, smoke-filled dream, he went from bed to bed and woke the boys, shaking them gently. One by one, without a fuss, they sat up, rubbed their eyes and stared around. Then, without a whisper or the slightest expression of surprise, they got out of their beds in their red and white striped pyjamas and put on their dressing-gowns and slippers . . . as though they had been waiting for Ian to come for them. Without a word, the boys followed Ian out of the dormitory, along the corridor, down the stairs and into the firelit dining-hall.

There was no one at the table. The hall was deserted. Silent, solemn, their eyes glittering and their hair tousled, the boys stared at the feast and the candlelit Christmas tree. One by one, they sat at the table. Only Ian remained standing, holding his breath, listening to the silence. When he heard a knocking and scratching on the front door, like the knock and scratch of the cedar branch on the dormitory window, he went to open it.

A boy was standing on the doorstep. He was lean and tall and frowning, barefoot; his pyjamas were wet. He said nothing to Ian, but he seemed to stare straight through him at the boys who were waiting to start their Christmas feast. A wolfish, wonderful smile lit his face. He flicked his hands and spattered the snow with a little blood from his fingers. He walked past Ian and took his place at the head of the table. He smacked his hands together, beating off the cedar needles which had stuck to the blood on his palms . . . and this was the signal for the feast to begin. The boy beckoned Ian to come and sit beside him.

It was a glorious party. The fire was ablaze, heaped with logs and fir cones, spitting the blue flames of holly. The Christmas tree twinkled. The oak panels were lit by golden flames, leaping with great, dark shadows. The boys shouted and laughed. They ate and drank until all the food and drink was gone and the plates were littered with crumbs and bones. Then, still seated at the table, they sang carols, their sweet boys' voices high and clear. From time to time, Ian caught the eye of the boy sitting beside him at the head of the table; and the boy nodded back, lifting a bloodied hand.

Outside, the snow fell softly, heavily, muffling the world in a thick, white blanket. It drifted on the open downs, weighing on the deep, dark woods. The fox limped through the trees. The deer coughed and shuddered. The hare was huddled in a snowdrift. The owl floated in the moonlight, its cry echoing in stillness.

At last the feast was over. The carols were done. The fire burned low. Together, as though at a given signal, the boys stood up, blew out the candles on the table and the tree and made for the foot of the stairs. All but one . . . Dimly lit by the dying embers, the boy at the head of the table did not move as the others stepped silently to the top of the stairs. There they paused. They turned to watch as the remaining boy stood up and crossed the hall to the front door, opened it and trod into the snow – still barefooted, in his pyjamas – leaving the door open behind him.

Ian followed the procession along the corridor. There was no sound of footsteps, except his own. Again, the corridor seemed endless, like a cold, dark tunnel. Again, the dormitory was swirling with a silvery mist, as dense and clinging as smoke . . . As the boys climbed into their beds, slipping off their dressing-gowns and stepping out of their slippers, Ian undressed too. He leaned out of the window, to see the world weighed down and smothered with snow. The cedar branch was out of reach.

Stretching as far as he could, he tried to grasp it and shake it, but all he could feel was empty darkness.

And below him, standing on the lawn, was the last boy, bare-foot, shivering in his pyjamas. He was staring up at the window, waving furiously, shaping his mouth in a terrible shout but making no sound, gesturing for Ian to make the leap himself.

So Ian climbed onto the sill. He was dreaming. The dormitory was dense with choking smoke. He had to get out. The boy below him was urging him to jump, to launch himself across the cold, black space between the window and the bristling branches of the cedar. Ian stood on the sill. His heart was thumping. The night was icy. He stood there and leaned out and he dreamed he was leaping ... flinging himself at the tree and grasping with his fingers, tearing his face and hands on the tough, sharp needles ... falling and falling through the branches and landing with a breath-taking thump on the drifted snow.

But then the boy was gone. It was only a dream, after all ... There was no smoke in the dormitory. All the beds were empty. Ian stepped down from the sill, shut the window and climbed into his bed. He fell asleep at once.

*

In the morning, he woke from the heaviest of all sleeps and sat up, rubbing his eyes. He had dreamed of laughter and singing and firelight. But now the dormitory was silent: the muffled silence of all the snow outside, the sunlight of a bright, cold Christmas morning. The other beds were neatly made-up. He got up, washed and dressed and made his own bed. When he looked around the room, when he looked out of the window, tantalising shreds of his dream came hovering to the edge of his memory ... but that was all. He could not remember it.

He went along the corridor and downstairs, into the dining-hall.

No. It wasn't a dream he'd had. On one of the refectory tables there were the remains of a splendid feast – all the plates and glasses and crumbs and bones, all the candles blown out.

There was a Christmas tree, whose branches were spattered with wax. The grey, cold ashes of a dead fire lay in the grate. Around the chair at the head of table, the floor was scattered with cedar needles.

Nobody there.

So cold! The front door was open, and a long drift of snow had blown across the hall. Ian went outside. The world was a crisp, dazzling place. He trod through the deep snow which covered the drive and the lawns. Something was moving there, whimpering at the foot of the cedar. It was Brutus. The dog was scrabbling in a great avalanche which must have fallen from the branches of the tree. Ian waded towards it, calling the dog's name, but it did not even lift its head to see the boy come closer. Whimpering, whining, Brutus worked to clear the fall of snow.

Still and frozen, Mr Hoddesdon lay half buried in a deep drift. The dog was licking his face. The man's hands were bloody and raw, prickled with cedar needles, and the tears were frozen on his cheeks. The yellowed photograph lay in the snow beside him.

The headmaster was not moving. He was not breathing. But, at the last, he was smiling a wolfish, wonderful smile.

ALSO AVAILABLE

With stories by:
Charles Birkin • John Blackburn • Michael Blumlein • Mary
Cholmondeley • Hugh Fleetwood • Stephen Gregory • Gerald
Kersh • Francis King • M. G. Lewis • Florence Marryat • Richard
Marsh • Michael McDowell • Christopher Priest • Forrest Reid •
Bernard Taylor • Hugh Walpole

ISBN 978-1-943910-51-9 (paperback), 978-1-943910-52-6 (hardcover)
Also available as an eBook
Available from booksellers worldwide or at ValancourtBooks.com

CPSIA information can be obtained
at www.ICGtesting.com
Printed in the USA
LVHW05*1430041018
592408LV00012B/291/P